Praise for Jon Hassler and *Simon's Night*

"Simon Shea, a retired professor of English at a small Minnesota college, has begun to forget things and has negligently set fire to his kitchen. Fearing the onset of decrepitude, he voluntarily commits himself to terminal residence at a private rest home. It's a serious mistake... but upon Simon's error hinges one of the most delightful novels I have read in years, a work of manifold virtues, felicitous, intelligent, and very often funny... Full of anecdotes, rich with scenes and characters of tremendous comic vitality."

– *Richard Bradford, author of* Red Sky at Morning,
The New York Times Book Review

"*Simon's Night* and its central character Simon Shea show Jon Hassler at his best, with his unique gift for giving voice, humanity, and dignity to the characters and landscape of the Midwest."

– *Nick Hayes, University Chair in Critical Thinking,
Saint John's University*

"What a marvelous gift from Nodin Press! Re-issuing one of Jon Hassler's finest novels, *Simon's Night*, is a gesture to be treasured.

– *Dave Wood, former Star Tribune book review editor
and author of the weekly column* Dave Wood's Book Report

"*Simon's Night* is a marvel. Out of Old Age, which our peculiar times have determined to view as a sort of generational sin, Jon Hassler has drawn forth a poignant, funny, wise novel about Eternal Youth."

– *Eugenia Thornton, The Cleveland Plain Dealer*

"[Hassler's] characters come alive, move and react, become new acquaintances... The world through Simon's eyes is richly humorous. This is an optimistic book... A remarkably good book."

– *Larry Batson, Minneapolis Tribune*

Simon's Night

&

My Simon's
Night Journal

edited and annotated by Joe Plut

Jon Hassler

NODIN PRESS

Cover painting and cover design: Chip Borkenhagen

ISBN: 978-1-935666-53-0

Simon's Night was first published in 1979 by Atheneum under the ISBN: 0-689-10981-4.

Library of Congress Cataloging-in-Publication Data
Hassler, Jon.
[Short stories. Selections]
Simon's night & My Simon's night journal / Jon Hassler, (edited by Joe Plut).
pages cm.
"Simon's Night was first published in 1979 by Atheneum."
"A small portion of this novel appeared as a short story entitled 'Smalleye's last hunt' in both Prairie schooner (summer 1972) and Blue cloud quarterly (vol. XIX, no. 2)"
My Simon's night journal (edited by Joe Plut)
ISBN 978-1-935666-53-0
I. Plut, Joseph, editor. II. Title. III. Title: Simon's night and My Simon's night journal. IV. Title: Simon's night. V. Title: My Simon's night journal.
PS3558.A726S575 2014
813'.54--dc23
                                2013037455

Excerpts from "The Lament of the Old Pensioner" and "Song of Wandering Aengus" are reprinted with permission of Macmillan Publishing Co., Inc. from *Collected Poems of William Butler Yeats*, copyright 1906 by Macmillan Publishing Co., Inc. renewed 1934 by William Butler Yeats. The excerpt from "The Well Dressed Man with a Beard" is reprinted with permission of Alfred A. Knopf, Inc. from *The Collected Poems of Wallace Stevens*, copyright 1942 by Wallace Stevens.

Nodin Press, LLC
5114 Cedar Lake Road,
Minneapolis, MN 55416

Simon's Night / 3

My Simon's Night Journal / 257

8/23/14

Ann —

It's good to ~~meet~~ meet a
Jon Hesslerian.

May you enjoy this _Simon's
Night_ combo.

Warm regards,

Joseph Plut

For James Casper

Simon's Night

After the final no there comes a yes
And on that yes the future world depends.
No was the night.

– Wallace Stevens

MONDAY

It was coffee time of an afternoon that promised rain but gave none, and Simon was sitting at the men's table in the dining room, finishing his cookie. He sat with Hatch and the Indian. Simon lacked five days of being as old as the century (born: 5 January 1900) and in his seventy-six years he had known a multitude of men whose company he preferred, but those other men were dead, and here at the Norman Home—a small institution (seven residents) in a small town (700 residents)—one made do; one passed one's days with Hatch and the Indian.

The Indian was cleaning his fingernails with a toothpick and Hatch was describing the several droughts he had survived as a farmer (the drought of twenty-eight, the drought of thirty-five, the drought of thirty-six, the drought of sixty) and Simon was struggling by force of will to overcome his boredom. This was only Simon's eighth day as a resident, and for three of those days he had been scarcely conscious, but he believed with the certainty of a lifelong faith that if he ever lost his mind—not merely his memory, which was deserting him anyhow, but every last marble—it would happen in this room, facing this wallpaper and listening to this prattle. All around the room, against a dead gray background, phosphorescent roses climbed the walls, roses neither on stems nor in bouquets but roses in an infinite duplication of the same tiny blossom, one blossom stacked tightly above another in scarlet stripes from floor to ceiling. After five minutes at table Simon noticed, in his peripheral vision, that the columns of roses began to advance outward from the walls while the mouse-colored background receded, and he was forced to turn left and right and look at each wall head-on in order to keep it from becoming corrugated.

And the stupefying conversation:

"In thirty-six you couldn't do your fall plowing without losing at least two inches of topsoil," said Hatch. "You'd go out to plow and your land would rise up behind the plow in a big cloud of dust, and if there wasn't no wind some of the dust came back down on your farm, and if there *was* a wind you never saw any of your topsoil again. It blew mostly into Wisconsin."

"I'd like to shoot a goose," said the Indian.

Simon swallowed the last of his cookie, a delicious cookie, large and dusted with sugar and heavy with chocolate chips. How ridiculous that thus far as a resident Simon had found nothing quite so enjoyable as his daily cookie. How suddenly his life had turned empty. In his forty years as a professor he had presided over the liveliest of classrooms and even in the decade since his retirement, even living alone in his cottage on the Badbattle River, his days had been full of reading and writing and walking and cooking and fishing and more reading. But now in the Norman Home he couldn't seem to read or write. He had no cooking to do and he had lost interest in walking and fishing. His soul had gone slack. His brain felt moth-eaten.

"I always worked hard, but I left two of my grain fields unplowed in the fall of thirty-six," said Hatch, fishing a pinch of stringy tobacco from his shin pocket. "Couldn't stand to see my topsoil rise up and disappear." Hatch was a short, neckless man with an enormous belly. The skin of his bony face was drawn tight and colorless—the sort of face, with its deep-set eyes and prominent jaw, that made it easy to imagine how someday his fleshless skull would look. "Of course in the *winter* of thirty-six we had moisture aplenty. Snow up to the eaves of the barn. But summer, nothing. Dry as dust."

The Indian said, "Every year about this time I get the urge to shoot a goose." He had finished his fingernails and was now probing, with his toothpick, his inner ear. He was a very old Indian. He claimed to be eighty-eight, but his daughter Tess, who showed up once a month to pay for his room, insisted he was eighty-two. Except for his joints, which were stiff, he might have been sixty; his hair was more black than white, he sat erect, and he heard most of what was said about him when he was considered out of earshot.

Although the Indian had been a resident of the Home longer than the other six, he seemed the least at home. He was aloof and restless and when he spoke it was to no one in particular. "I haven't shot a goose in twenty years. The mid-fifties. Fifty-five or -six. Shot four big honkers that year. Fifty-five, I think."

Hatch tucked the pinch of tobacco behind his lower lip, tamping in the strings. "But none of those years, not even thirty-six, was as dry as now."

Then silence. On cloudy days the dining room was dreary, the residents groggy. Their seven cups were empty and their seven cookies eaten, yet no one stood up to leave. All were held in their chairs by the bonds of lassitude.

"My niece Shirley's oldest boy has a mustache." This from the women's table. Simon turned and looked over at the four widows (one in a wheelchair), their heads four shades of blue.

"I have two grandnephews with mustaches," said Spinner.

"So do I," said Leep. Spinner and Leep were identical twins in their seventies. They were pert, nervous women who on brighter days than this fluttered and chirped and glanced incessantly about them with the black, darting eyes of small birds. Sparrows feeding in the grass cannot peck twice without cocking their heads at two or three quick angles, fearful of a stalking enemy, and Spinner and Leep reminded Simon of sparrows. Who was their enemy? What did they fear?

Mrs. Kibbikoski in the wheelchair said, "I once had a coat of Australian wool."

Then Mrs. Valentine Biggs felt Simon's eyes upon her and she came to life. Mrs. Valentine Biggs was sixty-nine and a flirt. Her defense against age was a wardrobe of tight skirts that revealed, when she sat, a tangle of garters and the dark bands at the tops of her stockings. These she turned toward Simon now, and she said to the room at large, "Everybody's getting divorced. Last time I was downtown I met Halvor Hinsilla. He said his daughter and his two sons are all divorced now, and at least two of them will be married again by Christmas. His oldest son was married to a Jap and his daughter was married to a cowboy and his younger son was married to a high school girl. He said that beginning this past July they all three got divorced a month apart." She gave Simon a smile that cracked her makeup.

"He must be kidding about the cowboy," said the Indian. "There aren't any cowboys any more."

"Aren't there indeed!" said Mrs. Valentine Biggs. "Well, all I know is what I'm told, I'm sure."

"There aren't any cowboys and there aren't any Indians any more," said the Indian.

"I repeat only what I hear, and what I hear from Halvor Hinsilla himself is that his daughter divorced the cowboy because she's been working in a jewelry store in Rookery and she has fallen head over heels for the jeweler's son, and his older boy divorced the Jap because he fell head over heels for the wife of another sailor, and his younger son is divorcing the high school girl because he can't keep her from chasing around." Mrs. Valentine Biggs winked at Simon, who pretended not to notice.

"In thirty-six the oak wilt took seven trees out of my windbreak," said Hatch.

"That Australian coat was the warmest I ever had," said Mrs. Kibbikoski, whose eyes were large and sad and watery along the lower rim: her eyes together with the tremor in her chin and the slope of her shoulders as she sat in her wheelchair suggested that she had long been acquainted with grief or regret or loneliness or some other spirit-dulling force abroad in the world. "I gave the coat to my daughter-in-law and it seems like I've been chilly ever since."

"Halvor Hinsilla says his daughter and his older boy will both be married again by Christmas," said Mrs. Valentine Biggs, "but the younger boy swore off girls. Like certain other men we know." She rolled her pouched eyes at Simon, and Simon chuckled unhappily.

Mrs. Kibbikoski sneezed.

"Bless you," said Spinner.

"Amen," said Leep.

Mrs. Kibbikoski sneezed again, harder.

"Bless you," said Spinner and Leep together.

Mrs. Kibbikoski had not set the brakes on her wheelchair and the thrust of her third sneeze—a mighty explosion of saliva—sent her rolling backward.

"Bless you," said Spinner and Leep and Mrs. Valentine Biggs.

Mrs. Kibbikoski started her electric motor (it whirred like a sewing machine) and shifted gears and drove back to her place. She wiped her nose and her eyes with a lavender hankie.

The Indian said, "Every year at this time I hanker for goosemeat."

"I never shot nor ate wild goose in my life," said Hatch. "Wild goose ain't eatable."

"You don't know that if you never ate one."

"I was told." Tobacco juice bubbled at the corners of Hatch's mouth.

Simon looked at his watch. Three twenty.

"*Tame* geese is different," said Hatch. "Many's the year I had tame geese and tame ducks on my farm, right in with the chickens. I tried pheasants one year, too, but you can't keep a pheasant to home. Clip his wings, I don't care what you do, you can't keep a pheasant to home. He'll run down between two rows of corn and never come back to the yard until after the first snowfall, looking for a handout."

Simon nodded his agreement. For several days now Simon, as a matter of principle, had been forcing himself to be attentive in the dining room, to listen, to say *yes, no, perhaps, indeed,* and *you don't say.* The talk was deadening, to be sure, but was it not his inescapable calling as a human being to endure the speech of his companions? He believed it was. No matter how clogged the ideas, no matter how asinine the assumptions, no matter how stale the platitudes and the breath that uttered them, Simon would listen. He thought of it as a vocation. By a trick of fate or the grace of God, age had led him to the Norman Home, where these six people were summing up their long years at the end of that longness. They mused and shook their heads and gave mumbling voice to countless memories, and he would listen like a brother. He would hear how

Hatch lost his pheasants and how Halvor Hinsilla's children—whoever Halvor Hinsilla was—had lost their spouses. All of this twaddle he was determined to hear and endure, for he believed that when he was born into the human race he had somehow given his tacit approval to this arrangement whereby he would spend his last years learning about the Great Droughts of the Twentieth Century. He would sicken and die to the sound of mumbling strangers. And was there a better way to die, after all? To the sound of prayers, perhaps, but the monks were a long way off. Surrounded by loved ones, perhaps, but who loved Simon? Certainly not his wife, Barbara, who had run off with another man so many years ago that the memory caused him no distress. Certainly not Linda Mayo, the lover he renounced in 1957. No, this would have to do. He would end his life in the company of these six strangers and as he lost consciousness perhaps the last shred of earthly knowledge to enter his ear would be news of someone's mustache.

"God, look at you!"

Hattie Norman was suddenly in the dining room, standing between the two tables with her fists on her wide hips. She was a stout, freckled woman of fifty, and single-handedly she ran the Home with a reckless efficiency and a voice like a hungry steer. "I swear you people are worse than garden plants the way you let the weather affect you. The barometer falls and you go to pieces. It's been overcast for a day and a half and you slouch over your coffee like a bunch of spooks. Up and out! Come on now, get up and get out of here!"

When Hattie Norman was a girl, her father had taken his considerable fortune and run away with an itinerant milliner, and that was when Hattie's mother had converted this vast and drafty house into a home for the elderly. That was forty years ago, and now after four decades of living with the argumentative, the forgetful, and the deaf, Hattie's customary manner of speaking was to shout at close range.

"Professor, you're due at the clinic in twenty minutes. Hatch, go somewhere and spit."

Hatch scurried out of the dining room and through the foyer

to the stairs. The Indian climbed stiffly out of his chair. The blue-haired women formed a procession to the TV parlor, Mrs. Kibbikoski leading in her motorized chair. Simon had been his own housekeeper for so many years that without thinking he carried his plate and cup to the kitchen and set them on the drainboard. He stepped over to the stove and lifted the lid of a steaming kettle and looked at supper. Cabbage and pork hocks, a meal to his liking.

Hattie Norman darkened the kitchen doorway, bearing the rest of the dishes. "Scram," she said.

Simon passed through the dining room and through the foyer, and as he climbed the broad stairway he heard the TV instruct the four women and the Indian: "Now remember, children, it takes four strokes of your pencil to print a capital E."

At the head of the stairs was a window, and Simon paused to look out over the prairie to the point where the plowed fields dissolved into the gloomy sky. Simon detested the prairie. He had lived all his life among hills where the eye—the mind—was not expected to take in so much all at once, where more was left to the imagination, where distant landmarks were memories and the weather building in the West was a mystery. But here, with hardly a knoll or declivity between himself and the curvature of the globe, he saw too much of the sky and earth. The Norman Home stood at the edge of town, and the window in his room, like this one, faced away from the houses and streets, and Simon was stunned each morning when he opened his curtains and took in the vast sweep of these flat fields and the atmospheric conditions prevailing over two states of the union and one province of Canada. He saw the truth in Hattie's remark about the barometer. In the Home, everyone's emotional changes were rung by the weather. Like the crew of a broken-masted ship, they were all at the mercy of nature, and their moods blended with the sky. Give me the hills of my youth and age, thought Simon. Give me gulches and steep grades. Give me bluffs and rolling pastures and winding roads beside winding rivers, roads like the one leading from Rookery to my cottage on the Badbattle River. Give me sandstone outcroppings and falling water and trails that lift me above the tops of trees and trails leading into ravines. Here, at a glance, is more than a man should see. Here, against the endless reaches of soil and cloud, I am puny.

He left the window and walked down the hall. He was a tall man with a slight list to the right, as though from a lifetime of bending his ear to people shorter than himself. There were ten rooms on the second floor of the Home, five to the right of the stairway and five to the left. Two were bathrooms and two were storage rooms, and what remained were the homes of six residents. Mrs. Kibbikoski lived downstairs, as did Hattie. Simon passed Hatch's room and the Indian's room and the bathroom he shared with them and he opened his door and stepped into the deep hum of cello music. He had forgotten to shut off his stereo. It played an Elgar concerto—a cheerless piece mourning the passing of the Edwardian era—and because the two speakers stood on the floor (there was nowhere else to put them in these crowded quarters) the somberness of the music was magnified by its being poured into the nap of the Persian rug.

He picked the needle off the record, switched off the turntable, and looked about him at the mess. He had brought along very few of his worldly possessions, yet the room was hopelessly crowded. Under the window were his favorite chair and his reading lamp. The stereo, a gift from his colleagues when he retired from Rookery State College, occupied the nightstand. Books teetered in stacks. His Persian rug was slightly longer than the room and the fringe had to be turned under at one end, but he had insisted on bringing it from his cottage; it had come from his parents' home in South Dakota, and though it was nearly as old as he, its reds and blues were lustrous and, as in his boyhood, he was still enchanted by the human and animal shapes he sometimes saw in its intricate pattern.

Simon readied himself for the clinic. He went to his dresser and, peering between the stacks of books piled before the mirror, he put on a fresh shirt and the flashiest of his three neckties and combed his wavy crown of white hair. He put on his brown tweed sportcoat (leather patches at the elbows, narrow lapels) and sat down and buffed his black shoes with Kleenex. His overcoat of Irish worsted was roomy in the shoulders; he was a huskier man twenty years ago when he had bought it in Galway.

On the stairs he met Mrs. Valentine Biggs, who made as if to block his way. "What takes you to the doctor?" she asked, giggling. Then, in a whisper: "Or is it something private you can't tell a girl?"

"Ah, the ever youthful Mrs. Biggs," said Simon, sidestepping her and not stopping. "I'm going to have my head examined. I want the doctor to tell me why I have waited so long to propose marriage to you."

She laughed like a child and called after him, "Who says I'd want you, Simon Pure? I never really cared much for you bookish types."

"You'd have me, Mrs. Biggs, don't be coy. It's no secret that I am your heart's desire." He crossed from the stairway to the front door, passing the TV parlor ("Get your mom to serve you Sugar-Bombs for breakfast!") and he let himself out into the gray afternoon.

The air was chilly and Simon turned up the collar of his coat. Standing on the broad front porch, he looked down Main Street, which ran straight as a needle through the center of Ithaca Mills and led nowhere beyond. At this end the street stopped at the front door of the Norman Home (the Home's circular drive was the eye of the needle) and twelve blocks away it narrowed to a point and ran up a weedy ramp to the receiving dock of an abandoned creamery.

Past the houses of no one he knew, Simon walked three blocks and came to the bridge over the Badbattle. He stopped and looked over the iron rail. This was the river he loved, yet here in Ithaca Mills it was unrecognizable. High in the hills, near Rookery, the Badbattle bubbled over rapids and twisted between boulders and widened itself into deep transparent pools, and in front of Simon's cottage where its bed was narrow it leaped and splashed and sounded like laughter. But having flowed out here onto the prairie, it fattened and slowed like a man full of age and its movement under this bridge was so turgid that you had to throw in a stick to see the current.

"To quote Housman," he said to the river, " 'we both would be where we are not.' "

He stepped off the bridge and crossed the street and walked past the small church where he had gone to mass yesterday morning. He had gone with Spinner and Leep, the nervous twins, and a florid-faced priest had delivered a rousing sermon on patriotism, this being election week.

Two blocks past the church, Simon came to the Ithaca Mills Medical Center, which despite its grand name was housed in a former restaurant and staffed only three days a week by a doctor from elsewhere. The restaurant had been known as the Busy Squirrel and its traces were yet to be seen: here on the ceiling a grease stain above what used to be the griddle, and there in the wall an opening through which the cook used to hand plates of food.

Simon hung his coat on a hook and stepped around the two people in the tiny waiting room and up to the opening in the wall and announced himself to a heavy nurse who sat at a desk.

The nurse asked him twenty questions. Yes, he was Simon P. Shea. P. for Peter. His address was the Norman Home. He was a retired professor. His last employer was Rookery State College. His social security number was 829–32–8229. His next of kin was his wife Barbara Shea of El Paso, Texas. No children. He had a savings account, meager as it was, in the Northern Federal Bank of Rookery and a checking account here in Ithaca Mills. Yes, he had had all the childhood diseases except scarlet fever. No, he was neither diabetic nor epileptic. Yes, he was troubled from time to time by constipation, bronchitis, dull headaches, hemorrhoids, and palpitations of the heart. No, he had never had typhoid fever, yellow jaundice, hallucinations, syphilis, shingles, ulcers, cancer, earaches, or false teeth. No, never any surgery. No, he wasn't allergic to penicillin. No, he was addicted to neither alcohol nor drugs.

"Please have a chair," said the nurse. "We'll call you shortly."

Simon sat on a hard chair and for twenty minutes he tried to occupy his mind with the news in the *Ithaca Miller*.

Ernie Fulson Reports Theft of Two Pigs
A. B. Cooper and Wife Sojourn in Bismarck

Finally the nurse called his name and led him down a narrow hallway and into a tiny room in which were crowded two stools and a spindly desk and an examination table.

"Undress and wrap this around your waist," said the nurse. She handed him a paper towel and shut the door.

Simon undressed and sat on one of the stools with the towel across his lap. He looked himself over. He was not pleased with the odd shape his body was taking on these days. He had always been lean, but now his flesh seemed to be getting away from him, seemed to be eroding from his arms and legs and piling itself up around his middle. His shoulders were bony and his ankles were those of a young girl, but everything between his collarbone and his belt seemed to be expanding. His belly was bloated and his breasts were pendulous, and while he had never set great store by the shape of anyone's mortal flesh, he was dismayed these days to see himself naked.

He waited a long time for the doctor. The room was chilly and he shivered. He looked at his watch. Four fifteen. When you undressed for a physical exam, did you remove your watch? Yes, he decided, and he unbuckled the strap and laid the watch on the desk. Then he changed his mind. Removing one's watch struck him as being oversubmissive. He put it back on his wrist. Then he noticed that he had not taken off his shoes and socks. What was medical policy on shoes and socks? Probably they should come off. But he was shivering and the floor was cold tile. He left on his shoes and socks and as a compromise he removed, once again, his watch.

Then a beautiful girl stepped into the room. She wore blue slacks and a white jacket and a necklace of small wooden beads. She placed a clipboard on the desk and Simon saw that it held the nurse's questionnaire with his name at the top. The girl sat down on the other stool and faced him across the desk and said that she was Doctor Kirk.

A joke? Simon had known women doctors but never one so young. Her brow was unfurrowed and her eyes were strikingly blue and clear. Her hair was the color of straw in sunlight. He was mortified that this young and lovely girl should find him sitting here dressed only in his shoes and a paper towel and he began to speak apologetically. "It isn't that I'm ill in any way. I'm here only because a complete exam is required at the Home."

"The Home?" She raised an eyebrow.

"Yes, the Norman Home. I'm new there. I think Hattie Norman, the proprietor, wants some assurance that she won't be inconvenienced by the state of my health. Or perhaps she wants you to estimate when my room will become available again. There's a waiting list, I understand."

"Exactly what is the Norman Home?"

"You aren't acquainted with Hattie Norman?"

"I'm new at the clinic in Rookery, and this is my first trip to Ithaca Mills. The duty falls to the novice, you see."

"Ah."

"My home away from home is the Thrifty Springs Motel." She looked very amused.

"Ah, yes, the Thrifty Springs Motel. And that isn't our only attraction in Ithaca Mills. Have you dined at the Open Soon Café? It takes its name from the sign hanging in the window. It has hung there, I understand, since before its grand opening three years ago."

Doctor Kirk nodded. She had seen enough of the boondocks to believe anything.

"Officially it's the Koffee Kup Kafe," said Simon. "With *K*'s instead of *C*'s, you know. That's what it says on the menu. But from the street all you have to go by is the Open Soon sign."

"And the Norman Home?" Doctor Kirk looked him intently in the eye, and he was enchanted. Not since his retirement from Rookery State, where beautiful girls were part of the daily traffic, had Simon been so charmed by a face. Her blue eyes and her cascade of glinting yellow hair moved something in his breast.

"The Norman Home has a reputation for the humane treatment

of the elderly," he said. "Which is to say that we are neither encouraged to become senile nor encouraged not to. And it costs only nine dollars a day, meals included, which is what attracted me in the first place. And except for those meals, which we take together in a perfectly depressing dining room, and except for our bedtime, which follows the ten o'clock news, weather, and sports, we are left pretty much to our own devices. Actually, I have been a resident only eight days myself, having moved there from my cottage in the hills. So you might say we're strangers here together, Doctor Kirk."

"Yes?" Her eyes never wavered from his and he was a little disconcerted. What did she mean *Yes*?

"There are seven of us at the Home," he offered. "Three men and four women. And of course Hattie Norman herself."

"Hattie Norman is a nurse?"

"Oh my, no. But why do I say that? Perhaps she *is* a nurse. Yet there is something about her slapdash manner that bespeaks a lack of training. She really does quite well, considering she runs the place alone. But she's very crude."

"What did you give up to enter the home, Mr. Shea?"

"Only my freedom." This he intended as a joke, and he chuckled to prove it, but when Doctor Kirk gave him only a perfunctory smile and then a look of intense concern, he felt suddenly very sad. He felt like weeping. *At nightfall weeping enters in*—the line of the psalmist flashed in his mind. He crossed his arms over his naked chest and he turned away, unable to face the compassionate blue eyes of this girl without losing control. He looked at the wall and addressed a crack in the plaster: "It's a great relief to be living at the Norman Home. You understand, there comes a time when you want the bothersome details of life taken care of for you. You want to be told what to eat, when and where to fall asleep. You reach a point in life—I'm seventy-six—when your memory goes, and you find yourself in trouble. I lived alone, you see, up until eight days ago. I always thought I could live out my old age alone. Be self-sufficient until the end. But no. Things happen."

A long silence. "What things?" Her voice rose on "what" and fell on "things," like the musical call of a robin.

"Well, in my case it's my memory." The crack he spoke to led to others; the wall was a maze of cracks. "I lose it from time to time. It's a frightening sensation. When your memory goes, a Home is the only place for you. My pension is modest, but it covers my room and board. So . . ." He turned to face Doctor Kirk. His surge of emotion had passed.

She looked down at the questionnaire. She took a pen from the pocket of her white jacket. "Is that your primary concern right now, Mr. Shea? Your loss of memory?"

"Yes, my memory is not to be trusted. It comes and goes. It will function just fine for a few days and then all at once it will go out from under me like an athlete's trick knee. One day last winter I took my mail from my mailbox—it's a rural mailbox along a country road—and between the mailbox and the house I set it down somewhere and I never saw any of it again. There was a letter from a former student and a retirement check and two or three other pieces and they all disappeared."

Her eyes again. Boring in. "So what? We all misplace things."

"But not with such abandon as I do it. Last summer I misplaced my car!" If she needed convincing he would convince her. "It was an act of sheer stupidity. I drove my car to St. Paul and I came home on the bus. Each year I make four or five trips to St. Paul—I review books for a newspaper there—and I was in the habit each time of taking the bus. But last summer I drove my car because I had something else to attend to along the way. And when I was finished with my business in St. Paul I took the bus home. I forgot that I had driven. When I got home and discovered what I had done, I called the St. Paul police, but it was too late. The car wasn't where I had left it. My sixty-six Ford Fairlane. I haven't seen it since."

Was she impressed? He couldn't tell. Her eyes were again on the clipboard. He moved quickly into his next example. "And later, in August, I got lost a mile from home. You see, I have this place on the Badbattle River. It's about fifty miles from here, upstream, near Rookery. It's where I've been living since 1941. A small place, nothing fancy, but it has all I need—needed. Bedroom, den, sitting room, bathroom, kitchen. Plus a screened porch. Well, the road out there is very remote and it runs along the river and I was always fond of walking it in the evening. There is the Odmer house and the Pribble farm along the way, but mostly you pass through wilderness and if you follow it far enough—slightly over a mile—you come to this hill with a fine prospect of the entire township. Of course I didn't go to the hill every night—it's two miles round trip—but I certainly went often enough to know the way. And one evening, wouldn't you know, I went to the hill and sat there on top of the world for half an hour, and then when I came down off the hill I took the wrong way home. I simply went walking off in the wrong direction. My mind was occupied, don't you see, and my native sense of direction deserted me, and by the time I realized my mistake it was dark and I was nearly two miles from my cottage. It took me half the night to get home. I couldn't walk a quarter mile without sitting down on the ground and resting. And the mosquitoes. You'd never believe the mosquitoes. Every step of the way I'd have to wave my hands around my head to keep away the swarms of mosquitoes.

"That was the night I first decided to rejoin my fellow man. I had lost a retirement check and I had lost my car and there I was trying to find my way home in the dark. I wished it weren't true, but I had no choice; I had to find a place to live where I would be fed and dressed and pointed in the right direction every morning. A place where if I became lost people would come looking for me. Not that I didn't have neighbors on the river. The Odmers lived a quarter mile down the road. But often many days went by between our visits and, besides, I didn't want to start relying on them."

Doctor Kirk shrugged—unsympathetically, it seemed to Simon. He said, "Are you unconvinced?"

Her face was without expression, her gaze steady. She said, "Yes."

"Then what would you say if I told you I nearly burned my cottage to the ground?"

She said nothing.

"Ten days ago I nearly burned my cottage to the ground. After supper one night I left one of the gas burners of the stove on, and I went down to the river and I was sitting there watching the ripples in the water while my house caught fire. You see, the dish towel that I had draped over the stove caught fire first, then the curtain on the window, and before I smelled the smoke and got the garden hose turned on, the whole wall of my kitchen was in flames. So now what you find when you step into my kitchen is one wall entirely gone and boarded up with plywood, and the other three walls caked with soot. That was the last straw. Two days later Kermit Odmer drove me to the Norman Home and helped me carry in my belongings. And what's wrong with the Norman Home for a man my age? After all, I'm seventy-six and I made it through eleven good independent years after I retired, and that's considerably more than some of my colleagues were able to manage. I had a friend at Rookery State who died of cancer the year he retired. For a while there we had a hell of a run of cancer through Rookery State."

"So you're Shea of Rookery State!" Her leaning forward as she said this was involuntary, gravitational. She smiled a broad smile.

"The same," he said.

"Well, in case you haven't heard, you and your poetry course have become a legend, Mr. Shea. I took my pre-med at Rookery, and the subject of poetry never came up that someone didn't say, 'Nobody's done justice to poetry around here since old Shea retired.' "

Oh, the joy. Smile warmly at an old man and tell him he's not been forgotten and his heart races with happiness. "Old Shea," he chuckled. "They called me Old Shea long before I was old. I never thought of myself as looking particularly decrepit, but I guess I projected that image. In the student newspaper I'd see a photo of myself standing in the graduation line or at a faculty reception and it would take me a second to realize that the fellow with the stoop was I. Then, too, my hair turned white in my early fifties. Twenty-five years ago I was already Old Shea."

"Yeats was your specialty, I believe."

"Insofar as I specialized. I tried not to be narrow. I offered my students the widest possible variety of poets, but it's Yeats I love. He's durable, don't you find? I've had other favorites fall apart on me after a long, close reading. But Yeats endures."

"I'm afraid I know very little Yeats. Only the standards. 'Innisfree' and so forth. In lit classes I felt more in tune with the women. Plath and Sexton. They fascinate me."

"What is it that fascinates you? Their poetry or their suicides?"

"Both. But their poetry first. Pointing as it does to their suicides."

Simon nodded. "Sexton I still read, but Plath I gave up on. For some years I was very enthusiastic about her, but I don't feel the attraction any more. With poetry, I go where I'm pulled."

He spoke at length about his enthusiasms and disappointments as a reader. The examination room became a classroom and Doctor Kirk was the pretty girl in the front row who had learned the trick of inspiring her teacher by looking absorbed and nodding her head at intervals. Her attention spurred him on. Never mind his nakedness, his bloated belly, his bony shoulders; this was a tutorial and he was full of his subject. He described for her how Walt Whitman had fallen from his grace and how he had lately seen an auction poster that struck him as more inventive than *Leaves of Grass*. He touched on Emily Dickinson and Anne Bradstreet (wasn't that the procedure nowadays—giving women poets equal time?) and he returned to Yeats for an explication of "The Lament of the Old Pensioner," which was much on his mind of late. Through his teeth he said, with force,

> "I spit into the face of time
> That has transfigured me."

He paused for breath and heard his voice bouncing off the walls of the cramped room and he felt slightly foolish. But Doctor Kirk seemed not to mind being lectured. She sat back on her stool, her head against the wall, in the pose of the patient listener, the honor student. Was her interest feigned or genuine, he wondered. Had she no other patients to see this afternoon? What about those two poor souls in the waiting room, sharing that single copy of the *Ithaca Miller*? Should he go on? Pound, perhaps? Wallace Stevens? No, he wouldn't press his luck. He would see her again. They would meet for coffee at the Open Soon Café.

"To return to the subject at hand," he said, "Hattie Norman sends me to you as her newest specimen."

Doctor Kirk was suddenly all business. She moved Simon to the examination table and read his blood pressure and probed and listened at places where he was ticklish, then she left the room. The heavy nurse took her place, wheeling in what looked like a footlocker with tentacles. Simon lay on his back and the nurse taped the tentacles up and down his front and the machine recorded its impressions on a length of paper that came rolling out of a hole in its side. Next the nurse drew from his arm a large portion of unhealthy-looking blood. Then she led him into another room and stood him before a photographic plate with his arms behind his head (his paper loincloth fluttered to the floor) and she aimed a ray gun at him. Before turning it on, she hurried around behind the sort of bunker Simon used to see in the war movies of William Bendix, and as she threw the switch and the ray gun hummed, he saw her looking at him through a small window in the bunker, the same aperture of bulletproof glass that William Bendix used to look through when he said, "Take cover, men, the Nips are coming back for more!" Then the nurse directed him to the examination room once again, where the beautiful doctor was waiting with her clipboard. She asked him if he was acquainted with the proctoscope.

"Only by hearsay."

She described its dimensions and function—all too graphically, it seemed to Simon—and said that on Wednesday morning, after an enema, he must return for this final stage of his exam. "And now you may dress," she said.

"How am I doing so far?"

"You'll get a full report when all the evidence is in. Your blood will tell us a lot. Offhand, I'd say you're sound for seventy-six, or even sixty-six, but of course I don't make judgments offhand. I'll see you Wednesday morning at nine."

At the door she turned and said, "And if you're really concerned about your memory, Mr. Shea, you'll leave the Norman Home."

"I will?"

"You'll go back to your cottage, where there's no one to wait on you. A year or two in the rest home and you'll be feebleminded."

"I'm never going back."

She was gone.

Simon dressed, smiling. He tucked in his shirttail and tied his tie and wondered if Doctor Kirk liked to go walking. When she was in town, they might meet for walks. Not often, certainly, for what was more irksome than an old man pushing himself off on a young beauty, but a walk now and then. A walk once a month. Something to look forward to. Lord, what an attractive woman. How odd to call someone who looked like that "Doctor Kirk." He must discover her first name and then ask her permission to use it. He must urge her to call him Simon. A lovely girl. A friend. Who else in Ithaca Mills would sit still for his chatter about Yeats? Who else was interested in his evaporating memory? How astonishing to have someone inquire after his happiness. How unsettling was that moment when he thought he would burst into tears, when he had had to turn away and choke down his emotion. He must guard against becoming a simpering old fool.

A lovely girl, a friend, but not altogether sound in her judgment. Not for all the world would he return to the cottage and risk another lost retirement check, another night wandering along the road, another fire. The fire was the worst. When he discovered his kitchen in flames he thought he would die of terror. Within minutes the smoke had attracted a mob of firemen and rangers, for it hadn't rained all summer and the forest was tinder. It didn't take them long to douse the flames—Simon, with his garden hose, had already done most of the dousing—but the firemen and rangers were very jumpy, and before they left they took turns giving him their most humiliating lectures. Then after the trucks cleared out and Kermit

Odmer sealed the wall with sheets of plywood, Simon collapsed into bed, and except for getting up to go to the bathroom and to eat some bread and cheese, he slept for nearly twenty-four hours.

Then he phoned Hattie Norman. She had an open room. He moved. And during his first days at the home he was in bed more than he was out of it, dreaming of flames and smelling in his sleep the pungency of charred wood and plaster and trying to overcome his excruciating fatigue. It was as though his terror at the fire, his disgrace before the gruff and hectoring firemen, had swept away the source of all his stamina, and it was three days before he could sit in a chair without dropping into a troubled nap. It was three days before Hattie Norman lost her suspicion that she had inadvertently taken in a basket case.

Simon put on his sport coat and combed his hair. A lovely girl. Doctor Kirk. As they got better acquainted he would tell her about his wife. Doctor Kirk would be interested in Barbara, for who could resist a love story, whether a tale of love requited or love gone wrong? In recent years it was only to the Odmers that he had spoken of his past. But although the Odmers were obliging and chatty, they were not the sort to whom you spilled out your heart. For years the Odmers had been living in the wilderness in a kind of mindless bliss. They chopped wood and gardened and fished and hunted and were generally at ease with the elements of nature. But of human nature they were wary. You could talk to the Odmers about poison ivy and eagles and thunderstorms, but if you brought up love, ambition, or grief their eyes went glassy. Describe some emotional experience, either happy or sad, and Felicity Odmer would draw back from the conversation with a humorless smile, as if to say that she had come up against such emotions in the books she was forced to read as a girl but she had met nothing in real life to confirm their existence. Mention feelings to Kermit Odmer, and he would excuse himself and go out and chop down a tree.

In Doctor Kirk, then, he would confide. He would uncover the part of his life he hadn't spoken of since he and his Rookery State colleagues parted company years ago. What lovely blue eyes.

Simon stepped from the examination room, and on his way down the hall he came to the open door of a small office. Walking past it, he saw Doctor Kirk and the nurse, their backs to the door, looking into the drawer of a filing cabinet. He heard one of them say, "He's just moved here from Rookery."

And the other replied, "Yes, he used to teach at Rookery State."

In recent years Simon's hearing had lost its edge, making it difficult for him to sort out voices, making it impossible for him to tell who spoke next:

"He sure is a windy old bird."

Oh, the pain. These words—considering that they may have been Doctor Kirk's—had the force of a punch in the chest; and judging by the way the man and the girl in the waiting room gaped at him as he put on his coat, the pain must have been apparent in his face.

The words were spoken, in fact, by the nurse, and had Simon lingered in the doorway he would have heard her add, "You were in there with him for almost twenty minutes, and whenever I went past the door I could hear him carrying on. What is he, some kind of crazy fanatic?"

"Not at all," said Doctor Kirk, "He's a man living among aliens. He needs someone to talk to."

"Aliens? What do you mean, aliens?"

"I mean anyone entering an old folks' home before he needs to is bound to find himself in a foreign country. They don't speak his language at the Norman Home."

"But of course they do. I know everybody at the Home—they all speak English."

"Never mind," said Doctor Kirk, "we're running behind. Let me see the next patient."

As Simon left the Ithaca Mills Medical Center, the phrase *windy old bird* flapped and squawked in his mind and caused him acute pain. If only he could be sure that the nurse had said it and not the doctor. If only his ears were as sharp as they used to be. There had been a time when he could listen to the college glee club and pick out the individual voices of his students, but lately he had lost the knack of identifying speakers simply by their tone and timbre. At the Norman Home, Spinner sounded like Leep, and—worse— they both sounded like Hatch. Gone were the days when he knew orioles from warblers by the songs they sang; now he couldn't tell a crow from a loon.

Windy old bird. Surely Doctor Kirk wouldn't have said such a terrible thing. Surely it was the nurse. But Doctor Kirk must have said it. It was to Doctor Kirk, not the nurse, that he had spoken— lectured—rambled. Oh, the pain.

But in his long life Simon had certainly suffered deeper wounds than this. As he walked along Main Street, he tried to remember such a wound. He recalled his shock at returning home last summer and finding his car gone, his sinking heart when the St. Paul policeman told him over the phone, "Sorry, no sign of a sixty-six Fairlane, but chances are fifty-fifty it will turn up someplace within the next year or so." Ah, there was a fine, deep wound—and now four months later most of the pain was gone and little remained but the scar. Wounds healed. Now think of another one. The fire. Yes, there was a fresher wound, and much more humiliating than being called a windy old bird. It was only ten days ago that his kitchen had burned, and already the pain was diminishing. Wasn't that the lesson in adversity? That we survive? What were our scars but notchmarks enumerating our struggles and testifying to our strength? Cruel, certainly, to be called a windy old bird, but hardly fatal. So he would return to Doctor Kirk on Wednesday morning, his wound healing, and while subjecting himself to the most demeaning of medical procedures he would wear the mask of good-humored banter. It was becoming clear to Simon that that was the primary challenge of old age: to maintain your dignity no matter what fix you found yourself in.

Simon proceeded down the street of strangers and he looked into store windows as he passed. In Sealy's Fashions a woman was trying on a coat. In Norris's Furniture and Funeral Chapel, Norris was asleep in a soft chair with $239 on the price tag. In Ollie's Food

Mart the checkout girl read a magazine. In the front window of the Open Soon Café a man was pounding catsup onto his heap of fried potatoes. Woody Allen was showing at the Plainsman Theater. As he came to Tess and Herbert's Bar and Lounge, a man in overalls stepped out the door and was trailed by the jukebox voice of Johnny Cash. Simon, on impulse, caught the door and went inside. He sat at the bar and ordered a whisky and water.

"Ain't you from the Home?" asked the barmaid, mixing his drink. She was a skinny woman with narrow shoulders.

"Right. Simon Shea is the name."

"I seen you there last week when I went to visit my old man. Smalleye's my old man."

"Smalleye?"

"Smalleye. The Indian."

"Oh. The Indian's name is Smalleye?"

She nodded. "But nobody calls him by his name. The Indian is all they ever call him, which burns me up. If you got a name, you ought to be called by it, otherwise why have one?" She set his drink before him.

"Here's to your father," said Simon, raising the drink. "I can't say I know him well, but I enjoy his remarks. Rare as they are."

"Nobody knows him very good. Not even us he fathered. One thing we never understood was why he wanted to sit on his ass out there on the reservation all his life. Me, I got away as soon as I saw my chance. I came to town and married Herbert and amounted to something. We own this place, Herbert and me. Made our last payment four months ago. The deed's ours, free and clear. We live in the back. I don't look like an Indian. Bet you'd never take me for an Indian if I didn't say Smalleye was my old man."

Simon studied her. Sure enough, the eyes were slightly aslant, the blond hair black at the roots. She had missed being pretty by very little, and he searched her face for the flaw. He decided it was her nose, which was not quite perpendicular to the floor.

"I think you look definitely Indian," he said.

"Oh, for Christ's sake!" She wiped her hands on the bar rag.

"The manners of some people!" She flounced off down the bar.

Johnny Cash gave way to Elvis. Simon stirred his drink and whispered, "A windy old bird." It still hurt. What he needed was the memory of another old wound that had healed—something serious at the time and slight in retrospect. Something like his lost car, only older. A wound from which even the scar had been erased. Barbara's leaving him? No, that was a wound of an entirely different magnitude; though the pain was gone, he still lived with the consequences. But the military examination of 1918, that was the very thing! Simon stirred and stirred his drink and gave himself up to the memory.

A troop train puffed into town and stopped to take on water and coal and to give its thousand passengers—all in uniform—forty-five minutes to stretch. This was in Redbank, South Dakota, where Simon's father was the hardware merchant and his mother the piano teacher and where Simon had grown to manhood in what seemed now, from a distance of nearly sixty years, like an amplitude of sunshine and peace. It was a Saturday evening in April. The stores were open, the high school band was playing in the square, and the townspeople were at first astonished and then thrilled by this sudden invasion at twilight. There were soldiers everywhere. The amazed bandsmen let their horns drop from their lips and the music stopped, but it didn't stop for long because Prof Pickett (bandleader as well as superintendent of schools) saw the opportunity of his life to instruct Redbank in the power of music. He conferred for a moment with an officer; the officer plucked from his troops a platoon of marchers; and to the tune of something by Sousa they put on a snappy demonstration of close-older drill.

The effect was tumultuous. Redbank cheered the army and the army cheered the band. Soldiers were kissed at random by girls and grandmothers. The officer climbed up beside Prof Pickett on the bandstand, hushed the crowd, and announced that the men on this train were bound for New York City, where ships to France awaited them. More cheering. More kisses. Some tears.

"We've got to enlist," said Simon Shea to Fred Lemm, his closest friend.

"Yes, we've got to go to France," Fred agreed. They were high school seniors a month and a half from graduation and they drooled with patriotic zeal.

Then Prof Pickett struck up "Battle Hymn of the Republic" and all of Redbank sang the words, and the marchers fell into step again and drilled and drilled through seven or eight verses, and when the shrieking whistle of the locomotive called the army aboard and the train chugged off into the night, the band kept playing and the crowd kept singing "Glory, glory, hallelujah" until long after the red light of the caboose had vanished down the track. Prof Pickett was high-strung, and throughout his performance that evening he whipped his baton up and down and around with such high emotion that he pulled open the underarm seams of his red and gold uniform. You would have thought, to watch him, that the music he was drawing from the lungs of his students and townsmen would deliver some cosmic victory into the hands of this army that had suddenly materialized on the prairie and then disappeared. And who knows?—perhaps it did.

The next day, Sunday, Simon Shea and Fred Lemm drew up their plans. They went to Central's switchboard at the back of the drugstore in order to place a call to Sioux Falls. Central in those days was Mamie Lemm, Fred's cousin. She gave them the oath of secrecy they demanded, then she helped them reach an army recruiter named Sergeant Green. He instructed them to arrive at the Federal Building in Sioux Falls the following Friday. He told them to bring a toothbrush and a change of clothes because after their physical exam they would be transported directly to camp. "Welcome to war," said Sergeant Green.

Now, how to tell their parents? And their teachers? They rehearsed every word, and when they confronted their parents and Prof Pickett, they found themselves overprepared. Of course Simon's mother wept and his father clapped him grimly on the back, but the glorious troop train at twilight was fresh in everyone's mind—it was all that Redbank knew of war—and permission was quickly granted. Prof Pickett went so far as to plan an assembly at the high school to see the boys off.

On Friday morning, then, adults as well as students gathered in the auditorium to pay homage to Simon and Fred. Rosemary Rosinski recited the Gettysburg Address and the band played "America." Prof Pickett read a telegram from the governor and the band played "Hands Across the Sea." Simon's father, representing the merchants of Redbank, gave each of the boys a silver pocket watch. Jane Willis, representing the students, gave each of them a gold fountain pen. Prof Pickett, representing the school board, gave them their diplomas six weeks early. The crowd cheered deliriously, then sang the National Anthem.

Then the fifers and drummers, with whom Prof Pickett had been working overtime all week, led everyone out of the auditorium and into the April sun and down the street to the depot. The ten twenty-five east-bound was applauded as it steamed into town. The two boys climbed aboard and looked down on the hundreds of waving flags and handkerchiefs, and they were glad when the train finally jerked into motion, for their smiles were becoming tremulous.

They took their seats and looked around. At least half the passengers in this coach were recruits like themselves, yet they might have been mourners or convalescents for all the spirit they manifested. Like Simon and Fred, they had all been served a rich diet of acclaim by their hometowns, and they had been walking all week with something of a strut, but now as the train sped over the swollen creeks and between the greening pastures and hove in sight of the chimneys of Sioux Falls, everyone was apprehensive and silent, and it was not an army of courageous young men who stepped onto the brick platform of the Chicago and Northwestern depot, but a cluster of homesick boys.

In the cavernous Federal Building, they remained a cluster throughout the afternoon. In their hands they clutched their billfolds, watches, and loose change, for they wore nothing but their underwear as they were passed from one clammy room to the next. First they were weighed and measured for height. The man tending the scale shook his head when Simon stepped up. Simon, at eighteen, was very thin. He was six feet tall and weighed scarcely a hundred pounds. His limbs were pipes and his joints were knobs. The man shook his head a second time as he noted his weight on a slip of green paper. Next a doctor looked into Simon's eyes and throat and another measured his blood pressure and listened to his heart. After that came the bone doctor and the hernia doctor and at the end of the line was the foot doctor, whose method of observation struck Simon as ingenious. This man was looking for flat feet, and he recognized them at a glance. After two hours of going barefoot in the Federal Building, the bottoms of your feet were either dirty in part or dirty overall, and if they were dirty overall your feet were flat.

The boys' confidence came back as they put on their clothes, and their chatter was loud as they waited outside the room where the final doctor studied their papers and passed judgment. It had not entered the mind of even one recruit that the army might find him unsuitable in any way, and thus Simon Shea was stunned when the doctor said, "Sorry, you don't weigh enough, and your feet are flat." It was several seconds before he understood, and when he did he broke down. Only a few hours before, in Redbank, it had seemed that he couldn't take a step without admirers breaking into song, and now he had to be guided, groping, out of the room, so blinding were the tears he was holding back.

Fred Lemm, who weighed enough and whose feet were nicely arched, nearly shed a tear of his own. He hadn't counted on going into the trenches with strangers.

"When you get home," he told Simon, "remind my folks to write. Tell them I'll send them my address by telegram."

"I can't go home!" said Simon.

"You can't?"

"How can I go home? I've got this new watch. I've got this new fountain pen. I graduated over a month early."

"Where will you go?"

"I'll kill myself."

But instead of suicide, Simon tried Minneapolis, where his grandparents lived. He arrived on the evening train and took a streetcar to their house. His grandfather, a butcher, promised him a job in his shop, and his grandmother, a magnificent cook, consoled him with a midnight snack of roast beef, wild rice, pickled beets, homemade bread, and rhubarb pie.

So Simon spent the summer of 1918 behind a meat counter. His parents came to the city to take him home, insisting that Redbank's pride in him had not diminished, but how could he go home? His hopes for military glory had been dashed, his pride severely wounded. He told time by the silver watch and he wrote with the gold pen and how could he face the citizens of Redbank without feeling wretched and unworthy? He vowed never to return.

Simon kept the vow for thirteen months, then in the summer of 1919 he went home for a visit. By this time he had finished his freshman year at the University of Minnesota; Fred Lemm was home from France unscathed; Prof Pickett was dead of influenza; and Redbank, in Simon's absence, had grown small and uninteresting. He stayed only three days but it seemed like a week. He spent a day in his father's store, he spent an evening with Fred and his girlfriend, he went to a recital performed by his mother's piano students, he fished in the river and caught a bullhead. This time when he boarded the ten twenty-five eastbound, he was eager to get away. From the train he watched Redbank disappear behind a hill and he wondered how any place that small and remote could have meant so much to him. A year earlier he had been obsessed by his place in the minds of his fellow townsmen, and now their opinion of him, whatever it was, didn't matter very much.

"Whenever I point out his mistakes, he gets super pissed." This from a woman who had come into Tess and Herbert's Bar and Lounge and taken the stool on Simon's right. It look Simon a moment to draw himself out of his reverie and another moment to realize that she spoke not to him but to a second woman, a redhead, who sat on his left.

"He makes mistakes so often I'm beginning to worry about his mental health."

"Jeez," said the redhead.

"I've been his secretary for eight years and I can read him like a book. I know when he's going to make a mistake before he makes it. He made a mistake last Friday and he made the same mistake today, and it's up to me to tell him. God, I hate to tell him. He gets super pissed."

"Jeez."

"What will it be, girls?" said Tess.

"Beer," they both said.

"How about you?" She sneered at Simon.

He hadn't realized his glass was empty. "Nothing," he said. "Do you sell whiskey by the bottle?"

"Down there." She pointed to a counter at the end of the bar.

"What would you do if you had a boss that got super pissed every time you pointed out his mistakes?"

"Jeez, I don't know," said the redhead.

"How about you, old man?" she said to Simon. "What would you do?"

"Jeez, I don't know," said Simon.

He left his stool and went to the bottle counter, where a swaybacked man with a soft, sagging belly (Herbert, no doubt) sold him a fifth of Jim Beam.

Outside, on the corner, a girl in a long coat was handing out messages and she put one into Simon's hand as he passed. It was a green and white strip of heavy paper. It said GRITS AND FRITZ.

"Mister," the girl called him back. "It's a dollar."

"This is a dollar?" He read it again. "What does it mean?"

"It's a bumper sticker for your car. It's for Carter and Mondale. Grits and Fritz. Get it?"

He handed it back to her. "Find me my car and I'll take two."

As he continued along the street, he saw his shadow moving

ahead of him. He stopped and turned around. The sun had slipped down from behind a fringe of purple cloud and was looking him full in the face. It was large and red and fifteen minutes from the horizon, and hanging over the flat land it seemed only a mile or two from town. Too close.

He resumed his way and came to the Badbattle. He stood at the bridge rail and enjoyed the short spell of fuzziness the whiskey was causing in his brain. "A windy old bird," he said to the river, and the pain broke through his light inebriation. Damn, it still hurt. He tried again: "You don't weigh enough, and your feet are flat." He laughed.

At the Home, Simon found Hatch and the Indian standing in the circular drive. Hatch wore his winter jacket zipped to his throat: his eyes were pink, reflecting the setting sun. The Indian scanned the sky for geese and said, "When I was on the reservation I used to shoot geese from the top of a haystack. Every night about sundown they'd come flying low over the field. I'd be lying on the haystack covered with hay, and when they got close I'd rise up and fire. Bam! I'd drop the lead goose in the flock. It's a lot easier shooting geese if you're on their level, shooting head-on."

Gabbling and the flapping of wings approached from the dark distance, and soon the silhouettes of a long line of geese passed overhead.

"Now if I was to shoot into that bunch," said the Indian, looking about for a likely place, "I'd want to be up … let's see. I'd want to be—"

"Fool idea to shoot a goose at your age," said Hatch. "I s'pose you'd stand in a tree. You'd climb one of these elms."

The Indian ignored Hatch's guile. "No, shooting out of a tree is bad business. Never shoot out of a tree. I'd want to be up on something solid."

"Maybe up on that balcony," said Hatch, and the men turned to examine the Home, its Victorian roofline complicated against the dim sky. Hatch was pointing to the small railed balcony over the front porch.

"Not high enough."

"It's twelve, fourteen feet—high as a haystack."

"Geese lift some when they fly over town," said the Indian. "But see there, up on the roof above the balcony. The big chimney. I could get up next to the big chimney and stand. Coming from the north, the geese would never see me standing behind the chimney. Then when they got close I could just edge around a little and fire. Bam!"

Hatch cocked his head. "I hear somebody chopping wood."

"The chimney's the likeliest place. I believe I'll try it."

"Somebody's chopping wood. Let's go look." Hatch was fascinated by all forms of manual labor.

"You two go ahead," said the Indian. "Walking hurts my joints."

"But it must be nearly suppertime," Simon told Hatch. He pulled back his coatsleeve. His wrist was bare. He had forgotten his watch in the examination room.

"Come on, it's this way. We got time for a whiff of fresh-cut wood before we eat." Hatch's voice cracked with excitement as he set off down the street and Simon went along, lured not by the prospect of sniffing wood but by Hatch's delight.

Hatch stopped and said, "What you got in that sack?"

"Whiskey."

Hatch nodded and they went on, following the sound of the ax. They turned at the corner. Here there was no sidewalk and they walked through the dry, dead leaves of the gutter.

"Hattie don't allow drinking in the rooms," said Hatch.

"Hattie needn't know."

Three blocks from the Home they found a man chopping wood in his driveway and a small boy picking up the sticks and stacking them against the house. It was twilight now, and neither the man nor the boy noticed the two old men who left the street and took a few steps into the yard and stood just inside the circle of fragrance.

"Smells like maple," said Hatch softly.

Simon nodded. He didn't know the smell of one tree from another but he recognized the scene before him. What he saw was Redbank, South Dakota, in 1907; the man was Simon's father and the boy was Simon himself; his father chopped and Simon threw the sticks down the coal chute into the basement; it was dusk and they worked under the lighted window of the kitchen, where Simon's mother was preparing supper; soon she would call them in.

So engulfing was this plunge seventy years backward that it took Simon's breath away. Unlike his earlier reminiscence in the bar, this memory came unbidden and all in a rush. He was seven once again and he wore a pair of his father's cotton gloves, which were too big and kept falling off as he handled the wood; it grew very dark as they worked, the Dakota sky going from pink to purple to starry; in his nose were the mingled odors of fresh wood and dead leaves and the pot roast in the kitchen; he was hungry for the meal his mother was about to serve and hungrier still for his father's praise at his doing a man's work; both hungers were certain to be satisfied. Standing beside Hatch, Simon closed his eyes and half believed that he would hear, at any moment, his mother calling.

A cry pierced the darkness. "Hatch! Professor!" It was Hattie Norman bellowing from the front porch of the Home.

The two men left the yard reluctantly, silently, and walked along the street. When they turned the corner and Hattie saw their shapes in the gloaming, she called, "You men are ten minutes late for supper! God, are you walking in the street? Get out of the street this instant!" She came down off the porch and along the drive. "God, it's a wonder you haven't caused an accident and brought a lawsuit on me. Don't let me catch you in the street again!"

Hattie's barking echoed under the bare elms as she herded the two men across the front yard and up the steps and through the open door of the Home.

In the dining room, over cabbage and hocks and strawberry Jello, the Indian said he never knew a man worth his salt who didn't shoot at least one goose a year.

Hatch said wild goose wasn't eatable.

Mrs. Valentine Biggs made several remarks designed to draw

Simon out on the subject of his health. "My blood pressure is 140 over 112, Simon Shea, how does that compare with yours?"

"I don't know," he said. "I didn't take notice as the doctor wrote it down."

The nervous twins were dressed alike tonight, in white blouses and blue pinafores. Spinner said that moneyed people understood money.

Leep said that Ford could have had their vote by keeping Rockefeller on his ticket, but she and her sister couldn't see voting for what's-his-name from Kansas.

Hatch said he had had an uncle once who farmed in Kansas.

Speaking of Kansas, Mrs. Kibbikoski in the wheelchair said that when she and her son used to travel to Colorado to see her sister they always stopped at a steak house in Grand Island or Emporia or one of those towns and had the nicest steak imaginable for two ninety-five.

Hatch said Grand Island wasn't in Kansas, it was in Missouri.

Spinner said they should all vote Democrat to show Mondale that Minnesota was behind him.

Leep said she heard Mondale had a brother who was odd.

Mrs. Kibbikoski said she heard Carter had a brother who was odd.

Mrs. Valentine Biggs said she had had a hysterectomy in 1954, but it didn't stop the pleasure she took in sex.

The Indian said damn near everyone he knew had a brother who was odd.

Hatch said he would vote for Carter because Carter was a farmer. Carter always worked hard.

Mrs. Kibbikoski sneezed and her eyes watered and she said her right foot was giving her a lot of pain.

Spinner and Leep bent under the table and took off Mrs. Kibbikoski's slipper. Goodness, they said, her toes seemed to be turning black.

Hattie Norman delivered dessert to the tables—peach slices in milk—and said that if anybody developed any serious ailments (she glared at Mrs. Kibbikoski) they would just have to pack up and leave. She was cook and housemaid and appointment secretary and groundskeeper and she didn't know what all, and she wasn't about to become a doctor besides. She said she was going to cast her vote as soon as the polls opened at seven A.M. and anyone who wanted to was welcome to ride along in the van, but if they wanted to vote later they would have to walk because she was damned if she'd take the van out of the garage twice in the same day. She said that next Friday night a crew of Public Health nurses from Rookery was coming to the Ithaca Mills Medical Center to give everybody in town a swine flu shot. She said everybody was expected to show up for the shot, especially old folks, unless they had pneumonia or something else that was going to kill them anyway.

News of the shot silenced the residents for a time. There were a couple of soft burps and the clink of tableware. Then Simon told Hattie that the peaches were tasty. Simon was conscious of having entertained a long series of negative thoughts today, and he wanted to say something positive for a change. He had found fault with the dismal wallpaper and the flat prairie and the sluggish river. He had been offended by the insult he had overheard at the Medical Center, and he had offended, in turn, the Indian's daughter by saying she looked like an Indian. It was high time he cast his attention over on the agreeable side of life. Hattie's cooking, for example. Her meals gave him pleasure because they were genuinely good and because after thirty-three years he was finally through cooking for himself.

"I applaud your cooking, Miss Norman." He applauded over his sauce dish.

Hattie threw him a suspicious glance and retreated to the kitchen. Surely this old professor was nuts.

"I always regretted not voting for Kennedy," said Spinner, "but my husband told me not to."

"*I* voted for Kennedy," said Leep.

"I could tell you a secret about *my* husband," said Mrs. Valentine Biggs.

"We had four apple trees in the grove behind the barn," said Hatch.

"About my dear husband Valentine."

"I never saw the inside of a polling place," said the Indian. "Never voted in my life."

"Valentine was potent till the day he died."

At Simon's cottage in the hills, the phone was ringing. It rang off and on all evening, for Barbara Shea of El Paso, Texas, was dialing his number and getting no answer. This was to be their second phone conversation in their thirty-three years of separation. She wanted to tell Simon that she was on extended leave from her job, that she felt a need for travel and diversion, that she was coming north for a change of scene and one of the first sights she wanted to see was her husband.

TUESDAY

Simon slept later than usual. His narrow bed was old and uneven, but this morning its contours seemed especially designed for his body, and each time he awoke he was tempted back to sleep. Between seven and nine he opened his eyes four times, feeling as though he had passed through a deeper stage of rest, had sunk deeper into oblivion, had restored yet another segment of the brain that deteriorates during waking hours, had plumbed dark dreamlessness so deep that he thought he heard music. He rose too late for breakfast. He sat on the edge of his bed and listened to the noises from the room next door.

Next door the Indian was opening and closing the drawers of his bureau, where he stored the remnants of the life he had lived outside the Home. He dug among tarnished keys and dog-eared snapshots and seven earrings belonging to his dead wife. He uncovered coins, pill bottles, check stubs, and the manufacturer's directions for a stove he bought in 1927. He found a comb with half its teeth and eyeglasses with one lens, and under a yellow necktie and a layer of yellow letters he found his last remaining shotgun shell. It was an old shell from the days when shell casings were made of paper, and the brand name, Winchester, was all but faded from sight.

The Indian slipped the shell into his pocket, then he picked up the shag rug by his bed and dropped it out the window.

The nearsighted Mrs. Kibbikoski caught a glimpse of the rug as it fell past her first-floor window. She thought it was a human figure and she burst into tears. She maneuvered herself from her bed into her wheelchair, and she motored into the kitchen and told Hattie that she had just seen a body fall from upstairs.

"God, what now!" said Hattie, hurrying to the kitchen door and looking out. "It's only a rug, Mrs. Kibbikoski, stop crying."

Hattie bustled through the dining room and foyer and upstairs to the Indian's room. She flung open his door and saw him standing beside his bed, his thumbs hooked in his suspenders, his gaze on the floor where his rug had been.

"How does it happen your rug is outside, Smalleye?"

"That's what I was wondering," he said.

"Well, see that you retrieve it." Hattie descended the stairs. She had been in the game long enough to know when the antics of old people should be investigated and when they should be ignored.

"So it was a rug after all?" asked Mrs. Kibbikoski, her engine idling at the bottom step.

"It's hardening of the arteries," said Hattie.

Later, when Hattie had finished the breakfast dishes and lay in her room with her feet up, the Indian stole through the kitchen and into the basement and brought up a stepladder. He carried the ladder through the kitchen and dining room and past the TV parlor (Hatch and Spinner and Leep were watching "Dinah") and up the stairs. His motions were slow and painful, his exertion having aggravated his arthritis. He stood the ladder in his closet. He put on his jacket. He stepped out into the hallway just as Simon came out of his room.

"On your way to the polls?" asked Simon, buttoning his black overcoat. "We'll go together."

The Indian shook his head. "Just downtown to see my daughter."

"Oh yes, that would be Tess, of Tess and Herbert's Bar and Lounge. I met her yesterday. She served me a drink."

The Indian made his way down a few steps with both his hands on the banister.

"Would you like to take my arm?" said Simon.

The Indian studied Simon's sleeve, considering the proposal. There was no precedent in the Indian's memory for such an offer of aid. He slowly brought his hand around and gripped Simon's elbow. Now his movements were greatly eased, yet his weight on

Simon's arm was imperceptible. The Indian seemed as light as a hollow-boned bird.

Outside, the Indian said, "Just a minute," and he hobbled around the corner of the house to pick up his shag rug.

Simon stood waiting on the grass, dazzled by the sunshine. This was going to be a grand day. The drought was unrelieved and across the prairie the vegetation was dead or dying as far as the eye could see, and here along Main Street winter was foretold by the trees standing birdless and leafless and by the lawns furry with morning frost and by strips of rags stuffed around ill-fitting storm windows—but this was going to be a grand day. It was that time between the last cold spell of fall and the first cold spell of winter when summer, given up for dead, seems to be gathering its strength to reappear. Simon was glad of this reprieve from winter. For most of his life he had tried to love the brittle cold of winter as much as he loved the colors of autumn, the birdsong of spring, and the warm rains of summer: but he had come, with age, to dread the ice and wind and drifting snow. Cold air made him wheeze. In December when the sun went down at four in the afternoon he felt lonely. In January when the temperature at noon rose to only twenty below zero he wondered if spring could possibly make it back before he died. He was certain that one of these winters—most likely on some bleak, sterile day around the end of February and the beginning of Lent—he would die.

Simon walked downtown, slowly, with the Indian. As they parted, the Indian said, "Will you be in your room this afternoon around five?"

"Yes, I'm sure to be."

"And you will do me a favor?"

"Glad to. Come a bit early and we'll have a drink of whiskey."

The Indian nodded, walking off with his rug over his arm.

Simon crossed the street to the Ithaca Mills Town Hall and presented himself to the three women serving as election clerks. All three were white-haired and stern, having been chosen, it seemed to Simon, from a roster of retired schoolteachers. Wasn't this one who ordered him to sign his name in her ledger wearing the same long and belted dress that Mrs. Driscoll had worn when she forced fractions on Simon in the sixth grade? And wasn't that a schoolteacherish stare he was getting from her companion, the woman handing him the green certificate which would admit him to the curtained booth? There were several voters ahead of Simon, and the third clerk—the one assigned to watch over him as he stood in line—was as dour and bony (particularly bony in the wrist and nose) as old Mrs. Wheelwright, Superintendent of Schools for Redbank County, 1894–1914. He handed this woman his green certificate and she studied it like a note from home explaining a long absence for a dubious reason.

Then it was Simon's turn to vote and when the bony woman permitted him behind the curtain, he was amazed to find not a ballot and pencil but a machine with twenty-five switches. Clearly this town of four or five hundred voters was overmechanized. On the face of the machine were printed four long paragraphs and a long list of names. Simon read the first paragraph, a proposed amendment to the state constitution, and found it unintelligible. Although he had lived his entire adult life in Minnesota, he knew next to nothing about its government. He knew only that it operated out of St. Paul, and that several years ago *Time* had described it as clean. His first instinct was to vote against the amendment, but he changed his mind at the last moment, reasoning that clean governing bodies quite likely proposed amendments for the public good, and even if this amendment was ill-advised, Ithaca Mills was a long way from St. Paul and quite likely out of harm's way. He bent the switch to yes.

He moved on to the other three paragraphs—municipal questions all—and he voted in favor of making liquor legal on Sunday (Tess and Herbert had conducted a door-to-door campaign for this); in favor of floating a small bond for the purchase of a second squad car and the hiring of a second cop (this in response to the nationwide rise in crime); and in favor of converting the local jail into a museum (the existing cop, Doodle Novotny, hadn't made an arrest in eighteen months). Never before had Simon voted in favor of so much. Where was his customary distrust of public servants, his conviction that the only good government was a paralyzed government? He looked at the four yes switches and he felt like a radical.

Then he came to the candidates for public office. For President of the United States in this Bicentennial election, Simon had decided to vote for Franklin Pierce, a man after his own heart and dead a hundred years. This was not a frivolous choice but one he had arrived at by searching his soul. After Vietnam, after Watergate, after countless books exposing the chicanery of diplomats and Presidents, Simon had lost his faith in the ability of the ordinary citizen to separate truth from tinsel in a political campaign. He had come to think of the first Tuesday after the first Monday in November as a holiday for swindlers. Why *not* vote for a dead President from the nineteenth century? Why *not* vote for one's ideal of the Presidency rather than for Carter or Ford—men purported to be flesh and blood, but how was one to know? Might not these candidates be straw men, prepared and paid for by a committee to elect a television image? Might they not have been born, like Ronald McDonald, in an advertising agency?

Franklin Pierce was Simon's kind of man. He had Nathaniel Hawthorne's word for that. Simon had read a good deal about the lifelong friendship between the President from New Hampshire and the author of *The Scarlet Letter,* and nothing in the annals of Presidential achievements impressed Simon like Pierce's gesture at the grave of his wife. Hawthorne later described the incident to a friend who wrote it in his memoirs, and the story had come down to Simon in an old book with a faded cover. It was on a bitterly cold day in December 1863 that Mrs. Pierce was buried, and among those at the graveside was Nathaniel Hawthorne, weakened and shrunk by a mortal illness of his own. As the coffin was lowered into the ground, Pierce saw, through his tears, that Hawthorne was shivering, and he turned and drew up the collar of Hawthorne's coat. Now there was the gesture of a true friend. Now there was a

President for you. Simon took his fountain pen from his pocket and printed Pierce's name in the write-in square.

He scanned the rest of the choices, the state and local offices aspired to by names he didn't recognize. He threw a couple of switches and ignored the rest. "For what it's worth," he said as he gripped the large lever and pulled, and the machine recorded, with the clangor of a heavy door going shut, his senseless opinions.

"What did you say?" asked the bony woman as he stepped from behind the curtain.

"I said, 'For what it's worth.' I was speaking to the machine."

"And exactly what did you mean by that?" The Redbank County Superintendent had never looked haughtier, and without listening for his answer she said, "This is a place of decorum—here is the voting booth, there is the flag—and hardly the place for smart alecks."

He smiled guiltily, and though he held himself erect as he stepped from the Ithaca Mills Town Hall, he felt as if he were slinking.

The sun, higher now, was turning the morning frost to water. The town hall flag was new and it rustled when it stirred like a taffeta gown. From the bridge Simon spat into the sluggish river, testing it for life signs, and regretted his cynicism in the voting booth. It was with excitement and a sense of weighty purpose that he had cast his first Presidential vote in 1924. That vote was for Coolidge, the one and only time in his life that he had voted on the side of the winning party. But though his choices came up short for the next half century (Smith, Hoover, Landon, Willkie, Dewey, Dewey, Stevenson, Stevenson, Nixon the first time, Goldwater, Humphrey, McGovern), he had maintained his faith in the system for most of those years, and it was only now during the Bicentennial that he was fully struck by the meaninglessness of his vote. There had been a time when he was secretly pleased to have children point to him and call him Uncle Sam. This happened with some frequency in the early forties when the "Uncle Sam Wants You" poster by James Montgomery Flagg was in vogue for the second time and Simon's hair was turning white over his angular, Lincolnesque face and the resemblance was striking. Now in 1976 while he still looked like Uncle Sam, albeit an ancient Uncle Sam, children were no longer familiar with the Flagg portrait, which was just as well because he was no longer proud of the resemblance. Why this sudden disillusionment? Were Vietnam and Watergate and Spiro Agnew the entire cause? No, he guessed he was bothered by other factors equally significant but harder to define. For one thing, seventy-six years was an awfully long time to believe in anything short of the Holy Trinity, and for another thing, 200 years was an unheard-of duration for a constitutional system to perpetuate itself, and for a third thing, the fire in Simon's kitchen had traumatized him into thinking that he was soon to die—and inherent in the thought of a man's own death is the suspicion that not much of what he holds dear can survive for very long without him. In other words, Simon feared that he and America were going down the tube together, and while Simon believed that he would move on to life everlasting, where did nations go when they died but into the thin air of museums? Moreover Simon harbored the impression (it was the vaguest sort of notion rather than a conscious thought) that the Bicentennial was being observed as much for his own sake as for his nation's, and this made him uncomfortable. How many times in magazines and news broadcasts had the populace been urged to reflect on the country's past and to meditate on the country's future, and didn't Simon always end up pondering his own past, his own future? Well, to tell the truth, he was sick of it. He had no future. It may be true that the unexamined life wasn't worth living, but the overexamined life was equally wretched, particularly if you were embarking on your fourth quarter-century and you had just set fire to your kitchen. Moving into a home for the elderly and leaving your self-determination behind was enough of a spur to meditation without editorial writers nagging you every day to examine your conscience and shape up.

From the bridge Simon walked home, facing the morning sun, and on the front porch he exchanged some happy nonsense with

Spinner and Leep and Mrs. Valentine Biggs, who were setting out for the polls.

"Though threatened with death and damnation, I would never vote for Sunday liquor," clucked Spinner.

"Nor I," said her twin. They wore old pillbox hats and new vinyl coats the color of pea pods.

"There's a certain party keeps a bottle in his room," said Mrs. Valentine Biggs, smiling. Her lipstick was vermilion, her eye shadow russet, her powdered dewlaps white. She had a dozen ways of smiling, and this one was devilish. "I repeat only what I hear."

"Lips that touch liquor," said Spinner.

"Will never touch mine," said Leep.

Indoors, Hatch called to Simon from the TV parlor. "Come see this. They've got the winningest voter in history on TV."

Simon stepped into the room. "What do you mean, the winningest voter?"

"This old codger's voted for the winner every time, beginning with Taft in ought-eight. Look at him, he's eighty-nine."

The poor man on the screen was being supported by two young women and a crutch. He was standing in a garden somewhere and was sweating and blinking under the hot sun. His eyes rolled as he mumbled something indecipherable into the microphone.

"He's voted for nothing but winners and where has it gotten him?" Simon murmured sadly.

"On TV," said Hatch happily.

Simon went up to his room, and because he felt that his patriotism needed rejuvenating he put Charles Ives on his stereo and looked for Walt Whitman among his books. He couldn't find Whitman but he ran across a volume of three young poets his editor had asked him to review for the *St. Paul Chronicle*. He had started the review two or three times, but though he sensed power and earnestness in some of the poems, the meanings were obscure and the essence of the book eluded him. Now he sat down with his clipboard on his knee and began the article over again and— lo!—he discovered what he wanted to say. He wrote through the morning and after lunch he took his portable typewriter out of its case and wrote through the afternoon.

Downtown, after parting from Simon, the Indian met an old woman in the middle of Main Street. On her face were a thousand wrinkles. She wore a black shawl. She said. "How are you, Smalleye?"

"Fit," said the Indian, stooping and peering closely into her eyes. "Gert? Aren't you Gert Cloud? I didn't know you were still alive."

"Well, I am. I'm your first cousin once removed, in case you forgot, and I'm still living. Where are you going with that shag rug?"

"To Tess and Herbert's. The rug is filthy and Hattie Norman won't wash it only once a year."

"Thank God I'm able to do for myself. I don't think I could stand the Home."

"It takes a thick skin all right."

They parted, then the Indian called her back. "Did you know that since Eve Horseman died you're the oldest squaw in town?"

"I knew that."

"And I'm the oldest buck."

"I knew that, too."

Along came a car and honked them off the street.

The Indian followed the sidewalk for a block and a half, then he turned into the narrow passageway between Tess and Herbert's place and the adjacent grocery store. He dropped his rug in the passageway and emerged in the alley behind. Without knocking he entered Tess and Herbert's apartment by the back door. He stepped into a long carpeted room furnished on one end with a sofa and chairs, on the other with a refrigerator and stove, and in the middle with a dining table. A gun rack hung on the wall over the sofa.

"You home?" he called. He closed the door behind him and inhaled the heavy smell of stale beer.

As he expected, Tess spoke from the bedroom: "Who is it?" The bedroom door was open, and the Indian saw an arm sticking out from the lumpy covers on the bed. Tess slept late because she tended bar till one each morning.

"It's me. I'm uptown on errands for Hattie. Thought I'd just say hello."

There was no reply. He squinted at the gun rack—two rifles and a twelve-gauge shotgun.

"Busy last night?" he asked, to break the silence.

"Not very."

"What time did you close?"

"The usual."

"I suppose Herbert's out front tending bar."

"He'd better be."

The Indian went to the sofa and glanced back at the bedroom door to make sure he was out of Tess's line of vision. He took the twelve-gauge from the rack and carried it to the back door.

"Just thought I'd say hello."

"Yeah."

"Hope I didn't wake you."

"Yeah."

"Well, good-bye then."

"Yeah."

He left, carrying the gun, but in a few seconds he reopened the door and called, "I seen Gert Cloud on the street. Looks damn old, if you ask me."

"Yeah."

"She's the oldest Indian in town, you know."

"Yeah."

"And when she goes, I'll be the oldest."

No answer.

He closed the door and carried the gun into the passageway between the buildings, where he separated the barrel from the stock and wrapped both parts in the rug. He carried the gun thus concealed to the Norman Home. Upstairs in his room he reassembled it and stood it in his closet beside the ladder. He spread the rug on the floor.

At noon the Indian asked Hattie, who thought he was joking, if she would cook his goose.

At five o'clock the Indian knocked on Simon's door. In his reading chair Simon had fallen asleep over his review, and it took him a few seconds to rouse himself.

"Come in," he said thickly.

The Indian stepped into the room and Simon stood up. "Ah, Mr. Smalleye, nice of you to drop in. Here, sit down." He removed some magazines and books from the low-slung easy chair that came with the room.

"Not there," said the Indian. "I'd never get up out of a seat that low."

The Indian sat down—painfully, it seemed—in Simon's reading chair. He studied the room. He said, "You read all this stuff?"

"Oh, no, I'm afraid I don't get around to half of it. I'm oversubscribed where periodicals are concerned. It's a carry-over from my life as an English teacher, a desire to be surrounded by the printed word." Simon sat on his bed. "It's a kind of insulation, you might say."

"Against what?"

"Ah, now that's the question, isn't it? I've wondered about that myself. Insulation against idleness, perhaps. Against ignorance."

The Indian nodded.

"But that's not the whole answer, Mr. Smalleye. At my age I wonder if all this reading I do isn't an insulation against thinking about what lies ahead, against—"

"How come you always wear a tie?" The Indian was scowling sternly.

"A tie? Oh, that, too, is a relic of the classroom. Just as your flannel shirt and suspenders are doubtless what you wore on the reservation."

"My wife asked me to wear a tie for our wedding," said the Indian, "but I never did. That was in twenty-two."

"And now you wish you had?" Was this the reason for the Indian's visit? To talk about his regrets?

"No, hell no. Why should I wish that?"

"I thought maybe as a concession to your wife."

"No, hell no. I gave her sixty years of my life. Isn't that enough? Without putting on a tie besides?"

"Sixty years is indeed a long time."

"I used to wonder what would happen if I died before she did. If she'd have the undertaker put a tie on me. I told her more than once I didn't want to be wearing a tie forever in my grave, but she was the kind of woman you never knew for sure what she'd do. And now I wonder the same thing about my daughter Tess. It would be just like her to have me laid out with a tie on."

"Certainly she must know your wishes."

"Tess? Hell, Tess has only one ambition in the world, and that's to be white. I don't think Tess's been back on the reservation since she married Herbert and they started up business. She doesn't even like to have Indians drinking at the bar. She's set on being totally white. She dyes her hair. Who do you think put me in the Norman Home with all you whites? It's Tess pays my room and board, and what choice do I have? Once I started to stiffen up I couldn't do for myself any more. Couldn't chop wood to feed the fire. Couldn't keep my driveway shoveled out in the wintertime. And just wait. You come see me when I'm laid out in Norris's Funeral Chapel and I bet a dollar I'll have a tie on."

Simon shook his head sympathetically.

"Unless somebody wanted to step up and untie it." The Indian looked hard at Simon. "Somebody with respect for a man's wishes."

"You mean me?" Simon drew back on his bed. He tried to imagine himself taking a necktie off a corpse.

"But that isn't what I came to ask you. I came to ask if you'd give me a hand. It won't take but a minute."

"Yes, of course."

"I'd ask Hatch, but he'd blab it all over the place. It's a secret what I'm doing."

"Mum's the word."

"Okay then, come with me."

"Have you time for a drink first? I was going to offer you a whiskey."

"Maybe later. This is urgent."

The Indian led Simon next door to his room, opened his closet, and drew out the shotgun.

"What are you doing with a gun?" said Simon.

"I'm hunting geese. Now wait till I put on my jacket, then we'll go out on the balcony."

"Are you serious?"

The Indian led Simon along the narrow walkway beside the stairwell and out onto the railed balcony over the front porch. Here the stepladder was already set up, standing under the eaves. A brisk wind was blowing. The sun was low. The Indian handed Simon the gun and began to climb.

"Once I'm up on the roof," he said, "you hand me the gun and then lay the ladder down flat so nobody sees it from the street. Then give me an hour and come back and set up the ladder again."

"Now wait a minute, you'll break your neck. And besides, it's against the law to shoot a gun in town."

"Come back at six, so I can get down." The Indian stood on the top step of the ladder. From there the edge of the roof was waist-high.

"But you're breaking the law, you know."

"I'll fire just once. I only got one shell."

The pitch of the roof was not steep, but once the Indian found himself on his hands and knees on the shingles he looked around rather desperately as though he wished he weren't going hunting.

"Come back," said Simon. "It's a damn fool idea." His white hair waved in the wind.

"Hand me the gun."

"I really shouldn't." But he did.

The Indian's jacket flapped in the wind as he crawled across the pebbly shingles, dragging the shotgun by the barrel. When he reached the chimney he pulled the old red shell from his pocket and sat down to load the gun. He saw Simon from the nose up, staring at him across the shingles. He waved him away.

"It's getting dark," called Simon. "By six it will be pitch black."

"Never mind. The streetlamp will give me enough light."

"But you've got no hunting license."

"I don't need a license. I got a gun and a shell and a taste for goosemeat. Now fold up the ladder and get off the balcony before Hattie finds out."

"It's a damn fool idea," said Simon, but he said it without unction, for the significance of the Indian's act was dawning on him. The Indian was not up there at the peak of the roof merely to shoot a goose. He was up there at eighty-two or eighty-eight, depending on whom you believed, pointing his shotgun into the face of Time.

Simon laid the ladder flat on the floor of the balcony and went indoors.

As he stepped around the corner of the hallway he saw a young man peering into his room, and he heard Hattie shout from downstairs: "If he isn't in there, he's probably in the john. He pees a lot. Just wait around up there and he'll be out."

"Are you looking for me? I'm Simon Shea."

He put out his hand and the young man took it warmly, bowing slightly as he did so. "Mr. Shea, it's nice meeting you. I wonder if we could talk for a minute. My name is Douglas Mikklessen." He was tall and strikingly handsome. He had dark wavy hair and dark serious eyes. He wore jeans and a blue shirt open halfway down his hairy chest. His voice was gentle, almost a whisper.

"Come in," said Simon. "I've been here nine days and you're my first visitor from the outside world. Pardon this mess. I'm not entirely unpacked. Haven't room for my books. I should give most of them away. Look at this, for example. *Symbols in the Fiction of George Eliot*. Are you interested in George Eliot, Mr. Mikklessen?"

"I'm afraid I haven't read him."

"Here, take it. Use it as a door jamb. I'm tired of literary criticism. My favorite book at the moment is *The Wind in the Willows*. Second childhood, you know. Here, sit here in my deep red chair with the broken springs."

"Thanks." Douglas let himself down till he hit bottom. "It's good of you to see me. I should have called ahead." Turning to look out the window, he revealed under his left ear a long purple scar.

"Good of me? Please don't play dumb, Mr. Mikklessen. In a home for the elderly the goodness is all on the side of the visitor. I'm finding that out. For ten years I lived on a remote riverbank and was never distressed by the lack of human contact, yet here in this household of eight I have been very lonely. Can you tell me why that should be?"

Douglas shook his head. "I'm sure you'll get used to it. It seems like a nice place." He cast about for something nice to comment on. "This rug. It's a nice rug."

"Yes, you're right." Simon regarded his rug and thought of the room it had occupied in his boyhood home. It was a spacious room with nine windows—the music room where Simon's mother gave piano lessons, a room full of sunshine and études and the relentless tick of the metronome.

"Of course, when I was living on the riverbank I had a car, and that was a great advantage. When I felt the need to rub shoulders with humanity I could drive into the city—Rookery—and mingle with people in stores and eat on a stool at some counter. And there were certain houses in Rookery where I was welcome. And the campus of course … the library …" Simon's voice trailed off; he was uncertain where these words were leading him.

"I'm from Rookery myself," said Douglas. "I go to Rookery State. I've heard you mentioned at Rookery State."

"Isn't that amazing."

'You're a poet, right?"

"No, no, heavens no. I was a teacher of poetry, not a poet. I tried my hand at writing poetry, but you should see the things I turned out. Atrocious. Sing-song poems. A rhythm so strict you could dance the polka to it. I simply couldn't master the modern idiom. Are you a reader of poetry, Mr. Mikklessen?"

"No way. I'm planning to be a civil engineer some day. But I'm just starting college. I'm a freshman at twenty-five. A late starter."

"Nonsense. I've known freshmen in their sixties."

"My life has been pretty tangled up since high school. I'm trying to get it straightened out." Douglas's soft voice got softer at the ends of sentences, and Simon had to strain to understand him. "What I came to see you about was your cottage on the river. Jean told me about it. Jean Kirk. You know, the doctor."

"Ah, yes, Doctor Kirk."

"Well, she and I go together, see. Or more than go together. Live together is more like it. Only that isn't entirely true either because now she spends half her time in Ithaca Mills. But anyhow, she said you had this cottage on the Badbattle not far from Rookery and nobody was living in it, right?"

"That's right."

"And she said it was in need of repair. So I was wondering if you would consider renting it to us. We have this place in Rookery, an apartment, but they're kicking us out because of our dog."

"I'm sorry, Mr. Mikklessen, my cottage is uninhabitable. One wall is completely gone. A gaping hole, covered temporarily with plywood. Heat would escape faster than you could produce it. Doctor Kirk should have told you that."

"That's exactly what she told me. I could fix it for you."

"You could?"

"It's my specialty. I've built entire houses. I've worked for building contractors off and on."

Simon considered this, his eyes narrowing. Douglas looked out the window and saw a flock of geese in the twilight sky.

Simon cleared his throat. "To be frank, Mr. Mikklessen, I had thought of putting the place up for sale, furnishings and all. I'm not at all well off, you know, pensions being what they were when I retired, and inflation being what it is now. River property is worth quite a little these days, I'm told, and I've about decided to sell the place as is, fire damage and all, and realize a tidy profit without going to the expense of repairing it. You can see my point."

"You're late for supper, professor! Have you lost track of time?" This was Hattie, shouting from the foyer, and Simon popped out of his chair. So did Douglas.

"I'm sorry, Mr. Mikklessen, at the Norman Home supper waits for no man."

"It's my fault, I had no business coming at mealtime. But I had class till four and it's a fifty-mile drive."

"Shea, you hear me?" This was followed by muttering: "I swear to God all I need in this house is an absentminded professor."

"I'd like to talk to you some more," said Douglas as they went together downstairs. "Perhaps I could come back tomorrow. If you thought it over you'd see it's a good deal for both of us. Jean and I and the dog would enjoy living in the country, and you'd have the place repaired and then next spring if you still wanted to sell, you'd get a better price. I could stop back in the morning. I'm staying at the Thrifty Springs Motel overnight."

"Save your talk till later," said Hattie at the bottom step. She took Simon by the sleeve of his suitcoat and pulled him toward the dining room. He followed her a few steps, off balance, then he stopped and jerked his arm from her grip.

"If you please, Miss Norman! I had not finished with my visitor." He turned to Douglas. "Have you had your evening meal?"

"No, Jean and I are just going to grab a hamburger."

"Shea, you have no business inviting visitors to eat here. We serve visitors only at Christmas."

"I wouldn't think of asking a visitor into your dining room, Miss Norman. I was about to ask him to dine with me downtown."

"Downtown! Your food is on your plate!"

"Give it to the Indian. He always has two helpings." Simon climbed the stairs for his coat.

"The Indian isn't here. He's probably gone to Tess and Herbert's again without telling me."

"Then dispose of it as you wish. I've paid for it. Tonight Doctor Kirk and Douglas Mikklessen and I are going out to grab a hamburger. I'm inviting myself along, Mr. Mikklessen, please bear with me."

"Fine. Only could you call me Douglas?"

Outside, Simon's eyes did not adjust quickly to the darkness, and he allowed the young man to guide him down the steps to an old pickup parked in the drive. On the front seat a short-legged, long-haired dog danced excitedly and bared its teeth.

"Your dog appears to be snarling at me," said Simon, stepping back from the window.

"That's not a snarl, that's a smile. Look at his tail."

Indeed the tail wagged, and when Douglas opened the door the dog leaped out and circled Simon, brushing against his leg and yipping with joy. Douglas picked up the dog and introduced him. "I found him lying under my truck one day on campus, thirty-five wood ticks clinging to his hide. I picked off the ticks and fed him milk, and he wouldn't leave me after that. I named him Tick."

Simon petted him between the ears. "He has a happy gleam in his eye."

"He's a great friend. High-spirited. Too high-spirited for our landlord. When he gets excited he barks and whines and piddles on the floor. I guess he's young yet."

"Possibly, although that can be a symptom of old age as well— at least in humans."

They got into the pickup, Tick between them and sniffing at the buttons of Simon's black overcoat. It was an old truck and the engine was loud, and when Douglas put it in gear the vibrations made Simon's nose itch.

"I told Jean I'd meet her at the café across from the Medical Center."

"Wise of you, since we have no other. It's where we all grab our hamburgers in this town."

They met Jean Kirk on the street. She wore jeans and a turtleneck sweater and a tan leather jacket and she greeted Simon warmly (walking toward the restaurant between Simon and Douglas, she linked arms with both of them), but Simon was guarded nevertheless, fearful of being a windy old bird.

The Open Soon Café was overlit and understaffed. They sat in the fluorescent glare and were served, in a manner of speaking, by a morose teenage girl who had plucked out one set of eyebrows and penciled in another. The lettuce salad was rubbery, the coffee strong.

"So how would it be if I picked you up tomorrow and drove you to your cottage and back?" said Douglas. "Just to look it over.

We could talk about repairs. I mean I'm not asking you to commit yourself one way or the other right now, but I'd like to see the place. I bet you would, too, if it was your home all those years."

"I would be glad to be driven anywhere. I have been without a car for four months."

"Great, we'll make a day of it. What time can I pick you up?"

"Are you sure you want to trouble yourself? We're nearly sixty miles from the cottage, you know. And what about your classes?"

"What time can I pick you up?"

"Well, at nine I have an appointment with our friend here. She's going to examine my innards by telescope."

"If you come in at nine," said Jean, "I'll have you out on the street again by nine fifteen."

"I'll be waiting," said Douglas. "The three of us will make a day of it."

"The three of us?" said Jean. "You're forgetting I have another day's work here."

"Tick."

"Oh yes, Tick."

"All right, if I survive the examination I will go," said Simon. "I look forward to it. And you won't need to drive me back. There's a bus from Rookcry in the evening."

The door opened as someone left the café, and there rolled in on the evening breeze the sound of a shotgun blast. Several diners looked up from their plates and one man remarked to another that it sounded close by, within the village limits, but neither Simon nor Douglas nor Jean look notice, the waitress having arrived with the main course and needing their help to sort out what they had ordered.

Soon after the Indian had taken up his station on the roof and Simon had laid the ladder flat and gone indoors, a large flock of honkers flew over town. The Indian stood up and took aim, bracing his shotgun against the chimney, but the geese veered off to the east and he held his fire. It was a long shot that he might have tried in the old days, but now he had only one shell. He sat down again to wait. He passed the time by picking loose mortar from between the bricks of the chimney. He shifted positions several times, for the rough asphalt shingles, through his threadbare pants, were wearing his seat raw.

The next flock flew directly overhead, but it was higher than the Indian liked (his best shot was always head-on) and once again he held his fire. As they passed over, he could hear the fanning of their wingbeats, the sinewy sound of their hardworking wingjoints. Reflecting the glow of the western sky, the thick gray down of their bellies looked like amber foam. When they were out of sight, the Indian regretted not shooting. They had been just within range. He might not get a better shot this evening, and his aching joints told him that he would never make this climb again.

Light died on the prairie. The wind was cold. The Indian squatted in the lee of the chimney, his gun across his knees, and he ran his hand over the bricks, which had retained a little of the sun's heat. Most of the bricks were loose and held in place only by their weight. With his finger he dug out more of the crumbling mortar. He must remember to tell Hattie that her chimney needed repointing.

Then he saw a pickup drive away from the Home, in the back window was a head of white hair like the professor's. What the hell, had the professor forgotten him?

The stars were dim in the hazy sky and the moon was late in rising. The Indian tried to identify constellations, but they blurred and disappeared when he looked at them. He opened his pocket watch and held it close to his eyes and saw, by the light of the streetlamp, that it was nearly six. Since the second flock, he had seen no geese, though now in the darkness he heard the rush and creak of beating wings, first to his left and then to his right. They flew in darkness. Six fifteen.

At six thirty the Indian began calling for help. Not since his boyhood had he come home from a hunt without game. Never in his life had he needed rescuing. Thus he was filled with chagrin as he stood on the ridge of shingles saying, "Hatch! Hatch!" into the night. The pitch of his cry rose an octave as his voice became strained, and to his only listener—a pedestrian two blocks down the street—he was a screeching cat.

After five minutes of shouting "Hatch!" and then "Hattie!" and then "Help!" the Indian grew breathless and woozy. He decided the only way to attract aid was to fire off his shotgun. He braced his right shoulder against the chimney so that in his weakened state the kick wouldn't knock him down. He released the safety. He pressed his cheek against the cold steel and looked down the barrel, and because he had never shot without a target, he aimed at what he guessed was the North Star. Then he saw geese. Suddenly hundreds of geese were skimming the chimneys and power poles of Ithaca Mills. By the light from the street lamp they were dimly visible as wildly flapping forms that seemed not to be moving in straight lines but to surround the Indian in a dizzy dance. As hard as he pressed himself against the chimney, he couldn't overcome the sensation that he himself was moving on air high among the gabbling geese. It had been his principle never to flock-shoot, but in all this dither and noise how could he pick out a single bird to aim at? He leaned hard against the chimney, and just as he had done as a nine-year-old when he first went hunting, he squeezed the trigger with his eyes shut.

The gun blasted and kicked, and the chimney fell apart. Bricks toppled and rolled with the Indian down the sloping shingles and fell over the edge of the roof to the balcony. The shotgun dropped straight down the chimney hole and when it hit the furnace grating in the basement it made a gonglike concussion that rattled all the windows.

Spinner, Leep, and Hatch were watching TV in the parlor, and the racket lifted them out of their chairs.

"Bombs!" said Hatch. "A bomb upstairs and a bomb in the basement." He pointed at the ceiling with one of his stubby forefingers, at the floor with the other.

"Save your valuables!" said Spinner. She rushed upstairs to her room.

"I'll tell Hattie!" said Leep.

"No, *I'll* tell her," said Mrs. Kibbikoski, speeding out of her room and through the foyer with both hands on the throttle. She careened through the dining room and into the kitchen, where she found Hattie on the phone and Mrs. Valentine Biggs leaning out the back door calling, "Who's there?"

"Send Doodle Novotny to the Norman Home," Hattie was saying to the operator. "We've got guns going off."

"Hatch says it's bombs," said Leep.

"Guns! Bombs! God almighty, what next?" said Hattie.

"Let me down the ramp," said Mrs. Kibbikoski. She drove to the back door and nudged Mrs. Valentine Biggs aside with her bumper and coasted down the ramp especially installed for her wheelchair. She came to a stop on the bumpy brick walk running through Hattie's vegetable garden.

Into the kitchen came Spinner, wearing her vinyl coat and pillbox hat and carrying her musical jewel box. She was followed by Hatch, whose eyes were filled with wonder. This put all the residents in the kitchen except Simon, who was downtown, and Mrs. Kibbikoski, who had made a U-turn on the brick walk and wondered why she saw no flames in the windows, and the Indian, who lay on the balcony, half buried in bricks. When the doorbell rang, they formed a procession, Hattie in the lead, and they met Doodle Novotny on the front porch.

Doodle Novotny weighed three hundred pounds. He patrolled the streets of Ithaca Mills in a black squad car that leaned left when he got in and righted itself when he got out; a car equipped with radar, a shotgun, a carbine, a .44 revolver, a spotlight, and a siren that screamed or whistled or popped, depending on how he played the buttons on the dash. It also had a two-way radio into which Doodle often spoke but from which, because he was the entire Ithaca Mills police force, he never heard a reply.

"There's something wrong in the cellar," said Hattie, and the procession led now by Doodle, moved back to the kitchen. At the cellar door he stepped aside for Hattie to go first.

"Don't tell me you're scared!" said Hattie. She unbuttoned his holster and handed him his revolver. She switched on the basement light. "Now get yourself down there and see what's up."

With his revolver at arm's length, Doodle squeezed himself noisily down the narrow steps, his black nylon jacket rasping against the rough stone wall, his breath rasping in his nose. From the bottom step he looked about at the shelves of canned vegetables and stacks of moldy magazines, and he returned to the kitchen.

"Nothing wrong down there," he said, breathless from the climb.

"The first bomb went off upstairs," said Hatch. The procession moved out of the kitchen once again (Hattie slammed the back door, stranding Mrs. Kibbikoski in the garden) and through the dining room and foyer and up the stairs. They looked into each room, beginning with that of Mrs. Valentine Biggs, for which two keys were required, one in the keyhole under the doorknob and another in the bolt she had had installed to thwart rapists.

As Douglas Mikklessen turned his pickup into the circular drive, they saw the squad car standing at the door.

"Shall we come in?" asked Jean, who held Tick on her lap. "Please do," said Simon. "Something is evidently amiss."

From the foyer they heard chattering on the second floor. Hatch called down to them, "There's been bombs and guns going off," and with that Simon remembered the Indian on the roof. He felt a panicky rush of blood to his head. He hurried up the stairs, beating his forehead with the heel of his hand, and as he opened the door to the balcony, bricks tumbled in on his feet. In the light cast out from the hallway he saw the Indian lying across the flat ladder. He was covered by rubble. His face was bloody and motionless.

Simon stepped over the body and stooped for a closer look at the Indian's face. Doodle Novotny shouldered him aside and turned on his flashlight.

"God almighty!" said Hattie in the doorway. "Where did he come from?"

Doodle Novotny put his ear to the Indian's nose, then struggled to his feet and announced, "This poor son of a bitch is dead."

"Like hell I am," said the Indian hoarsely. He opened an eye and closed it again.

"Let the doctor through," said Simon. "Let Doctor Kirk through."

Hattie said, "Where did all those bricks come from?"

"Stand aside, all of you, let the doctor through. Someone call his daughter Tess."

Hattie said, "Listen, professor, I'm the one who gives orders around here." She stepped out onto the balcony and took the flashlight from Doodle. She examined the eaves of her house.

Jean Kirk made her way onto the balcony and knelt by the Indian.

In the doorway now was Mrs. Valentine Biggs, who was beating her breast with Douglas's hand and saying, "Where on earth is a body safe from catastrophe?"

Spinner wound up her musical jewel box.

Leep went downstairs to phone Tess.

Simon shouldered his way through the hallway to his room.

Tess arrived in less than a minute and when she did, everyone's attention shifted from the body in the rubble to the shouting match at the head of the stairs. "What kind of a Home is this, anyway?" said Tess. "The authorities are going to hear about this, you can bet your life on that."

"Pipe down!" said Hattie.

"We expect a little *care* when we put our old folks in a place like this, not neglect."

"What am I supposed to do—tie all these people to my apron strings? Now pipe down."

"The authorities are going to hear about this, Hattie, and I'm starting with the attorney general in St. Paul."

"Pipe down, or I'll have Doodle Novotny throw you out on your ear." Hattie clumped down the steps and retired to the kitchen.

Finding no broken bones, Doctor Kirk asked Douglas and Doodle to move the Indian into the hallway, where in the stronger light she examined his bruises. She stood up and threw back her golden hair and said, "He has two deep lacerations in his scalp.

He may have a concussion. He's in shock and his temperature is dropping. Please bring blankets and keep him warm until the ambulance comes. I'll call the hospital in Rookery. Where's the phone?"

Spinner pointed downstairs. Her jewel box was playing "Some Enchanted Evening."

Tess followed the doctor to the phone. "What's the prognosis?"

Doctor Kirk dialed the phone in the foyer. "There are things we won't know till we get him to a hospital. His injuries wouldn't kill the ordinary person, but he looks pretty old. How old is he?"

"Eighty-two."

"That's against him. If he lives through the night he stands a good chance of recovery. Though he may have had a stroke. I can't tell."

Tess strode into the TV parlor and lit a cigarette. Jean spoke into the phone and when she finished she regarded the residents who were in procession once more but stalled now on the stairs—Spinner and Leep and Mrs. Valentine Biggs and Hatch and Doodle Novotny, one above the other, gazing over the banister at the doctor. Douglas was watching over the Indian in the upstairs hallway, and Simon had collapsed into his reading chair with his overcoat on.

"My stars, you mean she's a doctor?" said Spinner, hot in her vinyl coat and pillbox hat. Her jewel box melody was slowing down.

"You can tell she's the take-charge type, God bless her," said Mrs. Valentine Biggs.

"I'll bet that coat of hers cost a pretty penny," said Leep.

"Now tell me this," said Jean, "what was that poor old man doing out on that balcony covered with bricks?"

"That man is my father," said Tess, darting out from the TV room and gesturing with her cigarette. "And the reason he was up there covered with bricks was because of Hattie Norman's neglect. Listen to me, all of you. When I brought my father into this place—where's Hattie? I want her to hear this—when I brought my father into this place I could tell by the look on Hattie's face that she wasn't all that pleased to have a Native American living here, but she didn't have a leg to stand on, and I moved him in here and I've paid through the nose for the last five years just so he'd get cared for and wouldn't cause Herbert and me a lot of worry and grief, and what happens?" She pointed upstairs. "There, you see what happens."

"I can explain," said Simon, coming into view at the head of the stairs, a lock of white hair hanging in his face. "The Indian got up on the roof to shoot a goose. He asked me to help him up there, and I did! He asked me to return in an hour and help him down, and I forgot. So it may be entirely my fault that he has suffered these injuries, and I want you all to know that I am sick about it. I am literally sick." He turned away and hurried to the bathroom and shut the door. Douglas heard him retching.

Hattie Norman appeared in the foyer and announced that she was serving coffee and cookies in the dining room (a diversionary tactic) and whoever was interested had better step lively.

The procession of five moved from the stairs into the dining room.

Jean Kirk returned to the Indian and counted his pulse.

Simon went from the bathroom back to his reading chair and held his head in his hands.

Tess remained in the TV parlor, chain-smoking and fuming.

And Mrs. Kibbikoski (who would not be rescued until after midnight) remained in the back yard, weeping in her tilted wheelchair. She had made two runs at the ramp but the weakened battery of her electric motor lacked the power to climb it, and now one of her wheels was stuck in the little ditch along the sidewalk. It was a frosty night and Mrs. Kibbikoski shivered and quaked and her right leg throbbed with pain. Her cries for help were soft and tremulous like the warbling of a dove.

The ambulance covered the fifty miles from Rookery in forty minutes. The Indian was loaded aboard, and Doodle Novotny, his siren blaring, escorted the ambulance and Tess's silver Corvette to the village limits, one block away; from there he watched the flashing lights of the ambulance and the moonlit Corvette hurtle across the prairie like a meteor and its tail. "Come in, ambulance driver, come in, come in," said Doodle, testing his two-way radio. "Ten-four and A-okay," he said. "Come in, come in, come in." But the ambulance driver did not come in.

When the ambulance left, Jean and Douglas had climbed the stairs to Simon's room. Through his open door they saw him slumped in his chair. The room was full of shadows, lit only by the reading lamp that funneled its light onto Simon's white hair. Jean knocked softly and said, "May we come in for a minute?"

Simon removed his hand from over his eyes and tried gallantly to smile—did smile, in fact, for the sight of these two young people blunted his despair. "Yes, yes," he said. He stood and unbuttoned his overcoat and turned hesitantly in a circle, as though the problem of where they would sit was beyond him.

"Here, take my reading chair, Miss—er, Doctor Kirk. And here, Douglas, you are already acquainted with this chair with the missing springs. If I get down in that one I'm afraid I'd have difficulty rising out of it … I'll just sit here on the bed … Now, can you tell me anything hopeful about the Indian, Doctor Kirk?"

"The name is Jean."

"Jean. Ah, yes. And my name is Simon, if it's come to that. And I'm glad it has."

"The Indian's in good hands," she said.

"Yes, well, all we can do is hope and pray. And now my whiskey. I have a fresh bottle of Jim Beam here in my bureau." He rose from the bed and opened a drawer.

"No, please," said Jean. "We're just here for a minute."

"I could do with a drink myself," said Simon. "I'm afraid all I have are these tumblers. And no ice. And if we want water we go to the tap in the bathroom. If you had visited me at my cottage not only would you have had ice, you would have had highball glasses from Waterford. I brought them back from my tour of Ireland some years ago." He poured Jean a drink.

"None for me," said Douglas. "I'm off everything stronger than pop."

"Where's the bathroom?" said Jean. "I think I'll cut this with a little water."

"Here, allow me."

In Simon's absence, Jean said, "I guess he's all right. His color is back. But he looked so feeble and washed out before the ambulance came."

"I *hope* he's all right. I want to spend the day with him tomorrow. He's one old man I can relate to."

"Did he say if the cottage had running water?"

"No, but it must have. He doesn't look like he's been roughing it."

"And how is it heated? Be sure to check on that. And tell me about the kitchen—appliances and so forth. If the place is at all habitable and if it looks like you can repair the fire damage, do your best to make a deal with him. I love the idea of spending a winter in the wilds."

"Except you'll only be there half the time."

"Half the time is the best we can do till I get enough seniority at the clinic to drop Ithaca Mills. Or until you get your degree and we move on."

"I'll offer him my repair work as our first month's rent."

"Fine." A pause. "Unless, of course, he wants to move back there himself. He should be urged to do that; it's where he belongs."

Simon returned with her drink. He poured one for himself and held it in the air. "To the two of you. My new friends."

Douglas gave him a serious nod. Jean raised her glass. "We're here because we thought you looked so upset," she said. "But you seem to have recovered."

"Very kind of you." He sat on the edge of the bed and sipped his whiskey. "I don't mind admitting that I was absolutely destroyed by the sight of that man lying there on the balcony in such a dreadful state. I hope you won't think I'm indulging in self-pity, but I must tell you how deep was my despair. I wanted to withdraw from life. I had helped the man up onto the roof, which may or may not have been foolish of me, and I had promised to help him down, and then I put him completely out of my mind. On this cold, black night, I left him up there on that precarious roof to fend for himself. God knows what he went through to get down ... You see, I've done this before—suffered these terrible lapses, but never at the cost of another person. Only myself... Let me tell you what it feels like to lose your memory."

He lowered his eyes to the design in the Persian rug. "You know, it feels like death. I mean when your memory goes, it feels like every alternative in life has been taken away. You begin thinking that every action you take might lead to some unforeseen disaster. And then—worse—you begin thinking that your *inaction* might lead to some *other* disaster. You get to thinking that you're forgetting something even when you aren't, and so you go around all day expecting something to go wrong because you haven't been paying attention. I mean, if you go ahead and do a certain thing, you may be upsetting some balance that all the world is aware of but you have forgotten. So you hang back and you don't do it—whatever it was you had hoped to do—because you're not sure you've considered all the consequences. And then, in your idleness, you begin to wonder if you've forgotten some urgent reason *for* doing it. In other words, if you have forgotten the dire consequences of an action you're about to take, mightn't you just as easily have forgotten the dire consequences of *not* taking it?"

He raised his eyes from the rug to his visitors. Douglas coughed and crossed his legs. He had sunk so low in the springless chair that his knees were now higher than his head. Jean sat in her examination-room pose, holding Simon in her steady, expressionless stare. Simon finished his drink and poured himself another. He stood his bottle beside the bed.

"So that's what I mean by losing your alternatives. You feel unable to act and unable not to act. And isn't that a kind of death, after all? Backing yourself into a narrow space, losing the possibility of action, and losing the possibility of inaction? Giving yourself up entirely to the care and the mercy of others? In the Norman Home to the mercy of Hattie Norman? In the grave to the mercy of God?" He drained his glass in one swallow.

A knock at the door.

"Yes?" said Simon.

"The drought is on TV." It was Hatch.

Simon went to the door. "I'm sorry, not tonight. I have visitors."

"Yeah, well, I thought they might want to see it too." Hatch looked past Simon, studying the young couple. "There's pictures from this year and pictures from thirty-six."

"Some other time."

"One thing about this year, we ain't had grasshoppers. There was grasshoppers in thirty-six."

Simon left the door open, not wishing to close it in Hatch's face, and returned to the bed.

Douglas said, "Getting back to the Indian, I don't see where you're to blame. You didn't cause the chimney to break apart. The Indian probably pushed it over by accident, and it could have happened before you were due back on the balcony. You don't know when it happened."

"It happened halfway through *Wild Kingdom*, " said Hatch in the doorway. "Quarter to seven."

Jean said to Douglas, "Let's not minimize Simon's problem. If he's going to get over his loss of memory, he must not be prevented from facing it."

"But it's not something you get over," said Simon. "That's what I mean about there being no choices left to me. If I could help myself, that would be a choice." He poured himself a third drink.

"I don't believe that," said Jean.

Simon bristled. "What are my choices then?"

"Hattie doesn't like drinks in the rooms," said Hatch.

"Your first choice is to get yourself out of the Norman Home." She was speaking to Simon but looking sternly at the squat figure in the doorway. "If you don't, you'll catch a case of atrophy from your neighbors." She stood; so did Douglas.

She's hard at the core, thought Simon. For all her beauty, she lacks mercy.

She handed Simon her glass. "Thanks for the drink. May I borrow something to read? I've exhausted the collection of *National Enquirers* at the motel."

Together they looked over several poets on his dresser. She settled on Maxine Kumin.

Hatch made way for the three of them to leave the room, and Simon accompanied his visitors to the head of the stairs.

"I'll see you at nine in the morning," said Jean, her hair bouncing on the way down

"So will I," said Douglas, following her.

She called up from the foyer, "Remember, think of this place as only your temporary home. You're already of two minds about being here. I can tell that from the way you talk."

"You mean two fragments of a mind," said Simon. He waved good-bye.

In the meantime Hatch had entered Simon's room and sat in the reading chair. He adjusted the lamp and examined his fingers for slivers the way he used to after a day of cutting timber on his farm. He hadn't had slivers for ten years, and he missed them.

"Ah, Hatch," said Simon, returning. "Not watching the drought on TV?"

"Wanted to warn you about drinking in your room." Hatch yearned for a drink.

"A nightcap, Hatch." Simon poured him a generous portion, then one for himself. "To the health of the Indian. I've done him a great harm."

Hatch held up his drink, not as a toast, but to examine it for purity against the light, a carry-over from the days when he drank little but home brew, which had never been quite clear of foreign matter.

Simon, inebriated, regarded Hatch—his only male companion now the Indian was gone. He saw that Hatch was one of those rare men who wore their belts higher than their stomachs. Simon centered his fuzzy mind on this phenomenon. Whereas most men with large stomachs wore their belts very low, and a lesser number tightened their belts in the middle (producing an upper and a lower stomach), Hatch wore his belt very high; its buckle lay on his breastbone and the track of his zipper ran from his crotch nearly to his throat.

"At what stage in our lives do we decide how to wear our belts?" asked Simon. "Haven't you ever wondered, Hatch, about those strange men who divide their stomachs in half? How can they make that tight a cinch without doing damage to their innards? How does a thing like that come about, Hatch? When did I decide to wear my belt low, and when did you decide to tuck your entire belly into your pants? I mean it was probably our mothers who determined where our hair should be parted and our mothers who trained us in a certain style of nose blowing, but what about the position of our belts?"

Hatch ignored these inquiries. He drank his whiskey in three greedy swallows. He hit his chest with his fist and let out a long, satisfied sigh. Then he got up and waddled from the room.

Simon closed his door and undressed for bed. He took his drink to his chair under the lamp and aloud he recited a psalm beginning, " 'Have mercy upon me, O God, according to thy great mercy. And according to the multitude of thy tender mercies, blot out my iniquity.' " Early in life, Simon had decided that if he was going to retain his religious faith over the long haul he was going to have to nourish it with a daily prayer, and at his prayers he was going to have to say something more interesting than "Now I lay me down to sleep" and other prescribed chants of his childhood. Over the years, therefore, he had evolved this habit of beginning with a psalm and then improvising:

" 'Deal favorably with me, O God: have mercy on me according to thy great mercy.' These four drinks of whiskey have made me fuzzy in the head, Lord, and I feel as though a heavy blanket has been wrapped around my brain, insulating it from the bone of my skull and placing me far off from the alarms and the beacons of life. I have never been a heavy drinker, O Lord, and you know the reason as well as I. With me, the giddy lift of inebriation has always led too easily to the miseries of the hangover, and besides that, when you drink a lot, you miss a lot. You miss the beacons and alarms of life. Now the alarms I can do without, and that's why I have knocked back these four slugs of booze, but the beacons, O Lord, are not to be missed.

"I hope that the brave Indian who was struck down by my negligence is the alarm to end all my alarms, for I am confident that I have suffered my full quota of life's alarms (pardon my presumption) and I pray that during whatever brief time remains to me on this earth I may be spared anything like the utter despondency that came over me when I saw the fallen Indian on the balcony, covered with bruises and brickdust.

"But, dear God, I am feeling a little better now. I am a bit tight and I am feeling a little better. I have made two new friends: the beautiful and somewhat chilly Doctor Kirk—Jean Kirk—and her tall and soft-spoken lover Douglas Mikklessen. And another thing that makes me feel a little better is that I have determined that one of the conditions of a serious sin—namely premeditation—was absent from what I did to the Indian. My forgetting was not intended. So what you have here, Lord, once again, is a case of sheer negligence, and when I figure out how to atone for my negligence I will feel even better yet.

"The beacons, O Lord, let us dwell on the beacons. Young people are among the brightest beacons in the world. In parks and restaurants and on buses, I have seen children in the presence of old men and women. I have seen the old men and women reach out to touch the children, to grasp momentarily the young muscles of their arms, to feel the softness of their cheeks. I understand the urge. Introduce me to a six-year-old and I will immediately ruffle his hair and chuck him under the chin in order to feel, running through my fingers and up my arm, the electricity of youth. So it is no wonder that simply by their presence in the room Douglas Mikklessen and Jean Kirk, half a century younger than I, have rescued me from the slough of despond.

"Jean Kirk puts me in mind of Barbara. What, besides their attractiveness, do they have in common? Is it the distance they seem to be keeping from those around them? Or should I call it inscrutability? I believe I never really knew Barbara, even as my wife. And Jean Kirk, though she be sitting in the same room with you, has the knack of seeming far away. I guess Barbara had an easier time smiling than Jean Kirk does. When Barbara smiled, her eyes peaked like triangles. What do you make of my marriage to Barbara, Lord? Was our marrying a mistake? Our falling in love? I fell in love with Barbara during my first week at Rookery State. I courted Barbara. I married Barbara. I vowed to be Barbara's faithful husband, no matter what, for the rest of my life. A vow I have done my best to keep. With the exception of my eight days with Linda Mayo, I have been Barbara's faithful husband for thirty-five and a half years, while Barbara has . . .

"It's old business, isn't it, Lord? It's futile and old and boring in your ear. What a lot of old business you must have to listen to when night falls on the world and the human race looks back on its mistakes. The drone of empty memories. Well, I know what you must be going through, Lord; I have been taking my meals in the dining room of the Norman Home."

Simon finished his drink. He went to the bathroom. He went to the window and saw the moon over the dark, dry prairie. He went to bed.

In September, 1940, Simon chose his bank as carefully as a man might choose a wife. He was new in Rookery, new on the staff of Rookery State College, and he was anxious to plight his savings of twelve hundred dollars to the bank with the best reputation.

The Drover's National was recommended by his department chairman, and while Simon was impressed by its claim to have remained solvent throughout the thirties, it clearly suffered from old age, its large outdoor clock having stopped at 7:05 of some forgotten day and its gold window lettering having flaked away in some forgotten rain. The Savers' Security, according to its free matchbooks, was the People's Choice, but when Simon opened the door the place was empty of customers and the eight tellers turned as one to stare at him. So he chose Northern Federal because it was large and its granite facing shone like alabaster and when he climbed the broad front steps between the fluted columns it was not hard to imagine himself entering the seat of some government, or the treasure-filled tomb of a pharaoh.

The treasure of Northern Federal was a girl named Barbara. She sat at one of several walnut desks in an area fenced off from the rest of the lobby like a corral. The other desks were occupied by gray-haired women and gray-faced men, so the beauty of this girl with walnut-colored hair caught Simon's eye the moment he stepped through the door. He saw that the nameplate on her desk said BARBARA STEARNS.

He went to a teller and said he wished to open an account. The teller gave him a card with a number on it and told him to sit down and wait. His number was two. He sat in a chair by the gate of the corral and hoped it would be Barbara who opened his account. Over the low fence he watched her at her work, and it struck him that despite her commanding good looks she seemed too small for her desk, too small for her job. What she was doing may have been of supreme importance in the world of finance, but she was doing it in an almost childlike manner. She wrote with the stub of a pencil on a tiny scrap of paper and she bent her head over her work in the fashion of a little girl who is pretending to be grown up. After a while Barbara looked around, saw Simon, and pushed her work aside. She stood and straightened her brown wool skirt and her doe-colored sweater, and as she walked toward the gate she looked down at her breasts to see how they were riding. They rode beautifully, he thought, loosely and fetching and soft as puddings, and when she stood before him and asked if he was number two, it seemed a question not of banking but of betrothal, so probing were her deep, dark eyes.

"Yes, I'm number two," he said eagerly.

"Come with me." She led him through the gate to her desk, where they sat and spoke of the weather (it was windy) and the current rate of interest (it was three percent) and of his twelve hundred dollars.

Behind Barbara was a floor-length window, past which a procession of shoppers and school children were moving briskly through the cold autumn afternoon. Ordinarily Simon's eyes were helplessly drawn to any window and to the rectangle of life it afforded, but now this lovely girl filled his vision, and he could spare not a glance for the world at large. Her speech was soft, her nose faintly freckled. When she turned to her typewriter, he studied her figure in profile. Then she picked up the pencil stub and wrote something on a card and once again she bent to the task like a little girl, her dark hair falling like a tent over her work.

"There you are," she said, handing him the card. "Sign at the X."

That was when Simon noticed her fingernails. They were horribly chewed, some down into the quick, where thin scabs showed that blood had been drawn.

He signed at the X and gave her his money. What sort of life did she lead, he wondered, and what were her terrors, her defeats, that she should nibble so fiercely at her fingers? Was her little girl pose at this desk an unconscious retreat from whatever fear made her chew her nails? Was it her wish, despite her alluring breasts and lips and eyes and hair, to be a child again?

She issued him a savings book and thanked him for choosing Northern Federal. She said she spoke both for herself and for Henry Hamilton III, president of the bank.

"You're welcome," said Simon, rising from his chair and backing out the gate, wishing he could leave her with something to remember him by—something more remarkable in a bank than twelve hundred dollars.

That night Simon dreamed about Barbara Stearns. She was trying to hand him a scrap of paper—it seemed to be a newspaper clipping—and judging by the anxiety in her eyes, the message must have been urgent, but he was unable to take it from her and read it. Failing the simplest task is often the subject of our worst nightmares and the dream grew frightening as he tried again and again to reach out for the paper and failed. But, by morning, fright and failure had evaporated from his memory of the dream and what remained was a curious sense of intimacy between himself and Barbara. In the dream they had seemed to be lovers.

A week later Simon met Barbara in front of Mercy Hospital. It was a rainy twilight, and as he walked up the long sidewalk to the hospital entrance, Barbara sailed past him on a hike. With his umbrella he hurried to the bicycle stand and fell into step beside her, protecting her from the rain.

"Oh," she said, startled. "Thanks."

"We've met, you know. You took my fortune and promised me three percent."

"Oh," she said again. She didn't seem to remember. "Are you with the hospital?"

"No, I'm at the college. I'm here to visit my department chairman. Appendicitis. He's recuperating very impatiently, they say."

"Oh."

"Do you have someone here?"

She nodded.

"My name is Simon Shea, in case you've forgotten."

In the lobby they wiped their feet and Simon furled his umbrella and stood it in a corner, and Barbara removed her scarf and shook out her dark hair. Her presence at his side, her form buttoned and belted into her tight raincoat, excited him. Rain sparkled on her eyelashes. Her raincoat, he noticed, was patched at one elbow and frayed at the hem.

The receptionist sitting behind a cage was an elderly woman with a beak like a buzzard's. She greeted Barbara by name, then gave Simon a frigid stare.

"Doctor Franklin's room?" he asked.

"210," the woman snapped.

Simon and Barbara boarded the elevator. "Lovely woman, that," he nodded toward the receptionist as the door closed.

"Mrs. Farr," said Barbara.

"Why does she hate me, do you suppose?"

"She thinks you're with me."

"And what of that?"

Barbara shrugged. Her eyes were on the wall that was moving down past the grillwork of the elevator door.

Simon said, "I dreamed about you the other night. You were trying to tell me something."

The elevator stopped and Simon pushed open the heavy door. Barbara made no move to get out.

"Are you going higher?" he asked.

"Three."

"How about meeting on the way out? I'll tell you my dream and you can tell me about Mrs. Farr."

Her assent delighted him, though it was the vaguest of nods and she avoided his eyes. "I'll be forty-five minutes," she said as Simon let the door slide shut.

Later, when they met in the lobby, Mrs. Farr made a deprecatory noise in her nose, something between a sniff and a snort.

Outside, in the rain, Simon walked her bike. "Where to?" he asked. "I'm a stranger in town."

"To my house," said Barbara, carrying the umbrella. "Mother baked cookies today."

For a man of forty, Simon's experience in the field of romance was meager, and as he approached Barbara's house, expecting to meet her family, he felt like a teenager who mistakenly interprets a girl's casual attention as a promise of love. The difference between Simon and a teenager was that Simon understood his mistake as he made it. He knew better than to trust the stirrings in his heart as he stood on the front stoop, holding the umbrella, while Barbara searched her purse for a key.

"Mother's at bingo," she said, letting him in. "She goes every Friday night. There's a thirty-dollar jackpot."

She hung up his coat and showed him into the kitchen, where they sat at a table and drank strong coffee and ate oatmeal cookies and talked about the college as though it were a foreign province. This was Simon's first week on campus and he did not yet feel at home among the faculty. He had the heightened awareness of a stranger among natives, and he described his colleagues in terms that made Barbara laugh. He said that the three tenured members of the English department gave him gooseflesh, that he had never run into a group of people who looked so much like the cast of a third-rate horror film. There was the anemic Doctor Franklin with his bullet-shaped head and his terrible teeth. From Princeton he was, and chairman of the department, and he was toiling mightily—and in vain, thought Simon—to make this college in the jackpines the Princeton of the West. There was the sadistic Doctor Stemm with his cankerous cheeks and his runny nose and his every utterance laced with poisonous sarcasm. And there was the huge and lopsided Doctor Flora Corpulotta, who spoke with a lisp and whose eyes were crossed. Last year Doctor Flora Corpulotta had had a sabbatical and a stroke, and now she was returning to work refreshed but lame. She smiled with only half her mouth, producing, when happy, a sneer.

He told Barbara how, as a new member of the department, he had been called into a conference with these three gargoyles in order to have academic policies explained to him. They said that the moment a student declared himself an English major, they began pushing him to his limits, and beyond. They assigned the student readings by the hundreds and term papers by the score. They sent him on meaningless errands to the library to find out such things as the location of the first performance of Milton's *Comus* and the identity of all the people who attended. They demanded that the student discover for himself on what page of which issue of the *Journal of International Pedantry* there appeared its one and only and highly celebrated typographical error. (They told Simon it was on page 206 of the May, 1927, issue, in case he didn't know.) And the student must be able to recite from memory, in Middle English and without stuttering, the "Nun's Priest's Tale." They said they wanted a student majoring in English overworked until he dropped, and if the student came back for a second term they knew he was sincere, and if he came back for a third term they knew he must be very persevering indeed, and if he came back for a fourth term they began taking an interest in him and thinking of him as worthy of a degree in English.

"College doesn't sound like much fun," said Barbara.

"Have you attended Rookery State, by any chance?"

"No, I went to business college in Minneapolis. That wasn't much fun either, come to think of it."

"Well, this English department is something out of the Dark Ages. I said to the three of them, 'In what course are we allowed to show our students the pleasures of literature?' and their eyes got very large. They looked at each other as though they had hired a goon by mistake."

"Will you have to teach the way they tell you to?"

"It looks like they expect conformity from their underlings, all right. There are four untenured English instructors besides myself, and all four of them look harried and grim as death. But, I have made a vow!" Simon brought his fist down on the table and the cookie plate jumped.

"A vow? I love vows. Tell me."

"I vow that either I will let some sunshine into my classes at Rookery State, or I will lose my job trying." Years later Simon was to remember this vow and marvel at how easy it was to fulfill. In an otherwise dismal department Simon himself was the sunshine. His popularity among the students of Rookery State was almost instantaneous and it continued for the rest of his career.

"I'm with you," said Barbara. "There's enough grimness in the world without putting it where it doesn't have to be." She examined her fingernails and began to nibble.

"How are things at the bank? Is that a grim job or a happy one?"

"It's fine. I'm well thought of by Henry Hamilton III, and that's what counts."

"Is he your sweetheart?"

"Heavens no, he's in his eighties." Barbara laughed an odd laugh; she winced and cried out, as though her amusement were a stab of pain.

"How about our going out some night? This weekend? Dinner somewhere?"

"Well..." Barbara turned away.

"Saturday night. I'm thinking of buying a car. I might have it by then."

"I would enjoy going for a ride in a car. But dinner? In public? I don't know. It's just… I don't know."

Barbara's mother came home. She was chubby and short and soaking wet. "Tonight I came close to winning the pot," she said as she struggled out of her dripping coat. "I needed B-6 with three calls to go. I tell you that's the closest I've been to thirty dollars in cash since Hector was a pup. How do you do." She offered her hand.

"My name is Simon Shea." He took the hand. It was icy and wet.

"He teaches at the college," said Barbara.

Her mother was impressed. "Well, now, that's more like it."

More like what, Simon wondered. He said, "I guess I should be going. It was good of you to have me in. Delicious cookies, Mrs. Stearns."

"Name's Bemis," she said. "Vera Bemis. Happy to make your acquaintance and we hope you'll come again."

Simon was taken aback. Why was her last name different from Barbara's? Too polite to inquire, he supplied his own answer: Mrs. Stearns had remarried.

Barbara went with him to the front door, and as he leaned down to pick up his umbrella she raised her lips to his.

In casting about for friends, Simon had to look beyond the curdled personalities of his own department, and so it was to Jay Johnson, mathematician, that he recounted this experience with Barbara Stearns of the Northern Federal Bank. Jay Johnson, too, was a bachelor, but unlike Simon, Jay Johnson's cynicism ran deep and his appetite for the social life ran high and strong. Jay got himself invited to the president's teas and to the dean of women's ice cream socials and to the art department's salons. He never left a party until the last bottle was drained, nor a faculty meeting until the last candidate was denied tenure. He roamed the campus like a private eye, dropping into all faculty offices at least once a week, whether the doors stood open or not, and almost everywhere—because of his high spirits and quick wit—was welcome.

"Last night I went out with a former beauty queen," he told Simon at the coffee bar in the bookstore. "You talk about getting kissed by what's-her-name from the bank, this beauty queen was the most passionate number I've had out in weeks. But to tell you the truth, I don't care much for her looks. She's said to be pretty—she was Miss Rookery of 1937—but I can't see it. Her eyes are too big for her head and her head is too small for her body. In my opinion, she's a bug-eyed pinhead. You're new around here, Simon, so you might not have noticed, but there's a hell of a shortage of good-looking women in this city."

"The current Miss Rookery, in my opinion, is Barbara Stearns of the Northern Federal Bank."

"I'll look her over for you," said Jay.

And he did. Between his two math classes that afternoon, Jay Johnson drove downtown and went into Northern Federal to appraise Barbara Stearns.

"I don't know," he told Simon the next day (they were lunching in Jay's apartment), "she's a little on the young and innocent side for my taste, and when I went up to her desk and asked if she belonged to the harem of Henry Hamilton III (did you know, Simon, that Hamilton is a rake?) she showed me a very ugly side of her disposition. And then there's her looks. I agree with you that the face is superb. But the body. Have you really considered the body?"

"As much as possible in the time allowed me. I think the body's fine."

"It *is* fine. And yet... how shall I say this? You look at the body and you say, 'Ah, yes, the body is fine,' and yet when you're not looking at the body, when you've turned away and all you have is the *image* of the body in your mind... well, she's a bit of a chunk. You're a newborn babe in these matters, Simon; you're the next thing to a monk emerging from his cell; you're a hermit coming down off the mountain, and it's my duty to tell you that now in the twentieth century nobody wants a chunk. You've been looking at too many Renaissance paintings. Women in chunks died out with the Old Masters. It's 1940. What we want now are women thin of face, thin of flank. What we want now is Garbo."

"You're blind," said Simon. "Barbara Stearns is a beauty."

"Well, by comparison perhaps."

"By comparison with what?"

"By comparison with Doctor Flora Corpulotta."

Some days later the subject of Barbara's shape came up again, after Jay had gone back to the bank for a second appraisal. "*Chunk* is too extreme a word," he told Simon at the coffee bar in the bookstore. "I take back the word *chunk* and I substitute the word *oval*. Bear in mind that I teach geometry and *oval* is a word I know."

"What do you mean, *oval?*"

"I mean that from Barbara Stearns one carries away the impression of ovalness. She has an oval face, right?"

"Don't we all?"

"And she has oval breasts, right? And her hams are oval."

"Her hands?"

"I said her hams."

Simon nodded, feigning seriousness.

"And her calves are oval, Simon; all her component parts are oval, and when you put them together what you get is a very oval girl."

True enough, Simon decided, Barbara was basically oval, and he unhesitatingly became a devoted student of her ovalness. He dated her once a week, and in his secondhand Ford coupé they drove out to small towns in the vicinity to attend movies. Barbara was shy of being seen with Simon in Rookery, and though he thought this strange (was he not presentable? was he not somewhat of a personage among his students?), he didn't see that it mattered.

One night, driving back from Bette Davis in Ithaca Mills (or was it Carole Lombard in Staggerford?), Barbara asked him, her head on his shoulder, why a man as marriageable as himself had never married. Or had he?

No, no, he assured her, he had never come close. He said that as a high school boy in Redbank, South Dakota, he had been steered by his mother in the direction of Rosemary Rosinski, because Rosemary was Catholic and well scrubbed and far and away the best of his mother's piano students. But Rosemary hadn't struck Simon as very interesting in those days; nor did she now, as a matter of fact, so he changed the subject and invited Barbara to the Rookery State homecoming dance the following Saturday.

"But that doesn't tell me why you never married," said Barbara, changing it back.

"I don't know, I just never did," he said, unable to put into words how he seemed to be living his life backwards, how he happened to be one of those men who felt old at thirty and young again at forty. Up to this point in his life Simon had been, quite frankly, an egghead. From his boyhood on, he had been ardently fond of books, libraries, rhyme schemes, fountain pens, crossword puzzles, literary journals, notebooks, and chess—in short, all methods and devices of intellectual stimulation. With the blossoming of his mind in his teens and twenties and thirties, his emotions had withered. At the University of Minnesota he had been a single-minded student of literature; he had written his thesis on the mystical poet Thomas Crashaw; and by the time he was awarded his Master of Arts degree he had already developed the scholar's stoop and the researcher's squint and a halting, carefully considered manner of speaking.

At twenty-three, he took his first teaching position at St. Andrew's, a Benedictine college in the woods of central Minnesota, and although he never trespassed beyond the warning sign at the door of the monastic enclosure, he fell naturally and happily into monkish habits. He attended morning mass and evening compline, and he proctored students from his cell-like room at the top of a dormitory. With the passing of years he became a borderline mystic himself. Besides following the chapel liturgy, which grew to be as vital to his daily living as food and sleep, he developed some rigorous habits of personal prayer that brought him to his knees at odd hours in unusual places. He was occasionally seen praying in the cemetery and at the Virgin's grotto by the lake. Sometimes he strolled the campus by moonlight, saying his rosary. Once in the rain—though this was never verified—he was rumored to have prostrated himself before the statue of St. Andrew at the entrance to the monastery garden.

For his assiduous attention to his duties, Simon was hugely respected by the abbot, who doubled as the college president, and by his teaching colleagues, most of whom were priests. And for his eccentric manner of speech, he came to be mimicked by his students, though always good-naturedly and at a safe distance. Simon worked hard to make himself into the image of a certain kindly and ponderous professor he had admired at the University, and by the time he was thirty he had become so deliberate in thought and deed that it was possible (said the students) to carry on a daylong conversation with Mr. Shea without interrupting your normal round of affairs. On your way to class say something to him as you passed his office door, and when you returned after class you would be just in time for his well-formulated reply. At noon ask him his opinion of Dos Passos or Galsworthy or the weather, then go to lunch and return at one o'clock for his closing remarks. And what, they wondered, went on in his head during those long pauses in the classroom? Midway through a lecture you would see his thoughts suddenly swerve from the topic at hand and his eyes stray from his notes and come to rest on the rolling woodland outside the window. He would stand there transfixed for several seconds—for half a minute sometimes—as though he saw among the branches of the trees, as in a child's picture puzzle, the lines of a human face. How quaint he was, and likable. And how stuffy. He was an old man long before his time, and at thirty- five—as though he willed it—his hair turned gray at the temples.

Then he began to wake up. The same bucolic atmosphere of St. Andrew's that had made it so easy for Simon to grow prematurely old made it possible for him to grow young again, for inherent in the Benedictine life is the habit of self-study, and by studying himself Simon came to see what a fuddy-duddy he was. He grew impatient with his role as dear old Mr. Chips. By forty, he had lived through his old age and now he wanted to be young again. This change was most noticeable in the classroom, where he decided he had been taking himself altogether too seriously to be a first-rate teacher. He had learned that of the three elements a teacher must constantly be aware of—his students, his scholarship, and himself—it is hard to achieve a proper balance between the first two if one is totally absorbed in the third. He became disillusioned with the lecture method and in its place he substituted discussion or, as he called it, conversation. The change wasn't altogether welcomed by his students, for as Simon's classes became more vital and informal the students had to show up better prepared and on their toes. It was in this spirit of renewal and exploration (and second childhood) that Simon decided to expand his world by applying for the position at Rookery State.

These, then, were some of the facts of his life that Simon was hard-pressed to put into words for Barbara.

"And how about you?" he said in fun. "How have you come to be so old without marrying?"

"Twenty-three isn't so old," she said, and Simon was surprised. He had guessed she was nineteen or twenty.

Simon went to the homecoming dinner and dance alone; or rather, he went with Jay Johnson and Miss Rookery of 1937. Miss Rookery tried to teach him how to dance and Jay Johnson kept pressing liquor upon him, and by the time the three of them sat down to a midnight snack at a roadhouse outside of town, Simon was drunk.

Jay said, "Simon, tell me when you're sloshed enough to hear a piece of shocking news."

With his customary precision Simon said, "I'm slightly beyond the point of dizziness, but not yet to the point of falling off my chair." He fell off his chair.

Jay picked him up and helped him to a booth where, with the wall on one side of him and Miss Rookery on the other, Simon sat upright. Jay, facing him from the opposite seat, said, "Simon,

I've discovered something about your Barbara Stearns of Northern Federal."

"You're going to tell me she isn't oval after all."

"She's married."

"What shape is she now, Jay? By what geometric term shall she be known?"

"She's married, Simon."

"Married? I'm sorry, Jay, but you're mixing your metaphors. Married is definitely not a geometric term. Give me a geometric term."

"Triangle, Simon. You are part of a triangle. I don't know how she thinks she can get away with it, but she is currently married to a man who is lying in a coma on the third floor of Mercy Hospital. His name is Donald Stearns and he's been unconscious since July, and they say he's certain to die. But he never does. They say—"

"Who says, Jay? Is this what Pythagoras says?"

"This is what my landlady tells me and what most of Rookery knows. It's general knowledge off campus. Barbara Stearns has a husband who is about to die, and when he does, she wants to have a new one ready, and guess who that new one is going to be? Simon, you hear me? You're going with a woman on the brink of widowhood."

Simon cupped his hand over his mouth and spoke between his fingers. "I have always loved widows. God bless widows and orphans. God bless holy monks and hermits. I think I'm about to be sick."

Miss Rookery sprang from the booth and stood at a distance.

"For God's sake, get to a toilet," said Jay.

"I don't believe you," said Simon.

"It's the truth. My landlady swears she's married."

"I don't mean that. I mean about Miss Rookery here." Simon got to his feet and took Miss Rookery by the hand. "What I mean is, I don't believe what you told me about this lovely Miss Rookery of 1937. I don't believe she's a bug-eyed pinhead."

Simon lurched off in the direction of the toilet as Miss Rookery struck Jay savagely three times—right cheek, left cheek, right ear—with her heavy, pebble-grained purse; then she stalked away to find, in another booth, another ride home.

Simon, too, had to find another ride home, for when he came out of the toilet, Jay was gone.

Barbara denied nothing. Yes, she was married and, yes, she felt horrid about deceiving Simon, but he must remember she had never actually *denied* that she was married, and she never took the lead in this romance.

"What about that kiss the first night I walked you home?" he said. "That was very forward of you."

Barbara turned away and shed a tear that glistened in the moonlight (they were parked in the alley behind Barbara's house) and said, "You'll never know how starved I was for a kiss. Donald had been in a coma all summer."

Simon was unsure of what he should be feeling. Anger? Pity? He thought it remarkable that after this initial tear she never shed another as she told him the story of her tragic summer. She spoke steadily and at great length and appeared far less moved than Simon, who listened in wonder. Was she dispassionate by nature, he asked himself, or benumbed by what she had been through?

Barbara Bemis and Donald Stearns had been married in June. Mrs. Bemis, a widow with high expectations for her only daughter, had not approved of the marriage. Donald worked in a granite quarry for a very low wage while Barbara after all had been to business college. But Mrs. Bemis attended the wedding anyhow and she had to admit that Donald's muscular hug made her feel warm. She concealed her dismay when they set up housekeeping above Eiler's Hardware with nothing but two chairs, a table, and a mattress.

"Let the young ones go their own way," Mrs. Bemis was told by her friends at the American Legion Club, where she went regularly for bingo and Scotch on the rocks. "Barbara and Donald will be very happy together."

"Don't go fretting over Barbara and Donald," she was told by her beauty operator. "Just be thankful she didn't marry a Catholic."

"Or a Negro," said the woman at the next sink. "There's a Negro at the college this year, and they say he's a very dark shade of black."

The Legionnaires were right: Barbara and Donald were very happy together. Donald was loud and reckless and high-spirited, and Barbara, in her demure fashion, quietly adored him for his thunderous laugh and his bullheaded opinions and the shocking pleasures he taught her on the bedless mattress. Each morning Donald delivered Barbara to the bank on his motorcycle, and their parting kiss at the curb was long and lingering and commented upon by many. Then Donald roared off to the quarry three miles south of the city.

Barbara worked five days a week and Donald worked six. With their combined income they might have bought a used car, but Donald, for all his bluster and bravado, was tight with money and he insisted that his motorcycle would get them anywhere they wanted to go.

"But what about when it rains?" Barbara argued.

"When it rains we stay home," he said, and that settled it. In good weather they went for Sunday rides on the cycle—Donald goggled and Barbara hugging his ribs, her hair flying—and in bad weather they stayed home.

Barbara worried about Donald at the quarry, for he worked with explosives, and one Saturday when she took her mother's car for a spin she paused beside the quarry and saw him standing deep in the pit, with a massive block of granite swinging on a crane over his head. Whenever she heard the ambulance race past the bank toward the hospital, her first thought was of Donald, and she was relieved each day at five o'clock when she knew he would be climbing out of the pit and heading into town.

It was at ten after five one hot afternoon in July that Donald broke his neck. The sheriff concluded that he must have been traveling too fast on his cycle, for although the road was narrow and it twisted sharply through the woods, it was midsummer and broad daylight and if he wasn't driving carelessly why didn't he see the chunk of granite that had fallen from a truck and lay in the middle of the road? Donald flew headfirst over the handlebars and slammed into the broad trunk of a cottonwood tree.

Barbara had walked home and was preparing supper when her mother came to her with the awful news. Her mother drove her to the hospital and let her off at the emergency entrance.

"I'll be in after I park the car," her mother said, and she drove off to the Legion Club for two quick Scotches.

The first thing Barbara saw as she entered the emergency room was a wheeled cot covered from head to foot with a rumpled, bloody sheet. She thought the sheet covered Donald, that Donald was dead, and she grew dizzy and slumped against the wall. But she was wrong. Though the sheet was stained with Donald's blood, Donald was not under it.

"He's in the next room," said the nun in white who rushed to Barbara's aid.

He must not be seriously hurt, thought Barbara, otherwise how could this sister be smiling? She took heart. But her shift from despair to hope was reversed as soon as she entered the next room. She saw Donald lying under a bright light and a nurse cutting away his shirt and revealing deep, bloody furrows along the right side of his neck and along his right shoulder, openings of flesh so deep that Barbara could see ligaments and bone. In the corner of the room a doctor was threading a needle.

"Will he be all right?" said Barbara, cautiously approaching the cot, her heart pumping in her ears.

The nurse looked at the doctor. The doctor looked over his glasses at Barbara. "Please have a chair in the waiting room," he said.

"But tell me he'll be all right." She kissed Donald on the forehead. His eyes were closed. He felt cold. "Tell me he'll be all right."

"He'll be all right," said the doctor. "Now please have a chair in the waiting room. There are magazines out there."

The smiling nun who had been escorting Barbara steered her into the waiting room and toward a chair, but Barbara broke away from the nun and ran outside and vomited under a tree and paced about the grounds until her mother returned. The two of them went inside then and sat together in the waiting room.

"Oh, I wish I had ordered doubles," said her mother. "Usually two Scotches fortify me just fine, but right now I feel unfortified. I should have ordered doubles."

Beginning with her left thumb, Barbara chewed down all ten of her long and pointed nails.

It was nearly an hour before the doctor emerged from the sewing room and Mrs. Bemis stood up and said, "What's the news, Doc?"

The news was as bad as news can be. "He'll die," said the doctor. "I don't know exactly when, but he can't last many days. The spinal damage is too great. I'm sorry."

"Is he conscious?" asked Barbara. She had a forefinger in her mouth.

"No, he's not likely to regain consciousness. We're moving him up to the third floor where we can monitor his heartbeat and give him some nourishment. Room 312. You can visit him up there." The doctor left.

"Are you going up?" said Mrs. Bemis.

"Of course I'm going up," said Barbara. "Aren't you?"

"I'm going to the Legion. Call me there when you want a ride."

As they left the waiting room by opposite doors, her mother called, "You aren't pregnant, are you?"

Barbara said she wasn't.

Barbara's first sight of Donald in room 312 was strangely consoling. That he had the best of care seemed borne out by the siderails on the bed, the apparatus for intravenous feeding, the blanket pulled up to his chin, the tight white dressings covering the lacerations in his scalp. On his expressionless face it was not difficult to read serenity, and if the doctor was correct about this being a sleep beyond recall, it was—thank God—a sleep without pain.

It was evening now, and a woman came into the room to visit the man in the other bed. He was a frail old man with no teeth who lay with his eyes closed.

The visitor pointed to Donald. "Is that your man there?"

"Yes," said Barbara.

"How long's he in for?"

"I don't know." She felt her throat close, tears rise. "A few days."

"He's lucky. The doctor says Ezra here probably won't come out alive."

At this, Ezra sat straight up in bed and nodded proudly.

Barbara kissed Donald on the forehead, on the lips, then left the room. She gave her phone number to Mrs. Farr at the main desk and walked back to the apartment.

Later that evening, Barbara was visited by Mr. and Mrs. Henry Hamilton III, president and first lady of Northern Federal. Henry Hamilton was a wealthy old lecher with a bad case of asthma, and as he climbed the stairs over Eiler's Hardware his breathing sounded like the sputtering valve of a pressure cooker. He weighed scarcely ninety pounds. Mrs. Hamilton, brawny and bejeweled, helped him into Barbara's apartment, removed his hat, placed him on one of the two chairs in the sitting room, and stood at his side while he caught his breath. Barbara, in her dressing gown, had been ready for bed, and she stood uneasily before her boss, wondering what this visit meant and feeling the old man's eyes roam up and down her front.

When the noise of his breathing subsided to a steady wheeze, Henry Hamilton asked Barbara to sit by his side, which she did while he explained to her that as a valued employee of Northern Federal she could look to Northern Federal for aid and assistance in this difficult time, and that although neither the bank nor the granite quarry carried health insurance on their employees, Henry Hamilton himself would confer with the director of the hospital and arrive at a plan to ease the financial strain of her husband's misfortune. He said the reason for his charity was that he didn't have long to live and he wanted to be remembered as a generous man. When he finished this speech, Barbara thanked him and Mrs. Hamilton picked him off his chair and moved him to the door, where he turned and tipped his hat at Barbara (imagine a hat on a night this hot) and gave her a lewd wink (imagine lust in a man this old) and in the second or two before he turned away from her to descend the stairs, Barbara saw the truth in his prediction that he would soon be dead. She saw it in the way his lower lip sagged out from his teeth and she saw it in his green complexion, the color of old currency.

The next day, Henry Hamilton III, good as his word, called in Sister Theodora, director of Mercy Hospital, and discussed with her the Stearns case. Barbara was making four dollars a day at her job. Mercy Hospital was charging four and a half dollars a day for Donald's half of a double room. Henry Hamilton ordered Sister Theodora not to charge Barbara Stearns any more than three-fourths of her salary for the care of her husband. Anything over and above that amount would be paid for by the bank, and Barbara could repay the bank, at simple interest, after her husband was dead.

"But what if her husband doesn't die?" said Sister Theodora. "He might live on and on."

"He'll die," said Henry Hamilton, green shadows playing across his face. "We have his doctor's promise."

To make it official, Henry Hamilton had his secretary draw up the details of this agreement in a letter, and he carried it personally to Barbara's desk and laid it before her with a flourish, drunk on his own self-esteem. Helping the unfortunate made him feel profoundly good and he wished he had started earlier. His help, of course, was worse than no help at all, for the hospital would have charged Barbara no interest on her unpaid balance, and Mrs. Bemis was outraged by this measly show of generosity, but Barbara was too preoccupied to care, and how do we measure charity after all if not by the euphoria of the donor?

At first, Barbara visited Donald twice a day, expecting to find him either dead or awake. The doctor insisted there was no hope, but her friends at the bank told her encouraging stories of amazing recoveries they had heard of, people snatched from the maw of death by prayer or by the manipulation of the fingers and toes or by a magical tea brewed from crocus petals and pine sap; so on her way to the hospital she would try to imagine Donald propped up on a pillow and chatting with his roommate or eating custard or paging through *Collier's*. But Donald slept on, and after two weeks Barbara secretly quit hoping and reduced her visits by half. There was a certain relief in giving up. Now, fully expecting the worst, she felt no letdown each evening when she found her husband unconscious. The difficulty was that no one at work, nor her mother, would permit her the luxury of facing reality; they were determined that she should delude herself with dreams of Donald's recovery, that she should continue to look like the happy bride she had so recently been, and whenever she appeared the least discouraged they would take her aside and give her an absurd and wearying lecture.

Donald's roommates were replaced every few days (the frail, toothless Ezra walked out under his own power), and at first Barbara paid them some attention, inquiring after their care and chatting with their visitors. But after twenty-five or thirty trips to the hospital, she put an end to these polite exchanges and concentrated on Donald. Like a nun at prayer who has trained herself to fight distraction and focus on a crucifix, she directed her words to this head on the pillow—the closed eyes, the dry lips, the oily hair—and she didn't care who listened.

"Well, Donald," she would say, slipping out of her coat and sitting on the steel chair beside the bed, "you aren't missing much out there tonight. It's been perfectly miserable—rain off and on all day and a chilly wind and now it's raining harder." She liked to begin all her visits by mentioning some troublesome aspect of life; if the weather was pleasant she wouldn't bring it up at all, but would substitute some other piece of irksome news (muddy streets or the price of groceries or the flu) as if to imply that by lying here day after day in this hot room and being nourished by a tube running into his arm, Donald had cleverly chosen the better part. Then she would speak of her day—what she had had for lunch, what Mr. Hamilton said to Mr. Thompson at the bank, what her mother would say to Wendell Willkie if she had the chance—and Donald never made any response—not the twitch of an eyelash—to anything she said.

Some evenings the patient in the other bed, having spent the long day with this comatose roommate, would be starved for human contact and would attempt to make a conversation out of Barbara's monologue, not realizing that she was in some kind of mysterious communion with the stranger on the bed. "Yes, I have driven Second Avenue many times," the patient might say, upon hearing Barbara's report of some street repair. "I used to take Second Avenue to work when I was with Sorenson Tool and Die, and I always liked it because it passed through the park, but after a while I started taking Eighth Avenue instead because Second, park or no park, had so many bumps." Barbara paid no attention to such remarks; she was as deaf to the roommate as Donald was to her; and therefore what nurses sometimes heard when they passed the door of 312 was a duet, a man's voice and Barbara's voice harmonizing in a canticle of the daily round ("I paid thirty-two cents for a pound of coffee today." "I was with Sorenson Tool and Die for thirty-seven years."); and only when one voice paused for breath did the other voice go solo: "You'd never guess who wrote a check with insufficient funds today." Or, from the bed by the window: "My bowels have always been sluggish."

As the weeks passed, Barbara tried less often to imagine how Donald would respond to her words if he were able, and she began to examine her *own* response to what she was saying. Thus, what began as a mere recital of news grew into an exercise in self-awareness. During an early visit when she mentioned how much she paid for coffee, Barbara imagined Donald's displeasure (not only was he thrifty, he never drank coffee), but during a later visit, after the price rose again, she said, "I paid thirty-four cents for a pound of coffee today, Donald, but I don't think that's at all outrageous when I consider how much coffee means to me. I can get sixty cups out of that can, and what else gives me as much pleasure for half a cent these days as a cup of coffee? I don't believe in being tight about the small things, Donald. I don't mean I'm going to surround myself with luxury, for heaven's sake, but neither do I intend to cut back on the small pleasures of life: the books I buy, the coffee I drink. If the book club is going to charge two dollars for a good novel, I'll pay it. If coffee is going to forty cents, I'll pay it. I don't intend to be like Mrs. Crump, my mother's neighbor, and switch to drinking plain hot water. That's demoralizing. That's disgusting."

The more Barbara studied her motives like this—the more she explained herself to herself—the more she grew in confidence, and the hope she had lost for a happy marriage was replaced, at least in part, by her growing self-respect. Not that she wouldn't have given anything to have Donald back. When she thought of him hale and rolling with her on the mattress on the floor of the apartment, her spirit sagged with longing and she chewed and spat out her fingernails; but if that life was not to be, then she must learn to live a different life, and in the second month of Donald's coma—about the time Simon Shea came into the bank and opened an account— she began to think of herself as single again.

This was Barbara's story, the essentials of which she recited, dry-eyed, by moonlight.

Simon was moved to the very bottom of his heart. Now he *knew* what he felt. It certainly wasn't anger. It was not exactly pity. It was love. "You're brave," he told her, enfolding her in his arms. "Next time you go to the hospital, take me with you. I want to help you through this trying time."

"You'll have to face Mrs. Farr, remember."

"To hell with Mrs. Farr."

And the next evening Simon looked the buzzardly Mrs. Farr in the eye when he and Barbara passed her cage. They took the elevator to the third floor. They stepped out and Barbara greeted a nun by name and nodded at several robed convalescents doddering in the corridor. She led Simon into room 312. There lay Donald in the ninety-seventh day of his coma. He lay on his back—in perfect ease, it seemed to Simon. His eyes were closed. His breathing was slow and shallow. He was shaved only every third day, and his whiskers, like his eyebrows and hair, were very dark. The scars on his right cheek and temple were purple and healing. His hands lay palms-up at his side, his fingers slightly curled. The room was hot. The other bed was empty, stripped of its sheets. Tiny bubbles were rising in the bottle of fluid that was flowing into Donald's arm.

Barbara took off her coat and sat down and picked up one of Donald's hands. "Well, you aren't missing much out there tonight, Donald. Very cold, and it's supposed to get colder. They're predicting a hard frost. There's someone here I'd like you to meet. Simon Shea. He teaches at the college."

As Simon timidly approached the bed and took Barbara's free hand in his own, he opened his mouth to say something, but he didn't know what.

"It's all right," said Barbara softly. She looked up at him and nodded as though she understood his confusion. "It's all right," she said again, holding hands with both her men.

Two days later, Donald died.

For Christmas Simon gave Barbara a diamond ring. By this time Mrs. Bemis knew that Simon was a Catholic (albeit no longer a borderline mystic who prayed in public) and her regard for him had cooled considerably; but Mrs. Bemis's opinions meant nothing to Barbara, and if Simon wanted her to take instructions from a priest, so be it. Through the winter and spring she made periodic visits to the Newman Club chaplain at Rookery State, and she went to confession for the first time on Good Friday and made her First Communion on Easter Sunday.

On the Saturday after Easter, Simon and Barbara were married in the Newman chapel, Barbara's alluring ovals moving down the aisle in step with the booming organ, the wedding party forming an oval as it deployed itself in the chancel, the oval-bellied priest orating the circular sentiments of the psalmist ("God from God, Lord from Lord, true God from true God...") and Simon declaring "I will," and meaning it from the bottom of his pumping heart and looking eagerly forward to the sublime moment when he would gather—naked—this brave and pudding-breasted girl into the oval of his embrace.

In her apartment in El Paso, Barbara emptied her kitchen of all perishable food and gave it to the people next door. She wrote a postcard to the postmaster, instructing him to hold her mail. She poured herself a small glass of wine and took it into the living room and settled down in front of the TV to watch the election returns. She gazed at the screen, where a reporter with his collar open and his tie undone was reciting the names and numbers that were also superimposed across his face, but she paid no attention to the news. Her thoughts were not political.

"In the fourth ward, Miller leads Gonzales by thirty-two hundred and seven votes. In the fifth ward, it's Hagen by a landslide. In the sixth ward . . ." If I get to Rookery and Simon is gone, I'll inquire at the college. His friends will know where to find him. His friends must think me horrid for running off and leaving him. Not that Simon would have told them that I was horrid. No, it's a safe bet that Simon, in all these years, has never said a word against me; yet by his stubborn loyalty to our marriage vow he has made me look heartless. Who will believe that in the two years we were together on the river, Simon was as heartless as I?

"In the Eighth Congressional District, McMillan and Cordenza are locked in a contest too close to call at this time. In the Ninth District, we predict Sampson by well over fifty thousand votes. In the Tenth District . . ." No, if Simon isn't home, I'll go to the Odmers' house instead of to the college. I know the Odmers are still living on the riverbank because Simon spoke of them in his note last Christmas. They will know where he is, and they won't judge me harshly for having run off. The Odmers never judge anybody.

When they were neighbors, Felicity Odmer struck Barbara as the most uninteresting woman she had ever met; Felicity was absolutely incapable of gossip. For her the only important activities in life were gardening and hunting and piling up firewood for winter.

"Carter and Ford are running neck and neck." Barbara put

down her wineglass and picked up tomorrow's plane tickets. She double-checked the times of departure and arrival: El Paso to Denver, Denver to Minneapolis. *What brings you back to Rookery?* the Odmers would certainly ask, Simon would certainly ask, everybody would certainly ask; and how could she explain her motives when she didn't quite understand them herself? Now that her plans were made, she almost wished she weren't going.

Barbara went into the bedroom, undressed, and put on her nightgown and robe. She sat at her mirror and examined her face. Would Simon know her? When she left Simon, she was a girl of twenty-six. This winter she would be sixty. Did one retain, at sixty, anything of one's youth? Any lines of the face? Any mannerisms? Any single opinion or feeling? Barbara picked up the small photo album which she kept on her dressing table, and it fell open to the page she most often studied: side by side were three snapshots taken in the early forties. The one on the left was a wedding picture; she was twenty-three and the bride of Donald Stearns; her smile was tense, Donald's was silly. The picture in the middle was taken by Simon; she was twenty-four and Simon's wife and standing alone under the birches along the Badbattle. The picture on the right was taken by a street photographer in Cheyenne, Wyoming; she was twenty-six and walking arm-in-arm with Evert Metz, her lover. Looking back at the middle picture, Barbara bent closer to the page. This would be the way Simon remembered her: standing with one arm around a spindly birch trunk and wearing a white blouse and a pair of those homely slacks that were stylish during the war—slacks worn by Rosie the Riveter and baggy in all the wrong places, the thighs particularly; her face was animated, her eyebrows raised, her lips caught in midsentence. How fascinating it would be, thought Barbara, to know what the girl was saying as the picture was snapped. How fascinating it would be, now, to know the girl herself.

She closed the album and raised her eyes to the mirror. Her face was still good and firm, her eyes still dark and direct. She was happy with her new light hair, her new upswept permanent. Her cheeks were colorless, but with the help of cosmetics that was a secret easy to keep. Surely Simon would not be disappointed by her physical appearance. If he recognized her. What if she had to tell him who she was? How embarrassing.

She went back to the living room and switched off the lights and sipped her wine by the light of TV. The Presidential race was very close, said the harried young reporter, who then introduced a political scientist from the University of Texas. The professor said that he was puzzled by the Black vote, by the Catholic vote, and by the farm vote; he said that he was puzzled as well by the Chicano vote and the white-collar vote, and he didn't know what to think of the returns from California—but none of this captured Barbara's attention; she was puzzled by mysteries of her own. Why, at the height of her career in real estate, was she taking this leave of absence? Why had she stood firm against the pleading of Mr. Bernardson when he asked her to stay on at least through the winter? He had said that absolutely no one in the firm was her equal at selling property to retirees from the North. Wasn't she flattered by his praise? Wasn't she tempted by the increased and unprecedented rate of commission he offered her? At this time of year she would be heading north against the flow of travel. All Northerners who could afford it were coming South. Furthermore, she had never liked Minnesota winters. But she was going in spite of all this. She was leaving on impulse, driven by a strong conviction that now, at sixty, she must break out of the routine of the past twenty years and fly across the country. She would look for Simon, and if Simon wasn't to be found, or if he wasn't happy to see her, or if he was dead (God forbid!), then she would fly straight on to Detroit and Boston. She had a cousin in Detroit and a friend in Boston. She would keep going until she found somebody who was glad to see her.

Barbara finished her wine and went to the phone. She called Simon's cottage on the Badbattle one last time. Again no answer.

WEDNESDAY

The election had slipped Simon's mind, and he did not learn of Carter's victory until he was positioned in something of a headstand on an examination table at the Ithaca Mills Medical Center. Most of his weight was on his right cheekbone, and his bare behind was high in the air.

"Do you think he'll make a good President?" asked Jean Kirk, inserting the proctoscope. "Did you vote for him?"

"Yes. No." Simon was able to utter only a syllable at a time, for as the instrument inched intestinally deeper, it kept taking his breath away.

"Well, *I* voted for him. I like his vitality. Ford was such a plodder, don't you think? And don't you suppose a Democrat is likelier to push the Equal Rights Amendment?"

"No. Yes." How long *was* this appalling device anyway? It seemed to be nudging his diaphragm.

"I'm really quite politically oriented, but I didn't have time to get involved this year. I worked for Students for McGovern in seventy-two. We traveled around to several midwestern cities. Not that it did any good. Remember how McGovern got slaughtered? I suppose you voted for Nixon.

"Yes. No." His words were clipped cries.

"The rest of the staff at the Rookery Clinic all voted for Ford, I'm sure. They're all Republicans. They're mostly old and stodgy. How many votes did Carter win by, finally, have you heard?"

"Don't. Know."

"I'll tell you what all the Rookery doctors are afraid of. Nationalized medicine, that's what. But I say why fight it? Socialism is the wave of the future, don't you think?"

"May. Be." The instrument was opening up pockets of gas, and Simon was most embarrassed.

"Everything looks shipshape from this end." She withdrew the proctoscope and helped him down off the table. "There, that wasn't so bad, was it?"

"No." Then on second thought: "Yes."

"Not a sign of tumors. But I wonder, are you always that gassy?"

"Oh, I'm a windy old bird."

She seemed not to recognize these words as her own. She left the room while Simon put on his pants, then she accompanied him to the waiting room where Douglas was paging through last week's *Miller.*

He stood. "You ready to go, Mr. Shea?"

"Ready. I checked the bus schedule, and there's a bus leaving Rookery at eight this evening, so you needn't bother driving me back."

"As you like, but I could just as well."

"Nonsense. Now before we leave town, we'll swing by the Home and I'll inform Hattie."

"*I'll* inform Hattie." Jean picked up a phone and dialed the Home. "Hello, Miss Norman? This is Doctor Kirk at the medical center. We have no report yet from Rookery about Mr. Smalleye, which obviously means he's still alive, but I'm calling about Mr. Shea … No, he's fine. I just wanted you to know … Is that so? The police? … Did they give you the number he should call? … Yes, I'll tell him. Now the reason I called, I wanted to tell you Mr. Shea won't be home till late this evening … I don't *know* what time. He's a grown man and he'll be home when he gets there. Good-bye."

She hung up. "There, I untied Hattie's apron strings. You're free for the day."

"Thank you. I feel like a man on parole."

"She said the St. Paul police called for you this morning. They want you to call them back."

"The police? It must be about my car."

Jean dialed and handed the phone to Simon.

"Stolen vehicles"—the shrill voice of a man in a hurry.

"This is Simon Shea returning your call."

"Simon Shea, cripes, do you realize how hard you are to find? I've been trying for three days to reach you on your Rookery phone and finally I got the sheriff up there to go out and track you down. He says he spent half a day searching the hills up there for your place, and when he found it he had to go look for neighbors who might know where the hell you took off to. Let me remind you it's a misdemeanor not to register your change of address with the Bureau of Motor Vehicles. Now listen, we've got your car. It turned up in Como Park, and we had it hauled over to Sterling Towing, where it's being stored. When you come for it, check in here at police headquarters first. We'll give you an authorization slip so you can get your car. Got that?"

"Yes. What shape is the car in?"

"Let's see. It doesn't say here on this report. It must be okay."

"And when did you find it?"

"Let's see. It doesn't say. Probably last night."

"I'll come for it tomorrow."

"Whenever." He hung up.

"My car," said Simon. "It's been found."

"Step one in your recovery," said Jean.

"I beg your pardon?"

"Psychologically you're in the dumps, Simon, but I think you've already hit bottom. Bottom was probably last night when the Indian fell off the roof. Now recovering your car can be the first step in your comeback. You can use it to drive away from the Norman Home. For good."

"On the contrary, having my car will make the Home more tolerable. I can go for rides."

"It won't work. With a car you'll become Hattie Norman's errand boy."

"We'll see," said Simon. He put on his coat.

"We're off," said Douglas. He gave the doctor a quick kiss.

As they went out the door, Jean handed Simon his watch.

The day was sunny and brisk. Ten days before, riding across the prairie with Odmer, Simon had been looking entirely inward and he had not seen the devastation wrought by the rainless summer; but now, bouncing across the prairie in Douglas's rickety pickup, he noticed that the cattails and wildflowers of autumn were dead in the roadside ditches and row after row of dead corn—stunted and earless—stood abandoned in the fields.

Halfway to Rookery the highway lifted and twisted into the forested hills that Simon loved, and here the signs of drought were even more alarming. They passed dried-up swamps where underwater vegetation, exposed now to the sun, gave off a spicy pungency as it wilted and died. They passed a lake in which the water level had dropped a fathom and all the docks stood on dry land. They passed acres of burned-over forest where the trees were black sticks and peat smoke boiled up from the earth like steam.

In Rookery they went first to Mercy Hospital, which was much expanded and scarcely recognizable as the place where Donald Stearns, in 1940, slept his life away.

In a room on the fourth floor they found the Indian. He lay on his back with his head wrapped. He turned to Simon with a glassy stare.

"I came to apologize," said Simon. "I left you stranded on the roof and I can't tell you how sorry—"

"I think I shot one," said the Indian. "I saw its wings fold up just before I fell. Have you come to get me out of here?" He sounded half asleep.

"I'm as sorry as I can be." Simon closed his eyes and shook his head.

A nurse came in and said, "No visitors here, please."

The Indian said, "I shouldn't have shot from the roof. I should have shot from the balcony. Where's my clothes?"

"No visitors here, please."

"Good-bye," said Simon and Douglas.

"I'm pretty sure I shot one."

"Now settle down, Mr. Smalleye," said the nurse.

"Where am I?" said the Indian.

Douglas and Simon drove further into the city. They stopped for lunch and Simon bought a newspaper. On the front page were two photos, one depicting a troop of forest rangers bulldozing a firebreak; the other showing a huge tub of water dangling from a helicopter. There was a photo on page two of a ball of fire leaping from one treetop to another. An article told of a man who had driven a pipe into the ground for a well and struck smoke. Another said that Gerald Ford had lost his voice and his wife had delivered his concession speech. On the back page it said that Mrs. Babe Ruth, at seventy-six, was mortally ill.

Back in the pickup once more, Douglas said, "Would you like to see the campus for old time's sake? I'll drive you around."

"Yes, of course," said Simon, and they rode through the sunny, leaf-strewn streets to the north edge of the city and slowed to a crawl as Simon called the various buildings by name and told of their function.

"There's where I had my office, there beyond that corner window on the first floor." Beneath the window a shirtless boy and a barefoot girl lay in a pile of leaves.

"There's the Science Hall, where a good friend of mine named Bob Thomas was involved in a five-year power struggle for the chairmanship of the department. He was chairman but he was challenged every year by a hothead named Mulligan."

"Who won?"

"They both lost. The president appointed a new chairman and the new chairman fired them both. There's Engineering. I suppose you have most of your classes there."

"Only two, metalworking and blueprint reading. You know how they make you take other stuff you don't need."

"A liberal education. Want it or not, it's good for you."

"Freshman English is good for you?"

"It's mother's milk."

"It's not my dish. We're reading a novel by some old woman and we're writing a paper with footnotes."

"The novels of old women are the meat and potatoes of life, my friend. Freshman English is a veritable banquet, and footnotes are the nutcups." Being back on campus made Simon giddy.

"By December we've got to write a poem."

"By December you will have put the fires and the stink of the metalworking shop behind you, and you will have changed your major to English. You will be drugged by Keats and in love with the *P.M.L.A.*"

"I've been drugged, but not by Keats. What's the *P.M.L.A.*?"

"*Publication of the Modern Language Association.* A feast of footnotes."

They stopped for a red light, and Simon pointed to the math building. "That's Johnson Hall. Named after a friend of mine. Probably my best friend ever. Jay Johnson. He died of cancer the year he retired. They asked me to speak at the dedication of that building. A sad sort of dedication. Jay dead. No family. Jay had never married. It was like his funeral all over again. An odd funeral it had been. No close relatives in attendance because he had no close relatives. Strange how we hate to witness the grief at a funeral, and yet a funeral without that grief is somehow unsatisfactory. Oh, he had a cousin or two in the mourner's pew, but I guess the only real grief was mine, and I was clear in back of the church. Same at the dedication of Johnson Hall. All those tributes to his teaching, his scholarship, his way with students, but nobody feeling quite the way I did—plain sad that Jay was gone."

The light changed to green. They passed a row of dormitories and several houses with Greek letters over the doors and election signs on the front lawns. FORD-DOLE. CARTER-MONDALE. And for laughs: GOLDWATER-MILLER.

"There's the house we have our apartment in," said Douglas. "A nice place, till Tick queered it for us by messing on the rug and growling at the mailman and barking early in the morning. But that's okay. Jean and I both like the idea of living out in the woods."

"You talk as though I've already rented you the place."

"Jean says I'm supposed to offer you a rent you can't refuse."

Five miles north of the city, Simon directed Douglas off the
highway and onto a dirt road that wound along the river. They
climbed farther into the hills, trailing a cloud of dust. They passed
a fire warden's lookout tower. They passed a field of rusted farm
machinery. They passed a meadow that slanted up from the road,
and Simon pointed to the crest of the hill and said that that was
where he often came on his evening walks; he said the view from
the hill was a long one. They passed a small farmyard and a rocky
pasture and a field of dead corn; Simon said the farmer's name
was Pribble. They passed the house and sheds and garden of Mr.
and Mrs. Odmer, Simon's closest neighbors. Over the next hill
they came to a white mailbox on a white post and Simon said,
"This is it."

Douglas pulled off the road and parked in the bare spot
where Simon's car used to stand. He studied the place through
the windshield—white cottage, broad spread of lawn, birch trees.
"Hey, this is great," he said. Simon was already out of the car and
shuffling through the thick carpet of dry birch leaves. Tick and
Douglas followed him around the cottage and down a slope.

"Hear that?" said Simon. He was listening to the bubbling
Badbattle River where it was sweeping over the rapids at the
bottom of his property and calling to him like the voice of a loved
one. They continued down to the riverbank and watched the water
leap over the stones.

"It's low now. You should see it in the spring—treacherous
little piece of water here in the spring. Beyond the rapids, down
there, it's deep. You can catch big pike there in the spring and early
summer." They looked downstream to a pool of still water, and at
that moment a kingfisher dropped into the pool like a ball of blue
lead. It came up with a minnow in its beak and soared into the
woods across the river.

"Here in the hills there's always something to see," said Simon.

A crow called from the opposite bank.

"And hear," he added.

A pair of blue jays sprang out of a bare birch and flew upstream.

"It's sure beautiful here," said Douglas. "I don't see how you could leave the place. I can imagine how it will be in the winter. Snow on the riverbank. Does the river freeze?"

"No, the current's too fast right here. Down there you'll see ice on that pool, but it will be too thin to walk on."

"How could you move away? Jean says you never should have."

"I had to. Before I destroyed it, and myself with it."

"But maybe by spring you'll want to come back."

"No, never."

Douglas shrugged and looked at the sky. Tick drank from the river. Simon said, "Come, I'll show you the cottage."

He unlocked the door and they went into the soot-filled kitchen. It was colder indoors than out, and the floor creaked where they stepped.

"Not so bad," said Douglas, looking at the fire damage. "I'll put in new studs and wallboard. Insulation. Ship-lap siding on the outside... Some damage to the ceiling but not very much... I'll rebuild the eave and replace a few shingles. Hell, we're only talking about two hundred and fifty, three hundred dollars in materials."

"And your labor?"

"A month's free rent, how's that?"

"I don't know, Douglas. Where would you and Jean live in the meantime? That plywood leaks heat. You'd never stay warm."

"We've still got the apartment in the city. Our eviction doesn't happen for another week or so. By that time I'll have this place fixed like new." Douglas ran his hand over the exposed, charred wall studs. "I'll start work tomorrow morning."

"No classes tomorrow?"

"I can't sit in a classroom with a job like this on my mind. How about a look at the rest of the house?"

Simon showed him through the living room, pointing out the thermostat for the electric heat and pausing at the windows facing the river. They looked into the bedroom and the den. On the porch he showed Douglas the fuse box and the switch for the pump.

"Are you accepting my offer?" said Douglas.

"All right, the place is yours for the winter." Simon shook Douglas's hand, which felt not like the hand of a student, but rough like a carpenter's.

"Great. Let's go into Rookery right away and haul out a load of materials. Can we charge it to you?"

"Yes, at West End Lumber. They know me there. The manager flunked freshman English in the late forties."

"Let's go."

"You go ahead, Douglas. I want to sit by the river. And then when you get back I want to take you for a walk. I'll introduce you to the Odmers, and we'll go to that hilltop in the meadow I pointed out."

"Fantastic." Douglas and Tick left.

Simon was glad to be alone. He felt some strong emotion coming on like the surge of feeling in the clinic on Monday, and he didn't want anyone around if it grew more intense and caused him to weep or curse or break out in a sweat. What was going on, anyhow, that his heart should be pumping so fast? It was like the edginess he sometimes felt from too much coffee or too little sleep. An aimless urgency. A vague dissatisfaction with the world at large. He felt bilious. It was nothing but the agitation of homecoming, he told himself, and in order to divert his mind he went to his tool shed, unlocked it, and drew out a rake. For a few minutes he raked leaves into a pile, then he remembered the statewide burning ban. Fire was the only way to dispose of the leaves unless he picked them up and carried them across the road and dumped them in the woods, and that was hard work.

He put the rake away and went into the cottage. In his study he looked at the spines of the hundreds of books he had left behind. What would he do with them when he sold the place? He opened a drawer in the filing cabinet where he kept carbon copies of the reviews he had been writing for thirty-five years. What would he do with these? He pulled out the earliest review. October, 1941. The arts editor of the *St. Paul Chronicle* (who in those days was also fashion editor, society editor, and recipe editor) had asked Simon for a biweekly book review and this was his first: surely the only time in history that Scott Fitzgerald and Hilaire Belloc were brought together in the same article. *If the serious reader is going to find fault with these two otherwise estimable masters of English prose,* he had written, *he will find it in the tendency of Fitzgerald to be unnecessarily complex and in the tendency of Belloc to be unnecessarily simple.* Was there enough truth in that sentence, he wondered, to justify his attempt at cleverness.

He returned the review to the drawer and took out another. June, 1963. *Are not the dismal, violent, and hopeless stories of the present day traceable to the dropping of the atomic bomb in August of 1945? The bomb brought the war to an end and, with it, the general belief in the power and nobility of man. In a stroke, man was diminished.* Simon scanned the review for titles and found none; it was an essay rather than a review, and this disappointed him. He hadn't remembered using his biweekly column as a soapbox.

January, 1959. Another essay, concluding, *Any hack can give you truth. It takes a writer of talent to give you style. The genius gives you both.* "My how pompous," said Simon aloud in the chilly, echoing room. "And how talented."

He read for a half hour and wondered what would become of all these hundreds of reviews. Little or nothing, judging by the musty smell of the yellowing paper, judging by his editor's remark when Simon once proposed collecting some of the better pieces into a book. Like most of the men and women he taught with, Simon had harbored a lifelong desire to publish a book, and like ninety-five percent of them he never did. What he had seen in his dreams was a book entitled *My Life as a Reader,* but in 1965 when he proposed such a collection, his editor at the *Chronicle* discouraged him. "Crazy idea, Simon. What's your base of readership? St. Paul and its suburbs. You think that's enough readership to interest a publisher in a book like that?" His editor by this time was T. S. Testor, a harried man whose every utterance was a decree. "Do you suppose your casual book buyer, if he's got the choice between a Cheever novel and a collection of Shea's old reviews, is going to buy Shea's old reviews? Or a choice between Moss Hart's autobiography and Shea's old reviews? Or a choice between a sex manual and Shea's old reviews? Face it, Simon, your book's a white elephant before it's printed. What the world wants from you is your autobiography." Testor himself was working on his autobiography and was forever urging Simon to do the same.

"My autobiography would put the reader to sleep, T. S. The idea doesn't interest me very much. But a sex manual, T. S., now there you have something. I'm going right home and get started on a sex manual."

Simon chuckled to think of T. S. Testor. To this day Testor was his editor in St. Paul and still urging him to get started on his life story.

Simon shut the file drawer and went into the bedroom. He sat down in the chair between the double bed and the dust-covered dresser. He had slept here for thirty-five years. It was a good bed, and he wished he had it in Ithaca Mills. He wished he had this view as well. From this window he could see down the slope to the river and into the woods beyond.

What a short time he and Barbara had spent in this bed together. They had bought the house when they were married in 1941. In those days country living was considered suitable only for farmers, and they were thought to be out of their minds for turning their backs on Rookery's paved streets and magnificent new system of sewers.

"We're only eight miles out," they said, "come and see us." But save for Jay Johnson, people seldom came. Frankly, the Sheas were not a popular couple. They fought. They were married in April and they fought through the summer and into the fall. Then they called off the fighting and lived through the winter in the wearisome peace of indifference. Like most unhappy couples, they were left alone. Separately Simon and Barbara each had a number of colleagues at work of whom they were fond, but together they seemed to live in isolation. At first Simon had thought this was due to their disparate backgrounds; Barbara's acquaintances were from the business world while his were teachers; and he imagined that once each became more familiar with the other's friends, and the friends' spouses, then they would build friendships with the bank personnel as well as with the faculty. But this never happened. Time and again Barbara and Simon sought to establish social ties with people they worked with (dinner parties, dances, drives to the Twin Cities for plays and concerts), but no matter how pleasant the dance, no matter how many laughs they shared with their dinner guests, no durable ties were formed. During the second or third evening with a particular couple (the Thompsons of Northern Federal or the Lindemanns of the philosophy department) there were as many awkward pauses and strained attempts at joviality as there had been when they first met.

What was the flaw that kept the Sheas on the sidelines throughout the social season? Why, after wine and dessert, did their evenings out never advance from chattiness to warmth? What impediment precluded easy companionability, both between themselves and with others? Simon blamed Barbara and Barbara blamed Simon, each thinking—erroneously—that the other placed a high value on socializing, and each concluding—correctly—that the other was at fault. Both *were* at fault. Their flaw as hail-fellows-well-met, their impediment to companionability, was that they were both inclined to be loners. All his life Simon had been exceedingly self-sufficient. His upbringing as an only child, his diligent scholarship, and his secluded life at St. Andrew's had prepared him to be content with his own company. His joys in life—reading and writing and disappearing down country roads—were the pleasures of solitude. He seemed not to *need* companions, and what companion—or wife— is going to stand for an attitude like that?

As for Barbara, she began this marriage to Simon preoccupied by her memory of Donald. She was pensive. Though she never uttered his name, Donald was constantly on her mind. Donald's ruggedness. Donald's loudness. Donald's stubbornness. Donald's assurance. So different from Simon. Then, finally, Donald's stillness as he lay asleep in the hospital. Secretly Barbara began to relive her grief. She felt she hadn't done justice to her misery. Too soon after Donald's accident she had had to play the role of the strong and persevering widow-to-be. Too soon after Donald's death she had become again a bride. Now there was time to grieve. Now she was out in the country, away from her mother, away from the neighbors of her childhood, and she was free to feel bad. She brooded. She kept a certain area of her consciousness roped off and devoted to Donald. She kept her job at Northern Federal and she cooked meals and she cleaned house and she made love to Simon (pleasurable lovemaking all right, but not frightening and exciting in the style of Donald Stearns); yet all the while a segment of her thinking belonged, like a shrine, to the memory of her former husband, and when Simon threatened to intrude upon that memory, threatened to desecrate the shrine, she bristled and defended it with anger. Then after a few months, when she was finally able to put Donald behind her, when she had dismantled the shrine, she found Simon beyond reach, he having burrowed deeper into his scholarship and left her behind.

Thus they passed from phase one of their marriage (conflict) to phase two (indifference), and their quarrels diminished while their silences grew longer. By the time they were married a year their aims and interests were so vastly separated that they had all they could do to muster an occasional show of anger, and their latter-day spats were like memorized rituals, imitations of spirited fights gone by. Simon would tell Barbara over dinner that she was altogether too devoted to the pursuit of money (she had been promoted to manager of Northern Federal's loan department) and that she should broaden her interests with a college course or two; then Barbara would say that no one's interests were narrower than Simon's; then Simon would say that she could use a little training in art or music or literature to temper her hardheaded business sense; and then Barbara would turn up the volume and recite her customary list of Simon's failings (his nose in a book, his head in the clouds) and she always signed off by concluding that no woman in the world would have been able to live happily with Simon Shea, and the rest of dinner was marked by a few tears on Barbara's part and some tongue-tied scowling on Simon's.

Simon was not so indifferent toward Barbara as he appeared, at least not at the beginning of phase two. Rather, he was mystified. He had not been aware of her lingering affection for Donald and when she finally put her memory of Donald away for good and gave Simon more of her attention, he was not aware of how aloof he seemed to her, how far he had retreated from her. He wondered what was on her mind. She read nothing but cookbooks and mysteries and she didn't have much to say. She hummed a tune as she went about her household chores, the same tune over and over, perhaps a melody of her own creation, and she seemed unconscious of humming it. And gradually Simon, poring over his books, grew unconscious of hearing it.

For the most of that first year of marriage, the Odmers and Jay Johnson were their only visitors. The Odmers were their closest neighbors. They were Barbara's age, and the Sheas genuinely liked them, but liked them in the same way that they liked the chipmunks at the back door and the orioles nesting in the birches: they liked them as presences rather than personalities.

Jay Johnson was a personality. Jay Johnson drove out to the cottage almost every Sunday evening (Jay touched all his bases once a week) and drank beer and talked uproariously about his students and his girlfriends and the eccentrics among the college faculty. For all his cynicism, Jay was an expansive and good-hearted man, and his talk was not meant for Simon alone but for Barbara as well. With Jay present, Simon and Barbara were at their best, seemed in fact on the best of terms with each other, and when Jay got into his car to weave home in the wee hours, they made him promise to return the following Sunday.

Then in September, 1942, Jay introduced the Sheas to Evert Metz, a new member of the art faculty. Evert Metz was a broken man: his English was broken, his heart was broken, and when he smiled he showed you several broken teeth. He came limping into Rookery fresh from a broken marriage in Montana and Jay Johnson, to cheer him up, brought him out to the Sheas' cottage on the Badbattle. He brought him out four Sundays in a row and then, sensing that Evert Metz was working some kind of chemical reaction in the Sheas that threatened to destroy their old three-way friendship, he stopped bringing him. But Evert Metz, with neither an invitation nor a car, came anyhow. Sundays on the Badbattle meant so much to the lonely Evert Metz that he came out the next two weeks in a taxi; Jay had no choice but to resume the invitations.

Simon liked the art but not the artist. Evert Metz specialized in the buffalo. Hazy horizons, Indians, sagebrush, herds of buffalo—serene and pleasing landscapes that belied his agony. It was the sort of painting Simon most admired, representational and slightly romantic and tending to blue. He bought one of Evert's larger pieces for the cottage, a picture called "Hills of the West," and later he saw a smaller oil of Evert's that he couldn't pass up—a stream purling and bubbling down a snow-covered hillside—and he bought it for his office. This was the year that Simon served on the planning committee for the new library, and when the time came to consider the interior decoration, Simon swayed the committee and a two-story mural was commissioned of Evert Metz, whom Simon called "the Charles Russell of modern times."

But, oh, Evert Metz the malcontent. Evert Metz was fifty. He was tall and brawny and sour and loud. His face was concave and his nose was small—much too small, thought Simon, to give Evert's large and reckless opinions the resonance they needed in order to be convincing. His hair was sandy, his eyes green, his clothes wrinkled. On Sunday nights at the Sheas', Evert drank beer and roared. He roared first with laughter, telling the same off-color jokes week after week; and then after six or eight beers he roared with anger, cursing the man who stole his wife and cursing the head of the Rookery art department and cursing his shitheel students; and finally—spilling beer down his shirt—he roared with remorse, regretting his infidelities to his wife, regretting his decision when he was young to be an art teacher rather than a full-time painter, regretting his yearlong commitment to remain in Rookery, the coldest, dullest, most godforsaken, backward, stupidest hick city on the face of the earth. What Evert vented was mostly bile, but he was capable of affection as well. Near midnight, after a monologue of savage spite, he was likely to grip Simon's hand, or Jay's, and swear that he had never known such comradeship. He was likely to take Barbara up in his arms and give her a breathtaking, bonecrushing hug.

Barbara enjoyed Evert and Simon didn't, and that was what changed (to Jay's regret, and later to Simon's) the chemistry of those Sunday evenings. With Evert around they all drank in earnest and found a lot to complain about, and late in the evening the foursome always turned into a pair of twosomes: Simon and Jay discussing the aims and ironies of college teaching, Barbara and Evert discussing the pains and ironies of love.

It was Evert, not Simon, who talked Barbara into taking a college course. Evert's course. Spring semester Barbara studied oil painting, under Evert, in the tradition of Charles Russell. And beginning one Saturday afternoon, behind the locked door of the college studio, she studied lovemaking, under Evert, in the tradition of Donald Stearns.

And when the school year ended and Evert left for a new job at Wyoming State (more buffalo, fewer days below zero, to hell with the mural in the new library) Barbara went along. That was in June of 1943. Barbara was twenty-six. Simon was stunned. Evert was jubilant. Henry Hamilton III was angered. Jay Johnson was speechless for a change.

Simon heard Douglas's pickup in the yard. Nineteen forty-three, he thought, rising from the chair in the dusty bedroom. That was thirty-three years ago last June. Good Lord, for a married man he had certainly spent a lot of his life alone.

Douglas backed his pickup across the leafy lawn and unloaded lumber and shingles and paint. From his apartment he had brought his toolbox, which he carried into the screened porch.

"Give me three days and you won't know this place," he said.

"Thursday, Friday, Saturday. By Saturday night I'll be done. You ready to go for that walk, or do you want more time with your memories?"

"I've had more than enough time with my memories. Let's be off."

With Tick they left the yard and walked the dusty road over the hill. They found the Odmers painting one of their sheds. "This will be the last day for painting this year," Kermit Odmer cautioned, climbing down off his ladder. "Radio says colder tomorrow, then rain and sleet and snow."

Before Simon could introduce Douglas, Felicity Odmer hurried into the house to perk a pot of coffee and Kermit Odmer began showing them around his property—a tour on which Simon had been conducted a hundred times. "Come on, now, I'll show you my sheds. I've got seven sheds now. I built a new shed this fall. I like to have a place for everything and everything in its place." Odmer had a bristly brown beard and large teeth the color of whiskey. He spoke fast, as though afraid of being interrupted, and he never looked anyone in the eye––not even (Simon suspected) his own image in the mirror.

"Here's the shed for my mowers and rakes and hand tools." He opened the door and stood aside for Douglas and Simon to have a look.

Douglas and Tick peered in. Simon hung back.

"Step up and see," said Odmer, looking slightly to the left of Simon's face.

"I've seen it before." Simon was trying to engage Odmer's line of vision. He moved a little to the left. It was a game he had been playing with Odmer for years, and he knew he could never win.

Odmer quickly shifted his gaze to a spot overhead. "But you ain't seen my new mower."

Simon obediently looked at the John Deere riding mower, then they moved on to the six other sheds, and then they examined the stumps of live trees that had died in the drought and which Odmer had cut up for firewood.

"Now my garden," said Odmer, and he led them to a large rectangle of dirt. "Best garden I ever had in my life, honest to God. Pumped water up from the river and didn't spare the fertilizer and everything grew so fast we could hardly keep up with the harvest, Felicity and me. You never saw such cucumbers. You never saw such cabbages. You never saw such beans." Odmer took off his cap and held it over his heart and he approached the garden like a tomb. "Of course there's nothing to see now but them squash over there, and here under these here dried-up leaves—a few cucumbers. See? Under these here leaves? A few small cukes we ain't picked. Well, it's late in the season and what do you expect to see in a garden this late in the season? Honest to God, you should have seen our tomatoes. Succulent tomatoes. And peas? Why, you never saw such peas. And squash? We've got squash to last us all winter. What's better than hot squash with butter melting in? And beans? Succulent, succulent beans, I can't tell you how good." Odmer had a deep, wet voice that sounded like someone chewing delicious vegetables. When Odmer spoke, Simon thought he could hear, apart from his words, the crunch of mastication, the biting into crisp green beans, the coming down of the molars on rosy slices of tomato, the swallowing of juicy cucumbers. "Chard, lettuce, radishes, big russet spuds, honest to God."

Felicity Odmer called them indoors. Felicity Odmer changed shape with the seasons; she was heavy at harvest and spare in the spring. She was one of those rare women who look better fat. Her interests were primarily in wild game, and she took Douglas into the living room and showed him the antlers of four deer she had shot; the antlers hung on the wall and served as coat racks, hatracks, and gunracks. She showed him the stuffed and lacquered bodies of three large fish she had caught. With coffee, she served the men large chunks of venison sausage and bitter morsels of pickled pike.

"It ain't like it used to be up here in the hills," said Odmer, biting into an apple. "Every few hours somebody drives by. I bet there's been five people past here already today."

"Six," said his wife. "There was one this morning before you were up."

"Well, one was probably the mailman," said Simon, "and Douglas's pickup has gone by three times."

"Yes, and there's been at least two others besides."

"The crush of civilization," said Simon.

"You'll be seeing me go by quite a bit," said Douglas. "I'm going to rent Mr. Shea's house."

The Odmers sat back, shocked. Odmer brought his eyes down from the ceiling and fixed them on Douglas's hairline.

"It's to our mutual benefit," Simon explained. "Douglas is going to repair my fire damage."

"You going to live there alone?" asked Odmer.

"No, about half the time—"

"He will be sharing the house with a doctor," said Simon.

"A doctor?" said Felicity. "A regular medical doctor or just one of your college-type doctors?"

"Regular medical," said Simon. "From the staff of the Rookery Clinic." How incredulous the Odmers would be when they met Doctor Kirk.

Odmer said, "The woods is tinder, young man. See that you don't strike a match outside the house. You don't smoke, do you?"

"Now and then."

Odmer scowled. "Take care with your smokes. The woods is tinder."

"The fires are driving the game our way," said Felicity. "The past few days I've seen more deer and rabbits and partridges than ever before. I picked off three rabbits the other evening with my twenty-two. I already put up eight quarts of canned rabbit this fall."

"Nothing like canned rabbit in a stew," said Odmer, succulently, moistly. "Steam it up good with lots of carrots and onions and cabbage. Honest to God."

Simon and Douglas finished their snack and began to disengage themselves from the Odmers, who followed them out the door and into the yard and a short way down the road, enumerating all the animals and plants they had consumed in recent memory. Did they actually mention muskrat, or did Simon misunderstand?

Another half mile and they came to the Pribble farm, where they saw cows in the cornfield, Pribble having surrendered to the drought and turned his crop over to his cattle. The cornstalks rasped and cracked as the red cows, dripping saliva, grazed on the rough, papery leaves. The cows amused Tick, who ran to the fence and thrashed about in the weeds and barked. The alarmed cows walked stiffly away, and when they judged they were safe they stopped and looked stupidly back at the dog. Was there a more dim-witted look in the world than that of a puzzled cow? Their faces reminded Simon of a class he had once lectured by mistake. Early one semester at St. Andrew's he had stepped into the wrong classroom and had gotten well into his lecture on literary criticism—Yeats's view of the French Symbolists, to be exact—when a boy in the front row timidly raised his hand and said that he and the others had gathered there to plan the spring formal. Simon said he was sorry and folded up his notes and left the room, and until today—facing these cows—he had never again seen such dumbfounded expressions.

When they reached the meadow, Simon pointed the way and they left the road and followed their long shadows across the dead grass and thistles and gopher mounds. It was late afternoon. At the crest of the hill, Simon said, "Here it is, my favorite view of the world," and with a sweep of his arm he introduced Douglas to the surrounding hilltops, the river bottom, the steeples and smokestacks of Rookery. Overhead flew a hawk and a forest ranger's airplane. The sun was sinking. They sat down on a long, flat rock.

"The hills remind me of 'Nam," said Douglas.

"Of what?"

" 'Nam. Vietnam."

"You were in Vietnam?"

"Two years to the day."

"And you saw action?"

"Man, did I see action. I rode the choppers." Douglas changed his position on the rock and looked east, away from the sunset, away from Simon. He hung his head and spoke softly, as though to the silvery wildflowers scattered at his feet. "I was the guy who sat beside the pilot and shot gooks in the face when they tried to mess with us. A lot of the time we had body detail. We went out and picked up bodies." He lifted his eyes and scanned the horizon. "The hills were like this, only green. They say the hills in 'Nam weren't green any more toward the end. Everything green had been bombed off. But when I was there the hills were green. You never saw anything so green."

"When were you there?"

"Seventy. Seventy-one. Just out of high school. I've been back in the States five years. It's taken me all this time to get my head together. See, I came home from 'Nam with the idea that I was behind everybody by three years. A lot of the guys I knew in high school never went into the service, and by the time I got back they were almost through college or else they already had pretty good jobs. Some of them were married and had kids. I felt I had to move fast to catch up."

A thin line of cobalt clouds stretched from north to south in the western sky. Behind it, the sunset was orange.

"So I married the first girl I ran into. I was mustered out of the army in Missouri, and that's where I met her. Seventeen years old. Cute. Daughter of a judge. Sally Childers was her name. Inside of one year we had a baby and got divorced. We were blitzed half the time. You know, stoned. I was no more ready to be married than she was. We had this baby and neither one of us knew what to do with it. What do you do with a baby? You feed it and keep it clean is what you do. Jesus, that's a big job in itself. It tied us down like you wouldn't believe. I could see right away we weren't cut out to be parents. And so could the judge, I guess, because suddenly he stepped in and brought down his gavel and we were divorced so fast I didn't know what happened until it was over. One day I was married and the next day I wasn't. Both of those days I was half in the bag, and all I can remember is standing out in front of that courthouse in Missouri with five hundred dollars in my pocket and a bus ticket north. I guess I had signed away all my rights and responsibilities. I guess the court decreed I can never show my face around that baby or Sally, either one. As far as they're concerned in that county, I don't exist. I was married for a year, and what I got out of it was five hundred dollars and a bus ticket north."

Douglas leaned down and picked a flower. It came up by the roots, its stem tough as a tendon. He put the blue blossom to his nose. It smelled of dust.

"So I came back to Minnesota. Came back home to my parents' farm down near the Iowa border; you know, south of Minneapolis. I had been home a couple of times with Sally, so my parents knew we had a baby, and when I showed up alone it was pure hell. My parents don't believe in divorce. I don't suppose I believe in it either, but I hadn't given it that much thought. Or had that much choice. Anyhow, my parents thought of it as a case of a father abandoning his wife and child and they were on me about it all the time. That was bad enough. Then after a couple of days they found out I was pretty well stoned, and they went crazy. They called a doctor and they called a preacher and they called a cop they knew. But I never waited around for the invasion. I took off. I left the farm and took off for Minneapolis. What the hell, I had five hundred dollars—or about four hundred by that time—and I was independently wealthy. I went to Minneapolis and I looked up this old friend of mine, Delmer Dean. He was attending vocational school, studying auto mechanics. Delmer Dean was straight. That is, if you call being in love with engines straight. Delmer Dean had two beds in his apartment, and do you know what he had on one of the beds?"

"No," said Simon.

"He slept in one bed, and on the other bed he had this old engine from a V-8 Ford. I mean, right there sitting on the bed was this cruddy old eight-cylinder engine that he was rebuilding in his bedroom. To keep the bedspread clean he had a bunch of towels and rags under the engine, but they weren't doing the job. He had parts scattered all over the bed and all over the floor. I knew as soon as I walked into the apartment that it was no good staying with

Delmer Dean. It was an apartment for two, and Delmer Dean was sharing it with an engine. That was his idea of the good life."

The sky faded from orange to copper. The breeze died and the parched land became shadowless and still.

"So I left Delmer Dean and went out on the streets. Somewhere in the back of my mind I had the idea I'd find a job. But what did I know about finding a job? The only job I ever had was picking off Southeast Asians with my rifle, and there wasn't much call for that around Minneapolis. You might say my training was overspecialized. So I just sort of lived on the streets, slept wherever I got tired, sometimes in a room, sometimes not. I think I was picked clean of all my money inside of a week. I was high most of the time. Don't ask me what I did or who I met. I have no idea. Isn't it funny how a person can exist like that? Funny how you can go along practically unconscious for a week or more. I mean, you'd think you'd die or something. There you are at the mercy of the rain and the cold and the weirdos you meet in alleys, and you just stumble right on through and out the other side. Sally and I used to live that way in Missouri, just gone, man. In fact it seems to me I spent whole years of my life that way. Those years in 'Nam and that year married to Sally and that time in Minneapolis, all of it unconscious. And here I sit on a rock in a field and everything is just fine. Everything is clear and real. I can feel the rock and see the hills, and instead of thinking about where I'll get my next fix I'm thinking about how I'll repair the wall of your house. I'll space the new studs sixteen inches apart and I'll nail on the siding and I'll put up the insulation and I'll cover the interior with wallboard and paneling. Three days at the most. The place will look like new."

Something moved in the grass, a mouse or a gopher, and Tick jumped in a circle, trying, and failing, to pounce on it.

"What brought you this far north?" asked Simon.

"The state hospital in Rookery. The hospital for loonies and drunks and hopheads. After I hit bottom in Minneapolis, I ended up in the Veterans' Hospital down there. Then they sent me to the state hospital in Rookery—the chemical dependency section. Man, that's a wild place. You get in these groups and you talk things out, and it's wild. Everybody's nerves are outside their skin. It seems like everybody's either supercharged or depressed out of sight. I was there a long time. That's where I met Jean. She was in training there. Then after I got clean I stayed on as a counselor part-time, which shows you how bad off some of those poor guys are—depending on me for counsel. See, I'm still screwed up, Mr. Shea. Do you know I can't read any more? I can't write? I get an assignment in English to read a story, say, and I can't read farther than the first page. My mind's all over the place. I can't concentrate. I can't focus. My mind is just blasted all apart. Fragmented, you know?"

"I know. I had students like that."

"Did they come around after while? Did they make it through college?"

"One or two did. Most dropped out."

"That's what I'm afraid of. I'm having a hell of a time. I just can't hit the books. Even in blueprint class I'm falling behind. When I'm on the job, I'm fine. See, besides counseling at the hospital, I worked for a contractor in Rookery and did just fine. But in college I'm a mess."

"I remember one student in particular, Douglas. Physically he had the jitters, and mentally he had a case of fragmentation as you describe it, and what I did was require that he hand me a paper every morning, five days a week. Day in and day out he had to write me something and bring it to my office. I didn't care what, as long as it was in English and down on paper. The first day he gave me one line that said this: 'Skiing in my life was then.' That was all it said. That was the extent of his writing capabilities that day. 'Skiing in my life was then.' I went to the admissions office and said, 'How does someone like this qualify for college?' and they showed me his high school records. Peerless records. Top of his class. 'Skiing in my life was then.' What he was telling me, I learned later, was that for three long winters he had been a ski bum and lived a very un-structured existence involving drugs and all, and when he decided to come back to college and pick up his life again, he found himself with your problem. Only worse, to look at him. He even *looked* fragmented. He was in motion all the time. Not the shakes exactly, but shuffling his feet and twiddling his fingers. 'Skiing in my life was then.' Imagine being reduced to expressing yourself like that."

"I can imagine it. Was he one of the dropouts, or did he make it?"

"He dropped out. But before he did, he made some progress. He was able to write a coherent paragraph."

Douglas shifted his position and faced, with Simon, the dying light in the west. "I wish you were still at Rookery State. I'd try to write you something every day."

"Do it anyway. Send it to the Norman Home."

"You mean mail it?"

"A letter a day. And once a week I'll respond."

"No. I'd try it, but I know I can't write a letter a day."

"It's entirely up to you. Douglas."

They were silent for a time. They heard a moo from Pribble's cornfield, a siren from Rookery. The warmth of the sunny day evaporated and the natural coldness of November dropped from the sky and settled on the hilltop. They felt it on their faces.

Simon read his watch in the twilight. "We still have some time before my bus leaves. Am I keeping you from anything, Douglas?"

"Nope. Jean will pull in around eight. We're going out to dinner."

"Since moving to Ithaca Mills, I have missed this hilltop as much as my house."

"How long did you live out here?"

"Thirty-five years."

"Thirty-five years! Man, how is that possible? Since I was eighteen I've lived at twelve different addresses. Thirty-five years! You lived alone all that time? I get restless when Jean goes to Ithaca Mills for three days."

"At first I wasn't alone. I'm a married man, Douglas, though I don't appear to be."

"You are? Where's your wife?"

"The very question I ask myself every so often. Where is

Barbara? She's in El Paso. At least that's where her Christmas cards come from. I'm on my wife's Christmas card list."

"Man, you've got a weird marriage."

"Weird. Yes, it was weird from the start. I was forty and Barbara was a widow of twenty-four, and as soon as we married, Barbara went into some kind of emotional nosedive. She became dejected and acquired a rather violent temper, which came to the surface at the least provocation. And I, as though to match her, as though to compete, developed a temper of my own, and we fought. It's hard for me to recall what we fought about. It's hard even to reconstruct those two years in my memory, for although I have pondered my relationship with Barbara a thousand times, it is always our happy courtship I dwell on. The two years we lived together in marriage—those arduous years—elude me."

"That's like 'Nam. There's certain parts of my life in 'Nam I can't remember. Of course I was on dope a lot."

"Well, without drugs I seem to have suppressed most of my unhappy memories. The mind is equipped to drug itself. My memory of the first summer and fall of our marriage doesn't run in a continuous line. It skips around. I see episodes but in no particular order. For example, I see myself departing the house and heading over the hill toward the Odmers', with Barbara's voice at my back. I don't know what she's saying but she's calling after me in a voice tight with anger. I remember calling home from Chicago—the convention of the Modern Language Association—calling home simply to say hello and then listening to Barbara enumerate her troubles. On and on. A forty-five minute recital of hopelessness. When she finished, I hung up, exhausted. I remember spats in the bedroom. Spats in the kitchen. Spats outside under the birch trees. I couldn't believe she was the woman I married.

"Then after a few months, she changed once more. She became passive. I could hardly arouse her to love or to anger. It was winter by this time. Barbara had kept her job at the Northern Federal Bank—had been promoted, in fact. We drove into the city together and worked at our separate jobs and lived, despite our being married, what strikes me now as quite separate lives. Our fighting was over, and I guess we were relieved about that, but we didn't seem to be attached to each other any more. Teaching will absorb all your juices if you want it to, Douglas, and I lost myself in my schoolwork. Barbara lived for banking and cooking—she was fond of the kitchen—and we met at meals and in bed. Both our eating and our lovemaking became perfunctory, but I doubt if either of us was much concerned about it. Our love wasn't growing, but we were too busy to notice. Maybe from the start we were never in love. I can't say. I had had very little previous experience of love, nothing against which to measure my feelings for Barbara. Since then, I have been positively in love once, and the experience seemed so different from my marriage to Barbara—it seemed so smashing, so purely delightful—that I can't believe the love Barbara and I felt for each other, if it was love at all, survived the wedding."

"A bummer of a marriage," said Douglas. "I learned all about that sort of thing in the group sessions at the state hospital. I could tell you a hundred stories about rotten marriages."

"Some other time. Douglas. Now that I've started on this tale, I'm determined to see it through to the end. It's a quality of this hilltop—the perspective you get on your life. I daresay you wouldn't have told me so much about yourself just now had we not been sitting on this hill. But wasn't it clear, Douglas, that in each of the hundred rotten marriages you heard about, both the husband and the wife were to blame?"

"I can't say. It was our job in those sessions to dig down and find the cause of everybody's problem, but I was never convinced we found much of anything. It seemed to me those marriages just turned rotten the way fruit goes bad in the heat. You know how it is with bananas. One day they're solid and the next day they're soft. I'm leery of marriage, Mr. Shea. Marriage, to me, is a black banana."

"But *our* failure, Barbara's and mine, was not a case of rotting fruit. In retrospect I see how I contributed to our downfall. I should have been a steadier husband. More patient. That summer and autumn after the wedding, when Barbara turned moody and angry, I should have recognized the cause. Here was a woman whose previous husband had been fatally wounded in a sudden, shocking accident, and we married so soon after his long and lingering death that her bereavement carried over into our marriage. She wasn't fighting me, I've come to understand, she was fighting the fates that robbed her of Donald Stearns. She was coming up from a depths of worry and grief and she had a bad case of the bends. I am haunted by the suspicion that with my help, instead of my contentiousness, we could have passed through that worrisome time and come into a better time, a calmer climate that would have lasted down to this present day. But what did I know? Emotionally, I was an adolescent. I was forty years old and treating marital adjustment as though it were puppy love, and when those months of fighting were done, we were strangers to one another."

"So you got divorced," said Douglas.

"No, we separated, but we didn't divorce. We separated in 1943. Not long after our second anniversary we bade each other farewell, and Barbara went to join the man of her dreams."

"You mean a lover?"

"A lover. An artist named Evert Metz. I owned two of his paintings, which I have since given away."

"She had a lover and you didn't get a divorce?"

"I know it sounds implausible, Douglas, but I didn't want a divorce. And Barbara didn't need one, because she and Evert Metz never intended to marry. Barbara had been through two marriages that didn't work, and she swore never to try it again."

"But *you* might have wanted to remarry."

"Out of the question. My Catholicism, you know. It permits only one marriage vow per person. It allows for divorce in certain cases, and mine was certainly such a case, but I could not remarry as long as Barbara was alive. And she was seventeen years younger than I. By remaining married, at least married in the eyes of the law and the Church, if not married in fact, I reasoned that I would have an easier time remaining single."

"I don't get it."

"Well, as a married man I would not be so inclined to go prowling after another woman, would I? Nor would other women come prowling after me. See, I have always worn this wedding band. It would be more difficult for me—divorced—to abide by the law of my Church."

"Isn't that a Mickey Mouse law?"

"It's a law I've chosen to live by."

Douglas looked askance at Simon. "I didn't know anybody took religion that seriously any more."

"It's hard to say, Douglas; I think you might be surprised how many people live by the rules of their faith."

"Old people, maybe. I don't know anybody my age that's going to live the single life just because the Church says you can't have a second woman. In this day and age you'd have to be a fanatic to believe that. Really, Mr. Shea, don't you think it was old-fashioned of you to deny yourself the pleasure of another woman all these years? The pleasure of having somebody around? Instead of living like a hermit?"

"No, another woman would have brought me—did bring me—the turmoil of a troubled conscience."

"Aw, you can learn to live with a troubled conscience. In fact, if you ignore your conscience long enough, it will disappear. I've learned that much."

"Not mine. I have a very durable conscience. It's four parts steel and three parts stone. A very great blessing it's been. Or curse, depending on your viewpoint. Of all my faculties—my memory, my will, my appetites, my reason—it's my conscience that dominates. My conscience is a bully."

"That must be hell."

"It has its compensations. You have a sense of living your life within a prescribed set of rules. Your life has direction, a destiny in eternity. And of course you're seldom troubled by doubt or indecision where morality is concerned. You're driven to respond in a certain way. You might say you're bullied."

"Sounds like you're a *victim* of your conscience. Not your own man."

"I should say servant rather than victim. And a servant, Douglas, enjoys a peace of mind that a master does not."

"He does?"

"The master must continually decide. The servant merely acts on those decisions."

"Like me, in the service. I signed up for a second year in 'Nam because everything was so clear over there. They told us what to do and we did it. Civilian life, by comparison, has been tough. In 'Nam all you had to worry about was how to avoid getting killed, and even that became routine. Nothing to bother your mind about."

"That's why it's called the service."

"But it's childish."

"Childish?"

"I feel that every day I spent in 'Nam prolonged my childhood. And if you'll pardon me for saying so, Mr. Shea, that's what having a conscience like yours amounts to. It's childish."

"Not childish, Douglas. Child*like* perhaps, but not childish." Simon stood. "I think we should start back. It's getting cold."

Following Tick, they descended the hill in the dark, and as they made their way along the road they heard the swift movement of deer in the woods and they saw the flash of a meteor in the eastern sky and they smelled the smoke of distant fires.

"Look, Mr. Shea, I could see this self-denial of yours if it was doing somebody some good. I mean, the one thing I respect about religion is that it preaches charity. I believe in that. I believe in doing good for others, and if your sacrifice was doing good for others, if you were involved in some super act of charity, then your sacrifice would make sense. But what you're doing isn't any good to anybody that I can see. It's a dead-end sort of sacrifice."

"I'm not sure you're right, Douglas. For one thing, my first obligation is to myself. I have to be true to myself, as they say. True to my word, my vow. And who's to say that my fidelity to my word has not inspired someone else along the way? I like to think that over the years my example has caused a few people to regard marriage vows with the seriousness they deserve."

"What people?"

When Simon didn't answer, Douglas dropped the subject. They walked a long way before Simon spoke.

"Do I sound very sure of myself, Douglas?"

"Yep. You've obviously convinced yourself—if no one else."

"Well then, I'm not being entirely honest. Take everything I've just said about my conscience and balance it with this: I sometimes wonder if my conscience has always been reliable." Simon walked with his head bent toward Douglas, his hands in the pockets of his black coat. The road ahead was barely discernible between the dark trees on either side.

"Getting back to the woman I loved after Barbara left me— Linda Mayo was her name—I have to say quite frankly that I'm no longer as certain as I used to be that ending our relationship was the right thing to do." Tick barked at Pribble's cows once again; they were hidden by darkness but noisy among the cornstalks.

"Our relationship," Simon repeated, chuckling. His chuckle was a whistle in his nose, for his breathing was tight in the evening chill. " 'Our relationship' makes it sound like a long love affair, when actually it was very brief. It started quite suddenly on a Tuesday, in Dublin, and it came to an end a week later on a Wednesday—in Cashel, a town in the Irish midlands. I turned my back on her. It caused both of us extreme pain—we were deeply in love, Linda and I—but at the time I saw it as my only alternative ... And now I wonder ... "

A car came over the hill behind them, and they stood aside as it hurtled past, leaving them to proceed, squinting, in the heavy cloud of its dust. "My guide, as I have said, has always been my Church. The early fathers, the saints, the theologians down through the centuries, that mammoth collection of moral guidelines burgeoning and piling up for two thousand years—all of that has seemed to me the most reliable sort of philosophy to follow. On my own, I've never been much of a philosopher, Douglas, and therefore I have been satisfied—indeed, happy—to regulate my life according to Church law. But what is Church law, after all?"

"You tell me," said Douglas.

"It's based on natural law and divine revelation. I mean Church law is based on what we know by instinct and what we're told by our Father in heaven, who wants what is best for us. And here is where my misgiving creeps in. That God speaks through his Church I don't doubt, but what I've come to question in my old age is whether he speaks *exclusively* through his Church. Mightn't he sometimes speak to us directly, Douglas?"

"Why not?"

"Why not—exactly. I'll never forget how positively right and proper it seemed for Linda and me to be together in Ireland during that week in 1957, and I have since wondered whether that rightness we felt in our hearts was a sign—an indication from on high, so to speak—that our love was proper in the eyes of the world, proper in the eyes of God. That's a big misgiving for a fellow like me to entertain, Douglas."

"Now you're talking my language."

"Not that it matters any more. I only bring it up as an item of curious old business. I lost track of Linda Mayo twenty years ago."

"And you've been regretting it ever since."

"No, no, you overestimate the power of regret, Douglas." Simon put his hand on Douglas's shoulder. "This whole matter has become merely a mental exercise for me. No pain lasts forever. Live long enough and your life becomes a textbook—an outdated edition, full of lusty old exercises."

As they walked along, Simon took out his handkerchief and covered his nose and mouth, filtering out the dust that had been raised by the car.

The Odmer house was dark. "They're in bed," Simon explained.

"Already? It can't be much after seven."

"They're in there snoring among their taxidermy. Dreaming no doubt of pickerel and gooseberries, cabbage and hare."

At the cottage, they went inside for a last look around, then they climbed into the pickup and Douglas drove Simon to the bus in Rookery.

Later, before going out to dinner, Douglas drove Jean to the cottage to show her around. He drove her Oldsmobile rather than his pickup, and as he turned off the dirt road and parked near the mailbox and the headlights shone on the white birch trunks and the small screened porch and the golden leaves covering the lawn, Jean said, "Lovely." They went inside and Douglas turned on the yard light and they stood at the front windows looking down the slope to the river. "Just lovely."

They heard a car door slam. They went out onto the porch and looked into the headlights of a car parked next to their own, a car with a yellow light on its roof—a taxi—and now, cutting off the beams of light was the figure of a woman walking toward them through the leaves.

"Simon Shea?" said the woman. "Isn't this Simon Shea's house any more?"

Douglas and Jean stepped off the porch. "Yes, this is Simon Shea's," Jean said to the silhouette against the lights, a woman slightly shorter than herself, slightly wider. "But Simon Shea has moved to a home for the elderly in Ithaca Mills."

At this the woman whooped loudly, and Douglas and Jean were startled for a moment before they realized it was a laugh. As the three of them came together in the yard they made a quarter-circle turn so that their faces were sideways to the light. The woman put her hand on Jean's arm and threw her head back and laughed up at the dark branches overhead. It was a frosty night and the vapor of her laugh formed a little cloud. "I've been wondering all day," said the woman, catching her breath, "what our first words would be when I arrived here tonight—whether Simon would be happy to see me or irritated or stunned or what. And now he isn't even here. He's in a home for the elderly. When I last saw him he was forty-three. Well, it's probably the reception I deserve, and I should have known he was gone—I've been trying to phone him for days—but something told me to come ahead anyway. Something told me it was the right thing to do. I'm Barbara Shea, Simon's wife. I started this day in El Paso, Texas. I've been on two planes and a bus and a taxi, and I'm beat."

Jean patted the hand on her sleeve and said, "I'm Jean Kirk and this is Douglas Mikklessen. We're friends of Mr. Shea's—Simon's." She was about to add that soon they would be living in this cottage, but she didn't. Rather she said, "There's been some fire damage to the kitchen wall, and Douglas is repairing it."

Barbara gave her other hand to Douglas, who took it with a bow of homage and said, "Mr. Shea has told me about you. He'll be glad to see you."

"Do you really think so?"

"Let's go inside," said Jean. "It's cold."

"No, I guess if Simon isn't here I'll go back into Rookery for the night. I'll track him down tomorrow. That's how I've come to think of this visit—a tracking operation."

"We'll take you," said Jean. "Send your taxi on its way. We're going into Rookery ourselves."

"But I have two large suitcases—"

"I'll get them," said Douglas.

While Douglas transferred the bags and the taxi pulled away, Jean and Barbara went into the cottage and discovered in one another that intangible factor of personality, that indefinable turn of mind, that flash of recognition in the eye, which are the rare signals of unforeseen and immediate friendship. Within two minutes Barbara understood that Jean was a doctor and the daughter of a doctor and living with Douglas out of wedlock and buying him a college education out of her very substantial income from the Rookery Clinic. In those same two minutes Jean understood that this would be the winter Barbara turned sixty and that she was looking around for the right place to spend the rest of her life and that this was her first stop in a tour only vaguely mapped out in her mind—and, most fascinating of all, that Barbara was a pioneer in the field of unmarried cohabitation. The pitch of their excited voices carried out the door of the cottage and across the dark lawn and reminded Douglas (who was having trouble closing the trunk on the two large suitcases) of certain group therapy sessions where hope ran high.

When Douglas finally got the trunk closed and entered the cottage, the two women had opened a cupboard and were admiring Simon's set of Waterford crystal.

"How like Simon to keep all this in an ordinary kitchen cupboard," said Barbara. "Anyone with a speck of pride would have it out in the open to show it off."

To whom, Douglas wondered. To the Odmers?

"Mrs. Shea," he said, "have you had dinner yet? Jean and I are going out for dinner. How about joining us?"

"Yes, come with us," said Jean. "We'll take your things to our apartment. You'll have our second bedroom, which never gets used, and you can freshen up and we'll go out."

"I'd love to," said Barbara. "I'd love a large drink and a small meal, and I'd love to hear more about Simon." She stepped from the kitchen into the living-dining room.

"Maybe you'll want to call Simon from our apartment," said Jean.

"No, I think not." Barbara turned in a circle, wondering where the Persian rug had gone and taking stock of the furniture, most of it in need of polish and new upholstery. "I think now that I've come this far I'd rather step into Simon's life in person. There's going to be so much to say that I couldn't possibly get it all said on the phone. Tomorrow I'll take a bus to Ithaca Mills and see him face to face. My God, it's been thirty-three years."

"Tomorrow I'm off after my morning calls at the hospital," said Jean. "I'll drive you to Ithaca Mills."

"How kind of you." Barbara felt a series of pangs in her heart, little shocks of recognition, as her eye fell on certain furnishings— the antique clock on the shelf, the lamp with the parchment shade— things she hadn't thought of for thirty-three years. "Now let's get out of here before I get emotional," she said.

The streets of Rookery looked strange to Barbara. She might have been riding through Cairo or Lima for all the landmarks she recognized. Douglas parked in front of a large brick house near the campus, and Jean led the way around to the back door and into their apartment.

"How comfortable," said Barbara, casting her appraiser's eye over the spacious living room. Three twenty a month, she estimated, utilities included.

Jean showed her the guest room, and Douglas carried in her bags. "Would you like a glass of wine?" he asked. "Or something stronger?"

"Something stronger, if you please. I've been on two planes and a bus and I'm beat." She laughed. "And I'm repeating myself."

Freshened up and dressed for dinner, Barbara got her second wind. Over drinks in the living room, she asked about Simon. What did he look like? How was his health? How did he end up in a place like Ithaca Mills, which Barbara remembered as a nothing town?

"He looks a lot like a retired English professor," said Jean. "If you gave Mr. Chips a shot of adrenaline you'd have someone a lot like Simon. He's got that kindly bearing about him."

"And that soft-spoken humor," Douglas added, sipping a Coke.

"He's in excellent health," said Jean, "but if he stays where he is, he'll start declining fast. I've seen it happen. You've come back at the ideal time, Barbara. Simon has to be talked into leaving that awful place he's in, and you're the one to do it. I spent a lot of my training in geriatrics, and I saw dozens of cases where useful lives were cut short by the horrible places they throw people into. I don't know if you realize it, but Simon Shea is one of the most respected names on the Rookery campus to this day, and he reviews books regularly for the *St. Paul Chronicle,* and he's probably the only man in Ithaca Mills—which is a jerkwater village—capable of carrying on an intelligent conversation; and now, at the height of his esteem, he's gone and moved in with a bunch of cuckoos. He's like somebody getting up in the middle of a good party and saying good night. Your husband is saying good night and it isn't even his bedtime, Barbara. Wait till you see him at the Norman Home. You'll know what to do. You'll say the right things. You'll wake him up. He belongs back in his cottage, with his river and his Waterford and his books. And with you—if you're interested."

There goes country living, thought Douglas.

"Well, I certainly seem to have walked into the middle of something, haven't I?" Barbara laughed and squirmed. "I admit I was looking for some variety in my life, but I'm not sure I was looking for the kind of challenge you're offering me. To be frank about it, I'm totally without direction. And that's on purpose. You see, I have this thing—I guess most people have—about decade birthdays. It's a jolt to go from your fifties into your sixties, which I will do in February. It's the same jolt I've felt every ten years whenever I went from one decade to the next. Of course you two wouldn't understand what I'm talking about because it's obvious that neither of you has hit thirty yet; and when you do, you might not be the type that cares very much. But I care a lot. I told myself this fall that before I hit sixty I was going to take a leave from my job and do some exploring."

"What's your job?" asked Jean.

"Real estate. I've been with Bernardson Land Company in El Paso since the mid-fifties. I like the work, I like the climate, I've made some good friends down there, but I decided to shake loose for a while and do some exploring. So I'm on indefinite leave— for indefinite reasons, you might say—and now it looks like I've walked into the middle of something complicated right off the bat.

"I'm entirely without plans. When I left, my only plan was to be planless. I have a cousin in Detroit whom I've been meaning to visit for years—we were close when we were girls—and I have a friend from El Paso who moved to Boston, and I thought it would be fun to see Boston, but basically I'm without direction. For the past twenty years my longest vacation has been five days in Mazatlan, and this year I told myself it was high time that I took some of my considerable bank account and set off in whatever direction the wind was blowing."

"High time," Douglas agreed, finishing his Coke. "How about another drink?"

"Thanks, but not before dinner. I'd pass out on the street."

"Let's eat," said Jean.

They went to a quiet restaurant and were shown to a table in a quiet corner, where Barbara changed her mind about another drink. She put down two cocktails very fast, as though eager to loosen her tongue and hear what it had to say:

"I'm dying to know if Simon has lived the single life all these years, and if he hasn't I'm dying to know who he's lived with."

"We've known him only since Monday," said Jean. "I'm sorry if we gave you the impression that we're old friends of his."

"Only since Monday? Then you can't know much about his past."

"Only that you're his wife," said Douglas. "He told me that much. He appears to have been living alone ever since you separated."

"Of course he has!" said Barbara. "What else would one expect from Simon Shea? He has this tremendous capacity for self-denial. Odd in a man, don't you think?"

Douglas nodded. Jean did not commit herself.

"Where does a trait like that come from, do you suppose?"

"He says he's living by the rules of his Church," said Douglas.

"Yes, that's what I'd expect him to say. But his strictness, his self-denial, is so much a part of his nature that I maintain he was born with it, and it just happened to fit in nicely with his religion. I mean, I don't see how anyone could be as strict with himself as Simon—and, let's face it, as self-sufficient—without being born that way. No amount of religious training could make a man live the sort of life Simon has led. I swear he was born a monk."

Jean asked, "Are you a Catholic, Barbara?"

She looked puzzled for a moment, then said, "I don't know." She speared the olive from her drink and ate it. "I was a Catholic for Simon's sake, but I haven't gone to the sacraments in over thirty years. Does that mean I've excommunicated myself, or what? I guess you'd have to get a ruling on that from somebody who knows the faith better than I. Somebody like Simon. Not that the answer is important to me, if that's what you mean. I'm sure if I went back and read the catechism I wouldn't find much I believed in. Religion is all very indefinite in my mind. I put it all aside when I went to live with Evert Metz." She looked from Jean to Douglas. "You've probably never heard of Evert Metz."

"Simon mentioned his name," said Douglas. "He called him the man of your dreams."

Barbara smiled. "The man of my dreams." Then she frowned. "If you knew Evert Metz, you'd never call him that. The man a girl dreams of is Prince Charming, and there wasn't much that was princely or charming about Evert. What Evert had was brute strength and passion. And anger." Barbara lifted her glass and looked into her gin. "Imagine Simon's opposite, and you've got Evert." She put down the glass and looked at Jean. "Evert was half crazy with resentment. He had lost his wife to another man, and he felt that by teaching for a living he wasn't making any progress with his art—he was a painter—and he came along at a time when I was feeling a lot of resentment myself. Donald was dead, and Simon and I weren't hitting it off."

"Donald?" asked Jean.

"Donald Stearns, my first husband. He was killed. You see, there have been three men in my life: first Donald, then Simon, then Evert. I married Simon shortly after Donald was killed, then two years later I went to Wyoming and lived with Evert. I think that when I married Simon I was still full of resentment about Donald's death. Fate had given me a bad deal, and I was looking for ways to express my revenge against the world. And Simon couldn't understand that. You know how Simon is. He's always so accepting. Or at least he used to be. Take what comes, that was Simon's philosophy. Well, it's not mine, never was. I felt like crying and being angry. I guess I wanted Simon to curse the world with me, but he never would. Instead, he'd go for a walk or bury his nose in a book. He'd ignore me. Now, looking back, I can't blame him very much. I must have been as bitchy as they come. But at the time, his behavior only made me angrier. Then along came Evert. He had a lot of bluster and fire about him. He was mad at the world and together we made a great pair. We saw ourselves as two lost souls in the big cold universe. Evert used to come out to the cottage and get drunk and put his arm around me and curse and shake his fist at the moon, and I loved it. He made me feel strong. When Evert left Rookery and moved to Wyoming, I told Simon I was going along. And I did."

"What was Simon's reaction? What did he say?"

"Nothing. Nothing at all. I can see him as if it were yesterday. I think at that point if Simon had flown off the handle and ranted and raved, I might have stayed with him. I needed a man who was capable of a damn good fit of temper once in a while, and Simon wasn't that man. I said, 'Simon, I'm packing my things and moving out. I've decided to go to Wyoming with Evert.' Simon was sitting in his den when I said it—sitting at his desk. I was standing in the doorway. Simon got up and put his hands in his pockets and looked at his shoes. That's what I remember like yesterday: his standing there looking at his shoes, his arms stiff, his hands in his pockets. I said. 'Simon, do you understand it's over between us? Get a divorce, do what you like. I'm going to live with Evert. We aren't getting married, we're just going to live together. There I've said it, and I guess you have a right to hate me for it, but it's what I'm going to do.' Simon never looked at me. He turned his swivel chair around to face the window and he sat down with his back to me. And that was that. I packed my bags and Evert drove out and picked me up in a car he had borrowed, and we went to the depot in Rookery and got on the train, and that was that."

"So you were never really sure what Simon thought," said Jean.

Barbara shook her head. "I guess not. We wrote to each other once a year, but as you might expect, his letters were clever and chatty and there was really no telling what was on his mind. Except he called me up once, after Evert died. He said if I wanted to come back to the cottage, I was welcome. Can you imagine? Almost fifteen years had gone by and he was still keeping a place for me."

"But you never came back."

"No, I was getting off to a great start in real estate. Evert and I had moved from Wyoming to El Paso—and I was in charge of sales. It was a great opportunity. I was a career woman long before it was fashionable. I had been in business since I was twenty—not my own business, you understand, but handling other people's money—and I knew opportunity when I saw it. When Simon invited me back, I told myself that someday I might do it; but for the time being, he'd have to go on waiting. Not that I made him any promises, mind you. In fact, I urged him to find himself a woman."

"Were you teasing him?"

Barbara looked surprised. "I don't think so."

Dinner was served. Jean and Douglas ate hungrily, but the food made Barbara very tired, and after a few bites she put down her knife and fork and said, "Do you know what I think? I think all this talk about Simon has made me love him again." Her eyes were wet. Were they the tears of a stifled yawn or the tears of strong emotion? She herself was unsure. "All the way North today, I had this intuition that I was doing precisely the right thing, and yet I felt nothing in my heart. I didn't feel happy or tender or eager or anything. I felt cool as a cucumber. Now suddenly I'm overcome with feeling. I can't wait to see Simon."

"Do you want me to take you there tonight?" said Douglas.

"No, heavens no. I'm in no shape to meet anybody tonight, least of all my husband."

"I'll drive you there tomorrow when I'm finished at the hospital," said Jean.

"Wait a minute," said Douglas. "Tomorrow Simon goes to St. Paul."

"So he does," said Jean, pausing with a bite of steak halfway to her lips. "He's going to pick up his car," she explained to Barbara. "But he should be back in the afternoon. I'll take you to Ithaca Mills in the afternoon. That will give us some time to plan your strategy. I'm assuming that when you see him you'll want to get him out of the Norman Home and back in the cottage where he belongs. Whether or not you decide to stay, the cottage is where he belongs."

And so Barbara Shea (who for the past three decades had gone by the name of Barbara Metz) was unexpectedly enlisted in a plot to reclaim her husband from what Jean called his self-imposed senility. "Tell me what to do, and I'll do it," she said, offering Jean a shrug of surrender. "I've been on two planes and a bus and—"

"Yes, we know."

"I thought it was two buses and a plane," said Douglas.

"Finish your steak, dears—and show me the way to go home."

THURSDAY

Simon left the Home before dawn. It was a cold morning, moonless and very dark, and except for the barking of a distant dog, Ithaca Mills was silent. He wore his black coat and his black leather gloves and his gray hat. In his briefcase he carried, along with his review of the three young poets, his wool scarf, his rubbers, and a paperback book. He walked past several houses where he could see people at breakfast, their heads bowed over bowls and surrounded by cereal boxes, their shoulders slumped as though their night's sleep had been as exhausting as a day's work.

The bus stop in Ithaca Mills was the Open Soon Café, the only place doing business at this early hour. Simon pushed open the door and stepped into an atmosphere of consternation. The morning waitress had not yet shown up for work, and the cook, a bleary-eyed woman, was on duty alone and muttering bitterly. She condemned the new breed of waitress, the faulty switch on the coffee warmer, the tardiness of the sunrise, and the coming of winter. Her customers, some of whom, like Simon, needed bus tickets, were impatient to be served, but so acrid was her anger, so intimidating was the downward curve of her mouth, that they kept their counsel and hoped for the best. Along with his ticket to St. Paul, Simon asked for coffee and a doughnut. She served him with a grunt of disdain, the coffee partly in his saucer, the doughnut hard as bone.

The Twin Cities bus pulled up with a screech and a honk. Simon said good morning as he handed the driver his ticket.

"What's good about snow and sleet?" said the driver. "The weatherman says snow and sleet." The driver's face was pale and drawn, as though his night had been sleepless, yet his rumpled uniform looked slept in.

Simon took the front seat opposite the driver and switched on his reading light. He drew the book from his briefcase—the autobiography of Leonard Woolf, volume one—and as the bus left town he began reading. London: aunts, cousins, schoolmates, the rise and fall of family fortunes. Cambridge: Keynes, Moore, Strachey, the beginnings of lifelong friendships. Pages of old photos: everyone in high-button collars and high-button shoes; in the background of almost every photo the lines of a large stone house in the country, in the foreground of many Lytton Strachey looking comical. The photos were grainy and blurred at the edges.

Now and then Simon raised his eyes from his reading to watch daylight spread across the prairie. The ceiling of low clouds seemed to be held up by the silos and windmills. Farm children shivered in clusters along the highway, waiting for the school bus. Some of the children waved, and Simon waved back. Some of them stuck out their tongues. Behind them were the large frame houses they came from. A fine mist began to form on the windshield and Simon's view of the children grew indistinct and blurred at the edges.

Halfway to the city, Simon became drowsy. He slipped his book into the briefcase and spent the rest of the trip sleeping while the bus was in motion and waking when it wasn't. The bus reached the city at eleven A.M.

In a cab Simon rode first to police headquarters to pick up an authorization slip from the stolen-vehicle office, then to Sterling Towing to pick up his car. Sterling Towing was a shack and five acres of junkers surrounded by a fence of sticks and rusty wire. It was located at the edge of the city where a knot of four-lane highways came together, and the cab driver had to do some fancy lane changing and sudden braking to arrive at the door of the shack.

"Please wait," Simon told the driver. "My car is in here, and I want to make sure it runs."

In the shack, on two stools behind a counter, sat a man and a boy. The man, whose perfectly bald head was laced with blue veins, spoke into a microphone, dispatching a wrecker to an accident.

The boy had a shocking case of acne. The counter was littered with candy wrappers and official-looking papers smudged with oily fingerprints.

"What do you want?" said the boy.

"I've come for my car. A sixty-six Ford Fairlane. White." Simon presented his authorization.

"Oh, yeah. That's the one we've had for so long. It's back over there." The boy pointed over his shoulder to a window; the glass was opaque with grime. "Let's see your title card."

Simon produced it.

The boy pulled a slip of paper out of a recipe box and compared numbers. "You got an ignition key? There weren't no keys in it when we picked it up."

Simon showed the boy his key.

"All right, that will be a hundred and four dollars."

"A hundred and four dollars! For what?"

"Storage. That car's been sitting here for four months."

"No, you're mistaken. The police just phoned me yesterday morning."

The boy looked again at his slip of paper. "No, it's been here since July. I remember picking it up. It was left in Como Park by some guy the police were chasing." The bald man looked at Simon and nodded earnestly without interrupting his monologue into the microphone.

"But a hundred and four dollars?"

"I can do one of two things," said the boy. "I can write you a receipt, or I can keep the car."

The bald man nodded again.

Simon wrote a check.

He stepped outside with his receipt. The mist had stopped but the sky was even lower and darker than before. He walked around the shack and searched the aisles of the car lot for his Ford. When he found it, he groaned. Part of its rear bumper had been pulled away, and across the doors on the driver's side were the scrapes and creases of a sideswipe.

"My friend," he said aloud, "what have you been through since I saw you last?"

He got in and tried the ignition and the engine sprang immediately to life, but its pulse was irregular and he saw three red lights on the dash; one said OIL, one said DISCHARGE, and the other said HOT.

He switched off the engine and returned to the shack, where the bald man was still speaking; this time it was a soliloquy of numbers: telephone numbers, serial numbers, the numbers of houses and highways and insurance policies. The boy was eating a Milky Way.

"I need oil and water," said Simon. "I need my generator checked."

"We ain't no mechanics," said the boy, chewing.

"Then I will have to call someone who is."

"You got towing insurance?"

"No."

"Too bad. If you had towing insurance we could tow your car to a garage and your insurance would pay for it. This way, it will cost you fourteen bucks."

Simon took fourteen dollars from his billfold. "Let's go."

The boy poked the remainder of the Milky Way into his mouth and slipped into an oily denim jacket. As they stepped out the door the boy pointed across several lanes of traffic. "We'll take her to Olympus." He was pointing to a monolithic construction of concrete at the crest of a distant hill.

"Olympus?" said Simon.

"That's a big shopping mall, see, and they got this service station with all these mechanics on duty." His lips seeped caramel as he spoke.

Simon dismissed his taxi, then went into the lot and waited while the boy backed a wrecker into place and lifted the rear end of his Ford off the ground, further damaging the bumper. Then Simon opened the right-hand door of the wrecker, expecting to ride in the cab, but the seat was piled full of tools and dirty rags.

"You'll have to ride in your car," said the boy, "and whatever you do, keep your hands off the steering wheel."

Simon got into his car, which was tipped so precariously high in back that he had to brace himself against the dash to stay in his seat. The boy put the wrecker in gear and Simon rode backward through the aisles of Sterling Towing and out the gate and up a ramp to a highway where he found himself facing the radiator and headlights of a large truck. The truck driver was angered by the boy's cutting in front of him, and he honked his horn. Simon looked up at the windshield of the truck, and the driver shook his fist at him. Simon tipped his hat. The truck changed lanes and was replaced by a woman in a station wagon. When she saw Simon facing her, she laughed and pointed to him, and the heads of two children popped up from the back seat. They too laughed and pointed. Simon tipped his hat. By this time the wrecker had picked up speed, and when they turned suddenly onto an exit ramp, Simon was thrown across the seat, and not until they came to a stop at an intersection was he able to right himself. Here, waiting in the car behind him, was a gum-chewing man whose tendency toward eye avoidance was overcome by his curiosity. The stoplight was a long time changing, and the man, while pretending to be engrossed in something out his side window, kept peeking at Simon out of the corner of his eye. Simon tipped his hat, and the man, looking away, couldn't help the smile that spread across his face.

Then Simon found himself on another highway and the drivers who bore down on him responded to his gesture of greeting with either amazement or amusement, and then he was sailing across the vast parking lot of the Olympus Mall—forty acres of black tar with yellow markings. How fitting, he thought, that I should be transported to Olympus in this humble position, my eyes on the ground, my back to the gods. The wrecker whipped the Ford in a circle, stopped, and set it down on its four wheels, and Simon stepped out as though from a roller coaster, slightly off balance and glad of firm ground. This was Jupiter Service, with sixteen pumps and three mechanics and no business. The three mechanics, in green coveralls, raised the hood of the Ford and examined its dipsticks and pressure caps, its belts and hoses, and then held a consultation so earnest and lengthy that Simon was sure his car was in deep trouble. Next they wheeled up a boxlike device of gauges and dangling cords similar to the machine that had graphed the workings of Simon's heart at the Ithaca Mills Medical Center. They started the Ford, connected the cords to the engine, and the machine came alive with jumping needles and blinking lights. This seemed to tell the men a great deal of good news, for in their next consultation there was a tone of hearty confidence. They beckoned to Simon, and their spokesman—the tallest mechanic, with ALEX stitched on his breast pocket—told him he had a loose fan belt and a hole in his radiator. Also he needed a tune-up and new brushes (whatever they were) and five quarts of oil.

Simon's knowledge of engines was negligible, and he thought it marvelous that these men should understand such mysteries. He said, "I should have known that here on Olympus I would find the oracles and prophets of our time."

Alex, pretending not to be puzzled by this, said that if it weren't for the radiator, they could have him on his way in an hour. The radiator, however, would have to be sent to a radiator shop.

"And how long will that take?"

"A couple of hours." Alex looked at his watch. "By three o'clock for sure. Olympus is a good place for killing time. Why don't you go into the mall and kill a couple of hours?"

Simon toured Olympus, or rather he was enticed along its corridors the way Hansel and Gretel were lured into the forest, charmed by the promise of riches and sweets. Light and music came from nowhere and everyone's face was the same shade of green. There were seventy-four shops on three levels and all of them were designed like a stage and stuffed to the doors with the world's goods. In the Five and Dime it was Christmas while in Erickson's Jewelry the decor was autumnal, and in a few small places selling wall posters and belt buckles and icons, the lights were so low and the merchandise so random and purposeless that it was hard not to imagine oneself in the den of a pack rat. And Simon sensed that something moved down the dim, wide corridors besides people; he perceived it not with his skin or his nose or his eye or his ears, but with some primordial nerve at the base of his brain—something unearthly and nameless that carried with it the faint aroma of dry goods and popcorn and nervous breakdowns.

He came to rest on a bench next to a fountain where coins shimmered under the water. He sat facing the array of greenery and blossoms in the window of Faracy Floral. He closed his eyes and imagined that the noise of the fountain was the splashing of the Badbattle in the spring.

"Holy Christ, you ought to see what night security gets away with in this place," someone said in his ear. He turned and saw a security guard sitting beside him on the bench. He wore the same clothes as Doodle Novotny of Ithaca Mills, and the same arsenal of clubs and firearms hung from his belt.

"Holy Christ," he said, "I used to be on night security and the whole idea in those days was to work your way up to day security so you could sleep nights like normal people. And now I finally work my way up to day security and what happens? They bring in women at night."

"Women?" said Simon.

"That's right, women security guards. There's two women working nights at the present time and they pack revolvers and nightsticks same as us men, and they're a couple of hot numbers. I bet you never thought it would come to that, did you?"

"Never," said Simon.

"Neither did I. One in particular, she's a real tough blonde. A real hot number. I got this buddy works nights and he tells me about her. Holy Christ. Not that there's anything wrong with it. I mean what him and that blonde do together is their business, but what I'd like to know is why didn't the union bring those hot numbers in when I was working nights? That's the story of my life. I no more than put a rotten job behind me than it turns into peaches and cream. I spent three summers working for a sugar beet farmer up in North Dakota. I plowed and planted and drove truck. Driving truck I didn't mind, but plowing and planting was a killer. This farmer had a square mile of sugar beets and all he had was a little old tractor. Hotter than hell. I'd be out there on the tractor seventeen hours a day, dying of windburn and sunstroke. So finally I up and quit, and you know what that farmer went and did?"

"No."

"The very next year he went and bought a tractor with an air-conditioned cab. Holy Christ. Tinted glass, air conditioning, eight-track tape deck, the whole works. Whoever followed me on that job·sure stepped into peaches and cream. Well, I got to be on my way. Nice talking to you." He stood and hitched up his belt and strolled away.

Simon took his paperback from his briefcase and read to the end of volume one. His power of concentration, destroyed by the fire in his kitchen, seemed now to be restored. He went into a bookstore and returned to the fountain with volume two. Woolf's six years as Her Majesty's Civil Servant. Woolf as judge in Ceylon: murder trials, paternity suits. Letters from Strachey. Woolf's ambivalent feeling about the Empire. His affection for the natives. His tennis game.

A tall, stoop-shouldered man emerged from Faracy Floral and headed for Simon's bench. He wore a black suit and bright blue tennis shoes, the laces untied. He sat down next to Simon and hung his head. His shoulders shook violently, as though he were trying to suppress a fit.

"Pardon me," said Simon, "are you all right?"

The man raised his eyes. They were deep-set eyes, blue and cold. "I am fine," he said.

Simon returned to his reading.

"I beg your pardon," said the man. "I do not wish to bother you with my troubles, that's why I tell you I'm fine."

"Hmmn?" It was hard to quit reading, for on this page Woolf was opening a sacred tabernacle containing Buddha's tooth.

"You are obviously contented with your book, and I do not wish to bring my discontent into your life. Besides, I don't particularly enjoy talking to old men. How old are you?"

"Seventy-six." Simon, growing warm, removed his hat and his overcoat.

"If I had my choice I would talk only to young people. So would you. Admit it. You would be much more pleased to be sitting here talking to a young person than to someone your own age. You and I, we're over the hill. We're has-beens. Washed up. But who, among the young these days, can we talk to? Show me a young person who will bother talking to an old person. It's a rule of human nature that people want to talk to someone younger rather than someone older than themselves. Notice. See if I'm not right. Watch a conversation between two people of different ages sometime. Notice who starts it. Who carries it. The older one every time. Old people want to talk to young people, but young people want nothing to do with old people. Am I not right?"

"I don't think so. I spent my life talking to those younger than I. I spent my life in the classroom."

"That doesn't count. As a teacher you had a captive audience. I'm talking about everyday, willy-nilly conversation. See that young man and woman looking in that window? Now those are the kind of people I would like to talk to."

They were a couple in their twenties. They held hands and wore matching jackets of Tartan plaid. They sauntered dreamily from one display window to the next, absently pointing things out to each other and nodding, their minds obviously far away. Honeymooners?

"As I sit here in my dejection, that young couple could do me a world of good simply by saying to me what *you* said to me. You said, 'Pardon me, are you all right?' Weren't those your exact words?"

"I guess they were."

"Well, your being old and all, those words didn't do much for me, but coming from that young couple, those words would do me a world of good. But what are the chances of their asking me if

I'm all right? You can't get odds on a thing like that. It will never happen." The old man hung his head.

Simon opened his book, found his place.

The old man put his lips close to Simon's ear. "I pissed my life away. I could have become a musician. I was accepted at Juilliard. I could show you the letter. In 1925 there was a place for me at Juilliard, but I didn't take it. I pissed my life away."

Simon closed his book.

"I didn't go to Juilliard because Father got sick just then, and I stayed home and took care of things for Mother. We had a small grocery store attached to our house, and while Mother took care of Father, I took care of the grocery store. I had been brought up on the violin. Father gave me lessons from the time I was three. He wanted me to become a concert violinist. I auditioned for Juilliard and was accepted. I have the letter at home. But I didn't go. I pissed my life away." He sighed. "But that's neither here nor there."

"Your father didn't recover?" asked Simon.

"Father died. Father was ill for five months, then he died. Mother could have carried on without me after that. It was a small store off the kitchen of our house. I could have gone to school—she urged me to—but I got lazy. It was different around the house after Father died. It was more comfortable, if you know what I mean. Father had been a strong force in our house, and when he was gone it was easy to be lazy. I stayed home and helped Mother in the store. Pissed my life away."

The hand-holding couple came to the window of Faracy Floral and gazed at the blossoms.

"We ran the store, Mother and I, for many years, then closed it and lived on her savings and Social Security. Thirty years we were retired, Mother and I. Toward the end, she needed quite a bit of care. No problem. I was glad to care for her. She was my life. I cared for her till the end—which was yesterday. She died yesterday."

The old man stared at Simon. His shoulders heaved as before, but his eyes were stone. They were gray-blue, close-set eyes, devoid of emotion. The man's feelings appeared to be centered entirely in his shoulders.

"I'm sorry," said Simon.

"I just now went into Faracy's and ordered a wreath that says 'Mother.' She's in a funeral home on Skilling Avenue. She can be seen this afternoon and tomorrow morning before the burial, but of course no one will stop in to see her. We had no friends, Mother and I. The undertaker says it's customary to keep the body on view for a certain length of time, and I'm not one to fly in the face of custom, but between now and the burial if anybody stops in and signs the guest book I'll be surprised. She's there to be seen, but nobody wants to see her. It was the same when she was alive. We lived in seclusion. I said to the undertaker, 'We might as well close up the coffin and call it a day,' and I think the undertaker would have consented to do that, but his wife said, 'Nothing doing.' I think the undertaker's henpecked."

Simon was moved. He considered offering to go and see the body. Indeed, the old man seemed on the verge of inviting him. But there was something unconvincing about the man. The coldness of his eyes made Simon wary. In Rookery he had known an old woman with eyes like that. She was a shawled and toothless old widow who haunted the laundromats and the lobbies of banks and told sad stories that weren't quite true in exchange for sympathetic remarks that weren't quite sincere. Was this a similar case? And how could a man this old have a mother alive until yesterday?

The hand-holding couple drifted from the flower shop to the bench and sat down beside the old man. They stared, glassy-eyed, into the fountain. It was three o'clock. Simon stood up and put on his coat and hat. He said, "I have a car being repaired. I must go now and see if it's ready."

"There's no telling what will happen to me," said the old man. "There's little left of the savings, and of course I have no Social Security of my own."

"Can I give you a ride? My car is here at the Jupiter station."

The old man shook his head.

"Do you have a car?"

He shook his head again, then hung it down. There was another spasm in his shoulders. The girl noticed. "Pardon me," she said. "Are you all right?"

His head popped up. "I do not wish to bother you with my troubles. You two are obviously very contented with each other's company and why should I intrude into your lives with my discontent, but believe it or not I could have been a concert violinist."

The young woman settled herself against the young man's shoulder and the two of them listened attentively. They seemed to hang on his every word.

Simon went to Jupiter Service. His radiator was gone and so was Alex. One of the other mechanics said things were taking longer than planned. Simon should come back around five.

He returned to the fountain. The old man and the young couple were gone. As soon as he sat down, he knew he could not endure another minute on the hard bench, and he went to the Five and Dime to buy a chair.

The Five and Dime was decorated for Christmas. It was the fourth of November, and hanging from the ceiling on five hundred strings were five hundred faces of Santa with Buy Early and Save written in his beard. Simon had always considered himself as adaptable as the next man; he had nothing against the flared pants that were pressed upon him when he shopped for clothes, and he was as willing to take Holy Communion in the hand as on the tongue, but to find himself in a crowd of Christmas shoppers on the fourth of November took him off guard. He had trouble getting his bearings as he roamed the tinseled aisles. He walked beside vast displays of toothpaste and Christmas cards, and he came to a mountain of a kind of candy he remembered from his boyhood. Each morsel was in the shape of a pink peanut. He put a piece in his mouth. Yes, he nodded as he chewed, the taste was the same as seventy years ago—the taste of a chemical somewhere between an overripe banana and nail polish. He passed down an aisle with winter jackets on his right and summer sausage on his left and motor oil straight ahead.

"Chairs or stools?" he said to a clerk, and she pointed to a distant corner of the store. He made his way through tires and toasters and B.B. guns and extension cords and indoor plants marked down from eighty-five cents because they were dead. On a four-wheeled cart was a pile of lawn furniture obviously on its way to a trash heap. YOUR CHOICE: $4, said a sign. Simon chose a folding chair of green plastic webbing, and he carried it to the checkout counter, where the checkout girl seemed to be pouting.

"Advent is early this year, what?" said Simon.

"What?" said the girl, punching the cash register. On her blouse, her nameplate said DIANA.

"I say Advent is early this year, isn't it? At least here at the Five and Dime."

She frowned at him, an old guy in a black coat and a gray hat, carrying a briefcase and buying lawn furniture in November. Obviously some kind of nut.

"Four sixteen, with tax," she said.

He handed her a five.

"Eighty-four cents your change thank you merry Christmas." She taped his receipt to the chair.

He put out his hand for the change.

"It's down there in the chute," said Diana. She pointed to a coin dispenser at the end of the counter.

Simon put his coins in his coin purse, put his coin purse in his pocket, shifted his briefcase to his other hand and picked his chair off the counter; and because there was something vaguely feminine, not to say obsolete, about the coin purse, and because he was slow and holding up the line, Diana said, "Jesus!"

He returned to the fountain and set his chair beside the wooden bench. How restful was the sound of the water. How like the spring runoff of melting snow. He took off his coat and hat and sat down. In his book he returned to Ceylon and the early years of the century. Leonard Woolf rising in the ranks. Photos of Woolf in his white suit, posing with dozens of black tribesmen, robed and turbaned. Woolf returning to London on leave and keeping company with Virginia Stephen—and ultimately resigning his post in order to marry her.

"Excuse me, sir, but my oldest daughter is being married, and I have come to the end of my rope."

Simon looked up to see a large, red-faced man seated beside him on the bench. He wore a cashmere coat the color of rich cream and a brilliant red gem in his tie. He had a very wide mouth and when he spoke he bared his teeth, both top and bottom. They weren't much as teeth, thought Simon, but as a means of displaying his crowns and bridges of gold they were very impressive.

"Preparations for this wedding have been going on for over a year. Since a year ago September, nothing has been spoken of in our house except veils and ushers and invitations and punch bowls and what to give the pastor as a gift. And banks of mums. I've heard the phrase, 'banks of mums' exactly four million times in the past year. My wife is in Faracy Floral at this very moment ordering, finally, those banks of mums. My entire family have become monomaniacs. You think I'm exaggerating, of course, but let me tell you what happened the other day. I drove home this brand new seventy-seven Chrysler Cordoba and I said to my daughter, 'Lucy, this is your wedding gilt from your old man.' Sir, it was a beautiful car, a sleek, red car with opera windows and every automatic device known to the automotive industry. And besides being very expensive, it was very practical, because Lucy's husband-to-be is in medical school and he doesn't have a five-dollar bill to his name. He gets around on a bicycle. And so I said, 'Lucy, this is your wedding gift from your old man,' and I handed her the keys. And do you know what she said? She said. 'But Daddy, it's the wrong color. My attendants will be all in pink and so will Mother. All the flowers will be pink. This is a red car, and the theme of the entire wedding is pink. You *knew* that, Daddy. You *knew* it was going to be a completely pink wedding.'

"Do you understand what I am saying, Sir? Do you understand that in response to this nine-thousand-dollar gift my eldest daughter said. 'But, Daddy, it's the wrong color'? Sir, can you understand why I reacted as I did? Can you understand why I said to her, 'Lucy, you can take your precious pink wedding and you can shove it up your precious pink asshole!' and I went back downtown to my office and I turned out the lights and opened a bottle of Southern Comfort and I sat there watching night fall on the traffic over the Robert Street Bridge, and I got smashed."

The man's wife emerged from Faracy's. She wore a sable coat and diamond earrings and stood in the doorway of the shop, waiting for him to notice her. Finally she said, "Lawrence, I'm ready," and the man sprang off the bench and stood very stiffly—his jowls quivering—while he buttoned his cashmere coat. Then they came together with a slight bow and he gave her his arm and they strutted ceremoniously around the fountain and stepped grandly onto an escalator and were lifted out of sight.

At the end of the afternoon when Simon returned to Jupiter Service, the mechanics were turning off the lights and punching a time clock. The radiator, said Alex, would be ready first thing in the morning.

"But I had not planned to stay overnight in the city. My home is three hours to the north."

"Whereabouts?" said Alex.

"Ithaca Mills."

"Oh, yeah? A nothing town. I had a sister lived there once. She said it was a nothing town."

"If I stay overnight in the city, can I be assured of getting my car tomorrow? If not, I'll take the bus home and come back at a later date."

"First thing in the morning."

"Your word?"

"Cross my heart." Alex crossed his heart.

"I think you mechanics sometimes lose track of your important place in our society. You are the prophets and oracles of our time. We spend our life savings on our cars, and we turn them over to you for their well-being, and your slightest mistake or negligence can render us immobile and dead broke. Tomorrow morning you say?"

"Sure thing."

Simon put his chair in his car and went back into the mall to buy Leonard Woolf, volume three. Then from Olympus he took a bus downtown and checked into a hotel. It occurred to him that he should phone Hattie Norman and tell her of his whereabouts, but he decided to have supper first. He dined in a coffeeshop off the hotel lobby, reading as he ate, and by the time he went up to his room on the eighth floor he was so absorbed by Woolf's account of the two parallel catastrophes of 1914 (the breakdown of order on the Continent, the breakdown of reason in Virginia's mind) that Hattie was completely forgotten. He took off his necktie and shoes and sank into a soft chair and continued to read.

Hattie Norman, working at her stove, was stewing. She was emptying a bag of navy beans into a pot of water to simmer overnight, and she was calling into the dining room where Barbara Shea was eating tuna hot dish with the residents. "I tell you, you're going to have your hands full with that professor of yours! In the short time he's been here, he's caused me damn near as much trouble as old Mrs. Zimmerman, who used to walk in her sleep. She was the lieutenant-governor's mother, and she'd get up at night and walk through the rooms like a zombie."

Barbara dabbed at her mouth and laid her napkin beside her plate. She had eaten very little and all she wanted. She sat between Hatch and Mrs. Valentine Biggs. Tonight Hatch sat with the women because without Simon and the Indian he was desperately lonely; halfway through the meal he had carried his plate across the room and sat at Barbara's right hand, where he was now chewing with his mouth open and wiping his lips with his wrist and wiping his wrist on his thigh. Across from Barbara sat Spinner and Leep, straight as sticks, their eyes blinking and darting as they chewed.

"If you want my opinion," Hattie continued from the kitchen, "he's lived too long by himself and he's forgotten what it is to think of others. It takes somebody pretty god-awful selfish to leave the house in the morning and head for St. Paul before anybody's out of bed and never say where he's going or when he'll be back. It wasn't till you and that woman doctor showed up here this afternoon that I knew what he was up to. I've got half a mind to sic the sheriff on him. Or get the state police to track him down."

Mrs. Valentine Biggs spoke softly into Barbara's left ear. "Don't pay any attention to Hattie, she's such an old spoilsport. I think it's perfectly divine that you've come back to see your husband of years gone by. It's a storybook ending. Oh, I can hardly wait till he walks in and sees you." She stopped eating and laid her head lightly on Barbara's shoulder. "When he walks in the door, it's going to be just like a fairy tale." Her blue hair was oversprayed and smelled like glue.

With his mouth full, Hatch said, "You ain't taking the professor out of here, are you?"

Barbara turned to him—an excuse to move her shoulder out from under the head of blue hair—and said, "Whatever Simon does will be his decision, not mine." But she would try mightily to influence him, she was sure of that. Since arriving with Jean in the early afternoon, she had seen more than enough to convince her that Simon must move out. True, she hadn't yet seen Simon himself, but if he was as alert and vital as Jean insisted, then he had no business penned up in this awful place.

Earlier, riding down Main Street with Jean, Barbara's first glimpse of the Norman Home had been somewhat obscured by the bulk of Doodle Novotny, who stood at the end of the drive with his chubby hand raised to stop traffic. Behind him, an ambulance was pulling away from the door, its red lights flashing.

"Tell me I'm not dreaming," said Jean. "The *last* time I was here one of the residents was carried off in an ambulance."

The ambulance sped past them, and Jean rolled down her window and called, "What happened?" to Doodle Novotny, who was stuffing himself into his squad car.

"It's some old woman," said Doodle. "They're taking her to Rookery to see what's wrong with her foot."

Jean parked her car and led Barbara into the Norman Home.

They found Spinner and Leep and Hatch and Mrs. Valentine Biggs clustered in the foyer. Jean said, "I'd like you all to meet—"

"You're too late," said Hattie Norman, darting into the foyer and carrying the sheets she had just stripped from Mrs. Kibbikoski's bed. "She's off to Rookery by ambulance, and you missed her."

"Actually, I'm not here on a house call."

"Her foot's all black. Her toes are rotting off. I've never seen leprosy, but it looked like leprosy to me. I called your clinic in Rookery and told them what the foot looked like, and they sent an ambulance. What burns me up is that she hasn't paid me for November yet." Hattie looked from Jean to Barbara. Judging by Barbara's businesslike suit, Hattie assumed that she either represented Social Services or sold cosmetics door-to-door.

Jean said, "Is Simon back from St. Paul?"

Hattie blew up. "St. Paul! I swear to God, I'm the last one you should ask where that man is back from. He's in and out of here like a jack-in-the-box. He was gone before any of us were out of bed this morning, and if he isn't back by suppertime I'm calling the sheriff. What in God's name is he doing in St. Paul?"

"He's picking up his car," said Jean.

"So is he coming back for supper or isn't he?"

"I have no idea, but if he isn't you must *not* call the sheriff. Simon is perfectly capable of finding his way home. And now I'd like you all to meet—"

"Listen, it might not strike you as important that I know where all my old people are at all times, but believe me—"

"*Please*, Miss Norman, you're interrupting me!" Jean's raised voice and glaring eyes silenced Hattie. She took a step backward. Behind her armload of sheets, she looked chastened.

"Now," Jean continued, "I want you all to meet Barbara Shea, Simon's wife."

Barbara looked from one face to another, saying, "Hello, hello." In her smile, which was a bit too broad to be genuine, there was a hint of apprehension.

Spinner, Leep, and Hatch stepped forward—the twins to give

her a quick and sweaty handshake, Hatch to have a closer look at her teeth. Mrs. Valentine Biggs put fingertips to brow and said, "Oooooo," seeming about to swoon in the manner of Scarlett O'Hara.

Hattie came forward, recovering the ground she had lost. "You're the professor's wife? You want to move in? You sure you're old enough? The Indian's room is spoken for, but now there's Mrs. Kibbikoski's room. You don't really look that old. Nine dollars a day, two seventy a month, payable on the first. I've taken married couples before, and it hasn't worked out too bad. With a married couple, I find that one tends to ride herd on the other, and they both stay out of my hair. And the professor, Lord knows, could use some supervision."

"Thank you, I'm only visiting," said Barbara.

"Well, stay for one night anyhow. That way I'm nine dollars ahead and you're here when the professor gets back. Go right down the hall there: I'll bring sheets."

"Perfect," said Jean, and she hurried out to carry in Barbara's bags before Barbara could refuse. One night in the Home will do it, thought Jean. She'll see the empty life lived by these wretched people and she'll prevail upon Simon to leave. They'll leave together. They'll elope.

And so Barbara had moved in and Jean had returned to Rookery, and now it was six fifteen and Hattie was leaving her beans to soften over the fire and striding into the dining room to finish tattling on the deceased Mrs. Zimmerman. "She was the lieutenant-governor's mother and one night she walked out the front door in her sleep and woke up in the middle of Main Street wearing her nightgown. It shows you what a curse old age is. It shows you that once old age gets you by the short hairs, you can't help acting stupid even if your son *is* the lieutenant-governor. And I wouldn't be surprised to see the professor do something just about as stupid one of these days, what with his absentmindedness and the way he disobeys rules. Hatch! What in God's name are you doing at the women's table?"

Hatch lowered his head and shook it slowly.

When the residents had finished their dessert (peach slices in milk again), they rose in unison and headed for the TV parlor. Hatch and the three women were closer-knit today than ever before: it had been a frightening week at the Home—their numbers had been reduced by three, if you counted Simon's disappearance—and the four who remained seemed to be closing ranks in self-defense. Moving across the foyer like a chain gang, they called back to Barbara, asking her to join them for *Let's Make a Deal*. Barbara declined, claiming that it was time for her evening walk. At this the residents halted and looked at each other with raised eyebrows: what an ingenious and daring idea, an evening walk. Barbara was afraid for a second that the four would want to join her, but the pull of TV was irresistible, and they turned and filed into the parlor.

Actually, Barbara seldom went for walks. She had never shared Simon's interest in strolling along the Badbattle, and her longest walks in El Paso had been through the houses she showed to buyers, but tonight she walked around several blocks of the dark neighborhood while she sorted out her thoughts. Her short time in the Home had left her famished for fresh air and freedom. She wondered, half-seriously, if the residents might all have been lobotomized. If not, what accounted for their infantile simplicity? They were all single-minded in the worst sense, each of them dwelling for hours on a single topic. Four hours with the families of Spinner and Leep, the droughts of Hatch, and the loves of Mrs. Biggs were almost more than she could bear. Was this sort of lunacy—this monomania—the inevitable consequence of age? Was this what Simon was like? If so, Barbara knew what form his obsession would take: she imagined him reciting passages from literature. She recalled Simon's slightly irritating habit of sprinkling his talk with pertinent quotations, as though conversation were an exercise in matching life to books, and she feared that now, at seventy-six, his talk might have become an uninterrupted series of purple passages. And what about Barbara herself? At sixty, might she soon expect to exhibit the symptoms of a one-track mind? And what track would her mind take? Doubtless it would be the track of mortgages and closet space and two-car garages. Sixty scared her. Oh, to be fifty again. Or, as long as she was wishing, why not twenty-five, before Evert came to Rookery?

Barbara walked along Main Street as far as the bridge, and she stopped and peered over the rail just as the moon came out from behind a cloud and cast its reflection onto the water. She stood for a minute looking down at the bright oval. It glimmered and wavered on the slow current. Now and again a fitful breeze raised tiny waves that tore at the edges of the oval and threatened to pull it to pieces, but the moon was too cohesive to come apart—though rippled at the edges, it kept itself whole. One car, and then another, crossed the bridge, and Barbara watched to see if either would stop at the end of the street in front of the Home. Neither did. Neither was Simon's. She looked back at the water where now a sudden gust of wind kicked up waves that shattered the reflection of the moon and scattered its pieces across the black water like chips of ice.

She shivered and gathered her coat together at her throat and walked back to the Home—certain, for no reason she could name, that Simon would not return that night. She entered quietly and stole past the TV parlor ("Doctor, what can I do about my bad breath? It makes life such a drag.") and went into Mrs. Kibbikoski's room, which smelled of ointment and old shoes. She shut the door against the sound of the TV and against the risk of socializing with the residents. She was exhausted; last night in Rookery she had not slept well. She prepared for bed and sat for a few minutes with Agatha Christie's latest (and last) mystery open on her lap, but she couldn't read for sleepiness. She looked at her watch. It was only seven thirty, yet she could scarcely keep her eyes open. She turned off the light and got into bed and fell immediately into a deep sleep, at the bottom of which was a nightmare.

Barbara was standing up to her knees in a river. It was night and the river was covered with slivers of ice. It was her impossible task to keep the ice from slipping past her, for if the slivers floated further downstream they would surely be the death of many people. Donald was downstream, at her back, and he was afraid of the ice.

As were Evert, her mother and father, and whole throngs of people she didn't know. Was Simon downstream? Yes, she thought she heard his voice behind her. Barbara, in her dream, was taller than normal, and stronger. She was nearly as tall as the trees along the riverbank, and she was able to hold back great mounds of ice by stooping and spreading out her arms and cupping her hands, but she couldn't stop it all. Ice floated past her and people died. Where did all this ice come from, and why did the terrible responsibility for stopping it fall upon her? Why was there ice in the world at all? She sensed that someone she knew had introduced ice into the world, but she couldn't think who it was. "Whose ice is this? Whose ice is this?" she called, and as more ice pushed past her, she felt her strength draining away. She despaired of saving lives. She grew weary unto death. She turned from her task and waded toward the riverbank. Since she could not stem the tide of ice, she would devote her efforts to finding the culprit. She climbed the bank, crying, "Whose ice is this?"

The dream was brief. When it ended, Barbara slept on for a time, then came gradually awake. Lying with her eyes open, it took her a while to understand what she was doing in this bed, in this room. She was conscious of having dreamed but she remembered none of the details. She felt only a vague resentment against someone she knew but whose name she had forgotten. She drifted off again, and this time her sleep was interrupted neither by dreams nor by TV nor (after the news) by the four residents clumping upstairs in a cluster.

Simon, in his hotel room, climbed into bed in his underwear. He gazed at the city lights that flashed and moved across the ceiling.

"'Your ways, O Lord, make known to me. Teach me your paths. Guide me in your truth and teach me, for you are my savior, and for you I wait all the day long.' And turn not away from my questions, Lord, for tonight I am full of questions. Is my prose as cogent at Leonard Woolf's, O Lord, and where is the precedent for celebrating Christmas in November? I wonder if I was too quick to judge the old man in the black suit and whether his mother does indeed lie this night in her coffin; and if she does, how very old she must be. What accounts for the unbroken series of complaints and sorrows I have run into since early this morning? The cook at the Open Soon Café. The bus driver. Diana of the Dime Store. The security guard. The father of the bride. It has not been a good day for peace of mind. Are days like this caused by atmospheric pressure, or are they a hint of your displeasure with the way the world is going, Lord? Or are they caused by the chemicals the bakeries are putting in our bread?

"I have been to Olympus, and something is wrong. Strangers come up to me and pour out their hearts. I sit looking straight ahead like a priest in the confessional while they empty their anxieties into my right ear. It's doubtless my white hair that attracts them, together with the consoling sound of running water. White hair means age, and age—to a lot of people—means wisdom. Not true. Old age confers no wisdom. Most of my companions these days are old and there is nothing impressive about the wisdom of any of us—least of all myself, and I am almost as old as the century. The perceptive among the old were perceptive all along. Which was something I didn't know when I was sixty-five. When I was sixty-five and freshly retired, I decided to be wise overnight, and I began by trying to think of my past life as a series of artistic segments like the acts of a play. It was the sort of thing adolescents are known to do on boring summer afternoons, and I am still puzzled as to why I entertained such a notion in my seventh decade. Maybe you can't spend your career teaching courses like Modern Theatre and Literature of the Human Condition without imagining yourself the protagonist in a vital and weighty drama—a play to be reviewed and pondered in the leisure of old age. Well, if you're ever tempted to organize your past into segments, Lord, forget it. The acts overlap and people keep walking offstage before their time, and if your memory is like mine, the lighting is bad.

"But I stray from the point. The point is that if priests were smart they would move their confessionals and their power of absolution out of the churches and set them up in shopping centers, for it's there, while handing its precious money across those counters of jewelry and flowerpots and prewashed jeans, that humanity seems most vulnerable, seems least confident and most unsteady, seems about to weep for mercy. Coming out of shops, people stand and look into their empty billfolds and purses like sinners looking into their souls. A priest with a stall between the fountain and Faracy Floral could absolve a thousand penitents a day. In a month he could counsel every last wicked or despairing soul in Ramsey County. It's just an idea, Lord; take it up with your bishops.

"And now we come to the dead. It used to be that I could recite the names of the dead each night as I prayed for the repose of their souls, but the list has grown far too long for me to remember, and I can only trust that you are keeping the names in mind. You know the ones I mean. My mother and father and Jay Johnson and all the rest. Grant all of them the ineffable happiness of your presence, O Lord, and please add to that list the names of Virginia the novelist and her husband Leonard.

"What an interesting fellow is Leonard. When he was my age, he was toiling away at these five volumes of autobiography. Amazing. I find it unthinkable that one could muster the ambition, the energy, the willpower, the hope, to produce such a work at seventy-six. It's the very sort of thing T. S. Testor of the *Chronicle* is always after me to do. But my biweekly reviews for Testor are almost more than I can handle. And besides, at seventy-six, I am engaged in a different sort of work entirely. It's the very opposite of composing a book. It's called banking my fires. I am systematically closing up shop. I am reducing my inventory. I am trying to live with the barest essentials and the barest responsibilities. I am striving to like the Norman Home. The Norman Home provides me with warmth and food, and I keep telling myself that I require no more than that. What more could I possibly desire in my dotage than warmth and food? Ah, food and warmth, let me be content, O Lord, with food and warmth and nothing more.

"But an autobiography? Where would one start? One's earliest memory, I suppose. Being pulled on a sled over the snow. It was the sled my father built with the box for me to sit in, bundled in blankets. My mother was pulling me from the house to the hardware store in the afternoon. The sun was low and we passed through many long shadows where the snow was blue. Strange to think how much lay before me that afternoon in Redbank. It is my earliest memory, as if my consciousness came into being at that very moment in 1902 or '03, halfway between the house and the store. Strange, tonight, to think how much lies behind me, and how little ahead. One of these days my reason will go the way of my memory, and my conscious life will be complete, a closed book. That's why I must learn to like, or at least endure, the Norman Home.

"But an autobiography? The book would be dull. For one thing, I am by nature reticent, and wary of saying more than my listener—or reader—might want to hear. And for another thing, I am ashamed of my failures, my sins, my weaknesses, my stupidities. I would leave them all out. The best autobiographers put down their sorrows next to their joys, the dark next to the light, and they make no apologies, they seek not to justify. Everything, the good and the bad, goes down as flat fact. I couldn't do that. How could I expose to the world my affair with Linda Mayo, even though after all these years the Irish holiday we spent together looks almost innocent. But of course it was not innocent at all, and my conscience of steel and stone stood in the way at last.

"Linda Mayo. Her name calls up the beautiful west of Ireland, where the people are poor and the land rocky and the seagulls graze with the sheep. I see her in a prospect of stone, for that's where I left her, standing on a stony road by a stone wall, in the rain. I forget what I first loved about Linda Mayo. Was it her smile or her brain? Her smile was so open and full of good humor. Her smile, even from a distance, did something physical to me. It tickled the inside of my ribs.

"On some campuses there are elections for Teacher of the Year, O Lord, and I wonder why no one has thought to poll a faculty and honor the Student of the Year—the student who has most often challenged the faculty to go beyond their lesson plans and reach deeper into their intellectual resources than they have ever reached before. Linda Mayo was such a student. We moved through her senior year in perfect harmony, she and I. The world admires the grace of figure-skating partners and gives prizes in tennis to mixed doubles champions, but who has paid sufficient attention to the artistry of the perfectly matched teacher and student? Who sings of their measured movements through the reading list and into the stacks of the library and back to the classroom for questions and answers? Who applauds at the end of the term when they both come down on the same foot and part company full of insights and memorable quotations and look as though it had been no effort at all? Linda Mayo and I were such a pair."

Simon was seized by a tremendous yawn. He pulled the blankets up to his chin.

"That's it for tonight, Lord. I'm tired. And you know the rest."

Linda Mayo entered Simon's life through his nose. A clean breeze from the north was bringing down a slanting shower of elm leaves—registration day, 1944. Simon was crossing the Rookery campus with his head down (weighted with his plans for the new semester), and as Linda Mayo approached him, upwind, she was preceded by the scent she was wearing. This was on the sidewalk between the old science hall and the new gymnasium, and the scent, faint and pleasing, made Simon think of a blue flower. He raised his head and saw her blue skirt and her white blouse and her black hair and dark eyes. "Hi," he said, and she said, "Hi," and that was that. He thought no more about her until the next morning when she turned up in his nine o'clock class.

Her name, according to his class roster, was Linda Brennan Mayo, and because the name Brennan sounded more maiden than given, he assumed she was married. She was sitting in the front row—and wearing the same scent—whether of a violet or a vetch he couldn't decide, but definitely something delicate and blue. He guessed she was twenty or twenty-one, and judging by her tweed suit and plain shoes and the prim and overcurled condition of her black hair, he sensed that she wanted to be taken for older than that.

"Linda Mayo," he said, taking roll, and instead of answering, "Here," or raising her hand as the others had done, she smiled.

This was a class in creative writing—an innovative class in those days, established at Simon's insistence over the objections of the stodgier members of the department—and it wasn't long before Simon began to refer to it (over coffee with Jay Johnson) as the damnedest class of his career. By this he meant that the twelve people it drew together three times a week were the most disparate, colorful, abrasive, interesting students he had ever had. The class attracted a surprising number of nonacademic types, including five adults who hadn't been in a classroom for years. While his other three classes took only a day to settle into harness, this one took a fortnight. For one thing, most of the students couldn't decide where to sit. Each day when Simon entered the room he found the twelve rearranged in a different pattern. Some days they sat in clusters. Other days each student was an island. One day they all skipped class together, and he found them outside under a tree, reading their work aloud. When he crossed the lawn and stood at the edge of their circle, two or three of them nodded, as if granting him permission to sit, and the rest ignored him. He sat on the grass and listened to a girl named Catherine Magnus—an unmarried, shockingly candid girl—read a poem inspired by her recent discovery that she was pregnant. He saw that the class was absorbed in her poem, in her predicament, in the anguished tremor in her voice. At least *most* were absorbed; there was no telling what was on the mind of Mrs. Henry Hamilton III, for she sat with her back to the group and stared out across the hills; and there was no reading the mind of Tom Carney, a hotshot halfback who distrusted any emotion not connected with touchdowns and who doused all moments of seriousness with a squirt of his crude humor. "Hey, lookee here," said Tom Carney when Catherine Magnus finished reading her poem, "a blackbird dumped on my notebook."

At this Linda Mayo, sitting against the trunk of the tree, offered Simon a consoling smile.

At the end of the second week these twelve people arrived at a seating arrangement that proved what Simon was discovering in their papers: that he had a class of four writers and seven nonwriters and one in-between. The writers, having found each other out, now sat in a tight group by the door and wrote with an insane compulsion. All four were deeply troubled and they found writing therapeutic. Side by side in the front were Catherine Magnus, with child, and Gregory Altman, a burglar on parole who trembled for nicotine in the smokeless classroom. Behind Catherine and Gregory, and breathing down their necks, were Shirley Lance, divorced, and Mrs. Henry Hamilton III, widowed. On the recommendation of her doctor (this was ten years before the first psychiatrist set up practice in Rookery) Shirley Lance brought her knitting to class every day to calm her nerves, and she brought her four-year-old daughter Beatrice now and then. Class discussion was mostly impertinent and freewheeling, and Shirley Lance's talk was full of initials. She referred to her daughter as Beebee and to her former husband as her Ex and to Simon as Mr. S. She said that when she was P.G. with Beebee. Doctor Kaye was her G.P. She said that her G.P. suspected that Beebee's I.Q. was sky-high, but that, of course, was on the Q.T. She said that her Ex, who was 1-A, would soon be off to war, and thus he had quit his job and was behind in his child support; last month, instead of money, he had sent her an I.O.U., the S.O.B.

Mrs. Henry Hamilton III, decorated with ropes and rings and pins of precious stone and metal, was embarking—now that her husband the banker was dead—on her memoirs. This was something she had been meaning to write for years and years, but now as she dug into her recollections and put them on paper (surgery and tea parties and Caribbean cruises) she was dismayed by the emptiness of her life, and so she wrote with increasing speed and ferocity, as though by arching her elegant penmanship back over her days on earth she could infuse them, retroactively, with shape and purpose.

The seven nonwriters sprawled along the windowed wall and kept an eye on the weather and made the best of a course they considered silly, a course some of them had signed up for because of scheduling difficulties and the rest because creative writing sounded easy. These seven were an untroubled lot, and their ambitions were clearly defined; they knew where their college degrees would lead them, and if creative writing was unrelated to their goals in life, it wasn't as foolish as some other courses they had taken, say music appreciation, and they would bend to the task and hand in the required number of words—the most logical and uninteresting words Simon had ever read.

Simon's twelfth student, the beautiful Linda Mayo, was in a class by herself. She sat neither with the writers nor the nonwriters, for she was neither feverish about writing nor stone cold. Considering her attractiveness, Simon found her early writing a disappointment; although she wrote at length, her writing seemed artificial; it seemed like preliminary spadework of some kind, which didn't quite uncover what she really wanted to say. "This is all very correct and nice," Simon wrote on the third paper she handed in, "but I've had my fill of unpeopled landscapes. Let's see a little of your soul."

Linda's next paper was full of people. It was a perceptive analysis of her classmates. She said that Simon was teaching, in effect, two classes, and that she herself was sitting in the wide no-man's-land of desks that separated them. She described the writers and the nonwriters and their views of each other. She said that because the seven nonwriters felt no need to produce a single word more than was required, the writers looked on them with disdain. But at the same time the writers envied them, for the nonwriters seemed so stable, so infuriatingly sure of themselves. When asked about their futures—Linda had surveyed them—the nonwriters had the answers. Two planned to become lawyers, one a haberdasher, one a grade-school teacher, one a farmer, one a radio announcer, and one a loving housewife. And that was exactly what they *would* become, damn them, without ever knowing the agony of indecision. On the other hand, the nonwriters (Linda continued) tolerated the writers;

indeed they did more than tolerate them—they humored them. The nonwriters found writing easy, but they saw how hard it was for the writers. When a writer read a page aloud, the nonwriters smiled and nodded and said something like, "Boy, that sure was some great writing there, Mrs. Hamilton," for they knew how seriously Mrs. Hamilton took herself and her syntax. And Mrs. Hamilton, envying them and despising them, loved them.

"Loved your paper," said Simon, returning it to Linda.

"Next I'm analyzing the instructor," she said.

But she didn't. Her next paper was again full of her fellow students. She pointed out how everyone—judging by their remarks in class—seemed to be homing in on the subject of love. Parent love, spouse love, lover love, self-love, and, in Shirley Lance's case, ex-love.

It was true. Now in midsemester, love was bringing the writers and nonwriters together. Catherine Magnus was making her unborn child the subject of a sonnet sequence, and the halfback Tom Carney (had her poetry pierced his brittle shell?) asked her downtown for a beer. The blindest lover in class was a tiny blonde named Cynthia Wentworth, a nonwriter engaged to a shoestore clerk. Cynthia sat by the window, where the sunlight diffused her yellow hair into a halo, and demonstrated her grasp of logic by saying, "Herm and I are going to be married in June and it's going to be a perfect June day without a cloud in the sky because we're having the reception outdoors." She went on to say that her Uncle George would take the pictures and a cousin of Herm's would open the gifts. "Oh, I hope I don't get two toasters like my sister did, it's so embarrassing to get two toasters. My wedding dress is ready, Mom and I have been working on it for months, and Herm and his groomsmen will be in white coats with dark brown trousers. We have our apartment already picked out, just the loveliest little apartment over a grocery store on Fifth Street, and Herm will be getting a raise—he's already making twenty-seven dollars a week—and he'll be up over thirty by June. I want you all to come to the wedding, and if you can't come to the wedding come at least to the reception because I want you all to meet Herm, he's an angel. Oh, I hope we don't get two toasters." So small and radiantly blonde was Cynthia Wentworth, so unblemished was her skin, so misty were her eyes, that neither the divorced Shirley Lance nor the unwed mother-to-be Catherine Magnus (the two likeliest challengers to her utopian dreams) said a word in response. It was left to Tom Carney the halfback to break the romantic spell. "Herm the sperm," he muttered under his breath, and Simon ordered him from the room.

In years to come, particularly in the sixties, when self-expression was the fashion, love the watchword, and blatancy the tone, Simon was often reminded of these original twelve apostles of love, and he thought of them as precursors. And what eventually happened to all of them? Wouldn't it be interesting to know? As a matter of fact, Simon did know. Rookery was not so large a city that those who remained in the vicinity could lose themselves, and as for those afar, they turned up either in the alumni publication or at homecoming games.

Cynthia Wentworth had a perfect day for her wedding and she received only one toaster—a four-slicer from a rich uncle in Denver—but she turned out to be one of those women for whom the wedding, for all practical purposes, marks the end of life. Blame her mother, whose every instruction and word of encouragement seemed aimed at preparing her for the walk down the aisle. Blame her father, whose philandering made his wife weep and convinced Cynthia very early that the key to everlasting bliss was simply to find a better man than her father. Blame her Aunt Henrietta, who upon seeing her in her baptismal dress at seven weeks called her a bride. Blame the bridal magazines Cynthia began reading when she was thirteen, for in them no article or photo, not even the tiny hard-to-read ads on the back pages, hinted at any form of human existence following the wedding. Blame her husband the shoestore clerk, who was so kindhearted that he brought up the kids and washed and ironed their clothes and shopped for groceries and allowed Cynthia to lose herself in soap operas and sleep. She grew fat and shunned society, and so successfully did she remove herself from the joys and mishaps of daily life that one day years later when Simon met her in a dentist's waiting room, she looked— though heavy and glum—not much older than the morning she had invited his class to her wedding.

Tom Carney the halfback took his degree and went back to the farm he came from, and his agility in marketing was reminiscent of his footwork on the gridiron. When beef was high his pastureland was covered with fattening steers, and the day the price of pork skyrocketed he was already raising pigs. In his human relations he was equally efficient. None of his three wives got a fair settlement, and one time in anger he clawed the face and shoulder of one of his hired men with a thin-tined hayfork, and when it became apparent that the scars would be permanent and the man threatened to sue, Tom Carney shut him up with a gift of a thousand dollars, then he fired him.

The would-be lawyers became lawyers, the would-be haberdasher became a haberdasher, and so forth. Shirley Lance moved to Minneapolis and did O.K. for herself in P.R. for IBM. Gregory Altman stole a car and went back to prison. Catherine Magnus miscarried and joined the WACS. Mrs. Henry Hamilton III, who was born two years after the nation's Centennial, died two years short of its Bicentennial, and she left a thousand pages of memoirs lying loose in boxes and drawers and on the shelves of her closets—a Proustian remembrance of ninety-six years of minutiae: what streetcar to take from her girlhood home in Chicago to her grandfather's farm at the edge of the city (the farm was now mostly Interstate 90), who sat opposite her at the bridge table on the afternoon the President died (she couldn't recall which President), and what Gertrude Small said to the balmy Sam Garrison the day he proposed himself for membership in the Ladies' Garden Club ("No," said Gertrude Small). Mrs. Hamilton was laid to rest beside her husband, the lecherous banker who had been in the ground for nearly thirty years, and her only living kin was a grandson, Henry Hamilton V, who owned a carnival.

Linda Mayo spent another semester as Simon's student, this time in Poetry 400, and they grew very fond of each other. Her husband, Simon learned, was a marine fighting in the South Pacific. Poetry absorbed her the way creative writing had not, and her papers revealed such a fine grasp of poetic nuance that Simon poured his soul into mapping out her reading program. Her remarks in the classroom were so trenchant and witty that the other students boasted of her to their friends.

After her graduation in 1945, Linda kept in touch with Simon by letter. She wrote several times from California, where she attended graduate school and awaited her husband's return from the war; then she wrote once from Cleveland to say that her husband had been killed on Okinawa and she had dropped out of school. This was followed by a two-year lapse in the correspondence and then by a postcard from Dublin. The card was written on June 16, 1949—Bloom's Day; she had visited Davy Byrne's Pub and tried to drink a mug of Guinness in honor of James Joyce. She said it was very bitter and she only sipped at the foam. "Incidentally," she wrote, "I'm an airline stewardess."

Then it was 1950 and Simon was an honored guest at the Midcentury Dinner in St. Paul. He had been chosen, along with eleven other Minnesotans of revered reputation, to represent his profession and receive a bronze plaque for his contribution to "the Good Life in Minnesota." The dinner was held in the Great Hall of the Great Plains Hotel, and the speaker was Vice-President Alben Barkley. This was during Simon's twenty-seventh year of teaching, and although he knew a hundred men and women he considered more deserving of the honor (*The Epitome of College Professorship* was engraved on the plaque), he was not truly amazed to have been singled out. Simon, from the beginning, had been vastly successful as a teacher, and the energies he poured into his work, though considerable, never seemed to equal his rewards. Like a stirring line in a lyric poem, this Midcentury Award fit perfectly into the charmed life he had been leading in education, and as he sat at the long head table in the Great Hall and looked out over the 500 people who had paid twenty dollars a plate, he pondered the irony of his being so lucky in the classroom and so unlucky in love. He was struck by the great emptiness on the emotional side of his life. Barbara had been gone for seven years. He wished she were back, to share this occasion with him. Henceforth he would be known in the record books as Minnesota's Professor of the Half Century, but he thought of himself as the Loser of the Half Century in affairs of the heart.

When the twelfth and last honored guest (a preacher from Plainview) had been extolled and presented his award and the diners stood up and milled and circled and drifted toward the exits, there, coming forward to the head table and calling "Mr. Shea!" for fear the three or four people surrounding him might bear him away— and looking even more stunning than she had five years earlier— was Linda Mayo. Simon hurried around the end of the head table, and when he and Linda came together they were both aware of an awkward restraint that kept them from touching. Had he and Linda ever touched, he wondered. Most likely they never had. Then why would an embrace have seemed so natural here among the soiled napkins and empty ice cream dishes of the banquet hall? Certainly it spoke of their deep regard for one another, something akin to love, something ardent and flourishing that had been feeding, these five years, on next to nothing.

"Did you ever think it would come to this?" said Simon, leaning close to her ear, for the people around them were chattering noisily. He pointed to the engraving on his plaque. "Doesn't it make you wish you had appreciated me when you had the chance?"

"Listen, don't joke about that award," she said. "That's one award that has found its rightful recipient." She said this with her splendid smile, which at twenty-one had been captivating and now at twenty-six—with the smile lines etched permanently beside her eyes—made him tremble slightly with joy. Her black hair lay fulsomely across her shoulder, and her blue dress was full of tucks and billows, as was the fashion that year, and she was lovelier than she had been as the lovely bride of the doomed marine.

"Do you live here in St. Paul?" he asked.

"I live in Minneapolis, between planes. I'm still a stewardess."

"So what are you doing here? Who are you with?"

"I'm here to congratulate you. I shared a table with a couple from Duluth. The woman complained constantly about the mashed potatoes, and the man blew cigar smoke in my face. I'm alone." She touched her hair. "Alone!" she said again with gravel in her voice, and she rolled her eyes in mock seduction.

"Well. In that case we have a minute to talk." This lukewarm proposal was typical of Simon's strict decorum where women were concerned, and if Linda was disappointed at being restricted to a minute of talk (how could she not be?—she was dressed to the nines for a night on the town) she hid her dismay.

"How's your sister?" he asked, not caring in the least. Her sister, younger than Linda, had been his student as well.

Linda described her sister's state of mind at some length. Her sister was now the wife of a Cadillac dealer and very unhappy. "But still better-looking than I," she added, and this reminded Simon of how curiously uncertain Linda had always been about her looks. In her student days he had never spoken to her for long at any one time that she didn't let slip some subtle remark about the inadequacy of her appearance; not a self-debasing remark exactly, but a symptom of her being mildly insecure about the quality of her face and body—a throwaway line easy to overlook but which, when you thought about it, made her out to be second-best to some girl who had just walked by. She was married to the marine in those days, but the marine was on the other side of the world and she was obviously fishing for some slight attention to her womanhood. But Simon, in his customary guarded manner, never took the bait. It was unseemly, he thought, for a married man to comment on the appeal of any woman not his wife; and now, in the banquet hall, though unsettled by her beauty and by the blue scent she still wore, he paid her no compliment.

"Are you and your wife back together?" she asked with surprising candor. She swept the room with her eyes, as though looking for Barbara, but of course she wouldn't have known Barbara if she saw her.

"No, we're still apart."

She waited a moment to see if he had more to say about that, but he didn't. She said, "I think of you often."

Nervously he put his hand to his head and smoothed his white hair. He had been longing for a woman to share this evening with, and here she was. Under the circumstances, it was hard work to be funny, but he tried. "It's no wonder you think of me," he said. "I'm the epitome of college professorship."

Linda didn't think this was very funny, and her smile was sad.

Then Jay Johnson approached the head table. Simon introduced him to Linda. "Jay and I came down to the banquet together," he said, looking at his watch. "I suppose we should start back. It's a three-hour drive."

"Don't let me hurry you," said Jay, enchanted by Linda and willing to prolong the visit. Simon, sensing this, broke out in an unexpected rash of jealousy.

The three of them walked slowly to the door, their arms folded, their smiles slightly phony, their small talk hardly disguising their dissatisfaction with the way the evening was ending. Outside the air was hot and heavy, and Simon felt himself sweating under his shirt. He and Jay offered Linda a ride home, but she declined.

"I'm going to drop in on some friends as long as I'm in St. Paul," she said. "I'll catch a bus here on the corner."

They saw her to the corner, where she boarded the first bus that came along (without regard for its destination, it seemed), and then they crossed the street to Jay's car, Simon carrying his plaque through the cloud of bus exhaust and feeling more than ever like the Dolt of the Half Century.

They had not driven far when Simon proposed to Jay that they stop for a drink. In a dingy bar at the edge of the city they had two stingers apiece. Back in the car, Simon said that tonight he had met and rejected the only woman he really cared for. She was the love of his life. He said that Linda Mayo's beauty was stupefying and her brain had no equal and if he were a bit more gallant and a bit less scrupulous of his marriage vow he would turn right around and make his way back into the city and sweep her off her feet.

"You mean you'd throw the old blocks to her?" said Jay, driving eighty.

"I mean that she and I together would taste the golden apples of the moon, Jay, the silver apples of the sun."

"Lay off the poetry, Simon. Remember I'm in math."

"If Linda Mayo and I ever really got together, Jay, the music of our love would bring galaxies to a halt. Nymphs and shepherds, sporting on the green, would stumble in amazement, and the leaves of the forest would turn purple overnight."

"Does that mean you'd throw the old blocks to her?"

A few miles down the road, Simon proposed another drink, and they stopped in a small town where banks of lights over a softball diamond were being turned off. In the municipal tavern they found themselves surrounded by a women's softball team in sweaty red uniforms. On their backs they wore numerals and the team name: POTLICKERS. They had just lost a close one and they were thirsty. Simon and Jay bought the women several pitchers of beer, keeping to stingers themselves, and they were introduced to the coach of the Potlickers, a skinny little man with a thin black mustache and a lascivious cast to his eye. The team's best conversationalist was the husky first basewoman, who had an amazing memory for movies, but despite her great size she was clearly the heart's desire of the little coach, and Simon left them to their cuddling and went and stood at the bar.

He found himself next to the Potlicker shortstop, who he guessed was thirty-five and the mother of a lot of children. He could tell through her tight uniform that her body was still good, but her face, which had probably once been attractively austere, was now merely hollow, and her dark eyes were hard.

"I'm too old for the game of softball," said the shortstop, throwing her body into Simon, who stood on her left. Her erotic movements were hindered somewhat by a man standing on her right with his arm around her neck.

"I'm married to this woman," the man said to Simon, over her head. "She's my Dorie, and would you believe she'll never see thirty again?"

"I would not believe that," said Simon.

Dorie eyed him fondly.

"And would you believe she is the mother of five kids?" Her husband tightened his grip around her neck. "Four of mine and one from a previous marriage?"

"Not for a minute would I believe that," said Simon.

At this, Dorie reached under Simon's tie and opened a shirt button and lightly scratched the hair on his chest. Simon glanced at the husband, who seemed not to mind what she did as long as he had a good hold on her head. "I'm too old for the game of softball," she said softly.

"Nonsense," said Simon. "You can't be more than nineteen."

Had he been sober, he might have foreseen the effect of this remark, but drunk he was stunned by its potency—or rather by her husband's fist in his face, which followed her kiss.

"What the hell's going on?" said Jay Johnson, rushing over from a table where he had been talking to an outfielder.

The husband struck Simon again and knocked him to the floor, then stood over him and said, "I want you out of here by the time I count three. I'm the constable in this here town." He showed his badge.

"That's nothing," said Simon, getting to his feet. "I'm the epitome of college professorship."

Jay led him out to the car.

Back on the highway and speeding north, Jay chuckled. "Of all the dumb luck—to latch onto the wife of the town cop."

Simon rode with his head tipped back, a handkerchief to his nose.

Jay said several more things, to which Simon made no reply.

"What's the matter, Simon? You in pain?"

Silence.

"Simon? You all right?"

"I'm asleep."

"Okay, okay."

With the radio low, they traveled a hundred miles through the night before Simon sat up and turned to the darkness outside his widow and said, "Tell me this, Jay Johnson. Why did I not pay to Linda Mayo, whom I believe I love, one small fraction of the attention I paid to that dizzy shortstop?"

"That's easy," said Jay. "You're married."

The moon rose and Simon could see that they were nearing home. They were in the woods.

"Jay, everybody ought to be single at least twice."

But Simon would not permit himself to become single again. As the years passed, he remained faithful to his absent wife, remained faithful to the vow he felt he must keep as long as he and Barbara remained alive. "As long as you both shall live" was the agreement to which he had given his word on that April morning of 1941 before God and a holy priest and four dozen witnesses, and to violate that sacred promise would cut him off from God and the Church and render his word meaningless in the eyes of his fellow man. No allurement in the world, not even Linda Mayo, could counterbalance all that.

And Barbara Shea, as though to remind him of her continued existence, mailed Simon a note each Christmas. Barbara had embraced the rules and rigors of Holy Mother Church when she married Simon, but she had left them behind when she ran off with Evert Metz and quit believing in vows of any kind. How could anyone of sound mind make lifetime commitments in a world where husbands, without warning, turned cold or contentious or comatose? Her marriage to Simon had taught her enough about both Simon and the Church to know, without being told, that Simon would live a celibate life without her, and she pitied him for his inflexibility. She wished it were somehow possible to re-lease him from the old vow they had made together, but of course nothing short of her dying was likely to do the trick, and that was a bit much to expect.

So the best she could do, Barbara decided, was to send Simon a note each Christmas. Her notes had two purposes, both of which were lost on Simon. One, if she died before Simon did (which was unlikely, she being so much younger, but the world was full of surprises), then the discontinuance of these notes would be his notification, his release. And, two, by referring breezily to her life with Evert Metz, she might gradually convince Simon of the possibility of leading a normal, satisfying life outside the sacraments, and—who could tell?—he might someday put aside his strict dogmatism and go chasing skirts and have himself some fun.

Unlike Barbara's Christmas cards of the forties, all of which came from Grass Butte, Wyoming, the notes of the fifties traced Evert and Barbara's drift through New Mexico to Texas. Evert and Barbara were living in Taos in 1950, he painting portraits of the Pueblo Indians and she working in a bank. Evert and Barbara were living in Santa Fe in 1951, he redecorating the cathedral and she in training for a real estate license. Evert and Barbara were living in Albuquerque in 1952, he teaching at the University and she selling houses. Evert and Barbara were living in Socorro in 1953: he just barely, having suffered a heart attack, and she handling the sale of residential building lots in the Rio Grande Valley. Evert and Barbara were living in El Paso in 1954, close to a clinic; he had had a second heart attack and a serious case of pneumonia and when he regained sufficient strength he would have a tumor removed from his throat: she was with El Paso's largest real estate firm. Evert and Barbara were living in a suburb of El Paso in 1955: he was an invalid and she had been promoted by her firm to the office of Co-ordinator of Home Financing. Barbara was back in El Paso proper in 1956 and living in an apartment; Evert was dead.

On Christmas Day, 1956, Simon phoned Barbara and asked her if she wanted to return to Minnesota now that Evert was dead. Thanks, but she didn't think so. She had this good job in El Paso and she was on the verge of another promotion and she liked the warm winters in the South. She was forty (the age Simon had been when they met) and she was full of plans for the second half of her life; she would redecorate her apartment; she would oversee the promotion and sale of a new subdivision in the Valley; she had been meaning to go to night school and get her degree. She asked Simon to come and visit her.

Thanks, but he didn't think so. No, he had called only to offer her refuge if she was lonesome or grief-stricken or up in the air; it was his duty as a husband.

"Simon, I can't figure you out. How can you feel any duty as a husband after all these years? I ran out on you, Simon. You don't owe me a thing. To be frank, this onesided fidelity of yours makes you look kind of dumb."

"Everyone lives by his own lights, Barbara. I vowed to be your lifelong husband."

"But that vow no longer pertains. I broke my half of it."

"No, we took separate vows, Barbara. What you broke was your own vow, entire in itself and separate from mine."

"Now you're talking like that priest who gave me instructions. I think you and the priest are both all wet. I can just see you up there in the woods, pondering your duty as a husband thirteen years after I destroyed the marriage. To tell you the truth, it makes me feel guilty all over again to talk to you, Simon. I wish you'd loosen up your principles and be human like the rest of us. And when you do, call me back."

"I'm nearly fifty-seven. I'm set in my ways. I didn't realize you suffered from guilt, Barbara."

"Well, once a year, when I send you a Christmas card, I feel a twinge of something or other. Otherwise I seldom look back."

"Nor do I, Barbara. I don't want you to think of me as brooding up here in the woods. My teaching and reading and book reviewing occupy ninety percent of my time, and the house and yard the rest. I have a life quite separate from the one you and I began together."

"You had that before I left. Sorry! Forget I said that."

"All right, Barbara. I just called because I thought you might be upset about Evert."

"No, I'm not upset. Sad, I guess, but I've been sad before. It goes away. Evert and I got along fine, but he was no angel, you know. He had this girl in Juarez. But that was our agreement from the beginning. No bonds. That goes against your grain, doesn't it, Simon?"

"Everybody lives by his own lights."

"Simon, you're a dear man but you talk like a damn textbook. Thanks for calling. I'm doing fine; Evert needed a hell of a lot of care the last two years and so his passing is not entirely a bad thing, and now I've got to hang up and get on with the rest of my life." Somewhere in this sentence Simon thought he heard a sob.

"Just one thing before I let you go, Barbara. If you need a place—you know—if you ever want to return—"

"You'll take me back, right?"

"That's right. Good-bye, Barbara. Merry Christmas."

"Good-bye, Simon. I can't figure you out."

Since March of 1951, the year following the Midcentury Dinner, Simon had been receiving an annual St. Patrick's Day card from Linda Mayo, and he had been responding in kind. Her first card was written in a pub near Shannon Airport, where she said she was changing her opinion of Guinness; it was tasty, but she feared it was fattening. In the following years her cards came from Japan, Germany, Australia, Greece, England, and, finally, Minneapolis. This last card, in 1957, said that her airline had pulled her off the planes (had she lost her looks, she wondered) and increased her salary and put her in an office where she planned charter tours.

On the card Simon sent Linda in 1957, he said he was going to Ireland in June. This was to be his first time overseas and he was eager; moreover it was to be his first plane ride and he was apprehensive. He would stop in at Davy Byrne's on June 16 to see if Dublin was observing Bloom's Day.

The plane Simon boarded in Minneapolis had paint flaking from its fuselage and food stains on the seat he was assigned. He buckled himself in and clenched his fists, waiting for the takeoff.

The girl who sat next to him, by the window, was reading a gigantic book entitled *Siberia*. The couple in front of him had a crying baby. The man across the aisle had covered his head with a blanket and gone to sleep. Finally, when the plane lifted itself off the earth and banked steeply, Simon risked a glance out the window. He saw miles and miles of perfectly spaced dots, perhaps the trees of a gigantic orchard. Apple trees. But where in Minnesota was there an orchard that large? It seemed to cover several counties.

"Pardon me," he said to the girl, "is that an orchard down there?"

The girl turned to the window, then to Simon. "Where?"

"Down there. Those tiny dots."

The girl turned to the window, then to Simon, then back to her book. "Those are rivets on the wing," she said.

These were the girl's final words for the duration of the flight. Two or three times Simon tried to engage her in conversation and convince her that although he didn't know apple trees from rivets, he wasn't an absolute dunce; but the girl, deep in *Siberia*, seemed out of earshot.

The plane landed in Bangor and Gander and over the North Atlantic the sun went down in the west just in time to come up in the east. In Dublin Simon took a bus to a hotel where he slept for twelve hours. Then he rose and dressed with a high heart, for this was Bloom's Day afternoon and he was all set to throw himself into the excitement of merry Dublin. He stepped out into the rain. The tricolored flag over the General Post Office was torn. Dublin was gray with soot, and as he crossed the Liffey on a gray stone bridge a beggar with one leg asked him for five pence. Another, a boy whose sunken, hopeless eyes made Simon's heart ache, asked for ten. Simon gave them each a pound and then went into a church where the Virgin's altar was studded with gems. He said a prayer for the beggars of Dublin, for beggars everywhere, then he stepped out in the rain once more and proceeded up Grafton Street, asking his way to Davy Byrne's Pub. Where was the charm and spirit of this land of his forebears? Where was the Irish levity and laughter he had been hearing of all his life? He entered Davy Byrne's just in time to hear the barman's last call.

"Closing at this hour?" Simon asked, sitting on a barstool. "For a James Joyce observance, I suppose."

"We always close between two and six," said the barman, doing that Irish trick with his *l*'s that Simon loved to hear. "As for Joyce, you're the third chap to inquire of him today. I don't know the man Joyce, but if he's due in here he'd better hurry or the door will be locked. What's yours?"

Simon ordered a glass of whiskey and looked about him at the dozen or so people at little tables. They smoked and mumbled and looked depressed.

The door opened and in came a long-legged brunette with a copy of *Ulysses* under her arm. She was an American schoolteacher obviously, though Simon couldn't pinpoint his reason for knowing this, and she was looking for Bloom's Day action. She eyed the small clusters of people in the dark room, then turned on her heel and left.

Simon sipped his drink. The door opened again, and before he could turn and see who it was, he felt a hand on his shoulder and smelled the scent of a blue flower. Linda Mayo. She was removing a pair of dark glasses and beaming the smile that always made his heart thump.

"Hello, Simon."

As he stepped off his stool, she put her hand at the back of his head and kissed him quickly on the mouth, having determined that if she was to get anywhere with this man she had flown an ocean to see, she had better be quick off the mark. "Let's go to Sligo and recite 'Innisfree' over Yeats's grave," she said. "You're alone in this land and you obviously need a guide. Let's go to Galway and the Aran Isles. Let's go to Dingle."

Shock had tied Simon's tongue. "Sligo?" he said. "Dingle?"

Linda laughed. It was a clear laugh of pure joy, and it caused the drinkers at the tables to lift their heads and peer around through the fumes of their cigarettes. "And Cork," she said. "I've never been to Cork."

"Cork?" he said and then he, too, was taken by a fit of laughter, and they bumped shoulders and touched foreheads and Simon buried his eyes in the forelock of her black hair and the barman said it was closing time indeed.

"Aren't you curious about my being here?" asked Linda, walking with Simon to the door. "Haven't you any questions?"

"I have one. What are you doing with dark glasses on a day this dark?"

"Dark? This is Ireland, Simon. The dark and the light alternate twenty times a day."

They stepped out into sunshine. They held hands and sidestepped puddles and shoppers and they boarded a bus and climbed to the upper deck and sat in the front seat. They rode across the Liffey. Under the clear sky, Dublin looked much better. The beggars were still present along the rails of the bridge, but their faces had taken on a healthier hue. The flag atop the General Post Office was whipping itself further to shreds, yet the green and orange and white were cleaner now, in the sun.

The bus came to a stoplight. Simon and Linda looked down at a man filling a hole in the street. He wore a suit and tie. With her eyes on the man, Linda said, "Are you still married, Simon, or are you free to take me as your wife?"

"I'm married." He said this with no emotion. He might have been stating his age or profession.

The man was scooping tar out of a wheelbarrow. "But you *will* go to Sligo with me? And Galway? And Dingle?"

"I will, Linda. I will set off with you because it seems like the right and natural thing to do. It seems like an extension of Poetry 400, when you wrote your paper on Yeats. It's a field trip. At the present moment, in fact, I can't imagine going to Sligo without you. I think I've been in love with you since 1944. But you've got to realize—"

"Stop there, Simon. No contradictions to what you've just said."

"But you've got to know where you stand with me, Linda. We're suddenly here in Ireland together like lovers, and this afternoon it seems entirely fitting. I can guess at the iniquity we'll indulge in and I relish the thought. But, damn it, Linda, I'm likely to abandon you. The mood will pass and I'll be sunk in a deep state of guilt. My conscience, when aroused, is fierce. I'm likely to leave you."

"I don't care. Just so we have this vacation together."

The light changed but the bus didn't move. The driver, leaning out his window, was chatting with the streetworker.

"But I might abandon you before we even get started. Tonight I might leave you. Tomorrow. The day after."

"Try to make it tomorrow at the soonest." They kissed, and Simon was amazed at how right and natural it seemed for him to be holding Linda Mayo in his arms on a Dublin bus. Was this love? And if so, how could it have thrived on a once-a-year St. Patrick's Day card?

The bus lurched into motion and moved out from the center of the city and through neighborhoods of small, wretched houses of stone. They kissed again and then they sat up and wondered where they were going and they decided it didn't matter and they reviewed for each other the lives they had been leading since they met at the banquet in 1950. They rode the bus to the end of the line, then returned with it to O'Connell Street. They checked out of their two hotels and rented a car. Linda got in behind the wheel, claiming she was used to driving on the left, and in the first block she sent four oncoming drivers up onto the sidewalk. In the second block she pulled over to the curb and said, "Tell me *left*, Simon."

"Left," he said. "Left, left."

Linda nodded, trying to believe it. "Once more."

"Let me drive."

"No, once more will do it."

And it did. Simon said "Left," and they streaked off down Morehampton Road and out of the city without once crossing the center line.

"So much for Bloom's Day in Dublin," said Simon.

Linda said, "We're giving Bloom's Day one more chance." They came in sight of the sea and followed a dirt road along the rocky coast and parked at the base of a broad, round tower, a Martello tower, where Joyce had lived for a year as a young man, writing. It was Buck Mulligan's tower in *Ulysses*. A woman from a nearby house let them into the tower and said they could take the stairway to the top if they wished, but she couldn't for the life of her understand the attraction. She told them to pull the door shut when they left; she would be back later to lock up.

They climbed the circular stone steps and came out through a door onto the roof. On their left were the steeples of Kingstown and on their right was the blue Irish Sea. A dark blue steamship stood several miles out, under the dark blue line of its smoke. The tower was in sunlight and so was a distant headland, but there were two or three rain showers in between.

"I love high places," said Simon.

"Oh, yes? Then we'll go to the Wicklow Mountains. We'll go to the Rock of Cashel. I know a lot of high places."

From the sea they drove into the mountains. It was late afternoon and Simon found the beauty of the Wicklows literally breathtaking; that is, when they drove up over the first high crest and looked out over the green rolling valleys of pasture and hedgerow, he experienced a stoppage of his breath. Never had he seen a green so rich. A world of gleaming greenness, washed and rinsed in the rain and drying now in the sun. A green that turned blue in the shadows and gold in the light. Green fields laced with veins of blue gray rock and arteries of blooming fuchsia. They left the car and jumped over a stile and walked along the edge of a pasture containing one cow. The bleating of distant sheep came to them from four directions; they heard the sound of chimes from a steeple they couldn't see.

The cow retreated to the far limits of the pasture and watched them sit down on a flat wet rock. They kissed. They turned and sat back to back and gazed for a long time at the cloud patterns moving across the hollows and peaks of green. They kissed again. Linda took a picture of Simon sitting on the rock, then they changed places and as Simon backed away from the rock with the camera to his eyes, he stepped in a cowflop deeper than his shoe.

They drove into a valley and ate supper in one of the six pubs in a town of twenty houses. Behind the bar an old man and a girl of ten played cards. In the rest room a rosary hung on a nail over the toilet.

In the evening they went to Glendalough and walked through the shadowy valley connecting the two lakes and watched the sunlight recede up the steep hillsides and disappear, leaving the valley in twilight and filling with fog.

"I love exploring valleys," said Simon, leading Linda off the main path to a cemetery of high weeds and Celtic crosses.

"Ireland is full of valleys," she said. "We'll see them all. But it's night, Simon. Let's find a room."

In another valley they stopped in another small town and registered as husband and wife at a small hotel and drank large glasses of whiskey with the small proprietress in the small lobby. Then they climbed the stairs to a small room overlooking the narrow street and they undressed by moonlight and Linda guided Simon over her high places and eased him into her valleys, and considering his fifteen years of asceticism, they thought it nothing short of miraculous how right and natural were his skills of exploration.

Later Simon awoke. Linda was gone from bed. He sat up and saw her standing at the window. The room was cold and she wore nothing and the low moon was reflected off her shoulder and arm and the curve of her hip. "Something wrong?" he said, but she didn't reply. He went to her and found her weeping.

"I'm so happy, but it won't last," she said, looking down at the dark street. "I was this happy on my honeymoon with Merle, but Merle was killed and I never thought I would be this happy again. But I am, Simon. With you I'm as happy as I've ever been. But it won't last. You'll leave me."

"Come to bed." She was cold in his arms.

"It's not your fault, Simon. It's the way you are and I knew what I was getting myself into when I flew over here, and you warned me—" She turned away from him in a spasm of tears.

"Come to bed. It's cold."

"I *want* to be cold. I want to remember as much about this room, this night, as I can, including the cold." She pressed her face to the window and the cold glass turned opaque with steam. "There's no hope for us, is there, Simon? There's no way we can ever belong to each other?"

"Yes, there is. For a few days."

"But I mean forever. Tell me we'll be together forever."

"Forever is a long time."

"I *know* how long forever is! You don't have to define it for me!" Her sorrow had a sharp edge and she raised her voice. "You don't even have to *mean* it. Just say 'forever,' Simon. Just lie!"

"We'll be together forever," he lied.

"That's lovely."

"Now come to bed."

On the second day Simon drove. They crossed the midlands at a diagonal and rented a room in Sligo and then, packing along two bottles of wine, they went out to do Yeats. They went to Glencar Lake and rowed a farmer's boat across the green water to the tiny green Isle of Innisfree and recited Yeats. They drove to Glencar Falls and recited Yeats. They drove to Ben Bulben Cliff and stumbled—tight on wine—around its foot and gazed up at its bare rocky face and recited Yeats. They went to Drumcliff churchyard and found Yeats's grave, where Simon stood for a long time reciting Yeats to Yeats, as well as to the magpies and the sea breeze and the puzzled sexton who peeked out from the door of the church. It was nearly dark now and Linda was cold, and when Simon paused between poems she urged him to return to the car and to Sligo. But Simon said he wasn't finished. She sensed that he was caught up in something sacramental, and so she moved off to a stone wall at the edge of the churchyard and slipped off her shoes and sat on her feet and watched Simon's shock of white hair bobbing in the dusk and his long arms gesturing broadly as he called up verse after verse and dropped them like roses on the poet's grave.

When his memory gave out, it was dark, and he staggered

slightly as he walked with Linda over the graves toward the gate. They had drained the second bottle at Ben Bulben two hours earlier, so it wasn't wine that made him drunk; it was the poetry stirring in his head and his love for Linda stirring in his blood. They stopped and embraced and looked back at the small light over the door of the church and at the moon rising over the four-cornered steeple.

"It was Yeats who said we must obey our feelings, Linda, our deepest longings. He said we should trust our intuition and instincts because they're more reliable than the intellect, more sensible than custom and common sense."

"How wise of him," said Linda.

"And that explains why our being here together seems so right. It's right at the deepest level of our being. I see that now."

"How wise of you," said Linda.

They returned to Sligo and throughout this second night of their journey through Ireland, Linda's tears were forestalled by Simon's mentioning, early and often, the word *forever.*

On the third day—a cloudy day with mist in the wind—they set out across County Mayo, and at midmorning they came to Knock. Beside the highway was the old stone church where years ago a heavenly vision was seen. Simon said, "Let's have a look," and stopped the car.

Linda went with him to the door of the church, but declined to go in. "You go ahead," she said. "I want to look around outside." She knew that Simon's religious faith was her rival. She knew that his principles were Catholic and his scruples severe. She knew that his conscience, though amazingly lax at the present time, was suspended on strings pulled by Rome, and she was very uneasy as she watched the heavy oak door close behind him. How was a woman to compete against the wiles of a Church? How ridiculous of her to have carried the fight to Ireland, where signs of the faith were abroad in the land. Statues of Mary in kitchen gardens. Crosses of stone embedded in the hillsides. Rosaries in toilets.

As Linda waited in the doorway, sheltering from the mist, a line of several women and girls came striding around the corner of the church. They were praying aloud. They were circling the church reciting the rosary, and the wind was catching at their hair and their skirts and their mumbled words. Again and again as the minutes passed, they came around that corner, and Linda saw in each face the remote expression of the pilgrim; they were oblivious to the wind and rain, as though their prayers had put them in touch with a distant world.

Would Simon come out of the church distracted like this? Linda feared he would. She left the doorway and crossed the road, which separated the sacred from the profane. Here was a row of souvenir stalls, stick and canvas structures housing the merchandisers of mysticism. In each booth sat a man or a woman or a child shivering in the wind and looking out over a display of cheap and holy wares. Small statues, rosaries, crucifixes, dish after dish of religious medals thin as a dime, priced at a quarter, and worth a penny.

Simon called to her, and they got into the car. He gave her a kiss on the temple and said he was hungry and they would look for a place to eat. The shrine didn't appear to have worked the transformation she feared. Indeed, it was Linda herself who left Knock more solemn than before. She couldn't put from her mind the faces of those women and girls at prayer. They had seemed so removed, so otherworldly. She turned and looked back at Knock as they followed the highway into a valley and she sensed the mysterious magnetism of this place where the supernatural was said to have occurred, where a better life had been hinted at in a vision—a life without souvenirs, a life without tears or pain, a life where love never came to an end.

They spent two days and three nights in Galway, exploring the city on foot and the county by car. They each bought a winter coat of heavy Irish worsted; Linda bought gray and Simon black. On the second morning they made the three-hour crossing by steamer to the largest of the Aran Islands and hired a jaunting car driven by a man named Brown, whose slow and farting horse pulled them along the narrow road of the sheep-strewn coast. Brown told jokes from one end of the island to the other, and he told them very badly.

Simon and Linda didn't see the point of most of them, but they laughed as though they did, so infectious was Brown's delight.

"There do be a lot of jokes," said Brown, "and some folks don't like them, but I never see the harm in a joke." He laughed wildly, as though all the jokes he had ever heard were coming to mind at once.

At Brown's direction, they ate a big lunch for a small price in a tiny farmhouse, and when they returned to the jaunting car Brown told them—convulsed with joy at the trick he had played—that they had been fed by Mrs. Brown, yes indeed, his very own wife.

On the way back to the steamer it began to rain. Brown tipped back his wet face and laughed at the sky.

They passed a cemetery. "People die here, same as everywhere else," he said, and he laughed his mad laugh at the gray and crooked headstones.

Crossing back to Galway in the afternoon, the passengers shared the ship with a hundred crates of smelly salmon, so Simon and Linda moved out onto the open rear deck where the soft rain was just the right consistency to dilute their glasses of whiskey. Later, to warm themselves, they descended to the cramped lounge in the hold and discovered eight young men of Aran singing ballads. With two guitars and a vast repertoire of songs, they were returning to school on the mainland. Before they had too much to drink, their singing was exhilarating and beautiful; later it was mostly scatological. One of the young men—he had blue eyes and red curls—linked arms with Linda and sang her a cautionary ballad about the danger of marrying a dried-up old man. Nearing port, they sang seven different songs simultaneously, the eighth singer having passed out, and then as the ship docked they joined in unison once more and sang several verses about a blacksmith who shot sparks out of his ass. Four of the young men kissed Linda good-bye.

Linda, stepping from ship to land, sensed that she and Simon had passed the turn-around point of their tour. An experienced traveler, she recognized the hint of preoccupation in Simon's eyes; it was the look common to all tourists who are beginning to miss their own bed and table and the slant of sun peculiar to their own doorway. In the days following, they went to Dingle and Cork and they bought crystal in Waterford, but though Simon did his best to concentrate on the sights, half his mind seemed to be imagining how tall the grass was growing around his house and what mail he might be reading if he were there.

But the fervor of his love for Linda was undiminished, and the morning they set off from Waterford to Dublin their spirits were very high and they exchanged lines of the enchanting "Song of Wandering Aengus."

Though I am old with wandering
Through hollow lands and hilly lands,
I will find out where she has gone,
And kiss her lips and take her hands;
And walk among long dappled grass,
And pluck till time and times are done
The silver apples of the moon,
The golden apples of the sun.

They would have to part in Dublin, for Linda had business on the Continent, but the bond of intimacy they had fashioned in these eight days had all the signs of permanence. It was a bond too strong to weaken in separation, a bond easily transportable back to the States, a bond to build on.

The bond came apart at Cashel.

Leaving Waterford, it was Linda who had suggested going a bit out of their way to see the Rock of Cashel, where St. Patrick was said to have converted King Aengus to the way of Christ. Her motive, to some extent, was to prolong their last day together, but equally important, she knew that Simon, with his religious bent, would be interested in this magnificent pile of ruins—castle, cathedral, and tower, built on a hill of rock a thousand years ago.

Linda was at the wheel and Simon fell silent. Ordinarily the one with the guidebook read aloud to the driver, but now Simon, intent on the history of Cashel, read the book to himself with rapt attention, and when the Rock came into view—rising 200 feet above the surrounding plain—he sat eagerly forward in his seat.

They parked in the town of Cashel and walked a half mile up a winding road between walls of stone. They met an old man coming down from the Rock, and he gave them a quizzical look and said it would rain. There was no one to show them around the massive, crumbling ruins, but their guidebook contained a floor plan of the original buildings, and Simon paced the stone floors from room to room, from wall to wall, from window to window—in something of a trance. With his camera, he ducked in and out of the roofless cathedral, snapping pictures of it from every angle; he even attached his close-up lens and photographed the liver-colored lichen on the stones. Linda grew impatient, and when Simon finally put his equipment in his camera bag and buckled it shut, she took his hand for the walk to town. The sky had clouded and the wind was moist.

"Please, a little longer," he said, and he turned his attention to the round tower, to the chapel, to the cemetery. Linda was a little alarmed. Not only was she reminded of Drumcliff, where Simon had bent his mind to the grave of Yeats and she had had to wait her turn, she was reminded also of Knock, for now he wore the expression of those pilgrims at prayer; in his eye was a mixture of awe and purpose.

When he returned to Linda's side once more, his pants and shoes drenched from the knee-deep grass of the cemetery, he said, "I'd like to see the view from up there." He pointed to the peak of the cathedral wall over the altar and to the precarious stairway of stone leading up to it. "Want to come with me?"

"I think we should start back, Simon, before it rains really hard."

"Come on, it will only take a few minutes. I love high places."

"You go ahead. I'll stay here where it's dry." They were standing in a shallow, dark alcove, sheltering from the spit of fine rain. "And for God's sake be careful, Simon. The steps are wet."

The rain fell harder as he climbed, and when he reached the top and looked down at Linda in the alcove and saw how small she appeared, he became fully aware of how vast was the scale of this cathedral and how far he had ascended above the earth. He waved at her, but her eyes were elsewhere. The rain that fell between them grayed her complexion and her hair and the bright jacket she wore and she looked to Simon, in a moment of fancy, like a statue of aged limestone standing in its niche.

Then he caught sight—forty feet directly below him—of the tombs in the chancel. They were flat stones, laid flush with the floor, each the size of a coffin. He must have walked across them unaware when he was exploring at ground level and it was only now, shiny with rain and slightly canted with time, that the slabs became noticeable. Who lay buried there? Abbots, most likely. Kings. Saints. In his heart Simon felt a wrenching sensation as powerful as the surge of joy that Linda had brought into Davy Byrne's Pub in Dublin. He imagined the chancel as it must have looked centuries ago, candlelit and fogged with incense, the monks chanting their Latin orations. This scene in his mind's eye was more vivid than the presence of Linda below him in the alcove. He looked out across the rolling land. It was here in the fastness of the Irish midlands that civilization waited in repose while the wild tribes of the north and east sacked the rest of Europe, and at the close of the Dark Ages it was from this Rock and from other sequestered sites around Ireland that civilization began its movement eastward to the Continent, the Faith recrossing the old frontiers and reclaiming the old lands, classical learning doubling back over the way it had come in those earlier centuries when it radiated from Athens and Rome. So here, from the top of this slippery stone stairway, Simon saw a panorama of the Western World, and a panorama not of landscape alone, but of Time. He was standing at a pivotal point in the history of mankind, and he felt as never before a bond between himself and the multitudes of teachers who had kept the light burning down through the ages— not only the light of the classics, but the light of the Gospels as well. He felt like going to his knees and thanking God for making him a part of this tradition. In his fifty-seven years, Simon's most durable possession had been his religious faith; he cared little for money or material goods and his marriage had taught him not to spend too much trust in the uncertain market of friendship and love; but boy and man he had followed the rules and rites of the Catholic Church until they ran with the blood in his veins. This faith, to Simon, was more than a guide to behavior or a hope for eternity; it was a frame through which he viewed the world and his place in the world; it was the source of the light that made sense out of all creation; it was the miraculous order without which all was chaos; it was a gift of God.

And because his faith was all these things to Simon, and because though it preached love it forbade adultery, he knew—standing at this rainy height—that he must renounce Linda and the love they shared. Granted, his love for Linda sprang from the depths of instinct and longing where Yeats said truth abided; yet running even deeper in Simon's instinct was a current of longing for God and a love of His rigorous ways. He looked down at Linda now and his heart knocked with agony. He must descend to ground level and tell her. He must play the dolt once again. A dripping wet dolt in anguish.

Returned to earth, he took Linda's hand and drew her out of the alcove without looking her in the eye. They left the roofless cathedral and crossed the churchyard and passed through the outer wall under a mossy lintel of dripping rain.

"Simon, what's wrong?" she asked, beginning to know.

"Linda, it has to be over between us." He assumed a swift cut was less painful.

"Christ, Simon!" She stopped and stepped back and refused to move. They were at the top of the walled road, half a mile from the town, half a mile from their car.

"Come, Linda, we'll find a warm place and dry off. Have lunch. I've got to explain myself."

"It's nothing I want to hear." Looking down the road, beyond Simon, Linda saw the old man returning up the hill. What business could he possibly have on the Rock? Did he live in the ruins?

Simon tried to draw Linda along, but she stood her ground. She said, "Good-bye, Simon."

"Linda, this is no place to talk things over. It's raining. We'll go somewhere dry."

"There's nothing to talk over, Simon. If this is the end of things, then it's good-bye and good luck and please get the hell out of my sight."

"Linda."

"I thought it was safe to bring you here. I've never claimed to be attractive, Simon, but I thought I could hold my own against this ugly pile of moss-covered rock, for God's sake. You came through Knock all right. You didn't seem to have any visions at Knock."

"I said this would happen, Linda. I warned you. I said I wasn't to be trusted and you said okay. A day at a time. We agreed."

"Good-bye, Simon."

"I warned you and you said okay."

"I said okay because it was the best deal I could get. I didn't say that when it came time for you to reject me I'd enjoy it. Now what I wish you'd do is hurry back to the car and get in and drive yourself to Dublin. Please go right away, Simon. Right now."

Simon heard, at his back, the approach of the old man. He turned and they nodded to one another. The old man's face was deeply creased, like the stone wall he walked beside, like the crumbling stone walls at the top of the Rock—a man so old it was not hard to picture his climbing this hill when the castle was new, or even before that when the hill was occupied only by birds and wild goats and no stone had yet been placed upon another. As the old man trudged past Linda, she answered his nod with a blank stare.

"Listen to reason, Linda. Your bags are in the car."

"Please drop my bags at the bus depot. The bus depot shouldn't be hard to find in Cashel. I'll take a bus back to Dublin." She tossed him the car keys.

"All right, but if we go on separately, you take the car. I'll take the bus."

"Take the goddamned car, Simon. And good-bye."

Simon stepped toward her, holding out the keys. She stepped back. He gave up. He said, "I'll explain in a letter," and he turned and walked away.

"Simon," she called, and he spun around eagerly. "Simon. I don't want a letter. I'd much prefer never hearing from you again." She closed her eyes tightly.

He walked down the hill, turning several times to see her standing in the rain with the gray hulk of crumbling stone above and behind her. To avoid Simon's eyes and to avoid watching him leave, Linda had moved to the side of the road and was looking over the low stone wall and down on a pasture where a herd of white cows grazed in the rain.

Simon took his bags from the car and left the keys on the seat, intending to ride the bus himself and leave the car for Linda. Then he thought better of it. He would save her the trouble of driving in Dublin traffic and returning the car and paying what they owed. He left her bags at the bus depot and drove out of town.

It was Saturday afternoon, the hour of penance all over Christendom, and when Simon reached Dublin he drove to the church where he had prayed for the beggars. He went in and knelt at the gemmy blue altar of the Virgin and recited silently an Act of Contrition and rededicated himself to the sexless life a man of his state was expected to lead. For twenty centuries the Church had stressed the superiority of sexual abstinence, of chastity, of strict adherence to the marriage vow, and if celibacy was what it took to appease his exacting conscience, then celibacy it would be. In another twenty years, Simon would detect signs of compromise in the Church where old vows and new desires collided. If priests could rethink their vows and reenter the secular world without fear of everlasting punishment, then why not husbands and wives who had made bad marriages? Perhaps such people were not really married after all, said certain theologians on the left wing of the Catholic press. Perhaps there were mitigating impediments at the time of the wedding, said certain pastors from left-leaning pulpits. Impediments like immaturity, say, or lack of commitment. But this was 1957 and the rules were inviolable. The only place for a soul stained with Simon's iniquity was in the confessional, and that's where Simon went and knelt down and said, "Bless me, Father, for I have sinned. My last confession was three weeks ago and I have been committing adultery for the past eight days as though my life depended on it."

The priest was a boy fresh from the seminary. "And are you contrite, my son?" His voice was squeaky.

"I am, Father."

"Are you married?"

"I am, Father."

"And do you resolve never to commit this sin again?"

"I do so resolve."

"Let me warn you, my son, that this is no slight matter. The flesh has its enticements. As you go along through life you will find this a recurring temptation, and yet you must always remain faithful to your own dear wife. It is she who provides you with your home and happiness, and your proper place is at her side. If you find your carnal and illicit desires difficult to overcome, you need only ask help in prayer and you will be granted the power of heavenly aid."

"Yes, Father."

"And now let me say a word about your partner in adultery. Her welfare, too, must be considered. If your adulterous affair were allowed to continue, the two of you might begin to feel a strong attraction for each other. Spare her that, my son. Life is complex. Don't lead her on. If you do, your affair will end—as end it must—in tears and bitterness."

"I know, Father."

"You say you know but I wonder if you do. Let me warn you, my son, life is not simple."

"No indeed."

"Life is complex."

"Exactly."

"For your penance you will recite the rosary before the altar of Mary, Queen of Virgins, and at the end I wish you would add a little prayer for good weather on Sunday. We're having our summer bazaar. It will run from two till half past six. Perhaps you can come. I absolve you in the name of the Father and of the Son and of the Holy Ghost."

"Thank you, Father." It was emblematic of Simon's undivided mind and absolute faith that not for a split second did he doubt the power of this boy to remit his sin and save him from the fires of hell.

But if his mind was undivided, his heart was not. All night in his room at the Gresham Hotel he dreamed of Linda Mayo. She was on his lap, she was piloting a plane, she was in his classroom, she was in his bed, she was pulling him across the snow in the sled his father built, she was the daughter he and Barbara never had. And the next day, flying the Atlantic, he was swept up in a swirl of anguish when he pictured Linda as he had left her, standing in the road, in the rain. Over Iceland a stewardess in blue offered him a meal and he said, "No, thank you; I need whiskey more than food." He said this looking up at her with tears in his eyes, and she brought him four ounces of Calvert's in two miniature bottles. He drank as many more bottles as the stewardess permitted him, and by the time they touched down in Gander, Simon was weeping convulsively and the woman next to him arranged to have her seat changed. When they landed in Bangor, Maine, he had to be shaken awake for the customs check, and as he moved through the line with his bags, his fellow passengers gave him a lot of room, so repulsive were his bloodshot eyes and his tousled hair and his thirty-six-hour whiskers and his hangover breath.

The plane reached Minneapolis in the evening, by which time Simon had spruced up and regained his composure. He caught a bus north and rode over the same highway Jay Johnson had taken seven years earlier when they had met Linda at the Midcentury Banquet. As then, Simon was in pain. The bus driver made some remarks along the way that were intended for Simon, who rode in the front seat, but Simon did not respond. He was staring into the oncoming headlights and seeing Linda the way he had left her, in the road, in the rain, in a prospect of stone.

FRIDAY

Before leaving his hotel room, Simon opened the phone books of both Minneapolis and St. Paul and looked for Linda Mayo's name, but it was listed in neither book. He checked whenever he came to the Twin Cities, and her name had not appeared in these directories since 1957. That was nineteen years ago. Perhaps she had married. Maybe she had moved away. Simon would never know.

He checked out of the hotel unshaven, for he had brought no razor to the city. Outside, the promised moisture—rain, sleet, snow—had come to nothing, and the morning sun glittered sharply off the rush hour traffic. He crossed the street to a small café and ate an egg and a muffin and read the *Chronicle*, wherein a medical expert predicted that before spring 100,000 old people would be dead of swine flu.

Simon next went to the *Chronicle* building to see his editor, T. S. Testor. Months ago the *Chronicle* staff had been threatened by a phone call from a mad bomber who said he would blow everybody to hell unless *Dick Tracy* was restored to the comic page, and now Simon entered the lobby through a cordon of policemen who frisked him and examined the contents of his briefcase.

A receptionist phoned Testor's office to verify Simon's identity, then she turned him over to the policewoman operating the elevator.

On the fourth floor Testor shook Simon's hand and led him into his tiny office. "Have a seat," he said, tucking Simon into a chair between a filing cabinet and a coat rack. Testor's office was a cubicle of glass; his desk was a dump, behind which Testor sat on a swivel chair and faced Simon over a rounded heap of playbills, tearsheets, novels, mail, framed photographs lying on their faces, cold tablets, and sandwich wrappers; and over all this, like a layer of volcanic ash, were the grit and cinders Testor was forever knocking out of his pipe.

Testor was a poorly preserved fifty-five, and today he had a cold. He had red eyelashes and red eyes and heavy horn-rimmed glasses that kept slipping down his lean red nose. The front half of his red hair had fallen out and been replaced by freckles. He lit his pipe and dropped the match on the floor and said, "How's life in the north, Simon?"

"I've moved since I saw you last. I've moved into a small home for the elderly, and life is much easier."

"A home for the elderly! That sounds like a hell of a comedown from that nice place you had on the river." Testor's cold was thick in his nose and throat, and he pronounced each word with an extra syllable of phlegm.

"This place isn't bad. It's just what I need at my time in life. The river was too secluded. I was too much on my own."

Testor's smile was not really a smile. It was the stress of clenching his pipe tightly in his teeth. "There's something entirely wrong with your being in a home, Simon. Who did it? Who put you away?"

"I'm seventy-six, T. S. I put myself away. At seventy-six you get stupid. You need a lot of help." He opened his briefcase. "Here's a piece on those three poets you sent me. I hope it's suitable. I had a difficult time with it."

"Your stuff is always suitable, you know that." Testor did not look beyond the title page but folded the review lengthwise and poked it between two books on the shelf behind his head. From between almost all the books on all the shelves papers stuck out. This was Testor's filing system.

"You're buying it sight unseen?"

"Don't I always? We'll go down to the business office on your way out, and I'll have them issue you a check. Thirty bucks okay?"

"Well, thirty is acceptable, but it pays for only three days at the Home. And this piece was twice the work that most of my others have been."

"I'd love to give you forty, Simon, but my readers aren't big on poets. Poets don't amount to much in the marketplace, you know that. But maybe I can do better than thirty. What do they charge you at that old-folks' home?"

"It's not your regular old-folks' home, T. S. It's more like—"

"What do they charge you?"

"Nine dollars a day."

"Nine dollars! What the hell kind of a place can you get for nine dollars? What is it, a coal bin? I know a guy's got his mother in a home here in the city and he pays thirty-two dollars a day."

"That's my point, T. S. This is not what they call a full-care establishment. This is just a room and three meals. And the food is quite good, incidentally, and it's nearly an hour closer to the Twin Cities . . ."

"I don't know. I can't picture Professor Emeritus Simon Shea living in a home for the elderly. It sounds wrong. Are you sure you know what you're doing? Are you sure this isn't a crazy whim that's going to pass?"

"Growing old is not a whim, T. S."

"I'm not so sure. Did you ever read When I Was Old by Georges Simenon?"

"Is it a murder mystery?"

"No, it's a true-life account of a time when he was seventy or so and had the mistaken impression his life was over. He decided to crawl under a rock and die. Then lo and behold he got to feeling younger again. His feeling old had been just a phase, like a long sleep. He calls it When I Was Old. You ought to read it."

"Find me a copy and I'll review it."

"Or Thomas Hart Benton. Have you read Thomas Hart Benton's autobiography? The first edition ends with his farewell to the world, his farewell to art. Goodbye, folks. I'm bowing out— that sort of thing. Then you pick up a later edition and there's a new last chapter in which he tells how he bowed out too soon, how he took up his brush and paints again in his eighties and went to work on some of the best murals of his life. You ought to read that, Simon. Thomas Hart Benton."

"As you were saying, T. S., maybe you can do better than thirty."

"I'll buy you four days in that place, Simon. Thirty-six bucks, how's that?"

"Fine."

Testor sneezed, and four or five sheets of paper blew off his desk and wafted to the floor.

"How's your book coming?" asked Simon.

"Don't ask." Testor pounded his pipe into the palm of his hand, and with a sweeping motion he emptied the ashes across the desk, certain that his ashtray was somewhere in the clutter. "Don't ask. Every page is agony."

Testor was a frustrated autobiographer. For years he had been writing (and asking Simon to read) his life story. There wasn't room in the book for everything he wanted to say. He wanted to show the reader what it had been like to have had three wives and two divorces and a Purple Heart from the Normandy Invasion and the respect of men like Simon Shea and early signs of angina pectoris. He wanted to tell the world about the seven jobs he had held on seven newspapers and about his four children now scattered to the four winds. He wanted the book to contain every experience he had ever had and, beyond that, every thought that those experiences gave rise to. There was to be a chapter for each year of his life, yes, even the years of his infancy. It was to be the definitive portrait of life in mid-America from the 1920s to the 1970s, a Middle Westerner's odyssey through the middle of the century. But now, with the passing of time and more frequent chest pains, Testor was writing with an increasing sense of urgency and a diminishing sense of artistic control, and he was working himself into that worrisome state of mind common to artists who have taken an unsuccessful opus to the point of no return: he felt guilty when he wasn't writing and untalented when he was. Not a week passed that Testor didn't grind out and reject at least twenty-five pages of double-spaced reminiscence. He wrote late at night, stoking his pipe and gulping coffee all the while, and by the time he fell into bed he was too full of caffeine and smoke and old memories to go to sleep.

"Tell me, Simon, don't you ever get the urge, deep down in your heart, to put your life on paper?" Testor didn't understand why everyone wasn't eager to share his suffering.

"Very seldom. In fact, the idea never occurs to me except when you mention it."

Testor shook his head. He opened a drawer and drew out a thick stack of dog-eared paper. He held it at arm's length, as though it were putrefying. "I don't know why I feel this terrible compulsion, Simon, but it's driving me crazy. I'm afraid it's hopeless. You know what I mean, you've read most of it. Why is it dull, Simon? Why doesn't it have any zing? Why can't I put it behind me? Why can't I develop some innocuous little hobby the way other people do? I've got a neighbor who presses wildflowers. He seems happy. Why must this wretched piece of work rule my life? Tell me that, Simon."

"It's the star you were born under, T. S. Blame it on a star." It was hot in this cubicle, and Simon unbuttoned his coat.

Testor handed him the heavy manuscript. "Would you take it home with you, Simon?"

Simon frowned. "Again?"

"There are new parts in there you haven't read. Maybe if you read it through, you could tell me what to cut."

Simon examined the opening pages. "If I did, you wouldn't listen to me. I've already told you what to cut, T. S., and you never cut it. The first eighty pages, for example. I told you to throw out the first eighty pages, and you told me to go to hell."

"This time I won't tell you to go to hell. This time I'll listen to you." Testor restoked his pipe and both men watched the flame of the match until Testor waved it out and dropped it on the floor. "You see, the wife and I are taking a month off starting next week. A Caribbean cruise. If I know the manuscript is in your hands while I'm gone, then I won't feel guilty about not working on it. The wife says absolutely no writing on this trip. Says she's sick and tired of my writing. But the only way I can leave it behind is if I know you have it, Simon. If I think of it as in your hands, then I'll feel some progress is being made on it. If I have it here in my desk, I won't have a moment's peace. Day and night I'll feel like I should be writing. And the wife is right. She's not the only one who is sick and tired of this goddamn slave-driving piece of work. So please, Simon, take it with you."

It was a lot to ask. Besides being mostly dull, it was heavy to lift. "I'll take it," said Simon, trying to squeeze it into his briefcase.

"And you'll promise to read it through from beginning to end, right?"

"I'll read it through." To make room in his briefcase, he had to remove Leonard Woolf, volumes one and two.

"And promise you'll send it back by Christmas. We return from our cruise just before Christmas."

"I'll send part of it, T. S. I'll send you the worthy parts and I'll hold back the hot air."

"No, Simon, it's *my* work, not yours. That's my only copy you've got there."

"It's the only way you'll listen to me, T. S. I've told you before what to cut and you've never cut it. I'll send back the worthy parts and if you want the hot air you can drive up to Ithaca Mills and wrest it away from me."

"No, no, Simon, the writer himself has to be the final judge."

"You're blind to your faults, T. S. If I am going to the trouble of reading this work in all its flabby magnitude, I'm going to have to think my opinion counts." Simon stood and added Leonard Woolf, volumes one and two, to the mess on Testor's desk. "Say good-bye to your book, T. S. You'll be seeing part of it again at Christmas."

"But it's *my* book, Simon. It's my *life!* I have to have *all* of it back. Tell you what. I'll drive up to Ithaca Mills around Christmas and pick up the whole works."

"Very well. I'm not hard to find. Ask for the Norman Home."

"Here, Simon, you've left something on my desk."

"Keep them. Read them. They are models of conciseness."

Testor and Simon went to the business office and then to the elevator, and as the door closed between them Testor's last words were, "You've got my baby there, Simon. Guard it with your life."

Simon signed out of the *Chronicle* building and hailed a cab.

"To the Olympus Mall," he told the driver.

"Right on." The driver was a young man wearing hair to his shoulders and a red bandanna around his forehead.

They traveled out from the center of the city on Skilling Avenue and when Simon realized this he sat forward and said to the driver, "Do you know if there's a funeral home somewhere on Skilling?"

"Yeah, there's Marchand Brothers Mortuary. It's up ahead." The driver glanced in the mirror. "You want to go there?"

"I do. Just for a moment." He would verify the story of the old man in tennis shoes. If he found a guest book with no names and a single wreath that said Mother, then the old man spoke the truth. He would sign the guest book.

They pulled up in front of a three-story mansion. "Please wait," said Simon. "I'll just be a moment." He carried his briefcase, for it contained Testor's baby, and he crossed a pillared portico and stepped through gleaming white doors with hinges of brass and he knew that this place was too elegant for the mother of a man with a shrinking savings account and a misspent past. But he had come this far and so he went up to the tall young man in the foyer who wore the sad smile of undertakers everywhere and asked him if there was a very old woman in one of the rooms.

"Yes, sir, you must mean Mrs. Haverkamp. It's almost time for her service. She would have been eighty-eight next week." He took Simon gently by the elbow and moved him down the hall and opened a door on what sounded like a party and deposited him inside. There were fifty people here, and the noise of their laughter and chatter was deafening. The fashion this season was the layered look: red, white, and blue polyester; all the women wore it. The men wore leisure suits, mostly lime green or amber, and the children displayed large numerals and other printed matter across their shirts. On the chest of a ten-year-old girl Simon read IF IT FEELS GOOD DO IT.

At the far end of the room, under banks of roses, asters, carnations, ferns, and daisies, lay the corpse. Surely this was not the woman Simon had come to see, for the crowd was large and the old man in tennis shoes was nowhere about. Simon was just turning to leave when the door opened again and he was pushed further into the room by six or eight men and women whose arrival was met with shrieks of delight and kisses and hugs. Simon came to a halt beside a man in green who was selling a car to a man in rust. He stepped between them and headed again to the door but was intercepted by an elderly woman wearing a tall pile of black hair.

"Are you the preacher?" she asked.

"Don't be silly," said another woman, bewigged in red. "This is Uncle Francis."

"I'm sorry, I'm neither," said Simon. "I've come to the wrong funeral. I'm here by mistake."

He saw an open path of escape and was about to take it when the first woman took his right arm and said, "Come and see Thelma, how nice she looks," and the other woman took his left arm and said, "Uncle Francis, bless your heart." They steered him toward the coffin.

"Thelma always said the Marchand Brothers were the best in the business and now she's living proof. Doesn't she look beautiful?"

"Doesn't she look happy, Uncle Francis? Doesn't she look like she's having a pleasant sleep?"

Thelma looked dead. Her face was ivory and her hands were wax and one of her eyes was open a slit.

"Yoo hoo, look who's here," shouted a third woman bearing down on Simon. "It's Uncle Francis." She spun him around to put him on display and shouted again, "It's Uncle Francis, everybody, clear from California," and the crowd advanced upon Simon (someone bumped the coffin and Thelma opened her eye a bit farther) and they asked him how he had been and how long since he had been back to Minnesota and what ever happened to his children.

"Am I ever glad to see you," said a man with a tiny yellow mustache. "I've owed you twenty dollars since 1949, and I bet you forgot all about it." Into Simon's coat pocket he stuffed some currency.

"No," said Simon. "I'm not Uncle Francis. I'm here by mistake."

His well-wishers pressed in around him. "God, it's good to see you, Uncle Francis."

"Vincent was saying just this morning, 'I wonder if Uncle Francis will show up.' He said he just knew you'd be here."

"Uncle Francis, remember the time we weeded onions for old Charlie Henderson? Old Charlie Henderson's dead now. Been dead for years. His onion field is houses."

"Hey, Uncle Francis, how about a game of poker after this shindig is over. Remember how you and I and the Steele brothers used to play seven-card stud till three in the morning? How about a game of seven-card stud for old time's sake?"

"My Alice is in Seattle and my Billy is in Portland and my Carol Sue is in Memphis, did you know that, Uncle Francis?"

"All *my* kids stayed in Minnesota. Debbie's in Duluth, Eunice's in Mankato, and Philip's in jail."

"Do you remember my Jackie, Uncle Francis? Well, after college Jackie studied rabid skunks for three years on a government grant, but the grant gave out and now he's washing dishes in Adkirk's Restaurant on University Avenue."

"I told Vincent I didn't think you'd come all this way at your age just to shed a tear, but Vincent said if you knew how nice Thelma looked you'd come. Doesn't she look nice? I've never seen a bad one yet that the Marchand Brothers worked on. So peaceful."

"Let me take your bag, Uncle Francis, it looks heavy. God, what you got in here, bricks?"

Simon, struggling to keep his briefcase, said, "I have to go to the bathroom. You'll pardon me, please. I have to go to the bathroom."

"Uncle Francis has to go to the bathroom."

"Let Uncle Francis out, he has to go to the bathroom."

"Vincent, take Uncle Francis and show him where the bathroom is."

Vincent was the man with the yellow mustache. He cleared the way to the door.

In the quiet hallway the undertaker approached with solemn tread. "May I help you?"

Vincent said, "Show my Uncle Francis the toilet."

"I really don't need the bathroom," said Simon. "What I really need is daylight. Would you please point me toward the door I came in?"

"All right, show him outside," said Vincent. "He's my Uncle Francis and he always was a little funny. You never knew what he wanted from one minute to the next."

"I am *not* Uncle Francis. My name is Simon Shea and I never saw you before in my life, and everyone in that room is a stranger to me, including Thelma. The front door, if you please."

"This way, sir."

"Don't leave in a huff, Uncle Francis. If it's because of the interest I owe you on that twenty dollars, I'll make it up to you. You're going to upset a lot of people if you leave this funeral in a huff, Uncle Francis."

The undertaker opened the front door, and as Simon crossed the portico to the cab he heard Vincent say, "See what I mean? Same as the old days. Touchy. I guess there's one in every family."

The cabdriver looked up from a magazine as Simon got in. "Was this the right place?"

"No, but never mind."

"While you were in there, I happened to think, there's another funeral home on Skilling. It's behind this about ten blocks. An old run-down place. You want to try it?"

"No, you see I'm not even sure the corpse I'm looking for exists. I met a man yesterday—a complete stranger, a man nearly as old as myself—and he told me his mother lay dead in a funeral home on Skilling Avenue. He said he and his mother were absolutely without friends or relatives and no one was likely to come to pay respects."

"Hey, that's rotten, man."

"I'm not sure the old man was in his right mind, but I thought if he was telling me the truth, if his mother truly lies in a mortuary at this time, my name in the guest book might be some small consolation to the old fellow."

"Hey, that's cool, man. We'll try the other place." He started the cab.

"No, I've already done more than my duty. Let's be off to Olympus."

"No, let's go to the other place. I feel like cheering up a lonesome mourner. I'll go in with you. We'll both sign the book."

"I appreciate your compassion; your heart is obviously in the right place; but meanwhile the meter ticks away, and I am down to my last few dollars."

The driver switched off the meter. "This is on me. The fact is, I'm in a sociology class at the University, and this will give me something to talk about in our next discussion. The prof goes bananas over firsthand experiences like this, especially the problems of old people—dying and all." The young man removed his red bandanna and ran a comb through his long hair, then he made a U-turn and sailed down Skilling the way they had come.

In a neighborhood of dead elms and broken sidewalks they stopped before a tall narrow house. It was covered with sheets of asbestos which were designed to look like brick, but because the seams didn't match they looked like crooked wallpaper. A woman sat on the front stoop and spoke to a white cat on her lap. Above her, hanging crookedly from the eave, was a homemade sign:

ADrIAN HOOVEr, MOrTICIAN

Above the sign a man in his undershirt leaned out a second-story window. He was peeling an apple with a jackknife.

Simon and the driver went up to the front stoop. The cat flashed its pink eyes and raised its hackles.

"There, there, Gloria, don't be naughty," said the woman. She wore a bathrobe and sat on a straight-backed chair. Her face was crimson and her hair was white.

"Are you having a funeral here this morning?" asked Simon. "An elderly lady?"

"We got Mrs. Cruthers in the front room, if that's who you mean." She stroked the cat. "Service in about an hour, but her son wants it to be private. No guests, neither invited nor uninvited. Strict orders."

"Is the son here? We would like to offer our condolences. We won't stay for the service."

"Yeah, he's in the front room. I suppose it's okay, but he's probably closed the lid again."

Simon and the driver entered the front room, which contained a coffin, a couch, and a card table. The coffin was closed and on its lid rested a small wreath, the word *Mother* printed in silver on its black ribbon. The old man in tennis shoes snored on the couch.

"See what I told you," said the driver. "It's a weird place."

Simon turned in a circle, disoriented. He wanted to say a prayer for the deceased and a prayer for the bereaved, but meditation of any kind seemed impossible. On the walls were no pictures or other symbols suggesting eternal life; there were only stains in the wallpaper. The miserable surroundings, both inside and out, suggested the desirability of eternal sleep.

"Here's the book," said the driver. He stepped to the card table and wrote his name and handed the pen to Simon.

The old man on the couch opened his eyes and sprang to his feet. "What are you doing here? What's the idea?"

He took the pen from Simon. "What's the idea? We told the Hoovers, Mother and I, that we wanted nobody at this funeral. This funeral is something between Mother and me and no one else." He bent to study the guest book and saw the young man's name. His face turned sour—an expression of spoiled hopes.

"What's the idea, messing up this book? What good do you expect to do now at this late date? Where were you when she was sick and needed care? Where were you when Father was sick and needed care? Where were you when the tree came down on the house and we had to reshingle the roof? Where were you when they opened up that supermarket on Fifth and we had to close down for lack of business? All those years you ignored us and it's no use now trying to get on our good side. No use buttering us up.

What are you after? The savings account is down to nothing and I have no Social Security of my own."

He peered again at the hook, then asked the driver, "Who are you, anyhow? We never saw you before. Mother would die if she knew she was being visited by a hippie."

He turned to Simon. "I saw you yesterday at Olympus. Are you following me around?"

"Let's go," said Simon. He and the young man went out the door and the old man, scolding, followed them and said to the woman on the stoop, "It's a fine how-do-you-do when you try to spend a little time with your mother and the place is overrun with strangers."

The cat jumped off the woman's lap and ran around the corner of the house.

"Imagine my shock when I opened my eyes and saw that old has-been and that hippie standing by the coffin."

"Here, Gloria. Here, Gloria. Here, Gloria."

As Simon and the young man got into the cab, they heard the old man raise his voice: "He's an over-the-hill has-been. I met him yesterday at Olympus. Something ought to be done about people like that. They follow you home."

"Here, Gloria. Here, Gloria. Here, Gloria. Here, Gloria."

The driver tied his bandanna around his head. "So I guess we found the right place."

"Yes, thank you for your trouble. Maybe this will teach me not to meddle."

"I told you it was weird, even from the outside."

As the cab pulled away from the curb, Simon looked back to see the old man shake his finger at him. He saw a bright red coil of apple peel come spiraling down from the upper room. The woman called, "Here, Gloria. Here, Gloria. Here, Gloria."

It was late morning now, and Alex of Jupiter Service reported that Simon's radiator wasn't expected back from the repair shop for two or three more hours.

"I am coming back here only once more," said Simon, "and if my car isn't ready I will take the bus to Ithaca Mills and return only when I have a notarized statement that my car is driveable."

"Come back at three," said Alex. "You have my word."

Simon opened his car and took out his folding chair. He locked T. S. Testor's manuscript in the trunk. He carried the chair to the fountain and removed his coat and hat and settled down with Leonard and Virginia and their Hogarth Press. He finished volume three and he went to the bookstore for volume four, and when he returned to the fountain his chair was occupied by a woman in tears. She was fifty or so, stylishly dressed, and at her feet were sacks and a purse and a box tied with string. Her weeping was so blinding, so copious, so wet, that Simon assumed she had just been told some terrible news. Death of a dear one. Dismemberment. A burning house. Because his last good deed had been so completely thwarted, he walked twice around the fountain before he settled on the bench next to the chair and worked up his nerve and said, "Excuse me, perhaps I can be of help."

"Oh, this is insane," said the woman. She turned to him, a handkerchief to her eyes. "It's absolutely insane that I should be sitting here so out of control, but I just now went into Faracy Floral and ordered a bouquet for the christening of my granddaughter— our first grandchild—and as I came out of the shop I was overcome with emotion. Her christening is to be Sunday in the Cathedral. She's two weeks today, and she's a perfect little angel and no matter what I do I can't stop crying. I think I'm crying for joy, but it doesn't feel like joy. It feels like sadness. All I can think about is our daughter Louise. Louise is the little angel's mother. Louise is our only daughter, our only child. Louise was a perfect little angel herself all the while she was growing up. She sucked her thumb a little, but she stopped when we told her to, and she began stuffing fuzz up her nose instead. It was Louse's constant habit to pick fuzz off her blanket or her teddy bear as she was falling asleep and pack it into her nose. One afternoon when she was falling asleep in her crib she picked a hole in the fabric of her teddy bear and she drew out shreds of foam rubber and stuffed them into her nose. She was half asleep, poor thing, and she kept stuffing this foam rubber up her nose until it disappeared somewhere between her eyes, and by the time she began to cry and I discovered what had happened, the foam rubber had to be removed by a doctor."

"But she survived, obviously."

"Oh my, yes," the woman wept. "Today she's the best little mother you ever saw."

What, then, was the tragedy? Was the baby's father a bum? Or unknown?

"And Louise's husband is the perfect father. He thinks the world of that baby, and he clears thirty thousand a year at 3M. What grieves me is how Louise was once a baby herself and now she's a mother and where have all those years gone? Oh, I remember so little about her childhood. It's as though those years never existed. Those years are nothing but a blur of crayons and birthday parties. I don't even remember who her teachers were. Let's see, in the fifth grade it was Sister Cordelia, the strictest, most demanding teacher you ever saw. Sister Cordelia wasn't everyone's cup of tea, let me tell you. Less dedicated students than Louise suffered under Sister Cordelia; some transferred to other schools. But for a few conscientious girls in that class, like Louise, Sister Cordelia was just the thing. She took Louise's intelligence and her strong sense of duty and made an outstanding scholar of her—an honor student from that day forward, through high school and college."

The woman moaned and wiped her eyes. "Oh, I could tell you a few other things about her childhood, I suppose, but those years are mostly a blur. I mean she's twenty-five, and where have those years gone? Sunday we're christening her baby, and where, oh where, have those years gone?"

"I know what you mean," said Simon. "Myself, I've misplaced three quarters of a century."

At this, to his amazement, the woman's recovery was instantaneous. She took a mirror from her purse and straightened her hair, then she stood up and straightened her coat, and when she stooped to pick up her packages and Simon made a move to help her, she glanced at him not at all fondly, but with the look one reserves for busybodies, or boors.

When she was gone, Simon sat in his chair and opened his new book. Alas, Virginia's suicide. He read until he felt hungry, then he got up and wandered the corridors until he found a snack bar. He sat on a stool and ordered a hot dog and milk.

Behind the counter were two girls in short skirts and short aprons. They were about sixteen, and they chattered as they worked.

"My doctor says I'm fine, but I've got to start taking my blood pills again."

"My doctor says I'll always have that scar behind my knee but I shouldn't let it worry me."

"I was over at my boyfriend's house last night and his mother served us supper on paper plates. *Paper plates,* can you imagine?"

"I was out with my boyfriend last night and we had a fight."

"After work I'm going to the Y for a swim. Why don't you come along?"

"I can't. After work I'm going to have my ears pierced."

At this moment, chewing his hot dog and sipping his milk, Simon fell a revelation coming on. Three or four times in the past, Simon had had revelations that changed the course of his life. These were not divine revelations—no angels climbing ladders, no visions of paradise—but rather they were sudden, clear-eyed insights into the meaning of life generally and the life he was leading in particular. So it had been in 1918. Several weeks before the troop train pulled into Redbank and he suggested to Fred Lemm that they join the army together, Simon had been feeling certain prickings and urgings below the level of consciousness, whispers from nowhere warning him that the curtain was about to fall on his childhood and adolescence and he would do well to find a graceful way to take his leave of Redbank. So it had been in 1940 when he resigned his position at St. Andrew's; he was forty that year and he decided almost overnight to put behind him the secluded life prescribed by sainted abbots and move into the mainstream of the world, and thus he went to Rookery. So it had been at the Rock of Cashel in 1957, when he stood in the rain and looked down at the tombs in the sanctuary of the ruined cathedral and imagined the march of Christianity down through the ages and imagined himself—because of Linda Mayo—out of step. So it had been last month on the Badbattle the night his kitchen caught fire, the night he decided to move into the Norman Home.

Redbank, St. Andrew's, Cashel, the Badbattle. In each case his revelation had led to an act of rejection—turning his back on a way of life he had thought desirable. What was it to be this time? Simon didn't know, for his revelation was not yet clear. He knew only that it was on its way. Sitting here on a stool while these two girls spoke of their boyfriends and blood pills, he felt an upheaval in his head, as though his random thoughts and impressions since leaving Ithaca Mills yesterday morning were building toward a momentous conclusion. Light was about to dawn. He quit chewing and closed his eyes, trying to help his revelation along. He systematically went over the events of the last day and a half, for surely the pithy disclosures assembling themselves at the back of his brain were somehow triggered by the bustle and buffetings of the city.

Twice this morning he had looked death in the face, and into both funeral homes he had carried T. S. Testor's baby. Was that what had engaged his subconscious and set it in motion? In the funeral home where he had no business he was warmly welcomed, and in the funeral home where he intended to perform a corporal work of mercy he was chased out the door. Was there something in that? By placing himself outside Faracy Floral, he had witnessed the high emotions of death and marriage and birth. Was there something in that? He had seen the tears and sensed the anxieties and heard the complaints of strangers, all to the accompaniment of the splashing fountain and the calm and measured memories of an old Englishman. Was there something in that?

Yes, there was something in all of it taken together. He saw it now. He saw the revelation, and it had to do with Ithaca Mills. It had taken this trip to the city to jolt him out of his rut, to show him the staleness of his recent thinking, the staleness of the Norman Home. Here at Olympus he was faced on every side with people in touch with life and busy about their joys and sorrows, and he had only to compare this to his life at the Norman Home to see the awful difference. Jean Kirk was right, the Norman Home was wrong for him, wrong for anyone who had more life to live. At the Home the only champion of life had been the Indian, who had proclaimed his vitality from the housetop—and now the Indian was gone. How could Simon return to Hatch and Mrs. Kibbikoski? To Spinner and Leep and Mrs. Valentine Biggs? To Hattie? To that dreary dining room with those dreary people picking over the crumbs of their memories?

Simon opened his eyes. He drank the rest of his milk but left his hot dog half-eaten. He returned to his chair by the fountain, pondering his next move. Should he leave the Home immediately, having already paid for his November board? Should he move back to the Badbattle and rescind his promise to Douglas Mikklessen and Jean Kirk? Could he survive another winter alone? No, none of these choices seemed advisable.

What then? Well, he would work a transformation on the Norman Home. That's what this revelation meant, that he should go back there and change things, instill in Hatch and the four women a zest for life. The Indian, if he returned, would help him. The Indian knew what life was about; his goose hunt was proof of that. Upon arriving home tonight, Simon would call together the residents and challenge them. Tell them they were acting like over-the-hill has-beens. Tell them their decline into uselessness was unnecessary. Tell them to look sharp. Tell them to start functioning again. Tell them to pull the plug on the TV. Tell them to go around and make house calls on those who were *really* old and senile. Tell them to go out and do good works for others instead of turning in on themselves and dredging up foggy old memories. If they needed transportation to do these things—fine. Simon had a car. He'd take them around. Pick them up. Drop them off.

Yes, that was the plan. He saw the Norman Home transformed,

he himself the transformer. Well, why not? He had always succeeded as a teacher. He would return to Ithaca Mills and put his powers of education to the test, school the residents, turn the dining room into a classroom.

He tried to read, but his revelation distracted him. He closed his book and rehearsed what he would say to Hatch and Mrs. Kibbikoski and Spinner and Leep and Mrs. Valentine Biggs.

At three, he carried his chair and his book to Jupiter Service, where—wonder of wonders—his Ford was ready. The cost was greater than his bank balance, so he paid for it partly by check and the rest by credit card. One of the mechanics backed the car out of its stall and another washed the windshield and Alex gave him directions out of the city. Simon's was the only car in the station, and as he got behind the wheel the three mechanics gathered at his window to wish him Godspeed. They looked sorrowful, like T. S. Testor at the elevator, as though his departure would leave them forever idle.

It took him three hours to drive home. He drove through snow flurries and sunshine and fits of sleepiness and a dozen small towns. He drove through grassland powdered with snow and cropland lying fallow. He passed within reach of several small radio stations broadcasting news of small consequence and music painful to the ear. He drove through the long shadows of grain elevators and pine trees standing beside the highway and through moving shadows of windblown clouds that spanned the sky like soiled fleece. The rolling hills gave way to flat tableland. When the sun went down, the night was instantly black and the oncoming headlights seared his eyes. He saw the lights of Ithaca Mills from thirty miles away, lights in a flat line along the highway, the lights of streets and houses where life was flat. He turned off the highway onto Main Street and pulled up in front of the Norman Home and listened to the idling of his engine for a moment before he switched it off. Then he patted the dashboard a couple of times as though to convey his gratitude to the mysterious pistons and gaskets that had brought him safely home through the black and chilly night.

He got out of the car and locked it. He stretched slowly, like a cat, for he felt stale and stiff from his three hours behind the wheel. Approaching the front door, he went over his opening remarks. He would get the message off his chest this evening. He would go into the TV parlor and switch off whatever they were watching and say that he had come down from Olympus with important advice for every last one of them, that they were capable of more than they were accomplishing, that they could make better use of their time, that what they lacked were useful goals.

Lights shone in the foyer and dining room but both rooms were empty. The dark parlor was lit by the gray light of TV. Simon peered in and saw only one chair occupied, the recliner chair in the corner where the Indian used to fall asleep before the ten o'clock news.

"Hello, Simon." A woman's voice.

"Hattie?" he said into the shadowy room.

The woman switched on the lamp beside her chair. "Your wife," she said.

It was Barbara. He was stunned.

"I know you're shocked to see me, Simon, but I tried to give you fair warning. I called the house on the river all last week and got no answer. Why didn't you tell me you'd moved? Or at least notify the phone company?" Barbara worked the chair into its upright position and got to her feet. She had been worried about how they would act during these first few moments together, and she had decided to keep her distance and refrain from any false and awkward show of affection, but now, seeing Simon, she was drawn to him involuntarily. And he to her. They took each other's hands. They looked each other over. Barbara smiled and Simon chuckled. Then they both grew serious as they examined each other's eyes, searching for clues to their thinking.

"You look good, Simon. The years have been good to you."

He was taller in her memory than in fact, but his white wavy hair and his kind eyes were as attractive as ever.

"You too, Barbara." She was shorter in his memory than in fact. What would she be now, sixty? She wasn't heavy. Just oval. The suit she wore was of a nubby, expensive material and perfectly tailored. Her eyes, when she smiled, still came to peaks, like triangles. He pressed her head to his breast and his eyes became teary, and so did Barbara's.

Then they studied each other some more, and Simon saw that her hair was all wrong. It was no longer dark. It had evidently thinned and turned gray and she had put it through one of those unsuccessful rinses where the aim was blonde but the result was pink. He lifted both her hands and said, "You've stopped chewing your nails."

"What do you mean, stopped chewing my nails? I never chewed my nails. Now tell me where you've been, Simon. Jean Kirk said you went to St. Paul for your car and you were to be back last night. Hattie's quite upset with you." Barbara dabbed at her eyes with a hankie, Simon with the backs of his thumbs.

"My car was out of whack. I suppose I should have phoned. I haven't yet trained myself to report my whereabouts to Hattie."

Simon took off his coat and Barbara turned off the TV. They sat on the edges of two chairs.

"You're wondering what I'm doing here, Simon. You're wondering if I'm back in your life to stay or if I'm just passing through. Well, I don't know. I'm on leave from the realty firm in El Paso. I just got the notion one day to pick up and move around for a while. They were very good about it, but after all there's hardly anyone in the office with more seniority than myself. I just woke up one morning and discovered I was about to be sixty and decided to take an extended vacation and look around and see if I was missing anything by staying in El Paso for the rest of my life."

"And what have you found? Are you missing anything?"

"I don't know yet. This is my first stop. I thought I'd begin with Rookery and go out to the house on the river and get reacquainted with you, Simon. I don't know what it is, but I've been feeling kind of sentimental the last year or two, especially in the autumn. It was in the autumn that we met, remember? I've had this very strong desire to see that cottage again where I was a bride. You said I could come back any time, Simon. I don't know if you remember that, but you said so over the phone after Evert died."

"Of course I remember. I've forgotten a lot, but I remember that."

"So I flew into Minneapolis and took a bus to Rookery and went out to the river in a taxi—that was Wednesday night—and what did I find out there but this young doctor and her boyfriend. Jean and Douglas. Douglas was showing her around. They told me all about you, Simon. They're really a lovely pair, don't you think? Jean is so sure of herself and smart, and Douglas is such an earnest young fellow, and so pleasant. I liked them both from the start. Well, Jean—I guess she's told you—thinks your being in this Home is a great mistake. We had a long visit. I stayed overnight at their apartment. They said I turned up at precisely the right time to urge you back to your house, Simon. 'Lure you back' is the way they put it. Jean is one of those people who figure out how other people should live their lives, and she has the two of us and their dog—you and me and Tick—moving into that cottage together. Tomorrow, in fact. Douglas has finished repairing the outside wall and all that remains is the decorating inside. She says we both belong there."

"And what did you say to that?"

"I laughed." Barbara's eyes peaked and she laughed again.

Simon laughed too, then frowned. "Why did you laugh, Barbara?"

"I don't know. It was all too sudden. I mean maybe that's what we should do: live together again, but I had to think about it and I didn't know what to say, so I laughed."

"Did they tell you how the kitchen was damaged? Did they tell you my memory is shot?"

"They told me your memory is fine. They said it's only your confidence that's shot."

"My memory is shot, Barbara. Some days I'm a basket case. Let me tell you about the retirement check I misplaced and about the night I got lost a mile from home and about how my car happens to have spent the last four months in St. Paul."

"I've heard it all, Simon. Jean Kirk told me all those stories, and I can understand your fear or whatever it is that drove you here to Ithaca Mills, but now that I've seen you—and this place—I agree with Jean. Those stories don't justify your being in this houseful of ghosts. I've spent thirty hours here, Simon. Jean drove me here yesterday expecting you'd be back from the city, and I spent the night in a room formerly occupied by a Mrs. Kibbikoski, and I've spent the day with Mrs. Spinner and Mrs. Leep and Mrs. Biggs and Mr. Hatch and that awful, awful Hattie Norman, and it makes me sick to think of you in this house. Jean's plan makes sense. Before you came in I was sitting here imagining what it would be like to move back to the river, Simon, the two of us. If it's the lack of a companion that bothers you, that made you forsake the cottage, then I'll be that companion. I'll be your wife again, Simon."

He lowered his head as though weighing her offer, but when he raised it and spoke, he was adamant. "No, no, Barbara, it's too late for that. You're giving me the same speech I got from Doctor Kirk and from my editor in St. Paul, and to all of you I say a thousand times no. I am where I belong, and if the Norman Home hasn't the most pleasant of atmospheres I will work to change it. I have a plan, in fact, for revitalizing these people. By the way—where is everybody?"

Barbara hid her chagrin at being so soundly rejected. "Hattie Norman drove everyone downtown for their flu shots. Except the woman whose room I'm in—Mrs. Kibbikoski. She was taken to the hospital in Rookery yesterday for the amputation of her foot. A horrible thing. Her toes were turning black. It's a case of gangrene and her foot has to come off."

"Oh dear, the poor woman."

"Yesterday she went to Rookery in an ambulance and this morning they determined that her circulation to that foot was hopelessly impaired, and tomorrow morning one of the doctors in Jean's clinic is performing the surgery."

"The poor woman. I'm afraid Hattie won't permit her to return here. Hattie bars the bedridden."

"Hattie has already sent out word that she has an opening."

"You're here for another night then?"

"Well, obviously I wanted to wait till you got back. Yes, I told Hattie I'd be here one more night."

Simon sat back in his chair and so did Barbara. They both relaxed together, as though satisfied that this encounter was going as well as possible. They heard Hattie's van drive up outside and the doors slam.

"Your voice is still pretty," said Simon. "Do you still sing?"

"Sing? You're thinking of someone else. I never sang."

"You sang around the house, Barbara. You sang little melodies by the hour as you worked around the house."

"Not me," she laughed. "Are you sure you haven't been living with some other woman in the meantime?"

Her tone was facetious, yet it was a question she hoped he would answer.

"You sang, Barbara. You sang and you were always on key."

The residents filed into the TV parlor, removing their wraps.

"Oh, lookee, the lovers have found each other," said Mrs. Valentine Biggs. "Lordy, Lordy, Simon Shea, imagine our surprise when this delightful little woman came in here and introduced herself as your wife. And we didn't even know you had one! We thought you wore that ring as a memento of a dead wife and here she is alive. What kind of a devil are you anyway, Simon Shea, keeping this woman a secret? And how could the two of you stand being separated this long is what I'd like to know. I tell you, whenever Valentine and I were separated we just pined and pined to be back together again."

"That your Ford Fairlane out there?" asked Hatch. "I had a Ford Fairlane once but it didn't have them scratches and dents along the side."

"Do you know what they gave us with our swine flu shots?" chirped Spinner.

Her twin said, "They gave us a slip of paper saying that although the shot might be fatal, swine flu wouldn't be the cause of death."

Hattie poked her head in the room and said to Simon, "Where the hell have you been? It's getting so I don't know how many roomers I've got from one day to the next, what with this one falling off the roof and that one losing her foot and this one running off to the city. Did your wife tell you about Mrs. Kibbikoski?"

"She did. It's tragic."

"It's tragic and she better not come around here thinking she'll find a place. I called her son and told him to clear her stuff out of her room by the first of the week. I can tolerate old folks but only so long as they can do for themselves."

Mrs. Valentine Biggs said, "Let's have coffee and cookies, Hattie, in honor of the reunion of Simon and Barbara Shea. This lovely, lovely reunion. Oh, it makes my heart skip."

"All right, come and help."

"The women left the room, and Hatch sat down in his accustomed chair and because the TV was off he turned his gaze on Barbara.

Simon asked him, "Have you met my wife?"

Hatch nodded, his eyes on her face, causing her to stir uneasily in her chair.

"I had a wife like that, only bigger, " said Hatch. "She always worked hard."

"Let's go to the dining room for cookies in our honor." Simon took Barbara's hand.

Hatch followed them from the parlor. "Wives run bigger on farms. For chores and all, you want wives that run to a pretty good size."

As on all extraordinary occasions, namely birthdays and Christmas, the men's and women's tables were pushed together in the dining room and the Home sat down as one. Ice cream. Oatmeal cookies. Decaffeinated coffee. Hattie's rebuke:

"Professor, I've got to have rules in a place like this. I've got to know where my old people are from day to day. I've got to know if you're going to be gone for meals or gone overnight or whatever. When you didn't show up by bedtime last night I didn't know if I should take it in my stride or call the sheriff. You're lucky I didn't set off a statewide manhunt. You're lucky I took it in my stride."

"Let's sing something," said Mrs. Valentine Biggs. "Something romantic in honor of these two sweethearts. Let's sing 'The Sweetheart of Sigma Chi.' " She began to sing.

"I have a feeling we're in for a terrible time," said Spinner. "Terrible things are happening and it's the wrath of God."

Leep said, "The drought and the Indian's concussion and Mrs. Kibbikoski's foot and the swine flu. The wrath of God."

Hatch said, "I farmed through four droughts and the worst one by far was the drought of thirty-six. My soil was powder."

Mrs. Valentine Biggs stopped singing and said, "I know what. Let's have a speech from the sweethearts. A speech, Mrs. Shea."

Barbara smiled generally around the table and said, "It's been a long day and I really don't feel up to a speech."

Mrs. Valentine Biggs clapped. "Now you, Simon Shea."

Simon put his napkin to his mouth and cleared his throat. He said, "Thank you Mrs. Biggs. A speech is exactly what I had in mind. In fact, as I drove north from the city I rehearsed it. It's a speech about all of you. It's a bit of advice. A challenge." He cleared his throat again. Except for Hattie's bombast, speeches were rare at the Home, and all eyes were fastened on him.

"Were living in a rut, my friends. Here in the Norman Home we let ourselves become aimless and lazy and good for nothing." He looked from one to the other of his four housemates. Three days ago there were six.

"On Tuesday night the Indian went hunting on the roof and we all assumed he was out of his mind, but I daresay his goose hunt was probably the most sensible act ever performed by a resident of this house. The Indian tried to prove to himself that he wasn't aimless and lazy and good-for-nothing, and I say more power to the Indian. I can imagine what was going through his mind as he sat here in this dining room with us day after day. He said to himself, 'Good Lord, am I like the rest of these aimless people, old and useless before my time?' And he crawled up on the roof to prove he wasn't."

"What are you driving at?" said Hattie. "Don't give these old people any ideas. My chimney is costing me a hundred dollars to repair because my insurance is a hundred-dollar deductible."

"This is not a call for anyone to climb up on the roof, Miss Norman. What I'm getting at is that we are all capable of living fuller lives than we are doing at the present time. I have just spent two days in the mainstream of city life and I have become infected with a strong fear of becoming lax and seedy and broken-down. Mrs. Valentine Biggs and Mrs. Spinner and Mrs. Leep and Mr. Hatch, don't you realize that among our generation we are five of the lucky ones? We aren't ailing or bedridden or particularly senile. We're able to move our arms and legs and talk sense most of the time. Well, if that's the case, why are we sitting around watching TV all day and acting as if a trip downtown were a flight to the moon? It's high time we found ourselves a goal of some kind and went to work to reach it. And if transportation stands in your way, I have a car."

Mrs. Valentine Biggs clapped.

Hatch examined his hands. No slivers. No calluses. He mumbled. "I myself have been thinking along that line. I always used to work hard, and now I don't do anything. But there's nothing to do."

Spinner and Leep whispered to each other.

Hattie said, "You're asking for trouble, Professor. I've run this place for more years than I care to remember, and my motto has always been 'Let sleeping dogs lie.' Old folks are *supposed* to sit around watching TV. Every time somebody old tries to do something they screw up. My job's been a lot easier since cable TV came to Ithaca Mills. I've said more than once, God made TV to keep old people quiet."

"I won't argue with you, Miss Norman. I simply want to state my case and let these four people decide for themselves. If they want to get a new grip on life, they'll come up with some new goals for themselves."

Spinner and Leep fluttered nervously, one urging the other to speak. Finally one did. "Would you explain what you mean by goals, Mr. Shea?"

He was a teacher again and this was the lecture method, but as he spoke he began to lose faith in the lesson. His lines weren't making as much sense as they had in rehearsal. "By goals, I mean anything you would like to accomplish but have been putting off because you're reluctant to exert the effort. I'm convinced each of us has any number of things we've been putting off and blaming it on age."

Hattie said, "It's no good, Professor. You've got a pipe dream there that's going to lead to trouble, mark my words. I had an idea like that about five years ago. The outside trim on this house needed painting, and I put an old fart to work painting it. Curtis Murchison. He was a retired painter. He fell off the ladder and broke his wrist."

Simon ignored her. He looked at Spinner and Leep, who were hatching something. He looked at Barbara, who was stifling a yawn and looking into her empty coffee cup. Poor Barbara, he thought, returning to see the house where she had been a bride and winding up in this dismal, dead-end dining room, eating cookies with a group of over-the-hill has-beens, her husband possibly the furthest over the hill—for wasn't he behaving like an ass this evening? Wasn't he a fool for observing the occasion of Barbara's return by playing the commencement orator and delivering this futile speech about goals to his housemates? It struck him how ridiculous he was acting. How rude to Barbara. Where was his sense of the occasion? His grace? He swallowed his coffee and pushed back his chair. He was about to stand and ask Barbara to come to his room for a glass of whiskey and a good talk, when Spinner said, "Wait."

Leep said, "My sister and I have a goal." His lecture, though delivered in doubt, had sounded like sense. "My sister and I have had this little chore in mind all day, and we had just about decided to give it up because we didn't see how on earth we could do it, but now you've convinced us that we must find a way."

Her sister took over. "It's about Mrs. Kibbikoski's foot. You know, my sister and I are Catholics and so is Mrs. Kibbikoski and we're very concerned about the disposition of her foot."

Everyone studied the twins, Hattie with a sigh, Mrs. Valentine Biggs in wide-eyed excitement.

Spinner and Leep continued:

"You see, Church law is very specific about the disposition of body parts."

"You see, body parts, when they become unattached from the body, are to be buried in consecrated ground."

"And if Mrs. Kibbikoski's foot is removed in Rookery, who is going to see to its disposition?"

"Certainly not her son. He's a fallen-away."

"And although Mercy Hospital is run by nuns, we heard of a case last year where somebody's arm was removed and it wasn't buried in consecrated ground."

"It was thrown out with the garbage."

"Not all nuns believe alike anymore."

"At least not when it comes to body parts."

"So we see it as our duty, especially since you're a Catholic yourself, Mr. Shea, and since you've offered to drive, to be present tomorrow morning at Mercy Hospital and get ahold of the foot and bring it back here to Ithaca Mills and bury it in the Kibbikoski plot."

"It's best if body parts end up in the same grave with the body."

"It makes it easier on Resurrection Day."

"You're a Catholic yourself, Mr. Shea. You understand."

"The operation is scheduled for ten o'clock. We called to find out."

"All you need to do is drive us to Rookery and back. We'll deliver the foot to Father Kerwin at the parish house. He'll know what to do with it."

Everyone turned to Simon. Hattie's expression said *I told you so*. Barbara's said *Let's see you get out of this*.

"Oh, how religious," said Mrs. Valentine Biggs. "I'm not a Catholic, but it's clear to me where Mrs. Kibbikoski's foot belongs. Oh, I think it's a lovely goal. Let it be my goal too. I'll ride along."

Simon gave Barbara a crooked smile and wished with all his heart that he hadn't thrown down this insane challenge. Now what was he to do? He couldn't imagine driving these twins fifty miles to retrieve somebody's foot. On the other hand, he couldn't bring himself to say their goal was crazy and morbid. How could he presume to judge the rightness or wrongness of other people's goals? And for all he knew, they might be right; somewhere in canon law there might be a page concerning body parts and hallowed ground. Much as he might regret it, he had roused Spinner and Leep to action, and now with the irrepressible Mrs. Valentine Biggs on their side there was no deterring them. He wished he had never heard of the Norman Home. He wished he were alone with Barbara so they could talk. They had a lifetime of catching up to do, for heaven's sake, and they were trapped in this god-awful room with the stacks of phosphorescent rose blossoms in the wallpaper—the room that always turned him into an idiot the moment he crossed the threshold.

He glanced around the table. Everyone waited for him to speak, to pronounce this goal a worthy one, to come down in favor of burying body parts in hallowed ground. Mrs. Valentine Biggs was nodding piously. Hatch looked deathly tired, his mouth sagging open. Barbara's smile contained now, besides amusement, a hint of pity for her earnest and misguided husband. *The same old Simon,* her smile seemed to say. Hattie had set her fat elbows on the table and was pressing her face into her hands, whether with weariness or laughter he couldn't tell. Spinner and Leep sat across from him, erect and unblinking, their lips pursed like beaks.

"It won't take but a couple of hours," said Spinner.

"We'll be back by noon," said her twin.

"All right," said Simon with a lack of enthusiasm, "we'll start promptly at eight thirty."

At this everyone rose; it was time for news, weather, and sports. Hatch and the three women retired to the TV parlor, Mrs. Valentine Biggs asking Spinner and Leep, "Now do you Catholics dress for burying a foot? Do you wear your veils?"

Simon said, "Come, Barbara, we'll go up to my room and have a drink."

"I've seen your room, Simon. There's no place for two people to sit. Let's go to mine," and they went and sat among the earthly belongings of Mrs. Kibbikoski—her figurines and her photographs, her magazines and her medicine, her wheelchair and her rhododendron—and they talked about Rookery and El Paso and the North and the Southwest and the Badbattle and the Rio Grande. At first their conversation took many sharp and unexpected turns, as in talk between strangers; but before long their remarks grew more predictable and at the same time more interesting, as in talk between friends. Barbara said, "You're the same old Simon, the one I used to love." Simon said, "You're wrong; we're strangers, but it's time we got acquainted." They spoke of Donald Stearns and Evert Metz and Jay Johnson and Mr. and Mrs. Henry Hamilton III and Miss Rookery of 1937, and they tried to remember the name of the forbidding receptionist at Mercy Hospital. Barbara said there had been no one else in her life since Evert and she left an opening for Simon to tell her who, if any, his lovers had been since 1943, but he had nothing to say on this subject. Maybe some other time he would tell her about Linda Mayo. They spoke of selling real estate and of teaching English, of Wyoming and of Ireland, of the deaths of parents and friends. They talked until midnight, and when they stood and stepped into the dark foyer Simon kissed Barbara tenderly and a bit shakily and said, "What's to become of us, Barbara?"

Her hug was brief but tight. She said, "You don't belong here, Simon, and I don't think I belong in El Paso. We're aimless. Don't you see, we're exactly what you accused your fellow residents of? We're aimless and without goals. Let's go back to the river, Simon, at least for a while."

"I've said no so often, I don't see how I can say yes. But I'm tempted, Barbara. We'll talk more tomorrow. Will you ride along to Rookery?"

"At eight thirty? For a foot? Yes. I will if you'll let me off at the cottage and then come back there yourself after the foot is taken care of. Let's spend the weekend there, Simon."

"Well, that sounds entirely possible."

"Let's spend several days there. You can always come back here and I can always go back to El Paso, but let's have some time together in our house."

"Well, yes…but you realize I promised the doctor and her lover—"

"They're more than willing to stay in their apartment if we want the cottage. They're urging us to go back. We simply take their dog and move in. Say yes, Simon."

"Yes," he said.

They parted at the stairs. The house was dark and quiet, he went up to his room by the light of the moonlit windows, and as he prepared for bed he pondered Barbara's return. How did he feel about Barbara's return? First and foremost, he felt tired. The day had been long and full of surprises, and as he buttoned his pajamas he was seized by a yawn so abrupt and gaping that he nearly lost his balance.

He got into bed.

" 'God of my fathers, Lord of mercy, you who have made all things by your word and in your wisdom have established man; give me Wisdom. Indeed, though one be perfect among the sons of men, if Wisdom, who comes from you, be not with him, he shall be held in no esteem.' In particular, explain to me the signs and nature of love, O Lord, for beneath my heavy layer of weariness tonight I feel things stirring in my breast, a mixture of emotions, a bubbling stew, and I want to know if it's love. One thing I feel is joy at seeing Barbara again. I know joy when I feel it, and this is joy. Another thing I feel is conceit, or rather pride, at being taken seriously by her. Everyone needs to be taken seriously by at least a few other people in life; no one can tolerate being lightly dismissed day after day. Hattie Norman has developed the ugly skill of dismissal. It is no less withering to bend one's will to the tyranny of Hattie Norman than it was to be ordered out of that seedy mortuary this morning by the old man in tennis shoes. But now along comes Barbara and raises to four the number of people who I believe take me seriously. Doctor Kirk and Douglas Mikklessen and T. S. Testor are the others.

I know pride when I feel it, and Barbara's attention nourishes my pride. A third thing I feel is anxiety because I'm aimless. Barbara says we have no goals, she and I. Before she showed up, I had a goal, and it was to adapt myself to the life of the Home. I really believe I was making progress. As I drove north tonight I looked forward to the comfort of this bed. Put that together with Hattie's chocolate chip cookies and you have two things I have become fond of in Ithaca Mills, bed and cookies. Surely with time I can increase that number. Maybe one of the new residents Hattie takes in will prove companionable. But Barbara throws me off course by suggesting we go back to the river. To leave the security of the Home and risk independence once more—the prospect makes me nervous. And a fourth thing I feel is a desire to spill out my soul to Barbara. This talk we had tonight has whetted my urge to tell her all that I've thought and felt since we separated in forty-three, and it has whetted my urge to hear more of how she herself spent these thirty-three years, and then somehow to intertwine our thinking and feeling and make it hold fast this time, make it last. So that's what I'm feeling, Lord: joy, pride, anxiety, desire. Are those the ingredients of love? Don't bother telling me now, Lord, because I won't be awake for the answer. This day began long ago and far away, and I am weary unto death."

SATURDAY

"I feel so holy," said Mrs. Valentine Biggs, riding in the back seat between Spinner and Leep. "Isn't this what the Crusades were all about? Going on long trips to bring back the body parts of saints? Oh, I feel just like I'm on a Crusade."

Spinner and Leep said nothing. Their pillbox hats and their watchful eyes framed Simon's view in the mirror.

Barbara, in front with Simon, dozed.

"There's a religious side to my nature, you know. I don't wear my religion on my sleeve, but it's there. Valentine was never very religious, so during my married life I kept my feelings about God and all that pretty well bottled up, but now I think I could be born again if the opportunity presented itself."

Halfway to Rookery, where the prairie ended and the hills began, Simon drove into a trace of rain—eight or ten drops on the windshield per mile. It was an unusual morning for November—strangely warm and humid—and the sky was a single oppressive cloud which in ordinary times might have let down a heavy, all-day rain.

"I had a neighbor one time, a Mrs. Anderson, who liked nothing better than to talk religion, and I learned a lot from her. We'd get together for coffee and she'd talk religion every time. She used to say you couldn't beat the Baptists for gospel music, but the Methodists had roomier pews. She said if she was to become one thing or another she would become a Catholic because Catholics always served the best family-style dinners at their bazaars and they didn't care if you smoked when you were through eating."

Lo, it had rained in the hills. The highway was wet and the brown weeds in the ditches were heavy with moisture. "Look, ladies, it's been raining here!" Simon hadn't seen or smelled rain since early June, and he rolled open his window to hear the sound of water under his tires. The wind swirling into the car felt damp and caused Spinner and Leep to hang onto their hats. He drove into the mist kicked up by the car ahead. He saw a flash of lightning. "The curse is lifted," he said. "We are delivered."

Barbara roused herself and put her hand to her blowing hair, and Simon rolled up the window. "Sorry," he said.

"Don't be sorry, Simon. I love the rain. It never seemed to rain in El Paso."

"There was a time when I could sometimes get Valentine into a church for a wedding or a game of bingo or some other special occasion and he never put up a fuss, but that all came to an end the day they buried his sister. The day his sister was buried, Valentine said, 'That's it!' Never again would he have anything to do with religion. I'm talking about his older sister Sophia, who died of cancer. That was in the days when they used to lower caskets into the ground while the mourners were standing all around. Well, one of the ropes broke that they were lowering the casket with and it was just a big mess. He said, 'That's it!' and he lost what little religion he had."

Simon drove into Rookery and parked in front of Mercy Hospital. "We'll see if Mrs. Kibbikoski is in surgery yet. Will you come in?" he asked Barbara.

"I'll wait here," she said, and Simon went up the walk with Spinner and Leep and Mrs. Valentine Biggs. Barbara had not expected, when she left El Paso, that her journey north would take her to the site of Donald's death, and she sat pensively in the car, remembering.

Simon and the three women were allowed into Mrs. Kibbikoski's room on the third floor. She lay on a bed behind a curtain. She was due in surgery in a few minutes and had been given an injection that slurred her speech and made her woozy. She recognized her friends from the Home, but unless they spoke loudly into her ear she kept forgetting they were at her bedside. Also in the room was a man wearing a silky mustache and the uniform of Blue Sky

Dairy Products—Mrs. Kibbikoski's son. He paced and said to the ceiling, "Let's get this show on the road." His concern seemed not for his mother—he neither approached the bed nor glanced in her direction—but for his interrupted milk route.

"We've come for your foot," said Spinner or Leep; Simon couldn't always tell them apart.

"We'll bury it in hallowed ground," said her twin.

Mrs. Kibbikoski, on her back, smiled faintly.

A nurse came in and asked Mrs. Kibbikoski how she was feeling. She gave the nurse the same faint smile.

"Her foot looks horrible," the nurse explained to the visitors. "She had been wearing a tight garter around her leg because she said it helped the pain—and she cut off her circulation."

Mrs. Valentine Biggs told the nurse, "My husband Valentine came here for surgery in sixty-one. Prostate, you know."

"Let's get this show on the road," said the milkman.

Simon asked the nurse about the Indian.

"Mr. Smalleye went home yesterday. His daughter came for him about noon."

"His condition is improved then?"

"Wonderfully. He has headaches and sees double, but the doctor says he's in wonderful shape considering. The doctor says he never saw a man that old with such powers of recovery. When a patient gets up and dresses and tries to sneak out of the hospital two nights in a row, you know he's recovering. Our policy here is, don't hold them if they don't want to be held. I'll have to ask you all to go down to the waiting room now. We're about ready to take her to surgery. We'll let you know the moment it's over."

The milkman hurried away.

"Will you see that we get her foot?" said Spinner or Leep.

"Pardon me?" said the nurse.

"Her foot. We're going to bury her fool in hallowed ground."

The nurse looked at Simon as though he were in charge of this crazy delegation. Simon stepped out into the corridor.

"I'll send Sister Theodora to talk to you," said the nurse.

Downstairs Simon showed the three women to the waiting room. Mrs. Valentine Biggs sank into a soft couch. Spinner and Leep sat on matching chairs flanking a niche in the wall where Simon remembered years ago a blue Madonna standing. Now the niche held a display of Blue Cross pamphlets. He assured the women that he would soon return, and he went out to the car.

"Remember the night we met here, Simon?"

"Indeed, you were on your bicycle. It seems like yesterday."

"It seems like a thousand years ago."

The moment Simon and Barbara pulled up beside the mailbox, the door of the cottage opened and Jean and Douglas hurried across the wet brown grass and welcomed them and ushered them indoors and served them a cocktail and a submarine sandwich. Simon and Barbara sat on one side of the narrow dining table, Douglas and Jean on the other.

"You've come back to stay, haven't you?" said Jean. She looked stunning, Simon thought. When the sky was overcast, her eyes were a lighter shade of blue, her hair a darker shade of gold. "We're just out here for the day while Douglas does some finishing work on the wall and we don't intend to stay. The place is all yours. I've dusted and turned up the heat because I was positive you'd come. I brought some food for your first day or two. This is wonderful, just the way I envisioned it—the two of you back here to start your lives over together."

Simon chuckled and his eyes danced. He was positive now that he had misread yesterday's revelation at Olympus. It was not his mission to revitalize the Norman Home. How could he reverse the irreversible, move the immovable? No, the message in the revelation was that he must get the hell out. "You know what you've done, don't you? You've signed your own eviction notice."

"Without Tick we can keep our place in the city," said Douglas between sips from a can of Coke. He had sawdust in his hair.

"You and Barbara take the dog," said Jean, "and then when we want country living we simply come out and visit you."

"It really makes a lot of sense," said Douglas. "Our apartment is near the campus and near the clinic. And instead of a month's rent for repairing your kitchen, we'll take skiing and hiking privileges."

"Reserve us the evening of the first snowfall," said Jean. "I'll bring the snacks and the four of us will sit here and watch it snow. It's got to be lovely here when it snows."

Barbara said, "Our plans aren't long-range. We've just decided to come out here for a few days and see how it goes. I'm not crazy about the winters in Minnesota, and Simon isn't sure of himself yet, so ... "

But Simon was sure of himself now. At the thought of Barbara and Jean and Douglas and himself sitting there eating snacks and watching it snow, he felt weights shifting in his head and the scales tip. He imagined hot brandy and Hi-Ho Crackers and Colby cheese in the late afternoon of the first snowy day. He imagined it snowing on the roof of the cottage, snowing on his brown lawn, and snowing among the boughs and twigs of the birches. He imagined it snowing into the river, while the four of them watched from the front windows. He saw himself turning on the yard light as night drew on and the snow falling out of the black sky and into the bright circle under the light. Then he tried to imagine himself at the Norman Home on the night of the first snowfall. Supper with Hatch. News, weather, and sports. Alone in his crowded room upstairs. The springless chair, the lumpy bed. Snow falling on the prairie. He couldn't imagine it. Against the alternative of being here on the Badbattle with his wife and these new friends, he couldn't imagine it. Yes, he resolved, he and Barbara must remain here in the house they bought when they were first married. Right here, if possible, till the day he died.

"Another drink?" asked Douglas.

"Please." Simon held out his glass of melting ice. He did not declare his resolution aloud, his determination to leave the Norman Home for good and all. With his customary caution he wanted to carry it around with him for an hour or two and see if it held up. See if it made sense. See if it was the product of reason or of the cocktail he had been served. "And then I must be off."

Jean said, "Where to?"

"You won't believe this," said Barbara. "It's like something out of *Frankenstein*. Tell them, Simon."

Simon explained his business in Rookery—Mrs. Kibbikoski's foot. "So you see, the Home has answered my call to action. I am a knight-errant and my ladies have set me a task. The grail we seek is a human foot."

Douglas laughed and Tick barked and Jean shook her head in wonder. Barbara said, "Isn't that the last straw?"

Simon said. "The irony is that it might be exactly what my Church expects of me. I've never heard of any such rule in canon law, but it could well be true that amputated arms and legs are to be buried in consecrated ground. We'll find out when we confront the priest in Ithaca Mills and hand him the foot."

As Simon was about to drive off, Barbara called, "My bags," and Douglas went out and took them from the trunk of the Ford and brought them into the house.

At Mercy Hospital, Simon found Spinner and Leep still in their matching chairs. Sitting with Mrs. Valentine Biggs on the couch was an old nun in long white robes. Word was that Mrs. Kibbikoski had not yet been taken into surgery, that her surgeon was in the midst of an emergency operation, that he was helping a specialist repair the brain of an injured motorcyclist. Mrs. Kibbikoski had been put on hold. Spinner and Leep had just been up to her room, where she still lay behind the curtain, drugged and murmuring.

Simon took a seat and listened to Mrs. Valentine Biggs tell the old nun about her sister-in-law's burial.

"Sophia Cochran was her name and she was Valentine's sister, and as they were putting her down, the strap under the head end of the casket broke. Well, you can imagine what happened. The casket dropped into the grave and stood on its head and we all insisted that it be brought up and opened and Sophia be straightened out and made comfortable, because we thought probably she was lying in there all twisted around and you hate to think of anybody lying that way for eternity. So the undertaker and the pallbearers lifted out the casket, getting their suits all dirty, and when they opened the lid there was Sophia lying just as flat and nice as you please, but she was totally bald. Not a hair on her head. Well, that was a terrible shock to everybody, including Valentine. You see, she had been totally bald for some time, which none of us knew, and she wore a wig to fool everybody, but the wig had been removed by the undertaker when he closed the casket at the mortuary and there she lay without a hair on her head. It was just hideous to see her. It was too bad they ever opened the lid because as Valentine always said after that, you'd prefer to think of her lying twisted in her grave than to think of her lying there bald."

The nun patted Mrs. Valentine Biggs on the wrist and said, "There, there, the way of all flesh." Simon recognized her as Sister Theodora, the director—thirty years ago—of Mercy Hospital. It was Sister Theodora with whom Henry Hamilton III conferred about the medical bills of Donald Stearns. She must be nearly ninety now; her complexion and her chin whiskers were as white as her wimple. She said. "Now, are you the one who is interested in Mrs. Kibbikoski's foot?"

"Well, yes and no," said Mrs. Valentine Biggs. "I'm interested but I'm not of your faith. They are the ones to talk to." She indicated Spinner and Leep—and Simon.

"We've come for her foot," said Spinner.

"We're taking it to Father Kerwin in Ithaca Mills," said Leep.

"Bless you," said Sister Theodora.

At twelve thirty Mrs. Kibbikoski went into surgery and Sister Theodora came down twice with reports on her condition. Poor. Good.

At two, Sister Theodora said that the patient was in the recovery room, that the four of them should go up to the third floor, that the doctor wished to see them.

"Are you her family?" asked the doctor. He was a short man with perspiration in his beard. His green surgical smock was stained with sweat and blood.

"We're friends," said Simon. "She has a son, but apparently he's gone."

"Well, I just wanted to say that all the signs are good. I had to take more of the leg than I had hoped and she's going to be a long time getting her strength back, but she has a strong heart and all the signs are good. She'll be in a good deal of pain for a while, and perhaps even shock, but all the signs are good. Her heart is strong." He withdrew through a swinging door, wiping his brow.

Through the same door, carrying Mrs. Kibbikoski's leg, came Sister Theodora. Spinner and Leep flew to her side and hovered over the package and exchanged with each other a couple of peeps and coos.

Simon stepped back and so did Mrs. Valentine Biggs. The package was shockingly large. Wrapped in a green plastic bag, it was much bigger around than a human leg and over two feet long.

"I've wrapped it in a lot of newspaper to soak up the blood," said Sister Theodora. "I'll have an orderly carry it out to your car. Bless you all. Stevie! Stevie!"

Stevie was a high school boy in a white T-shirt. He took the leg from the nun and so jauntily did he move with it to the elevator and out through the lobby and down the walk to the car that Simon was sure the boy didn't know what he carried.

"Do you know what that is?" said Simon, unlocking his trunk.

"Sure, it's a leg. Sister Theodora is always doing this. Last month it was somebody's thumb."

It was after three when they reached Ithaca Mills and Simon turned into the driveway between the church and the rectory. No rain had fallen on the prairie, but the sky was low and the east wind blew and the radio reported showers on the way.

Spinner and Leep got out of the car and started toward the house. Simon unlocked the trunk and stood waiting by the car.

"Please come with us, Mr. Shea. Father Kerwin is new in town and we don't know him very well. We think you should tell him, man to man."

When Simon headed for the house, so did Mrs. Valentine

Biggs. The four of them walked across the wiry grass and rang the doorbell. The wind was strong, and the twins held onto their hats.

Mrs. Valentine Biggs covered her ears and said, "Wind gives me sinus."

Father Kerwin came to the door eating a dish of ice cream. He may have been new, as the twins said, but he was old. He was large and pink and hairless. Up close, his pinkness was vivid and startling, as though he had spent the day submerged in hot dishwater. Behind him were the sounds of football on TV. He said, "Yes?"

"Were from the Norman Home," said Simon, "and one of our residents—one of your parishioners, a Mrs. Kibbikoski—has just had a leg removed at Mercy Hospital in Rookery."

"How unfortunate," said the priest. "But Mercy has a full-time chaplain. I'm sure he'll be seeing her." From TV came the noise of rising excitement and Father Kerwin cocked his ear.

"We have Mrs. Kibbikoski's leg in the car," said Simon.

"Her leg?" Father Kerwin's facial expressions were not entirely contained in his face. When he looked surprised he was able to wrinkle the skin from his eyebrows to the crown of his bald pink head. "Why?"

"Is it not proper to bury body parts in consecrated ground?" asked Spinner.

"It's what we were always taught," said Leep. "We'd like to give you the leg."

"Now wait a minute." As the priest stood in his doorway formulating his response, he tipped his dish slightly and ice cream spattered on his shoe. "It is permissible," he began, then stopped as though he had lost his place on a page of fine print. "Regarding the removal of arms and legs...it is permissible...actually, it is advisable...actually, as long as I've been a priest this has never come up."

Simon said. "You're obviously no more fond of this business than I, Father, but we'd better do it and be done with it. We have the leg in the car and you no doubt have a shovel and you could ride with us to the cemetery. It will take only a few minutes."

Across his high forehead, the priest displayed resignation. "I'll get my jacket," he sighed.

At that moment in Rookery, the young orderly in the white T-shirt followed the sound of moaning to Mrs. Kibbikoski's room and found her in a state of massive hemorrhage, her strong heart pumping her life out into her scarlet bed. The orderly summoned the nurses. Sister Theodora sent word to the chaplain and then she phoned the rectory in Ithaca Mills, but Father Kerwin was riding off in Simon's Ford, his vial of holy water in the pocket of his black windbreaker, his shovel in the trunk, his phone and his TV echoing through his empty house.

Mrs. Valentine Biggs asked from the back seat, "Sir, is there a ceremony?"

"It will be slight," said the priest. Then to Simon he said, "Going to be tough digging, dry as it is."

A mile from town lay the cemetery, flat and treeless and open to the vast clouds sagging over the prairie. On the western horizon the sky was black and pierced by lightning. Stepping from the car, Spinner lost her pillbox hat to the wind and she hurried off to retrieve it. Mrs. Valentine Biggs, guarding against sinusitis, stayed in the car.

Standing at the trunk, Father Kerwin shouldered his shovel and asked Simon, "Where do we dig?"

Simon looked to Leep for the answer. Leep, holding her hat, shook her head.

Father Kerwin worked his scalp into the dimples and bumps of puzzlement. "You mean we have to go through the whole cemetery looking for the family tombstone?"

"There is no tombstone," said Leep. "The Kibbikoskis have a plot but there's nobody in it yet. You see, Mr. Kibbikoski's been dead since forty-four but he's in Belgium. He died there in the war and he's buried there. We thought you would have a cemetery chart with names on it."

"There is such a chart, but I don't have it," said the priest. "It belongs to Sid Norris, the undertaker. We'll have to contact Sid

Norris." He was explaining this to Leep, but Leep paid no attention. She had turned to watch her sister, who was being led by her hat out of the cemetery and across a strip of plowed earth. The round hat rolled like a ball.

Meanwhile, Sid Norris, undertaker to Ithaca Mills, took a call from Mercy Hospital in Rookery. Mrs. Kibbikoski, he was told, had died. He said he would come for the body immediately. Before he left his office, Sid Norris opened his scroll of cemetery plots and phoned Ignition Jones, a free-lance mechanic who lived in a little house on the north edge of town surrounded by five dozen old vehicles. Ignition Jones was under contract to dig graves with his diesel-powered backhoe. "Ignition," said the undertaker, "you have thirty-six hours to dig a new one. Southwest quarter, plot eight, bed one."

Thunder rumbled over the cemetery. Simon said, "Let's not bother with Sid Norris. This is all consecrated ground, isn't it? Let's just bury the leg somewhere and get it over with." He crossed a dozen graves to the life-size figures of Calvary. Speckled with bird droppings, the Blessed Virgin and St. John knelt at the base of the crucifix. Simon pointed to the ground next to St. John. "We'll dig here."

Father Kerwin said, "Good idea." He put the point of his shovel into the brown grass and stamped several times on the blade to no avail. The earth was baked like a brick.

"It's no use. It's like digging in a sidewalk."

"If we could just get down two feet, that would be enough," said Simon.

Father Kerwin handed him the shovel.

With his heel, Simon stamped on the shovel and lost his balance and recovered it by throwing his arm around the neck of St. John. The thunder was rolling closer. Simon turned to Leep. "This was a downright crazy idea and I should have said so from the beginning. We should never have gone to get the leg."

"The sisters in Rookery might have thrown it in the dump," said Leep, her eyes still on her twin, who was now entering a field of oat stubble and gaining on her hat.

"But what are we to do with it? It's impossible to dig."

The priest said, "Maybe we could put weights on it and sink it in the river." Was this man a comedian, Simon wondered. The priest's expression was serious.

Out from town came Ignition Jones riding his rusty backhoe. He steered it carefully through the cemetery gate, the diesel engine beating a fitful pulse and coughing out a smear of black smoke which was whipped away by the wind. He bounced along the narrow drive and when he reached Simon's car he stopped and stood up to judge his chances of getting past, then he sat down and maneuvered his way between the car on his right and a leaning shaft of polished granite on his left. Passing the statuary, Ignition Jones looked once, then twice, astonished to see living people standing shoulder to shoulder with the figures of Calvary. He tipped his cap.

Simon and Leep and Father Kerwin watched the machine crawl into the southwest section, where Ignition Jones stopped it, jumped to the ground with a scrap of paper in his hand, and sighted down a line of tombstones.

"Somebody died," said Father Kerwin.

"We'll ask him to dig for us," said Simon. They set off for the southwest section, Simon carrying the shovel, Father Kerwin the leg.

From the tool box under the seat, Ignition Jones took out a tape measure and four iron stakes with orange ribbons tied to them. He drove the stakes into the ground at the four corners of the grave he was about to open. Then he climbed back to his seat, steered into position, and began to dig, moving his hands deftly over the many levers before him. The sharp teeth of the square-jawed scoop chewed into the ground and came up with an overflowing bite of dirt and stones. Conscious of an audience, Ignition Jones dug, in ten minutes, the slickest grave of his life. The walls were smoothly perpendicular and the extracted earth was heaped in a symmetrical pile. When he switched off the engine and hopped to the ground, the sudden silence throbbed in Simon's ears like a great noise. Ignition Jones lifted his oily cap and smiled and said, "Howdy." He had a small grimy face and only one visible tooth.

"We have a favor to ask of you," said Father Kerwin. "We want you to bring your machine over next to those statues and take up one or two scoops of soil. A hole two feet deep will be sufficient."

"A hole among them statues?" What little Ignition Jones knew about priests had always mystified him.

"Yes, where you saw us standing."

"No good. No room for me to get in there. Too many gravestones. I can only use this fellow where there ain't no gravestones in the way." He patted the scoop of his backhoe like the nose of a horse. "Where it's tight I have to dig by hand, same as you. Last year I chipped a corner off a gravestone and caught hell."

Simon stepped to the edge of the new grave and looked in. There was moisture at the bottom. "We'll bury it here," he said. "Could you take out one more scoopful of dirt down there? Then we'll drop in our parcel and you can cover it over and no one will be the wiser."

Ignition Jones pulled the bill of his cap low over his eyes and looked narrowly from Simon to Leep to the priest and wondered if this was legal.

"Whose grave is this?" asked Father Kerwin.

"I wasn't told. There ain't no names on the chart I keep. Only numbers. Sid Norris, he called up and said plot eight, bed one, so I looked it up on my chart and saw it was in the second row, seven spaces from the end, and I hopped in the saddle and came right over and dug." He patted his backhoe. "Sid Norris said there wasn't no rush, he said I had till Monday morning, but the wife says no use getting dirty on Sunday, so I came right over." He studied the heavy green package which the priest was shifting in his arms. "Now whatever you folks got in that bundle, I ain't asking no questions. I can put it down there all right, but this fellow won't reach down any further. His neck stretches just barely to the bottom of your regulation-size grave and that's the furthest. So if you don't mind I'll borrow your shovel and dig it out myself."

At the edge of the grave, poised to jump with the shovel in his hand, Ignition Jones glanced once more at the package, judging the size of the hole he must dig, then he nodded and dropped out of sight and dug it. He reached up for the leg and buried it, gently tamping and smoothing the dirt at the bottom of the grave.

"Okay?" he asked, looking up and grinning slyly, certain that he was involved in something illicit and not wanting to appear naive.

"Fine," said the priest. He gave Ignition Jones a hand and helped him out. Then he sprinkled holy water into the grave and mumbled a brief prayer beginning. "Let us pray," and ending, "Amen, let's go."

Ignition Jones climbed to the controls of his backhoe and Simon, seeing his devilish smirk, said by way of explanation, "It was a leg," but with a burst of noise and smoke the machine was already lurching down the drive.

Simon looked at his watch. It was four. Barbara was waiting. He had spent eight hours on this stupid mission while Barbara waited. No one stayed behind to comfort Mrs. Kibbikoski, he thought, but instead we have spent the afternoon with her leg. It is to such moronic behavior as this that my challenge to the Home has led. Farewell to the Home.

He and Leep and the priest got into the car.

"Is it buried?" asked Mrs. Valentine Biggs.

"It's buried," said Leep with a long sigh. "It's at the bottom of a stranger's grave."

Simon drove a quarter mile down a dirt road and picked up Spinner, whose hat had been stopped by thistles in a ditch. Her face was ruddy with exertion and her stockings were torn. She got into the back seat and said, "Is it buried?"

"It's buried," said Leep. "It's at the bottom of a stranger's grave."

"Thank God," said Spinner. "Sorry I couldn't have been there."

Simon turned the car around and headed into town.

Mrs. Valentine Biggs said, "Now I've seen how it works, who do we tell?"

"What do you mean?" said Spinner.

"No one," said Leep.

"But certainly we tell Mrs. Kibbikoski, don't we? I mean wouldn't you want to know the whereabouts of your leg? And what about the people who will bury that stranger in that grave? Shouldn't they know what's under the casket?"

"I say no one must know," said Leep.

"I agree," said Father Kerwin, turning to face the women. "Let's the five of us pledge ourselves to secrecy." He looked at Simon. "Don't you agree?"

But Simon didn't answer. Simon, as he drove toward town, was casting his eyes across the prairie and bidding it farewell. Good-bye, prairie, forever. If he proved incapable of surviving in his cottage, he would not allow himself to be carted off to a prairie again. Stash him away in a home if need be, but it had better be a home in the hills. Farewell to the prairie for good and all. On the prairie he could see thirty miles in every direction (the sky was darker now, the lightning brighter) and he was puny. His heart was high at the thought of leaving Ithaca Mills. His escape had been a narrow one.

"Father?" asked Simon, "do you remember the psalm about deliverance: 'You drew me clear. You brought me up from the nether world.'?"

"Yes, it begins, 'I will extol you, O Lord, for you drew me clear and did not let my enemies rejoice over me. O Lord, you brought me up from the nether world; you preserved me from among those going down into the pit.' You mean that one?"

Simon nodded, continuing, " 'Sing praise to the Lord, you his faithful ones, and give thanks to his holy name. For his anger lasts but a moment; a lifetime his good will. At nightfall weeping enters in, but with the dawn rejoicing.' "

"A wonderful psalm of thanksgiving," said Father Kerwin. "One of the most stirring."

But Simon wasn't through: " 'You changed my mourning into dancing; you took off my sackcloth and clothed me with gladness, that my soul might sing praise to you without ceasing; O Lord, my God, forever will I give you thanks.' "

At the rectory Simon opened the trunk and handed Father Kerwin his shovel. "Good-bye, Father."

"It was nice meeting you. I didn't catch your name."

"Simon Shea." They shook hands.

"And you live at the Norman Home?"

"No. These three women do, but I don't. I'm just a visitor in Ithaca Mills."

"And how long are you staying?"

"About twenty minutes. Good-bye, Father."

He drove to the Home and parked at the front steps. In the foyer, Hattie Norman gave each of them hell as they entered. They were four hours overdue and she had been about to call the sheriff and report them missing. She had a good mind to withhold their suppers.

"Never mind," Leep explained to Mrs. Valentine Biggs. "In this life, good deeds often go unrewarded."

"Never mind," Spinner said to Simon. "You did us a great favor and you will be rewarded in heaven."

"Never mind," Simon said to Hattie. "It's no use dressing me down because I'm leaving the Home this very instant, never to return as long as I live. The food has been good and my room has been adequate, but you, Hattie Norman, have been a challenge to my sanity. You, Hattie Norman, have been a great obstacle to my peace of mind, and unless you tone down your shrill and haughty ways, I wouldn't be surprised if the rest of these people walked out on you as well. I have said this about only one other person in my life, Hattie Norman—I said it about the man who stole my wife from me—and now I say it about you. Hattie Norman, you are wicked."

The three women, half out of their coats, stood astounded along the wall of the foyer.

Hattie came up to Simon and dropped her head as though to butt him. She scowled up through her eyebrows. "You can't leave, smarty. I'm entitled to two weeks' notice!"

"My room is paid for through November. That's nearly a month's notice. Good-bye Hattie Norman. I thank you for the warm room and the good food, particularly the chocolate chip cookies, but the human soul longs for more than food and warmth. The human soul seeks refuge from wickedness, and you are basically a wicked person. Good-bye, Hattie Norman."

This exchange brought Hatch out of the TV parlor. With him was a stranger, a skinny, angular man with hair growing out of his ears.

"Hi, all," said the stranger. "I'm Jacob R. Gross. I'm living in the room the Indian used to live in."

"Oh, how marvelous," said Mrs. Valentine Biggs. "Another man."

"I'm happy to know you," said Simon. "I wonder if I could ask you two men to give me a hand. I'll just take a few of my essentials tonight and come back some other time for the rest. Perhaps Douglas Mikklessen will bring me in his pickup."

A few minutes later the three men came down the stairs with two suitcases, a box of books and a briefcase—and, rolled up and balanced on Simon's shoulder, the Persian rug.

Simon bade farewell to the women on his way from the stairs to the front door. "Good-bye, Mrs. Spinner and Mrs. Leep, I admire your orthodoxy. Good-bye, Mrs. Valentine Biggs. I'll never forget you."

Outside it was dark. The men packed the things into the car and shook hands. Jacob R. Gross started back inside, but Hatch stood by the car, puzzled. "Are you going to the hospital?" No one had ever left the Home for anywhere else.

"No, I have a bride, Hatch. I've tried old age for a while and now I think I'll try marriage. I did this one other time. About forty years ago I was old for a while and then I took myself a bride. I'm repeating myself." He took Hatch's hand with both his own. "Good luck to you, Hatch. I know you always worked hard and you deserve a good many relaxing hours in the TV parlor. I'm sure you'll get along fine with the new man."

"He was a farmer himself," said Hatch. "He always worked hard and he remembers the drought of thirty-six, but he doesn't remember the drought of twenty-eight."

"Maybe it wasn't dry where he was."

"That could be."

"And speaking of droughts, Hatch, I believe the drought of seventy-six is over. There was rain this morning in the hills." They looked at the sky. The wind had died, but the stillness that hung over the prairie was not like the dry stillness of the previous autumn nights. This was a menacing stillness, promising storms.

"Yep, I been smelling rain all day," said Hatch. He climbed the steps and joined Jacob R. Gross at the front door.

Simon drove downtown and went into Tess and Herbert's Bar and Lounge, where the earliest of the Saturday night drinkers were already slouched over their beer. The soloist on the juke box was loud and heartbroken and off-key. Tess approached to wait on Simon, then saw who it was (the man who had said she looked like an Indian) and she sent Herbert instead. Sag-bellied Herbert said, "What'll it be?"

"I just came to inquire about Mr. Smalleye."

"What about him?"

"His health. How is he?"

Herbert pointed across the room. There in the dark corner booth was the Indian. He was half-sitting, half-lying on the cushioned seat and his eyes were fixed on the TV screen over the bar. The color was faulty and the face of Lawrence Welk, who spoke inaudibly, was the color of V-8 Juice.

"Are you feeling all right?" asked Simon.

The Indian turned to him with pain. He wore bandages on his head. He said, "I think I shot one. I saw his wings fold up just before I fell."

"What about your wounds? Can you walk?"

"I shouldn't have shot from the roof. I should have shot from the balcony."

"What's to become of you? You don't intend to live out your life in this booth, do you?"

"Tess tried to get me back in the Home, but there's no room. My old room is taken."

"Mrs. Kibbikoski's room is open. It's on the ground floor."

"That's spoken for too."

"Well, there's my room. I'm leaving. Have Hattie put you into Mrs. Kibbikoski's room. She can put the newcomer upstairs. That way you'll be on the ground floor."

"Tell Tess about it." The Indian's attention moved back to Lawrence Welk.

Tess stood beneath the TV and averted her eyes as Simon spoke to her. What he said was helpful, but that didn't mean she had to give him the satisfaction of looking grateful. He explained about his room and Mrs. Kibbikoski's room and he urged her to call Hattie. She nodded curtly and went to the phone.

Simon went back to the corner booth and said goodbye.

"Next time I'll shoot from the balcony," said the Indian.

It was raining on the prairie, raining in the hills. Lightning stood out in the sky at three-second intervals, flashes so blinding and close that Simon flinched as he drove, jagged streaks of light with one end high in the clouds and the other end dancing along the barbed-wire fences beside the road. Rain ran down his windshield and blurred the oncoming lights; rain washed south to north in sheets over the highway; rain stood in depressions in the pavement and drummed against the bottom of the car as it was thrown up by the front tires. He drove through Rookery in a cloudburst and when he turned off the highway, the dirt road to the Badbattle was mushy with rain. Falling rain obscured the forest ranger's tower and the hill in the meadow and the Pribble farm and the house and sheds of Kermit and Felicity Odmer.

Simon turned in at his mailbox and drove across the grass and parked next to the cottage door and ran inside with his coat over his head.

Barbara kissed him in the kitchen.

Simon said he felt newly married and shy, and Barbara said she felt newly married and bold.

"The cottage is lovely, Simon, and I don't see why I ever left, but if we should ever leave again I'm sure it will bring at least eighteen thousand."

"I don't know why I left either, Barbara." He took off his coat.

"For some reason I decided to go into a kind of premeditated decline, but I should have known it wouldn't work." He took out his handkerchief and wiped the rain from his nose. "I went to the Home thinking that between life and death there was an intermediate form of existence. Like sleep. We see a lot of old people living in a dormant state, and I thought it was my turn."

"And it wasn't," said Barbara. She went back to the meal she was preparing.

"No, it wasn't." He stepped into the next room and hung up his coat. "And as it turns out, that dormancy is a kind of death in itself. . . ." In the living room, he stood for a moment with his mouth open—interrupted by the exquisite sensation of homecoming, of his life fitting, once again, its mold. "There is no intermediate existence, Barbara. Short of death, there's no alternative but life."

No reply. Barbara was busy at the stove.

Returning to the kitchen, he said, "And short of despair, there's no alternative but hope. Instead of Franklin Pierce, a dead man, why didn't I vote for Carter or Ford?"

"I didn't even vote," said Barbara. "By the time I remembered what day it was, the polls were closed. Simon, where do you keep your cooking oil?"

The thunder and lightning passed and the rain settled into a steady rumble on the roof. Barbara served supper—something hot and Mexican—and they ate with the door open in order to hear the rain splatter on the car and feel the breeze waft through the cottage, a breeze so full of moisture that their paper napkins were soggy the moment they spread them on their laps. Barbara said she hadn't realized until today how much she missed the rain while living in the Southwest. Simon said that this late in the year the rain was likely to turn to snow and if it did they must call Jean and Douglas out from town. Barbara said she had never been crazy about snow and she hoped she could endure a Minnesota winter but if she couldn't surely Simon would come with her to El Paso for a month or two; they could return in March. Simon said he would go any place where there were hills and a light to read by, but he wasn't sure he had the price of a ticket. Barbara said money was no problem, what did he think she had been working for all these years; and speaking of work she might see if any realtors in Rookery were looking for part-time help; she was sure that after a few weeks of idleness she would want to find something to keep her mind occupied. Simon said yes, everyone needed an occupied mind, and while he thought of it there was something he must put in writing tonight before it slipped his mind. The breeze grew chilly and he got up to shut the door.

After supper, they did the dishes together, then while Barbara put fresh linen on the bed Simon went out to the car and brought in his briefcase and books. In the den, he put the books on the shelf over his desk, then he sat down and opened the briefcase. He drew out his scarf and rubbers and Leonard Woolf volumes three and four, and the massive manuscript of T. S. Testor's life. He sat for a minute with Testor on his left knee, Woolf on his right. How different the writing skills. How controlled and astute was Woolf; how sprawling and dull was Testor. The gap between them was vast. And inspiring: couldn't an amateur like Simon try his hand and hope to fall somewhere between? He set aside Woolf and Testor and he drew a sheet of paper from his desk. He uncapped his pen and with scarcely a moment's hesitation he wrote:

> *Strange to think how much lay before me that after-noon in Redbank. It is my earliest memory, as though my consciousness came into being at that very moment. My mother is pulling me, bundled in blankets, on a sled over the snow. It is a sled my father has built with a box for me to sit in. She is pulling me from our house to the hardware store where Father works. The sun is very low and we pass through many long shadows where the snow is blue.*

Simon put down his pen and sat back in his chair, staring for a few moments at nothing. Then he got up and went into the front room and turned on the yard light. Mingled with the sound of rain was a melody coming from the bedroom—Barbara singing as she worked. Past the rain streaming down the window, Simon watched the rain falling on the slope under his yard light. And beyond the light it was raining into the Badbattle, a bubble where each drop of rain struck the moving water. And beyond the river it was raining in the woods, falling into bird nests and gopher holes, glazing the smooth bark of birches and soaking into the rough bark of oaks. Across the county rain fell steadily into fields and streets and rain gauges and birdbaths and it fell into garbage cans with their covers off. Rain fell onto the campus of Rookery State and into the not quite empty grave of Mrs. Kibbikoski, and it fell into dried-up creek beds like the third day of Creation. Rain fell onto hillsides and it ran brimming into streams, and water rose to a great depth in ditches where culverts were plugged. Rain fell across the land as unbidden and broad as the hope for good harvest, it fell onto everyone's roof like a blessing, it fell into everyone's life like the promise of love.

My Simon's
Night Journal

Jon Hassler

Edited and annotated by Joe Plut

Acknowledgments

If it weren't for my administrative assistant, Barbara Bendson, there would be no *My Simon's Night Journal* to be published. Jon had given me his typed copy of the *Journal*, which I then—over the years—edited and annotated. Barbara corrected, typed, retyped (some sections a number of times), and made copies until, finally, the *Journal* could be published. Thank you, Barb, from me and from Jon's readers who will be appreciating your labors.

And my appreciation to Gretchen, Jon's widow, and Liz, Jon's daughter, for their constant support and encouragement over these many years.

– Joseph Plut

The Genesis of
My Simon's Night Journal

Joseph Plut

In 1999 Ballantine Books published Jon Hassler's *My Staggerford Journal*. Now, with *My Simon's Night Journal*, the reader is once again privy to Jon's thoughts, daily routines, creative roadblocks, successes, and doubts in the birthing of a novel. However, not much documentation has been published about the origin of these journals/letters. In a small way, I hope to remedy that here.

In his introduction to *My Staggerford Journal*, "In Preparation," Jon began with this background: "Before I began to write fiction, I had started keeping a journal. Early entries I made in a large, hardbound record book with pen and ink and a fairly legible hand, but soon I discovered that I was capable of a shade more vitality and wit when I wrote to friends—and one friend in particular—than when I addressed myself. Thus my journal gradually became typewritten carbon copies of letters to Dick Brook clipped into a loose-leaf notebook. I now have perhaps thirty such notebooks lying about my den, with at least 95 percent of the pages—and many of the entries in this book—addressed to Dick, a friend from my college years with whom I enjoyed a steady forty-year correspondence."

Jon had dedicated *My Staggerford Journal* to Dick.

The two met when both were undergraduates at Saint John's University in Collegeville, Minnesota—Jon (1951-1955 with a major in English) and Dick (1952-1955 with a double major in English and Philosophy). Both graduated with a Bachelor of Arts Degree in spring 1955, and both later aspired to write fiction. Their dates of birth were close: Jon, March 30, 1933, and Dick, April 29, 1933. Dick and his wife lived in New Hampshire; Jon visited them and I know that at least Dick but probably both returned the favor. In a letter to me dated September 19, 1980, Jon wrote: "Here at the Brooks' I'm editing, walking, reading, sleeping, eating, visiting. No sailing yet because of the weather: fog. Maybe this weekend."

My Simon's Night Journal begins on January 8, 1977, and ends on November 22, 1978. Jon hadn't dedicated it to anyone when he gave me the manuscript to edit and annotate in late 2003. All the letters are addressed to Dick with the exception of four: Memorial Day, 1977, to Brother Benet Tvedten, O.S.B, at Blue Cloud Abbey, Marvin, S.D.; August 23, 1977, to Judith Kern, Jon's editor at Atheneum; and December 27, 1977, and October 2, 1978, to Gail Coufal, a former student at Brainerd Community College. Jon had typed this *Journal* on his typewriters (his typewriters are almost secondary characters in this *Journal*).

I recently found an undated audio cassette of a short interview I had with Jon about *My Staggerford Journal* (late 1999)—I'll quote two excerpts. I: "Your *Journal* contains letters and parts of letters to your college friend Dick Brook. Were these letters written as journal entries or did that happen afterwards?" Jon: "They were written as letters primarily, but I saw them as entries in my journal once I wrote them. I mean I would send them off and then I'd keep a copy of each letter and put it in a notebook since I was doing my best writing to him—seems like I write better when I have a particular listener in mind. And so after a while I confessed to him—I said I am saving your letters as part of my journal. I was a little self-conscious about that since I didn't know how he'd take that. And he said he had been doing it for years." I: "Would you ever think of having another journal published about one of your other novels?" Jon: "I have a *Love Hunter* journal; I have a *Simon's Night* journal; I have a *Green Journey* journal—I have journals of all my books. I'm hoping if this book [*My Staggerford Journal*] takes off, I'll come through with those, too."

When Jon gave me *My Simon's Night Journal* to edit, he and I skimmed through it making almost no changes or corrections. We changed some wording in one entry. Then, working on it this past fall and spring and now summer, I replaced some of the names of actual people Jon used in developing his characters with fictional ones to preserve their anonymity.

Jon penned this in a *My Simon's Night Journal* entry dated January 17, 1977: "They [the pages he had recently written] were written so spontaneous—like our letters to each other—that they are sound, unfettered, worthy writing. It's the unfetteredness of our letters, Dick, that make them such a pleasure to write, such a pleasure to get." "Dear Reader," as Jon sometimes addressed you, the reader, in his nonfiction, I hope that you will accept this *Journal* as a pleasurable reading gift from Jon.

– July 2013

My Simon's Night *Journal*

January 8, 1977 Brainerd

I wish I could absent myself from the classroom from now until I
die. Not that the classroom isn't comfortable: when I'm in it I enjoy
it, but it's nowhere near as exciting as being in the middle of a novel, which was where I was a year ago right now. I was in the middle
of *Staggerford*, which came to completion in March and came to
the attention of Atheneum Publishers in August and is scheduled to
come to the attention (I hope) of the reading public next August or
September. Atheneum has given me a small advance against royal-
ties, which has the effect of making a writer feel like an author and
making him feel like writing another book. And that's what I'm doing. But God, it's an arduous life when it's interrupted by students
sitting in desks. And today, Saturday, I must get started on a piece
about Ireland ["Dingle Drenched, Dingle Dry," published in *The
New York Times* Travel Section, May 15, 1977, p. 9], for I have
had some luck with travel writing and I would like to do it again.

January 17, 1977

But as I was going to say on the top of page 1, there you sit in the
evening, thinking that now at last you will get your life in order,
you will get your writing underway. And I believe you will. But
not quite yet. There are too many distractions: legal documents to
sign, wood to chop, a new landscape to get used to, a new room in
which to write; it's probably like being on your sailboat [in New
Hampshire] and pulling into a harbor to write before you're used
to writing on a sailboat.

But as I said once before, I firmly believe that when one is distracted from writing, one must write about the distractions. I re-

member a couple years ago being pulled away from my writing at the beginning of a day I had intended to devote to writing. My wife was in the hospital for one of her myriad ailments and the kids were occupied elsewhere and I was going to write.

And so I did what I always do when I see a whole day of writing ahead of me: I started slow. I devoted at least an hour and a half to coffee and musing. My sabbatical days began that way, Dick. An hour and a half for breakfast and looking out windows and turning the work-in-progress over in my mind—easing into the day's work. (Ah, it makes me hanker for those sabbatical days once more.) And that day at the end of the hour and a half, when I was about to set my typewriter in motion, there comes a call from the hospital. My wife was ready to come home. She was being released. She had had her tests. Would I please hurry along. And I did. I got to the hospital in time to wait for almost two hours before she was free to come home.

When I got home I could not bring a single word to mind that I had intended to write. Those two hours in the hospital were so distracting, not to say tiring, that my day was shot for writing. That's what I thought, at least. But what I did was I began writing about the hospital when I got home—a catalogue of unsightly sights: tubes in this old lady's nose, the frown on that nurse's face, etc. Pages. And I looked at those pages the other day, and they proved to be quite satisfactory as writing. Some day they will fit precisely into a piece of fiction. I swear they will.

They were written so spontaneous—like our letters to each other—that they are sound, unfettered, worthy writing. It's the unfetteredness of our letters, Dick, that make them such a pleasure to write, such a pleasure to get.

January 19, 1977

The deep snowfall we had today made people happy. The woman from an office down the hall laughed for the first time in weeks. I think she's having trouble with her husband, who is running around with someone prettier than his wife, and she has been looking pretty grim of late. But this afternoon she stood in the middle of the parking lot and laughed like a girl and said, "Which car is mine? They all look alike."

January 30, 1977
Evelyn Waugh. If he were alive, I would write and tell him how he has influenced my writing. No, I take that back. I wouldn't tell him *how* because I can't say how; I would simply acknowledge his place in my brain, his place in my first drafts, his place in *Staggerford*.

Me. Yesterday, at the behest of my kids, I bought a pair of Levi's. My first since 1952. I'm no longer a Republican.

I want to write. Writing is on my mind at all times. And I *do* write, at least when I can come into this room and shut the door. But I can't write as much as I did last year because of teaching. But I feel very good about writing anyhow, because during those three or four times a week when I am able to come in here and shut the door, I am not at a loss for words. I don't really believe I have been stymied for words since my sabbatical.

My sabbatical was like lancing a boil. I have been able to squeeze stuff out damn near at will ever since. I don't mean in torrents—I think I'm naturally too reticent for that—I mean trickles. Which are fine. Trickles are fine, as long as the trickle is clear. And steady. Especially steady. And clear.

February 13, 1977
Invigoration. That's what I went out looking for, and found, along the path that leads from my house through the woods to the small clearing on the bank of the Mississippi. Enervation. That's what I sought to leave behind. My enervation today was the cause of the following, which occurred in close succession over the past three days: going to Staples and trying to start up my parents' furnace in preparation for their return from the South, and the furnace failing to start and needing attention, which I will have to find within the next few days; going to Backus to visit a colleague recuperating from cancer surgery and discovering myself a day late, she having

been carted off to Rochester once more with complications; working on my taxes and discovering that I owe the state and the feds a total of $650; driving over to the other side of town (between paragraphs two and three of page one) where my daughter was stranded with a flat tire and discovering in the trunk no spare. This sort of thing gets me down. Malfunctions, mechanical and anatomical. The taxes, too, but not so much. Taxes are only money. But malfunctions—mechanical and anatomical—they get me down. What's wrong with that furnace? What's wrong with Virginia's innards? Where is my spare tire?

So the walk was invigorating. The temperature was 21, the sky was clear, the breeze was steady out of the north, the sun was sinking. There is a phantom snowmobiler who drives through the woods just often enough to keep the path hard-packed and easy to hike and just seldom enough so that I never see him, hear him, or smell his exhaust. From the clearing on the bank of the river my route home leads me through the cemetery the long way—a quarter mile of leafless elm and oak and polished stone where there are always, no matter how frequent my walks, two fresh graves [Evergreen Cemetery in Brainerd—please refer to April 20, 1978, entry—third paragraph from end].

I can't spend much time thinking about food. I know people who talk about meals they've had as though they were symphonies they'd heard. I know people who like to listen to talk like that. I've never felt that I could afford to devote myself to every possible attraction in life, and food was one attraction I struck off my list. Years ago. When, God willing, I someday live alone, I'm going to buy myself a case of Wheaties and a jar of honey and some milk. And a spoon. I don't know what I'll buy next, but whatever it is I won't buy it until my case of Wheaties is gone. Maybe it will be something for which I'll need a fork.

When it comes to writing, there are two currents that run through a writer. There is the surface current and there is the deep current. The surface current is the one that carries you from one word to the next, from one sentence to the next, from one page to the next of the novel or story you're working on. It is the current that can be, and is, interrupted often by the exigencies of the moment, by the telephone, by a cold in the head, by fatigue; and these interruptions have little effect on the current: if this surface current stops for a day or a week, it will start up when the interruptions disappear.

Then there is the deep current. This is the current that makes you believe in what you're doing, that gives you the strength to do it, that carries you through the days, weeks or months necessary to complete what you're working on. This is the current of man's desiring. This is the one you want to maneuver yourself into. This is the one you can't do without. This is the one that keeps flowing while the surface current is interrupted. This is the current that renders the surface interruptions harmless.

When you feel the deep current running, you have nothing to fear. The story will be there, the words will be there when you get back to them. The last time my deep current quit running was two years ago when the novel I was working on died on page seventy-five. After that, I don't think I wrote much of anything for almost a year. Then, after my trip to New Hampshire in the fall of 1975, my deep current started running again. [Letter to Dick Brook, "I am home now, Dick. From your home in Ashland, New Hampshire . . .," September 30, 1975, *My Staggerford Journal*, p. 28, Ballantine Books, 1999.] It sustained me through *Staggerford*. It has sustained me through 104 pages of this young people's novel I've been working on [*Jemmy*]. I hope to God it keeps running for years to come.

I just opened to page 257 of Volume 3 of my journals and found this: A List of Happenings in the Lives of People and/or Characters. I remember making this list. It took me three or four days in August of 1975. That was before I drove to New England. I listed one hundred things that might befall a person, that a person might do—things that might come in handy when writing fiction.

Now I will go through this list picking out every tenth item to give you an idea of what this list is all about. Or, rather, to give myself an idea.

Item #10 says: A young librarian advises the lovelorn. That's all it says. Most of the items are no longer than that. A young librarian advises the lovelorn. It isn't much but it could be enough, in the right place. I mean a story could turn on that if the story needed that kind of a detail and the deep current was running. Now I will continue.

#20: A man guides visiting lecturers. #30: A man loses the friend with whom he read poetry on snowy evenings [*The Love Hunter?*]. #40: A man, about to marry, sees his future in a dream. #50: First-year teacher gets contrary advice from father (ignore insulting student) and from husband (sue insulting student). #60: Man fails as a teacher—no personality. #70: Black army officer fathers child of white WAC—later visits child in village, refuses to marry. #80: Drunken Christmas party for neighborhood old folks [*The Dean's List*]. #90: Man grows melancholy in shopping mall [*Simon's Night*]. #100: Man takes wrong bus [*Simon's Night*].

March 4, 1977

If Plymouth State [NH] is a blacking factory, Brainerd Community College is the woodshed. We don't actually turn out any product; the raw material simply passes through here on its way to other places. Last Thursday I asked the President for a leave of absence without pay for fall quarter. He loved me for it. My absence will save money.

My replacement, if there is one, will come a lot cheaper than I do. I earn damn near $20,000 (not that I know where any of it is), and so I am giving up nearly $7,000. I was undecided for a time about this leave of absence. How will I support myself and my family, I said to myself. Don't be stupid, I answered. That's the same dumb question you asked before your sabbatical, and you lived through that, didn't you.

Indeed I did, I said. So I went to see the President. And then, after I saw the President, as though to endorse my decision, I got this phone call from my editor at Atheneum. Are you ready for this, Dick? She said Book-of-the-Month Club has taken *Staggerford* as an alternate selection. Isn't that a pisseroo?

So I am looking ahead to six months of writing time. June, July, August, September, October, November. Six months divided between Brainerd and Nevis [Jon's cabin seventy-three miles from Brainerd]. Six months divided between reading and writing, between walking and sitting, between happiness and ecstasy.

Now, if I am to get out of this woodshed for ten days of writing, I simply must bring this letter to a close and correct these tests lying on my chair. I must read them and grade them and average up quarter grades and record them on IBM sheets and turn them in to the registrar and go uptown and, using brandy and vermouth, wash winter quarter out of my innards. [Jon and I would drink Manhattans with dinner at Harold's Club in Baxter during these years. Before Jon went to Saint John's in 1980, he and I both independently of each other stopped drinking "hard" liquor. Jon said that drinking the evening before dulled his sense for writing the next morning. See second to last paragraph of January 15, 1978, "D."]

March 11, 1977

Yesterday I drove 200 miles through the rain, from Marvin, South Dakota [Blue Cloud Abbey], to Brainerd: it was raining in Ortonville, Benson, New London, Paynesville, Cold Spring, St. Cloud, Little Falls, and Brainerd: a good, long-awaited rain (we've been waiting damn near a year) that fell slowly steadily evenly wetly generally droppingly now and then slantingly on fields and roads and roofs and on the tops of people's heads. It fell on farms and stood in the fields, it fell into ditches and rose to a great depth where culverts were clogged with ice, it fell on hillsides and gurgled down into creeks that wound into rivers that rose over the ice at their edges. It dropped down on my blue car, and when I stepped out it fell on my brown ski jacket, which, blotterlike, spread each drop "like gold to airy thinness beat" [John Donne's "A Valediction Forbidding Mourning"], and in a minute my brown jacket was a shade darker and my glasses were covered with water and there was rain dripping off my nose. It fell into snowbanks and cedar hedges and rain gauges, it fell into icy lakes and old bird nests and garbage cans with their covers off, it fell into everyone's life like a promise of summer and harvest and cleanliness. [This journal entry presages the ending pages of *Simon's Night*. "Q. This brings to mind the conclusion to James Joyce's story 'The Dead' with snow falling and covering everything. Surely, this must have influenced you. A. That's right. I remember reading that passage in Joyce. I remember driving home from Blue Cloud Abbey one time through rain like that. So I stopped the car and wrote some of those details down, like the rain falling in garbage cans and things like that. And it seems to me that stood for rejuvenation, the coming back of life." *Conversations with Jon Hassler* by Joseph Plut, p. 47, Nodin Press, 2010].

March 15, 1977

How is it that you can always write paragraphs of nearly half a page? Don't you ever have thoughts that die out after a line and a half? It's you, Dick, I'm speaking to. How come that is?

This letter is petering out. I've been at it for nearly two hours. Think of it. A page and a half in two hours. My mind is sterile. Clean as a picked bone. Smooth as a pearl. Empty as the sky. Hollow as a robin's fibula. Sterile. Incapable of production. Wiped clean. Wiped out. Sterile. Zero. You deserve better than this, Dick.

March 20, 1977

A few words about imagination. If it's measurable on a scale of one to ten, I think I can sometimes get up to eight. I mean, on a rare occasion, with the help of a good book to read, a manuscript half completed and four cups of coffee, I can touch eight. Up in the nines and tens are Shakespeare and Kafka and, more recently, García Márquez in *One Hundred Years of Solitude* (did you read that?); and down in the ones and twos are the inmates of the Brainerd State Hospital. I range from two to eight. Like everybody else, I'm usually below five, and like everybody else I will sometimes surge up to six and seven, but not as often as I used to.

I think imagination is better when you're young. I think I could be a better writer if I were ten years younger. My imagination isn't all that great at forty-four. I remember working on *Staggerford* and fearing from day to day that my imagination would run out. Could I maintain my imagination through the first draft? That's what I wondered. That's why finishing the first draft was such a triumph for me. When I saw the end in sight, I said "whoopee."

Now here's another thing I think: I think you have to build from two to eight in stages. I don't think you can jump from two to eight without being at four and six for a little while.

I haven't been above five for a long time. This short novel I'm finishing is not strong on imagination [*Jemmy*]. It may be that teaching takes imagination and doesn't leave much for writing. You know how it is in the classroom, you can't hold back, you can't conserve, because you're there with a roomful of people and your pride forces you to produce. It's the difference between the actor and the playwright. The playwright has the harder job. He has to be creative in solitude, he has to motivate himself. The actor has the audience to motivate him. All the school's a stage and the faculty merely players.

March 29, 1977

We have never asked much of each other. We have never asked for philosophical breakthroughs. We have never asked for earthshaking (or steadying) discoveries. We have simply asked each other for a friendly word. Isn't that true, Dick, that all we ever demanded of each other was a friendly word? If we had demanded any more than that, we wouldn't have stayed friends all these years. Demanders are not to my liking, and not to yours either, I expect. I have spent a certain share of my life getting away from demanders, putting some distance between me and demanders, while at the same time keeping my eye out for those who look like they might offer a friendly word. I suppose that's the route we take when we leave our parents and marry our wives. We think we are leaving our demanders and joining a friend. And that's the route we take when we leave our wives who have gone from being friends to being demanders. A convolutionary paragraph if I every [*sic*] wrote one.

I wish I would write things down when I think of them. I have this card in my back pocket for that purpose. It's been there for weeks. On it are such things as phone numbers and items needed from the grocery store. Once in a while I will stop in the middle of what I'm doing and write a thought, but not very often. If I did it more often, I would have more to say when it comes time to write in my journal or write to Plymouth [NH].

Today, for example, I had a thought. It was about writing. I was sitting in a classroom and a student was reading something she had written, and it suggested something to me about writing, but instead of reaching into my back pocket and writing down a word or two in order to preserve the thought, I said to myself, relax, you will remember it when you are home in your den. But now I'm home in my den and I don't remember it. I never do. I've said that to myself a hundred times, but it's not true. Very seldom do I remember one of those passing thoughts. Tomorrow perhaps another one will pass through my head. If it does I will say to myself, relax, you will remember it when you are home in your den. [I transposed two sentences that followed to the June 9, 1977, entry, second paragraph.]

"The sail was patched with flour sacks and, furled, it looked like the flag of permanent defeat." That's from the first of *The Old Man and the Sea*. It was just what I was looking for the other day. I needed to say something on the first page of a story to set the tone, some neat figure to stand for what was coming. So I went and had a look at Hemingway. That's something I haven't done much lately, look at Hemingway. But old Ernie's all right. I don't give a shit what the critics say (Pauline Kael says Ernie doesn't speak to our time in history); he's still OK by me. He has that sentence about Santiago's sail and that's good enough for me. ["Q. Your writing style always includes descriptions of nature, the woods, birds, the moon or sun, the breeze. Did any writer influence you in this regard? A. I think Hemingway where he takes on nature. I admire those passages a lot, and I think by bringing nature into it, you give your novel a little more scope. Q. You studied Hemingway in graduate school, didn't you? A. Hemingway got me through graduate school. I read everything five times that he wrote. I loved his writing more than anything else in graduate school. My master's thesis at the University of North Dakota was 'Moral Choice in the Novels of Ernest Hemingway.'" *Conversations*, p. 12.]

I remember reading Hemingway's *The Old Man and the Sea* about the same time that I read Steinbeck's *The Pearl* and how much alike I thought they were and how much I wished I could write at least one book in that same style. It's sort of a parable style. A sort of heightened style with the story rather transparent and the symbols large as boulders lying underneath. That sort of thing really appealed to me in my early twenties. (I see myself at twenty-three lying on a bed in Melrose [MN] reading *The Pearl*.) [Jon taught English at Melrose H. S., 1955-1956.] And you know what? It still appeals to me. I would still like someday to write a short book in that style. But it's not easy. Whenever I try it for a page or two, it comes out sounding either downright silly or like an imitation of Steinbeck-Hemingway. Maybe there is a new idiom for writing parables in the seventies and it hasn't been discovered yet. Maybe it's up to me to find it. There was this old fisherman who hadn't caught a fish for eighty damn days. I mean even the kids that used to help him with all his lines and bait and that shit, you know, split.

Talk about discoveries, I just discovered that if you transpose the first and last letters of *shit* you get *this*. And I thought this was going to be an insubstantial letter. As ever, old friend.

April 19, 1977

My father is languishing in the Staples Hospital with a heart that isn't working right, my youngest goes to juvenile court tomorrow with me tagging along to defend him for driving infractions, a friend and former colleague went to his grave Saturday with me providing one-sixth of the strength to get him there, the fiction editor of *McCall's* is angry with me after discovering that the piece of *Staggerford* she bought appeared one time in a quarterly. I discovered on April 14 that I had thrown away (by mistake, not in anger) my W-2 forms. There. That's a sampling.

May 10, 1977

I know the cause of my restlessness these days. I am wondering about novel number four. I have completed three novels, one long and two short [*Staggerford, Four Miles to Pinecone, Jemmy*], and I am wondering what number four will be. I want it to be long. I want it to be about some old people I've got stashed away in my journal and about some young people that are on my mind, but I don't know [*Simon's Night*]. I don't see it plain. What will the story be? I don't know.

May 20, 1977

Two weeks and school will be over. I look forward to freedom. I believe this school year has been harmful to me. The novel I finished a month ago is brief and anemic [*Jemmy*]. Too much of my creativity was drained off into the classroom. I will not go back to work until December (I will live on the few small checks I have gotten from three publishers and a magazine), and even that may be too soon to go back. If I were more of a daredevil, I would quit. I would stride into the President's office this morning and say, "See here, Bill, I quit."

"You quit?" he'll say.

"Yes, this very instant."

"But your classes. Final exams. Final grades."

"The hell with final exams. The hell with final grades. I quit."

"Now, see here—"

"I'll have my office cleaned out in an hour. Pay me what I've got coming and goodbye."

"Now if I were you I wouldn't be hasty. You may wish to come back when you've thought it over. If you quit like this, I can't guarantee we'll have a place for you."

"I have to be hasty, Bill. Don't you see it's my only hope? If I don't quit impulsively, right now, this instant, I probably never will. If I come crawling back looking for a job, I hope to God you don't have a place for me. The last thing in the world I want is a place for me in a classroom. I have been in classrooms since I was five. Subtract five from forty four and you get thirty-nine. Thirty-nine years in classrooms. To hell with classrooms."

"Your retirement benefits will be very small."

"To hell with retirement benefits."

"You'll find yourself paying much more for health insurance."

"To hell with health insurance."

"And you'll lose access to our credit union, and next year we're getting dental insurance. And more. You'll lose all your fringe benefits."

"To hell with the fringes."

"All right, if that's your final word—"

"That's it, Bill. My final word: quit. Quit is my final word. It comes after the word 'I.' As in 'I quit.'"

Writing that conversation has given me a great deal of pleasure. You'd be amazed, Dick, at how much pleasure it gave me. Before I sat down to write this letter, I had not given much thought to quitting, but once I let it out on paper, it tumbled and surged up from my subconscious. You know how it is when you happen, by chance, to open up a door at the back of your mind and you discover a compartment packed full of stuff waiting to be released. Well, it seems here that I have opened such a door. I didn't realize that I had been thinking this much about quitting.

But the conversation is not realistic. Bill would never say things like "Don't be hasty" and "You'll lose the credit union." No, Bill would be happy as hell to see me quit. For one thing it would save him a hell of a lot of money and for another thing he doesn't care much for me. No, a more realistic conversation would go this way:

"See here, Bill, I quit."

"Thank God."

Later

I've been reading books lately. Let's see what have I read. *Fergus* by Brian Moore [writer, Northern Ireland, 1921-1999], mildly interesting, half fantasy and half reality, the fantasy much better done than the reality, more convincing than the reality, more *real* than the reality, a man visited by the ghosts of his family and friends, whom he left behind in Ireland. Likable ghosts. The narrator isn't very likable, though, a wishy-washy writer, sort of indecisive, a dull Hamlet.

Can you write a good book with a main character that isn't very likable? I'm beginning to doubt it. I came dangerously close to having this sort of main character in *Staggerford* [Miles Pruitt]—not unappealing, but indecisive. I must remember to give my main character more personality after this, more conviction, more clear-headed purpose.

Memorial Day, 1977

Dear Brother Benet [friend at Blue Cloud Abbey, Marvin, SD],

I was disappointed in *Falconer*. I hope with his next book Cheever goes back to the suburbs. It looks to me like the wide-spread praise of this book was a Madison Avenue media blitz without much regard for what was between the covers. As [Saul] Bellow has said, we have no literary establishment in this country, and, thus, the success or failure of books is pretty much determined by promotion, or lack of it. Which leads me to wonder about *Staggerford*. Atheneum remains vague about the publication date, but they assure me advance copies should be out in a week or two. *McCall's* will publish a chapter in its July issue. Andre Deutsch, Ltd., will bring the book out in England. If I'm not well into my next novel by this fall, I'll be very frustrated.

I have armloads of papers to correct.

June 8, 1977

I'm having a hard time thinking of what book-length work to write next. I'm beginning to worry about it.

I never before wondered what good my reading was doing me. I always thought it was being stored away in my head and would some day put me at an advantage. I don't know what sort of advantage over other people, but rather at an advantage over the self I was before I read whatever book I was reading: you know, a sort of self-improvement view of reading. But that's not altogether true either. I did not overlook the pleasant aspects of reading, the fun of being carried along on a good story well told. So let's say that for forty-four years I have read for fun and profit. But yesterday, reading Bellow, it didn't seem that I was reading for fun and profit any more. I asked myself why it was that I was reading this book and the best answer I could come up with was that I was reading it to finish it. Is this true of *all* my reading lately? Am I only reading books to finish reading them? It seems to me the profit is no longer there. I don't believe I carry one single mite of knowledge away from Bellow, except that now I can say in a sentence (as one is sometimes asked to do in the classroom) what the book is about. That and the fact that I admired one simile. That's my harvest. [Jon's agent, Harriet Wasserman, was also Saul Bellow's agent at the same time. From my interview with Jon in *Conversations* (pp. 41-42): "Q. Simon [Shea, *Simon's* Night] reviewed books by Scott Fitzgerald and Hilaire Belloc in the same review. He wrote, 'If the serious reader is going to find fault with these two otherwise estimable masters of English prose, he will find it in the tendency of Fitzgerald to be unnecessarily complex and in the tendency of Belloc to be unnecessarily simple' [*Simon's Night*, (129]. This passage brought back elusive memories of something witty you wrote about Saul Bellow which your agent asked you to change. Could you tell me about that? A. Simon comes across a review of a book by Saul Bellow. He says Saul Bellow is fascinating for five pages, interesting for ten, boring for fifteen, any five, any ten, any fifteen. Well, as soon as Harriet read that, she called me up and she said, 'Would you mind taking that out? Saul would be so insulted to read that.' So I took it out, as though Bellow would read my book."]

June 9, 1977

So now it's eight a.m. and the sun is already warm and burning the dew off the picnic table. I see a robin out there under my hedge. He has speckles on his breast and an uncertainty in his step, and yet he is as large as his mother. How is it possible that a few days ago he fit into an egg? Now he's sitting there in the grass, stock-still, his beak pointed north, his eyes glazed; he's doubtless dreaming the long daydreams of adolescence, the same daydreams I dreamed when I was fourteen. This robin in the fourteenth day of its life has achieved the same stage of development that I achieved in fourteen years. People sure grow up slow compared to birds.

Now if I had Saul Bellow's cast of mind, that paragraph would set me off on a six-page reflection on the subject of maturing. But my mind isn't that fertile. After saying something like people sure grow up slow compared to birds, my resources are completely exhausted. I have lamented this business in an earlier letter, Dick. I asked you why, on paper, you were able to think longer thoughts than I was able to think. Your answer was that you didn't indent very often. *So all these years I have been mistaking your aversion to indenting for sustained thought. Nice of you to fess up* [These two lines have been transposed from Jon's March 29, 1977, entry for clarity].

I yearn to get into another novel the way you yearn to go to sea. The analogy is apt. In passage, one cannot predict the currents and directions, and one must trust to one's acumen and experience to bring him safely into port. Furthermore, in passage, there is a distance between one and his fellow man, a turning to nature for diversion and consolation, the winds of nature, the winds over the water, and the winds of remembered voices in the mind.

There is no theme, no thread, in this letter, Dick. Nowhere has it settled for long on a single topic. It reflects the way my mind is working these days: fragmentation. My mind has the jumps, the staggers. This is the first week of extended term of unemployment. I won't go back to the classroom now until the 12th of December. Thus, I'm a bit giddy and unsettled. What I need to settle me down is to hoist the sail of my imagination and set off across a glass-clean sea of fiction.

June 27, 1977

I can't think of whom to write about in my next novel. At the moment nobody seems quite so interesting to me as those two robins. I'm beginning to understand the appeal of the fabulist. The end of the hour is now about to be crossed by my second hand.

July 6, 1977

In an hour from now I will stop typing and see how much I have written. That will be ten forty p.m. Ordinarily I am in bed at ten, but it is too hot to sleep so I will stay up those extra forty minutes. I have been sitting here at my typewriter for two days trying to write something. I have this theory that you can't sit at your typewriter for four consecutive days without getting started on a worthwhile piece of writing. John Updike says twenty minutes. I (and Joan Didion, in an interview) say four days. Well, this is the night of the second day and "Dear Dick" are the first words I've written. This letter, then, marks the halfway point of my experiment.

I say I have been sitting at my typewriter for two whole days, but I would not have you believe that. Not literally. I have gotten up and done things: gone to the can, heated a bowl of soup, taken my hedge trimmer to the sharpener, gone out to lunch [see note at end of this journal entry], cashed a check at the bank; but for the most part I have been within five feet of my typewriter. Some of the time I have spent on the other side of this table in that green chair, reading. [Jon and I had lunch that day at Harold's Club in Baxter, MN. In *My Staggerford Journal*, p. 55, Jon's March 30, 1976, entry reads: "My family announced that we were going out to dinner for my birthday. I had been looking forward to a can of sardines and getting back to my typewriter, but I graciously submitted to their plans. Mike, Dave [Jon's sons], Marie [his wife], and I ate at Harold's; Liz [his daughter], who works in the kitchen as the chef's assistant, came to our table for a minute to complete the family circle." Harold's Club served as the model for the Hub Cafe in *Staggerford* where Fred Vandergar's retirement party took place.]

I am currently reading *Seize the Day* by Bellow, *A Book of Common Prayer* by Didion, and *Falconer* by Cheever. *Seize the Day* is nothing as substantial as Bellow's later things (nor as hard to read), Didion has a smart-ass style which I don't care for, and I'm changing my opinion of *Falconer*. This is my second time through it, and I'm beginning to believe it's good.

I have spent some of the time over there in the corner at my filing cabinet, filing things away, though you wouldn't know it to look at the mess on my desk. This den is almost three years old (it used to be my garage), and for the first two years I kept it neat, but lately I can't keep ahead of the mess. Perhaps tomorrow, when I'm putting in my third day here at my typewriter, I'll clean up my den.

It's now two minutes to ten.

Trollope, they say, made it a habit of writing 250 [words] for each fifteen minutes of writing time. Trollope, they say, after finishing one of his novels, rested for fifteen minutes and began another. We'll see what I end up with in an hour. To equal Trollope, I should have one thousand words.

Now it's ten twenty-four. I think I'm on schedule. Trollope schedule. I think if I make it to the bottom of this page, another twenty minutes I'll have my thousand words. But this will not be guesswork. I will count them.

Morning, July 7. Or: 7/7/77

It is eight-fifteen. I have been up for forty-five minutes. Into the sack of my belly I have put two eggs, two slices of my father's oatmeal bread, one cup of Folger's instant coffee, and a delicious dripping spoonful of marmalade. I love the predictability of breakfast. It's my favorite meal. It's quickly prepared and quickly consumed.

This morning instead of robins there's a young blackbird meandering through the grass under my birch, watched over by an adult blackbird who is sitting on the branch above the abandoned robin's nest. This youngster hasn't been walking too long; there is a hesitation in his step that reminds me of a bride's progress down the aisle to her wedding, except that the bride hesitates on each step (is this symbolic of her subconscious reluctance to give it all away?) while the bird's hesitation is irregular, as though a trick knee were causing his leg to buckle. It is now eight-thirty. I am finishing my second cup of coffee.

This past year I was visited twice in my office by a man of twenty-three years whose name was something unusual from the New Testament: Simeon or Thaddeus or some such name. His last name, though I can't remember it, sounded Scot. Let's call him Simeon McPherson. He was strikingly handsome, of large scale and gentle voice, his hair dark and tending to curl, his manner polite. I was going to say that his manner was formal, but that impression was probably due to the serious problem he had with his back, an ailment he contracted in Vietnam while riding shotgun on helicopters and which now made it necessary for him to sit very straight and make no unpremeditated movements of his head and arms.

There was this same restrained quality in his voice, as though to speak loudly would cause him pain, and when I asked him to sit he told me, quietly and slowly, that he brought home from the war, besides a broken back, a drug habit and a mistaken but strong conviction that he was three years behind everybody else his age. After six months in a hospital for bad backs and hopheads, he was clean now of drugs, and that was all to the good; but he was having trouble from another quarter: in order to catch up to everyone else his age, the first thing he did when he returned to the States was to find a girl and marry her and have a baby. And now the girl, seventeen when he married her, eighteen last month, had decided that life had more to offer her than an old veteran with a bad back, and she had left him, but on the advice of her parents she wanted assurance that Simeon would pay her a lot of money every month before she would grant him a divorce.

Now all this would seem to be troubles enough, but there were at least two more. For one thing, his father was in such precariously poor health that Simeon felt obliged to stay with him, care for him, make up to him the grief he had caused him in his drug days. So they lived together, he and his father, in a remote lake home, thirty-five miles from the nearest college campus, where he hoped somehow to enroll in a few classes and where he was not sitting stiffly on my office chair. But the fifty-mile drive was killing pain and he was not yet ready to abandon his father, whose wish was to stay in the lake home till he died. So, although he had come to campus today to inquire about registration, he was certain before he stepped from his car that college was impossible, at least until after his father was dead. That was one thing.

Another thing was that his brain wasn't functioning right. He said that whenever he tried reading anything but a short poem his brain would not absorb the meanings of words. It was a problem of concentration, whether from drugs particularly or from his build-up of troubles generally he didn't know, but he was beginning to wonder if he would ever recover the power of concentration that had got him through high school in Minneapolis with better than average grades.

And why did he come to me? He came to me because, like most strangers who make their way down the dark underground corridor to my office, he had been writing poems and had been told by a counselor or a dean or someone else on an upper floor of this building (where light shone in windows and made clear divisions between sun and shadow) that I was the one to see if one was troubled by the urge to write, I was the one (like a math teacher solves equations) who could solve poems. [I'm not sure which school Jon was referring to. Brainerd Community College (now Central Lakes College) only added a new building with a second floor in 1997. Perhaps Jon was being metaphorical.]

It occurs to me, Dick, that I might have something here for my next novel. This young guy with a broken back, a broken life. And there would be a girl, of course. And the guy's dying father in that remote house. And of course the teacher, me, but me in the third person.

July 29, 1977

I too am going through my journal and letters, studying them for details and ideas which will give shape to this amorphous hulk that's crowding to the forepart of my brain. I too have forty thousand words of random writing, of which I must somehow find the handle. Here's what I've been doing. For the past week I have been compiling this raw material, first by making a list of the major topics in each letter and noting the date of the letter beside each topic, then by fastening the letters into place chronologically in notebooks, and third by browsing through the letters in the evening when my mind is not good for much else, thus becoming familiar with those forty thousand words, bringing them under some kind of control. It doesn't sound much like writerly work. It sounds more like something a file clerk should be doing. But it's worth the effort. When you come upon the good observation, the salvageable paragraph, the pure flight of fancy, you know it's worth the effort.

I got this idea during my sabbatical year when I made a compilation of things from my journal, which up to that time was written almost totally in longhand in large notebooks. I knew there were things in those journals, primarily figures of speech and descriptions of people, that I could use in my writing, and so I set about making that concordance, if you will, of my journals. The outcome was happy. There are dozens of details, figures of speech, turns of phrase in *Staggerford* that are lifted straight out of those journals. Now two years have passed since I did that and the job must be done again, and this time it's a double job, for besides the scribbling in notebooks I have these letters. The letters are not the more valuable of the two.

Another thing. It has seldom if ever been my experience to find a plot for a story in my journal/letters. What I find are smaller things than stories—faces, kinds of weather, digressions, etc., that fit neatly into the story I am writing. Until I made this discovery, that my journal/letters weren't going to supply me with anything BIG, I had expected that they could be converted easily into stories, but they can't. I find that the story has to be there before I can bring my journal/letters to bear on it. My journal/letters are the bricks and mortar, but not the blueprint.

The last writing I did was around the first of April and that was nearly four months ago. Around the first of April I finished that short novel called *The Maiden* [*Jemmy*] and I haven't done anything to speak of since. Incidentally, my agent is not having an easy time marketing *The Maiden*, and that, too, has me a bit anxious, fearful that I had only one book in me and now what's to become of me. What if I went to all this work to get the attention of New York and then couldn't write anything more that interested them? It's too early for me to get very upset about, but it's a thought. Graham Greene said that publishing one's first novel, difficult as it is, is not as difficult as spending the rest of your life proving yourself. [In addition to *Staggerford*, Jon had already written *Four Miles to Pinecone*, published by Frederick Warne in 1977. The *New York Times Book Review* printed a positive review in its May 15, 1977, issue. Maybe Jon was thinking of an "adult" novel as opposed to a young people's novel.]

Graham Greene is old, and not quite so interesting any more. He's like this guy in Proust that I came across the other day as I was sitting on the toilet. (Proust, like Bellow, makes good toilet reading; taken in short doses they are admirable and taken in long doses they make you numb.) Anyhow, there was this old writer about whom Proust says,

> The bulk of his thought had long since passed from his brain into his books. He had grown thin, as though they had been extracted from him by surgical operations. His reproductive instinct no longer impelled him to any activity, now that he had given an independent existence to almost all his thoughts. He led the vegetative life of a convalescent, of a woman after childbirth; his fine eyes remained motionless, vaguely dazed, like the eyes of a man who lies on the seashore and in a vague daydream sees only each little breaking wave.

August 20, 1977 [Saturday]

I have the feeling that I'm going to start my novel one of these days.
The day after tomorrow, I think. I hope you didn't think I was being coy in not talking about the plot that I have been imagining
these past few weeks, but I've lost plot by talking about them. But
this one grows firmer in my mind by the day, and I am tempted tonight to speak of it. Here's what I'm going to do. I'm going to walk
uptown in the twilight and mail some letters, and then when I get
home I will put down a few thoughts about the novel.

[Jon wrote the rest of this letter the next mornng, but he didn't
indicate this in the layout of the letter.]

And now it's ten o'clock of a chilly Sunday morning. I fell short of
the typewriter last night because on my way home from the mailbox a man and a woman who live in a big house painted orange
asked me in for tea and pumpkin bread. So I sat in their dark, high-
ceilinged living room as darkness fell on the neighborhood and we
drank tea together. And when I got home I lay down on my couch
and went to sleep.

   —you and I are old;
Old age hath yet his honor and his toil.
Death closes all: but something ere the end,
Some work of noble note, may yet be done.

Part or all of that quotation from Tennyson's "Ulysses" will be the
epigraph of my novel. Probably the last two lines will be sufficient.
[Jon instead chose these lines from Wallace Stevens: "After the final
no there comes a yes / And on that yes the future world depends. /
No was the night." To Dick Brook, July 31, 1977, *My Staggerford
Journal*, p. 93—"I've decided my fourth book will be about heroic
acts in old age. Some work of noble note before the end. Ulysses."]
It's going to be about four or five old people, residents of a nurs-
ing home, who decide to test their capabilities one more time. It's a
sort of a pact, and what brings them to this pact is Smalleye's last
hunt. When Smalleye goes up on that roof and shoots that goose

and is then carted off to the hospital, these four or five residents are inspired to act—each in his own way—lively once more. Gallant, brave, defiant. Rather than sit in chairs waiting for death, they determine to *do* something. A novel-length account, then, of five old folks proving themselves, beginning with Smalleye.

One of my problems will be the temptation to make it purely a series of episodes, a series of short stories. I don't want it to turn out that way. It must build and come together at the end.

Another of my problems at the moment is that I have not settled on the central character. I need somebody like Miles Pruitt [*Staggerford*] to move through the story, half thoughtful, half amused, and bring it all into focus for the reader. I guess that's my biggest task right now: to call up this crucial character. I had thought for a while that it would be a retired priest named Father Ferris, but I am leery of making the thing too Catholic. There's usually enough Catholicism in my writing without plunking the reader down in the lap of a priest. Should it be a retired schoolteacher named Simon P. Arnold?

That way I would have my classroom lore to fall back on whenever I felt the need for reminiscence. Yes, I think that's a good idea. An old schoolteacher.

Another problem. I seem to be writing from an idea, something I've never done before. My writing has always been to string together a story, and sometimes ideas, themes, leaked out of the story along the way. This time I seem to be overly concerned with the theme and making up a tale to fit it. I don't trust that way of writing, because I'm not an idea man; I'm a story man. My hope is that since the Smalleye section of this is already written, the story will be well on its way even as I begin to write and the theme will be sufficiently trodden underfoot by the story.

I have two devices in mind to keep the old folks' home from suffocating the reader. Linda is one device. She's eighteen and good-looking. I'm not sure of her place in the Home. A nurse's aide? More probably she's the girlfriend of Doug Arnold, a young man who visits his grandfather, the retired schoolteacher. Jimmy Carter is the other device. The story takes place in the fall of 1976 and ends on election day. I see these people following the last week of the campaign on the TV in the parlor, each city and state visited by Carter and Ford [Gerald], calling up memories in the minds of the old, causing them to chatter, none of them listening to each other, and then turning back to the TV about the time the news is over. Every night they miss 98% of the news because the Carter-Ford items are on first. They miss the avalanches, the coal-mine cave-ins, the Pope's illness [Pope Paul VI], the drought, and the gay-rights demonstrations, captivated as they are by their memories of the news of fifty years ago.

Dick, are you still reading this letter? I think your obligation ended at the top of page 2. What's more boring than the ill-formed blueprint of an unwritten novel?

Meanwhile. And what, you may ask, will these four or five people *do*? Smalleye has shot his goose and that is all very well, but what have these four or five other residents decided to do? Well, they haven't decided. They have difficulty deciding. And that will take up a lot of pages. I think one guy will run a mile. He used to run a mile a day when he was younger, and he'll probably try it again. One of the women, Bernadette Leep, will make it her business to see that her friend's amputated leg is buried in hallowed ground (Oh, grisly chapter), and another old lady, Dolly Spinner, will confront the parish priest with his misbehavior. She will do this in the confessional, where she will screw up her courage to go and tell him about *his* sins, not hers. That's three. One guy will vote Republican for the first time in his life, then he will spend a sleepless night worrying about what he did, and he will be greatly relieved to hear the next morning that despite his vote Carter won. That's four. I think there must be one more. A large one. And then at the end don't you suppose Smalleye should return? Bandaged and inscrutable, Smalleye will return.

Well, there you have some random ideas about Novel Next. Death closes all, but something ere the end, some work of noble note may yet be done. The town will be Ithaca Mills, Minnesota.

August 23, 1977

Dear Judy [Judith Kern, Jon's editor at Atheneum]:

Having poured so much of myself into *Staggerford*, I'm having trouble extricating myself from it. I'm having a hell of a hard time embarking on my next novel, in other words. But I have fall quarter off and I will put in the required six hours a day sitting here in front of this machine, and I trust something new and worthy will begin to appear on paper. I'm quite sure it's going to be about old folks. In my filing cabinet of short stories and in the back of my mind and in my growing up in the '40s, I've got a lot of old folks, probably enough to populate a novel if I can just figure out what to have them do. My agent has written to inquire what I am writing and I have replied that I will not issue any sort of report until Thanksgiving. If I am not on page 150 of something by Thanksgiving, I'll be the most frustrated man around.

Cabin—Nevis, September 2, 1977

Venables the King. [I don't know Jon's reason for choosing the name Venables as a possible name. Robert Venables (1613-1687) came from Cheshire, England. He distinguished himself in the service of Cromwell's army against the Royalists.] That's my working title for the piece I'm on now. I had a hell of a time getting started. I wrote the first two pages twenty-eight times, which must be a sign of how vaporous the story was in my mind. Then on the twenty-eighth try I broke through to page three, and thence to page thirty, where I am at present. I have gone back to the beginning again, and I'm coming at page thirty once more, taking words out of the mouth of one character and giving them to another, sharpening up the description of a dining room, trying to bring another pretty woman to life—things like that. It has me feeling good.

September 9, 1977, Brainerd

There's a fresh breeze blowing in Brainerd, too. At least in my den. I'm thirty-one pages into this novel and feeling very good about it. In fact, most of the next twenty pages have already been written and my weekend doesn't look busy, so I should be on fifty by Monday. My main character, Simon Peter Venables, age seventy-six, is beginning to interest me a great deal. In response to my probing he is yielding layers of character I didn't know were there.

The beautiful girl in this novel turns out to be his doctor. She's twenty-eight or twenty-nine. She has the clearest of blue eyes and her hair is the color of sunlight on straw. She wins Venables's heart at their first meeting and inspires him to speak at length about some of his past, some of his troubles, and then, later, he overhears her call him a windy old bird. God, he's hurt by that. Those words are like a punch in the chest; he stumbles out of the clinic wide-eyed and slack-jawed.

But through the winter in this village they will grow to be friends, and it will be at her urging that Venables leaves the Norman Home in the spring and goes back to his cabin on the Badbattle River. It will probably be May Day, and the Norman Home will be putting the residents through some stupid celebration, and Venables will doubtless be the King of the May when he stands up to declare his independence. I see him in his crown of crocuses and his mantle of crepe paper roaring "It little profits that an idle king, etc." He's a retired English prof. He would know those lines [the opening line from Alfred, Lord Tennyson's poem, "Ulysses"].

Two weeks ago I was up to page thirty, but then I went back and started over. I had no idea why. I couldn't seem to get to page thirty-one, and I wanted to be writing, so the only thing to do was to mark time by typing over the first thirty pages. That's what I thought it would be: merely marking time. But no, by God, my subconscious was telling me to go back and start over because I had done things wrong, and all the way through the thirty pages this second time, I am inserting new things, things my subconscious knew were missing, but which I did not.

September 14, 1977
That's what my writing has been like yesterday and today. Putt putt putt. Predictable and uninteresting. I suppose I have now worked a

total of twenty days on the novel—I'm on page fifty—and on only two of those days have I felt excitement. I got the old guy remembering an event in his youth, and at the end of each paragraph I had to get up from my chair and do that excited pacing that I remember from *Staggerford*. It turned out to be a five-page flashback and it fell into place very nicely, but when it was over and I brought the reader back to the present, there was a noticeable fading of color, a regrettable lumpishness in the language. Putt putt putt.

September 19, 1977

Rejection. Today the Frederick Warne Co. [originally an English publishing company which printed all of the Peter Rabbit books, the first one in 1902], publishers of *Four Miles to Pinecone*, wrote to say that *The Maiden* isn't a very good book and they don't want it.

Worry. Tomorrow I go to the dentist, and that causes me to worry. I worry about pain. I have feared the dentist since I was five, and I had hoped by writing that godawful toothpulling episode in *Staggerford* I would rid myself of this childish fear. But no.

September 22, 1977

I'm eighty-four pages into *Venables*. If it's like *Staggerford*, there will come a point sometime in the next few weeks when I will see my way clear to the end. Not that months of work will not remain to be done. But it will be joyful work because of my certainty of finishing it. Not my certainty that it will be good, not my certainty that it will be publishable, but my certainty that it is finishable. With *Staggerford* I was on page eighty or so when the end showed up on the horizon, and from that moment on, though I had 370 more pages to write, I knew I could do it. *Venables* is not showing me that much that early. I have the feeling that I will be approaching page 150 before I know if it's finishable. It is because I know both more and less about *Venables*. I know more because there will be a lot of flashbacks into this man's past, and I am already setting several scenes in my head for that purpose (many of them I have fished out of letters to Plymouth) [Jon's letters to Dick Brook in New Hampshire] yet I know less because *Venables* has not yet become as securely fitted into Ithaca Mills as Pruitt was fitted, from the beginning, into Staggerford.

In fact, three days ago a young man stepped into this novel and took a very prominent place in the foreground. The pretty twenty-nine-year-old woman doctor had to fight for her life, for her place in the foreground. It isn't clear yet, whether she will ever be the same, whether she has not suffered a diminishment of place, because while I used to think of her as the front-ranking secondary character, I now think of the young man, Doug Sutherlands [Douglas Mikklessen in the novel], as the front-ranking secondary character. There is only one primary character, and that's Venables himself, book reviewer, retired professor, and man of polite charm and failing memory and, God help him, the old age blues.

September 29, 1977

One of the best pieces of writing advice I ever got was the one I resented most when I got it. One time Gordon Lish at *Esquire* [see April 20, 1978, entry, third paragraph] responded to a story of mine by saying it sounded written. [November 10, 1976, letter to Gordon Lish, fiction editor of *Esquire*: "I have just sold two novels. . . . This is to acknowledge the part you played in my good fortune. After you picked me out of *Prairie Schooner* magazine nearly four years ago, I sent you several stories which were *almost* good enough, culminating in 'The Cheerleader,' which *almost* made it into the big sports issue of '74. . . . How fortuitous that instead of returning 'The Cheerleader' to me you gave it to Harriet Wasserman, who now represents me in the marketplace. How absolutely essential to my career that you were reading my stuff in those days." *My Staggerford Journal*, pp. 83-84.]

"Nothing wrong here except that it sounds written," he scribbled.

I was irritated by that. Of course it sounded written. I wrote it, didn't I? Why shouldn't it sound written. Well, if my reading and writing (mostly my reading) since then have taught me anything, it is that the writing of the '70s must sound extemporaneous. It is the style of our time. It is what is required of today's writer, required by today's reader. I mention this as a footnote to my comment on "Old Bones" [novel being written by Dick Brook]. It does sound written. It sounds extemporaneous. It is good.

I am amazed by these occasional lectures I send to Plymouth. It is not like me to hand down commandments. You must take them only for what they're worth. Maybe they're good for your writing. Maybe they're good for starting a fire in your stove.

October 6, 1977

It is possible to be on page 104 of a novel and still not be certain of whether it's going to work. I'm on page 104. The old man has spent a day with a new acquaintance, a man of twenty-four who is trying to make a comeback after Vietnam, drugs, a failed marriage, and skid row. Now at sunset the old man and the young man are sitting on a rock at the crest of a hill while the young man tells his story. It's like Beverly telling her story to Miles and Miss McGee [*Staggerford*]. It's like the Maiden telling her story to the painter and his wife [*Jemmy*]. Is this the book I am destined to write for the rest of my life? People reaching toward each other across a great span of years? The young needing the old? The old needing the young? I guess it's a worthy theme.

October 11, 1977

It pleases me how I can step into this room at eight in the morning with problems on my mind and slowly slip into my wetsuit and gradually let myself down into the swirls of my fiction and stay there for five hours and then emerge in the early afternoon, having written my eight pages for the day, my two thousand words, my new link in the chain of Venables's life. Today I took page 112 and linked it to page 120.

It pleases me in two ways. For one thing, my fiction takes wing and flies free of the encumbrances of my domestic life, and for another thing, for those five hours every day I, too, fly over (or, to keep my metaphors consistent, swim under) my domestic problems.

I told myself on Sunday morning that I would write for seven days and then pause. Tomorrow I will link page 120 to page 128, the next day 128 to 136, Friday 136 to 144, and Saturday 144 to 152. Then, having reached 150, a landmark I have been looking for since page one, I will take a week off and I will do three things.

I'll paint pictures for two days. I feel the pull of the paint. Too seldom in the last year have I felt the pull of the paint. I have kept up my inventory of paintings by painting under something like duress, but now that I feel like painting, I intend to devote two days to slopping around with my turpentine.

Then there's Fargo. This is one of those promotional trips. A half hour on TV and two autographing sessions at Dalton's [B. Dalton's, an American retail bookstore chain founded in 1966, liquidated in January 2010]. The trouble is that it will entail one day with a lot of empty time and two nights in a motel. To what end? Does Fargo buy books?

Then there's the sizing up of my novel. On page 150 I intend to size up my novel. Like *Staggerford* this novel has interesting episodes and dull episodes and good writing and poor writing, but unlike *Staggerford* something of its essence eludes me. It isn't form exactly, for I am the sort of writer who can't get beyond page five of *anything*, whether my own or someone else's, without a pretty fair grasp of form.

I think I see the form of this thing as well as I saw the form of *Staggerford*. Where the latter was eight days of one autumn, this will be three seasons of one year: autumn, winter, spring. I have already finished autumn (in a rough way of speaking) and I am edging into winter and I have enough episodes in mind (including the all-important climax) to carry me through spring, yet here I am on page 120 and I don't yet know if it's a finishable work. By 150 its finishability (or lack of same) should be apparent.

October 14, 1977
I gave up on that page. For one thing I was tired, and for another thing I had the carbon in backwards. But that was a couple days

ago. Now I feel like a million dollars. I raked leaves all day yesterday. I slept twelve hours last night. I went to a football game this
afternoon. I just now polished my shoes and ate two apples. At this
moment according to my predictions, I should be on page 144. I'm
still on 120. I have lost three days and twenty-four pages of writing.
How come I feel like a million dollars?

I wonder if the name Venables will last. It seems to give people
trouble.

October 30, 1977

Impossible to tell, Dick, if that will remain when I revise *Venables the King*, but that guy Testor came out of nowhere the other
day and allowed me to express what it feels like to be glutted
and unsatisfied because one's project, one's novel, is insufficiently
trimmed down—unwieldy due to elephantiasis of purpose. In the
act of writing, I don't think our purpose should be to aim at uni-
versality; I think it should be to aim at the specific; we shouldn't
try to say what all of life is like; we should say what today is like.
I think occasionally, if we do it just right, our specifics will suggest
universals and the day we describe will suggest all of life, but that
sort of largeness isn't possible (at least in fiction; poetry might be
different) unless we start by thinking small. Anyhow, T. S. Testor
thinks too large. And so do I when I'm beginning a book. I want
it to be the Bible [T. S. Testor—the name of Simon's editor at the
Chronicle].

Son of a bitch. My typewriter broke down. This morning, between pages 151 and 152 my "E" letter quit working right. On the
paper, the lower half of all my "E's" disappeared from view. I typed
seven lines of lower case "E" and got nothing but half moons. My
"E" key seemed to be bent. It looked like something I could fix with
my screwdriver. I picked up my screwdriver and went to work and
broke the "E" key off its arm. "E" of all letters. My Smith Corona
Portable Electric "E"-less. Son of a bitch. Two weeks, the repairman says. I left him the typewriter and went to the college for help.
No help. No extra typewriters. So *Venable* [sic] *the King* is arrested

on page 152. I don't think I can write fiction with my right hand. I haven't tried it for six years. But wait a minute. Why don't I rent a typewriter? I never thought of that when I was in the repair shop this morning. I'll go back tomorrow morning and rent a machine. I'll be back in business. By ten a.m. I'll be on page 153.

I have just decided to junk the name Venables. It's a problem with people. The name Venables. I have tried it out on a few people and you, Dick, are about the only person who had ever heard the name, and you didn't care for the association it called up in your mind. Other people say, "Venables? Don't you mean Venable without the 's'?" One guy, seeing it in print, said, "How do you pronounce that?" The title of a book has to be eminently pronounceable. I've decided to go with an Irish name. Callihan or O'Malley or some such name. Both strike me as much more colorful than Venables. O'Malley the King. I believe O'Malley actually *was* a king, centuries ago, in the west of Ireland. One of my great grandfathers was an O'Malley, from County Mayo. When the potatoes gave out, he came, penniless, to America. Callihan the King. I like the alliteration, and although it wasn't exactly my mother's maiden name (her name was Callinan), it's close enough to make me fond of it. But I think I lean toward O'Malley right now. Let's say it's O'Malley.

And I predict that because this guy's name will now be Irish, he will be a more spirited fellow than heretofore, simply because Irish names excite me. (Venables may be Irish for all I know, but I think of it as English.) If Miss McGee's name had been Smith, she wouldn't have been nearly as forthright and strong.

I am approaching the point in this novel where the hero is going to experience a sort of revelation. He has been elected king of the old folks' home in which he lives—an absolutely empty title thought up by some officious social worker—and at first he shrugs off his kingship as his predecessors have done before him; but after a two-day trip to the city, during which he is dropped suddenly into the hectic mainstream of city life, he sees how tomb-like the Home really is, and arriving there late at night he picks up the dinner bell and rouses his fellow residents and challenges them in a stirring speech to look alive.

November 2, 1977
Lookee here, Dick, a Royal the size of a Patton tank with no electrical current to help me press down the keys. It's exhausting work; I'm out of breath after two lines.

Flannery O'Connor is forever describing some character's revelation (usually religious), and either because I wasn't brought up in the Bible Belt or because mystical experiences have passed me by I think they sound phony. Sebastian Dangerfield is not given to revelations [main character in J. P. Donleavy's *The Ginger Man*, Irish American novelist, 1926-]. Miles Pruitt has no revelations. I guess the closest we come, you and I, to a revelation in our fiction is Mad Jack's determination to end it all [one of Dick's characters]. I am convinced by that one. I'm talking about the sort of revelation that turns the character around on the path of life and sets him off in another direction. A new set of possibilities dawns on someone and, by jingo, life looks different.

Falling in love is probably the most common vehicle for this sort of fresh vision (most common in life as well as in fiction), and that's why love stories are never out of fashion, and if the writer is on his toes, love stories are always convincing. The reader brings his own experience with love to the story, and when the main character falls in love and every day is lovely and all of life is charming, the reader says, "Yes, I believe this; I have been in love and this is the way it is."

But there are other turn-around experiences in life, and although they aren't so common as falling in love, the writer should probably put them in his books once in a while in order to remind the reader that such possibilities exist. I mean, once in a while we run into somebody who decides to stop being a dean and to clear away a lot of brambles so that he can devote more time to writing, and that is very exciting, not to say inspiring, for those who look on [Dick Brooks quit being a dean at Plymouth State College]. But it isn't easy to write about because it is rare. It isn't typical of human nature. Most people sit on their dreams until they are flat.

Another swatch of fiction, in which I will practice using the name O'Malley [Jon used Jay O'Malley as his main character in the short story, "Underground Christmas," and in his unfinished novel, "Jay O'Malley"]. O'Malley is in the city and his car is broken down. Except for taxi rides away and back, he is virtually a prisoner in this shopping mall near the garage where his car is.

November 4, 1977
Oh, how much easier it is to read than to write, how page ninety-four where my bookmark, a toothpick, sticks out. The novel is James Baldwin's *Go Tell It on the Mountain*, and my lazy mind begs me to drop into my reading chair by the window and pick up the novel. "You can finish the book by noon," my lazy mind tells me, but I know my lazy mind for the deceitful wretch it is and I say, "Get thee behind me, thou deceitful, lazy wretch," and I pick up the folder containing a fraction of my own novel. The fraction is one-third, if my estimate of the finished product is correct. I'm guessing that the finished product will amount (like *Staggerford*) to something between 400 and 450 pages. I had originally thought that I would write something 300 pages long, but that was before I started writing it. I pull my hard chair up to my writing table and I begin reading what I wrote yesterday, and here I resist the second temptation, which is to do this revising in my convertible reading chair by the window. Just as my lazy mind first wanted that chair, now my lazy body wants it. "You could just as well be doing this revising in that nice chair by the window," my lazy body tells me, but I know my lazy body for the deceitful wretch it is, and I pretend to be too absorbed to listen to this urging.

Yesterday's work amounts to five pages, by no means a record-breaking day's production, but at least average—if not better, considering the eliteness of this rented typewriter. I spend an hour revising and thinking. It is nine-thirty. I make myself another cup of coffee and I roll paper into my machine and I am ready to roll. I sit for a half hour with my arms crossed, thinking. I make another cup of coffee. I sit for another half hour, thinking.

It's what I have been doing since Labor Day, sitting on this hard chair making up a story in my head. You wouldn't think that would be enough to make a man happy, keep a man happy all his life, but damn it, Dick, I don't know what I'd rather do with my life than sit here moving my eyes from window to wall and make up stories in my head. I sit motionless for another half hour, then make myself another cup of coffee, and I begin to write. It is eleven o'clock. I write five pages between eleven o'clock and three. I stop midway to eat a cracker and a candy bar and I stop again, about two, to answer the phone. It is Brad Teslow, a former student [Brainerd Community College], who wants me to autograph two copies of *Staggerford*. I tell him how to find me and I return to the typewriter but his impending visit makes writing impossible. I pace through the rooms of my house. I move from window to window like a sailor's wife watching for a mast.

He arrives in an orange Vega and I call to him as he heads for the house across the street. I lead him into my den and he hands me the books and suggests what I should inscribe. They are for friends of his in Minneapolis, twin sisters, and he says one of them is having a birthday.

"What about the other one?" I ask, and we laugh like ninnies.

The inscribing out of the way, we talk about college classes and real estate. Brad has a real estate license. Brad has started many college classes but finished few. He is thinking about taking ten credits; I talk him into thirteen, which is uncharacteristic of me, for even in the role as advisor at the college I seldom care what students do.

If you want to know the truth, Dick, I seldom care what anybody does, and this thought lingers in my mind after Brad drives away in his orange car. I am downright non-directive (a favorite term of a counselor I know). Generally speaking, people can do what they please and that's fine with me. I care too little. I tolerate too much. If I had stronger opinions about what other people do with their lives, I would have been a better father, especially during these latter years when my kids were in their late teens. I don't seem to stand for much in their eyes. At least in *my* eyes I don't appear to stand for much in their eyes. Maybe I stand for more than I think I do, but it can't be much more.

I'm going to drop out of college, a student tells me. Fine, I say. I'm going to move to the cities where drugs are easier to get, another student tells me. Goodbye, I say. I'm going to take two thousand dollars of my savings account and invest it in a Mexican company that makes hovercraft for mountain climbing. Invest, I say. But to get back to my day ...

It is three and I have written five pages and all that remains to do is to pick them up from the floor (when I finish a page I pull it from my typewriter and drop it onto the floor) and put them in order and clip them to the pages in my folder. I calculate that today I have passed the 40,000 word mark. The last 7,000 words have gone very smoothly, but I see trouble ahead. At about 45,000 I'm going to have to do some clever inventing. Inventiveness is not my strong suit. This will require several hours of sitting here with my arms folded and looking from window to wall.

November 10, 1977

I had a student once whose husband was in a coma. Her name was Betty, and I found her very attractive. Her husband had had a stroke at about the age of twenty-five, and when I first knew Betty he had been lying senseless for eleven months. Although she was the mother of a three-year-old, she looked like the rest of the eighteen-year-olds in my composition class, but when it came her turn to read her paper for the week, you could see the rest of the students pull back slightly from her, as if they were backing up from the edge of a chasm.

Her paper was a supplication: "Oh please, Kent, open your eyes and look past me for just a moment so that I know you recognize me when I talk to you. I have just computed the number of times I have come to this bedside and sat in this chair for forty-five minutes and told you what Meg [their daughter] and I have been doing since our last visit. I have done this 252 times. During the first two months I came twice a day except for the day I moved from the house into the apartment and the day Meg was so sick with a cold. Then the next two months I came once a day and never missed a single visit. I made lists of things that happened during the day so I wouldn't forget to tell you everything. I've got those lists at home in a box. Then after the fourth month, at the urging of the doctor and my mother, I cut my visits down to three times a week.

'Let's face facts,' the doctor said. 'Kent hasn't heard a word you said to him in all this time. I'm afraid you're going to have some serious problems of your own if you insist on coming in here day after day and spilling out your life to someone who can't understand what you say. I'm afraid you're going to lose touch with reality. Don't come quite so often, Betty; if there's any change you'll be the first to know.'

And so for the past seven months I have come to see you only three times a week, but even at that my visits now total 252, and I feel guilty to have to admit that my purpose in coming here is no longer to visit you, Kent, but to continue this recitation of my life. Today's installment begins with my enrollment at the community college in Brainerd."

Right now I don't know if I'm writing a letter or a novel, Dick, for I have need of this girl in my novel, and maybe as I describe her to you I am moving from page 168 to page 169. And what are we to make of this long-standing habit of mine of centering my attention each semester on a particular co-ed? Indeed, what are we to make of this series of letters which seems to be a catalog of pretty girls I have known. My second adolescence? My change of life? I think neither. I think I am merely auditioning these girls for possible use in fiction. I guess that's innocent enough.

But anyhow, to get back to Betty, there was composition class, where her classmates were awestruck by the hopelessness of her situation, and the next quarter there was creative writing, where she began for the first time to shift her attention from that hulk on the bed and her smiles came easier and she picked up a boyfriend.

Tom was on-again off-again, both as a student and as a boyfriend. It was obvious in her eyes that she was Tom's if Tom wanted her, but the strange thing was he wanted her only at intervals. They moved into a house together and then he moved out. They went to California together, then they came home separately. Maybe he was put off by the three-year-old daughter she always carried on her arm. Maybe he was spooked by that comatose hulk in the rest home, afraid that the hulk would momentarily open his eyes and sit up and stretch and talk in sentences. Then, for Tom, it would be so long, Betty.

To make a long story short, toward the end of that school year when Betty was a freshman and often on my mind, the hulk died. I saw it in the evening paper, HULK DIES, or some such headline. When I met her three days later in school, her relief and grief were evident, for she greeted me with red eyes and a broad smile.

"Be strong," I said. I have arrived at this phrase, be strong, to cover all situations, Dick.

You may recall that Miles Pruitt never knew what to say to people who were in the extremities of pain or sorrow. That was because I hadn't yet thought up the phrase "be strong." Miles Pruitt was me, Dick. I never knew what to say either. But you may recall that at the end of the book Miss McGee's former students come up to her and offer her their condolences and what they say is, "Be strong."

The instant I heard them say that to her I knew I was saved. From now on, I determined, I would say that to people in trouble, in pain, in sorrow, in jail, in the hospital, in the ditch. It's a much better phrase than "I'm sorry." I've never found it easy to say—in funeral parlors, in cemeteries, or at beheadings—"I'm sorry." It was what everybody else was saying, and by the time it came my turn to say it, the phrase seemed to have been drained of its meaning.

It's hell sometimes to be a writer, Dick, and shy of overused phrases. I realize that "I'm sorry" is what the bereaved wants to hear, expects to hear, and it's a pretty good phrase for all people on all occasions, but I can't say it. So for years I said nothing, and the anguish in my face as I stepped up to the bereaved and said nothing was taken to be a sign of my sorrow, but actually it was a sign of how hard I was straining to find a substitute for "I'm sorry."

Well, now I've found it. I clasp the bereaved by the upper arm and I say, "Be strong." When they hear that, you can almost feel strength enter their body. Hearing the word strong makes people strong. If you called me up some night, Dick, and said, "Be strong," then I would really be strong. Not that I am not strong already. What I mean is I would be even stronger. I would finish my novel before winter quarter begins.

So Betty, red-eyed and smiling, stood facing me beside the mimeograph machine. "Kent died," she said.

"Yes, I saw it in the paper."

She closed her eyes and there was a slight seepage through her lashes.

I said, "Be strong, Betty."

She nodded tearfully, still smiling. She wiped her eyes. "I am," she said and she walked away.

Now she was free to be Tom's, and Tom rented a house and moved into it with Betty and the three-year-old, and they lived there very happily for part of a month, and then Tom moved out and moved on, West, I think. Then Betty moved out and moved on, East.

The hulk is dead. Where is Tom? Where is Betty?

I didn't get myself involved very much in that story, did I, Dick? It's all about Betty and the hulk and Tom, yet if it's going to be any good in my novel my hero is going to have to be more important than the hulk and Tom. He's going to have to do more than stand there by the mimeograph machine and say, "Be strong." At the very least he's going to have to undress her and make love.

Yes, in these letters I have been auditioning girls for fiction. Fiction needs pretty girls. Pretty girls need fiction, too, I suppose, but not as much as homely girls need fiction. The first round of auditions is over now, Dick, and I am posting the call-back notice.

I hope I haven't thrown away my grade books from my days of teaching high school. I have been fond of saying that in my old grade books every name is a story, a potential short story, a potential novel episode, and I have envisioned those lists of names in my mind, twenty, twenty-five, thirty names to a page, and yet I can't put my hands on the grade books. I know I saved them, for I have seen them in recent years, but now I can't find them. They may be upstairs behind a door I hate to open because it leads to a realm of spiders and mice.

Yesterday snow, today grosbeaks.

Be strong.

November 12, 1977

Let's say Hemingway and I and Robby Wilson [friend of Dick Brook] and Old Man Wittgenstein [Ludwig Wittgenstein, Austrian British philosopher, 1889-1951] were witness to that scene in your office where the department chairman broke down, and let's say that after it was over we each set about describing it in writing, and when we finished we would have five accounts, including yours. The more those five resembled each other, the less could be said of us as writers; the more they differed, the better writers we would be, for it would prove that each of us values our filtering mechanism and we keep it in good repair.

In *American Artist* a few years ago they sent eleven watercolorists to a farm and asked them each to paint a picture of the barn and the surrounding trees. I paged through the results, and although I saw the barn eleven times, I was no less interested in #11 than I was in #1. And I suspect that if I were taken to the spot and shown the barn itself, it would interest me less than these eleven visions of it.

Yes, I think Betty, the wife of the comatose hulk, will work in my novel. Callahan will marry her. (Callahan is now my hero's name, Dick; *Callahan the King* is now the title.) Her name will be Trudy. She will be childless, both with the hulk and with Callahan. She will be a single-minded woman, concentrating all her attention, all her good will, all her energies, on no more than one thing at a time. It comes, at least in part, from that year of sitting at the bedside of the hulk.

November 13, 1977

How can this girl be named Trudy? I don't know any Trudy's except two or three thick matronly types, and my experience teaches me that that would make my fictional Trudy thick and matronly at twenty-four. I have unconsciously stereotyped every given name, male and female, and when I name one of my fictional characters, I can't help the dreadful weight of associations that name calls to mind.

November 15, 1977

I think her name will be Carolyn and the hulk's name will be Donald. Donald had a job in a granite quarry, and he traveled to work and back on a motorbike. He had made it himself. It was a regular bicycle with the pedals removed and a small gasoline engine mounted between the wheels, and it ran a hundred miles on a gallon of gas, which in those days cost nineteen cents. This was in 1940. During the first weeks of their marriage, Carolyn worried about Donald when he was at work, because he worked with explosives and she had been to the quarry herself and had seen him going about his business deep in the pit, with huge chunks of granite swinging over his head on a crane. Between the quarry and the highway was a rough stretch of dirt road that wound through a wood, and it was here, in the twilight after a heavy rain, that Donald, at thirty-five miles an hour, steered straight into a deep chuckhole that stopped the bike and sent him flying over the handlebars. He hit a tree and broke his neck.

   Dick, I have been thinking about interrupting my novel to write a couple short stories. Part of my reason is to prove myself. Since publishing *Staggerford* I've written a novel that doesn't seem to be publishable (*The Maiden*) [published in 1980 as *Jemmy*], and so now I want to see what my agent might do with a short story. Another reason is money. I haven't had a paycheck now for about nine weeks, and that fantastic price the national mags pay for stories looms large in my thinking.

November 18, 1977

Dear Dick, See that bit at the top of the page? See this good old pica type? My beloved Smith Corona is back, its "e" in place once again—or almost in place—it looks slightly raised and tipped. But a raised, tipped "e" is better than no "e" at all, said Gerard Manley Hopkins [English poet, Jesuit priest, 1844-1889] in a poem called "Inscape on a Skateboard." [I could not find a Hopkins poem by this title—this probably was Jon's humor.]

"Oh not heavenlier 'e' raised and tipped/Nor for unforeshortened greenglow haze." Those, if memory serves, were his very words.

What I like about this machine is that I can look down on what I write. I'm in command. That machine I rented for two weeks had a superstructure like a battleship, and my fiction was always at eye level, staring me down. Now watch me sail through my novel. Haste is now essential, for it's countdown time: I'll be back in the classroom on December 12. I'll go from writing what Callahan said to Vera [?] the night they were married to teaching the difference between to, too, and two. On the night of December 11, I'm going to count my pages, count my words. Oh, I hope it's page 225. Oh, I hope it's word 58,000.

November 25, 1977

Rex Stout said that he wrote detective novels rather than serious novels because in writing serious novels one must reveal his own personality and character and he didn't think his personality and character were sufficiently attractive. I don't know anything about Rex Stout's personality and character, but I do know that I stand revealed here and there in *Staggerford*, and I remember how as I worked on it I first discovered parts of myself being sucked onto the paper. I had not expected that. I thought one could get serious about writing and keep himself to himself. I had done it in *Pinecone*, why not in *Staggerford*? But no, one can't hold back, and I have come to believe it's best this way. To see the writer in the writing is what makes reading worthwhile.

I suppose we all have traits that lend themselves to storytelling and other traits that impede storytelling. I suppose one of my traits of the former kind is a high regard for stories, a lifelong appetite for tales told by people I meet. I suppose one of my traits of the latter kind is a reflexive pulling back from anything new. To speak to a stranger, to enter an unfamiliar building, to board a bus on a route I haven't taken before—in any new experience, my first, unthinking reaction is no. Usually I can easily overcome this reluctance but that's not the same as eagerly seeking out the unfamiliar, the novel, the change of scene and viewpoint.

Sitting down at a coffee counter, I harbor the hope that the persons on my right and left will keep their noses buried in the newspapers and not try to strike up a conversation. This foot-dragging attitude of mine has a bearing on writing, and it is that I would much rather work on a second draft than a first; I would rather revise yesterday's work than push forward with today's; in every word that I put down I have to overcome a tiny voice that says no. NoI nohave noto nolop nooff noa nocertain nonegation nothat nocomes nowith noevery noword noI nocall noto nomind.

November 27, 1977

I stopped this letter to have the flu. It was a streamlined case, the kind you always want if you have to have the flu. It struck in midafternoon, caused me to shiver and puke through the night, gave me a small headache in the morning, and twenty-four hours later I was out shoveling snow. I think "flu" is one of the homeliest words in the language; it sounds gaseous. Researchers may someday discover that what makes the flu contagious is that people say the word "flu" to each other. The virus is in the word, spoken at close range.

This is my father's eighty-first birthday.

Look at that last period. Ever since I got this machine back from the repairman, my periods have been irregular. Now I'll have to take it to a gynecologist.

December 6, 1977

This is now Tuesday of a week with nothing on my calendar, the last week of my leave of absence, and I feel like bringing it to a close with a bang. I have decided that tomorrow morning I will do what I did the day I finished writing *Staggerford*, and what I have done on certain other celebratory occasions: I will go out to a restaurant and eat breakfast.

Yesterday I finished the first draft of a short story unrelated to my novel. I guess (on page two of this letter) that it would end on page twelve and it ended on page seventeen, which is about the upper limit of a short story these days, and because I wrote it with *McCall's* in mind I'm not sure it avoids being sappy and a little bit contrived. The ending needs a good deal more work. I will type up another draft and then during Christmas break still another, and if it holds up under all that construction, I will mail it to my beloved agent. It was fun. I haven't written a short story for a year and a half, and it was fun.

I think so rarely of suitable plots. Plot is my weak point, even in this one, a plot that still needs a lot of bracing and support. My characters come easy, plot comes hard. "No News in Culver Bend" is the title. It's a Christmas story [published in *Keepsakes & Other Stories*, Afton Press, 1999].

So anyhow, three days remain of my quarter off, Dick. A most excellent quarter. Very little in the way of frivolity, but duty hath its rewards, and here I sit with fifty thousand words of *Callahan* behind me. Each week I will try to chisel out some time to add to that total, and if I can advance the plot in spite of teaching, it will be because I have that substantial foundation to work on. Goodby, leave of absence, goodby.

My electric pica is back in the repair shop, and you are reading the work of a manual, finger-bruising Royal.

Brainerd Community College, December 15, 1977

I'm at the college now. I'm sitting in my office at my office typewriter. I'm sitting on my office chair surrounded by my office walls—an office so small that two people can be in here only if one quits breathing. There isn't room for the expansion of two breasts, four lungs. It's a claustrophobic office.

My free time is over, past, gone. It was nice. I will do it again as soon as I get enough money. I wrote fairly steadily from Labor Day till last Sunday and produced fifty thousand words on two hundred pages. Coming back to the classroom after that is like stepping ashore after spending a day in a canoe. The solid ground feels so natural, so steady; but it won't get you anywhere.

Our football coach just stopped by my office to tell me that he has spent the day stamping out ignorance. Says his foot hurts.

December 27, 1977

Dear Gail [former student, "a pretty girl in Albuquerque," in August 27, 1978, entry],

Since writing *Staggerford*, I have written a shorter novel, which no one wants to publish, and I am now halfway through yet another—something more ambitious than *Staggerford* in which (so far) I am well pleased. To get to page two hundred (where it stands at the present time), I took off fall quarter and wrote to my heart's content, but now the need of a paycheck has drawn me back into the classroom, and I may not get to page 201 until next summer.

The classroom, though not so exhilarating as writing, is really not a bad place to be. It's warm in there, and on a good day there are enough minds awake at one time to keep things interesting. But oh how I love to be sitting here at this machine. If there weren't so many people depending upon me to do other things, if I were responsible to no one but myself, I would sit here typing till the day I died. [This is just about what Jon did. Jon's morning schedule would be to get up at 8 A.M., take a shower, dress, and then work on a novel. On the morning that he was taken to the hospital, March 17, 2008, he was planning to follow this same routine, but after he took two steps, both he and his wife Gretchen knew that he would have to leave for the hospital. He died at 3:20 a.m., Holy Thursday, the 20th.]

Writing is bottomless. The more you write, the deeper you are lured, and you find yourself descending to level under level, this level rewarding, the next level frustrating, the one under that rewarding, the one under that frustrating. Down, down. How deep do you wish to go, Gail? So deep that you begin to wish you had made no commitments in your life except to your pen and paper? So deep that you want to marry the piece of fiction you're working on? Those are some of the levels, Gail. Dive in. Or turn back while there's still time.

January 1, 1978
It is no longer possible to buy *Staggerford* over the counter, *Pinecone* never did appear in a bookstore that I know of, *Jemmy* is unpublishable, my last travel article on the West of Ireland is unpublishable, two of the three short stories I sent my agent last year are unpublishable, my beloved Smith Corona has been a month in the repair shop without being looked at, and I feel great. Don't ask me why. I sometimes think my writing, and my happiness at writing, follow an annual cycle. I seem to crank it up in the fall and go to beat hell in the winter and fade away in the spring. I haven't made good use of a summer yet. Right now I am at the height of my powers. I am invincible. If someone else hadn't beat me to it, I would begin tonight to write *Moby Dick*.

January 15, 1978, "A" [Jon had both this and the following entry dated the same with no explanation. I added the "A" and "B."]
Jemmy has at last attracted the attention of an editor. But I must be guarded in my joy. This editor has written three pages enumerating its flaws. I think she is right in most cases. It is a flawed work. Something happens to the characters about midway through the novel; they become robots or something; they cease to be convincing; the theme seems to change. I spend three hours reading the ms. I ponder. I make notes. I conclude that the first third is sound. The second third needs adjustments, one or two large ones, several small ones. The last third must be entirely rewritten. I think I

can do it. I have faith in my ability to iron out flaws once they are pointed out. The question is, when shall I do it? Shall I interrupt *Callahan* and go to work on it, and produce a fresh draft of *Jemmy* by spring, say April? That's what I will do. For *Callahan* has been interrupted already. I haven't added a word to it since December 12. I let it lie for a while in order to write short stories, and I might as well let it lie a while longer, say four months, before I go to work on the second half. And how could I work on *Callahan* knowing that an editor in a receptive mood was waiting to read a new version of *Jemmy*. Amazing, isn't it, that a person 1400 miles away, a person whose voice you have never heard and whose face you have never seen, can dominate your thinking like that, can alter your course like that.

I sip a cup of hot chocolate as I page through the new *New Yorker*. Ah, a review of Evelyn Waugh's *Diaries*, which I am reading each night as I lie in bed, the volume resting heavily on my chest and crashing to the floor when I grow drowsy. The reviewer, V. S. Pritchett, seems to be amazed at the large number of pages produced by a lifelong diarist, and I am amazed at this amazement. Doesn't he realize how voluminous one can be simply by applying oneself steadily to writing? Our Brainerd-Plymouth correspondence, for example. Our 1977 letters alone fill a notebook. A shelf of Maugham is a big one, and Maugham wrote only three hours a day. Life is short but the days are many.

January 15, 1978, "B"

Now it's Sunday noon. Although the sky is almost light enough to cast shadows, it is snowing lightly—a snow so fine you can't see it without your glasses. Soon I will get into my blue car and drive to Staples and spend the afternoon with my parents; probably I will paint a picture over there. I keep my paints in Staples now, for I find it impossible to paint in my den. So overpowering is my desire to write, that a secondary pursuit, such as painting, can't be accommodated in a room this small. The only way I can paint in this room is if I paint with my left hand while typing with my right. We will probably eat supper on TV trays while watching the first half of the Super Bowl, and my mother will make two or three condemnatory remarks about the length of the football season, and my father will say (as he has said every Sunday since the regular season ended in early December) that this game brings the season to a close, and he will really believe he is speaking the truth, and he will be more surprised than my mother next Sunday when he discovers the Pro-Bowl on TV.

Why do my father and a hundred million other men like to watch football on TV? I think it's the quality of exaggeration. It shows confrontations between people in an exaggerated way. No verbal confrontations, no subtle gestures—just knocking each other down. And I think writing, to be popular, should not be too subtle. It should have some of this exaggeration we find in football—jarring events, exciting turns of plot, broad humor. Once every fifty pages there should be a fantastic pass reception or a shoestring tackle. Once every hundred pages there should be a loose live ball on the goal line.

I don't like rooms without windows. My office at the college has no window. I am negotiating for an office with a window. The offices with windows are very cold, but I would rather have bronchitis than claustrophobia.

I may never drink again. Two months have passed since I last had a drink, and not once have I felt a strong urge. When I have a medium or weak urge, all I need do is imagine the headache that would result, and the urge is gone.

If I were a sparrow depending on me for seed and suet, I would be a very disillusioned bird. I would sit on a twig and shake my head, the way that sparrow outside my window is doing at this moment. He looks over at my feeder, then he turns to face my window and opens his beak and closes it without making a peep, as if to say that my criminality makes him speechless. I see a story entitled "The Man Despised by Birds."

January 31, 1978

You may be at the University, but it is here at BCC [Brainerd Community College] that you see the University Women, the AAUW, showing up every morning for another day of sewing, ticket-selling, flat-painting, telephoning, and learning to dance on their toes. This, of course, is at the behest of our theater director, in preparation for *Fiddler* [*on the Roof*]. They bring their babies and set them in corners to cry. Just now I went into the hall for a drink, and a little boy grabbed me around my calves and said, "Lift me up there so I can drink." I have no idea how old he was because I can't judge ages that young any more, but he was out of the womb and not yet in school. I lifted him up for a drink, then he followed me into my office and said, "Give me some candy." I had a Payday on my desk, and I said, "That belongs to somebody else." Think of it, an out-and-out lie, and being shamed into it by an infant. "Then give me some money," he said. "I have no money," I lied. "Yes, you have," he said, hitting me in the pocket and jingling my change. "No money for you," I said. "Let me sit in your chair," he said, climbing into my chair. "Go away," I said, and he looked at me in disbelief. "You must go because I have work to do" (another lie), and I steered him out and shut the door.

February 6, 1978

I traveled to Rochester in 1948 [fifteen years of age] for my first, and last, art lesson. I registered and bought the required sketch pad and sat down among two dozen artists, mostly adults, and listened to a lecture on drawing, then tried to draw in the sketchbook what the lecturer advised (I still have that page from that sketchbook, and it strikes me as more geometrical than artistic), and then I got up and moved around the room, and when I returned to my bench there was a fresh oil painting lying there and I didn't see it, and I sat down on it. I forget how the woman registered her dismay—by shriek or sob—but I remember her dismayed, indeed, and rather elderly. When I stood up I lifted quite a bit of the paint off the surface of the picture, mostly blue and green, for it was a landscape, and I

went directly to the door and outside into the mild spring evening
and passed the time until my father came to pick me up by walking
the streets of the neighborhood and watching the passing cars and
listening to the starling shit splatter on the sidewalk. What kind
of a painter was that woman? Highly accomplished? A beginner?
Was this painting on the seat of my pants a work she dashed off
that very afternoon in order to have something for class, or was it
the labor of months? One thing I was certain of, and that was that
I would never be around to learn more about her. I would never
again enter that building, so mortified was I, so abashed.

The other day my dad asked me to deliver a note to the Staples
City Clerk, and I went downtown and into the city hall, and the
smell of the place transported me back to my childhood. I had two
childhoods: an early one in Staples and a later one in Plainview
[captured in *Grand Opening*], and this was the building in which I
had gone as a child, to the library. I went there with my mother in
1937 through 1942, and the smell was always the same, a smell of
books and old city records perhaps but mostly the smell that came
with the building, an overheated, public building smell with a dash
of dust. One whiff and I was back there forty years, sitting on the
floor for story hour, sitting at the base of the grandfather clock with
the loud, relentless tick—a clock so impressive in his walnut height
with a tick so stern and slow that I have never since felt the need to
investigate the nature of time; the tick of that clock taught me all
I needed to know. Time was stern, time was relentless, and it said
to me in a slow, loud tock, "Listen here, son, there's no outwitting
me. I am Time and I am very large and I control what happens in
the world, and although you are today only four, you will soon
be forty-four and then in the blink of an eye you'll be eighty-four
and your teeth will be gone." And the librarian's voice droned on,
reading us some tale I had been read at home countless times, a
lusterless tale that hadn't impressed me all that much—I think it
was about Rapunzel—but which had evidently been good enough
to be preserved in a very old book, a book in the librarian's hand
and under the very nose of Time, a book Time might someday get

control of but obviously hadn't yet. Was that the beginning of my urge to write? [Jon certainly would have felt honored and gratified by Central Lakes College naming its library the Jon Hassler Library on September 28, 2008. Jon had died on March 20, 2008.]

Shall I go to England in June, or shall I not? I am hung up on that question because the reasons on both sides are so compelling. The reasons for going are (1) I have a cousin in Scotland with whom I could stay for a few days, (2) my novel will be brought out by a London publisher in June, (3) a couple of friends from here will be touring England in June. The reason for my not going is that I am broke and in debt. I can't pay my bills. My quarter off put me in a class with panhandlers and ragpickers.

February 20, 1978

"How's your writing going?" a good-looking neighborhood wife asked—a black-haired, large-eyed, slim-flanked, highly desirable neighborhood wife.

"I'm at the top of my powers," I told her. I did a cartwheel on her front sidewalk.

"How's the writing going?" asked a high school English teacher, a bearded beetle-browed man in a corduroy suit.

"I'm at the height of my powers," I said as I did a few steps of Balling the Jack in the foyer of the high school.

But now it's the 20th of February, Dick, and I have been dulled and blunted by seven weeks of school. Asked about my writing now, I blink and flinch and pick my nose.

"How's your writing going?" says the highly desirable housewife.

I am lugging a briefcase of student papers past her house, and I slip on the ice and stumble into a snowbank.

"How's the writing going?" the bearded teacher asks. Suddenly I am mashed into the carpet of the foyer by thirty sophomores stampeding out of a classroom.

I'm dulled, blunted, filched, and picked.

But this summer, Dick. Ah, this summer watch my smoke, as they used to say in the funny papers. A high-gear summer if you ever saw one. I am not going to Britain. I am not going to teach at the Bemidji State Writers' Conference. I'm going up to the cabin and plug in my typewriter and let loose of a lot of fiction. One day in July you and Carol will come driving down the Belle Taine road, searching me out, and you will see this thin column of smoke angling up out of the birches, and you will say, "I recognize that smoke, that's the smoke of a smoking Smith Corona, Hassler's Smith Corona," and the smoke, like a star, will guide you to my stable.

February 28, 1978

I went into the president's office yesterday [not the same president referred to in the May 20, 1977, entry] and I said, "Let's talk about my future." He smiled. I sat down. "On the one hand there is my writing," I said, cupping my hands, palms up, over my left knee, as though holding a heavy head of cabbage. "On the other hand, there is my teaching," I said, moving the cabbage over to my right knee. "And I can't seem to do both at the same time."

He smiled.

"Now, what I'd like to know is how you feel about my taking a quarter off next year."

He didn't see any problem.

"Or what about this provision in our contract where a guy drops to 75% of a full load. How about if I did that?"

He hadn't heard of such a provision. He drew out his master contract and found the page and read about it. "Not a bad arrangement," he said. "Could you write while teaching 75% of the time?"

"I don't know. It might be possible if my classes were all in the afternoon or evening."

"We could work that out. We always need evening teachers."

"But, on the other hand, a quarter off gives me full time to write. That would be better. But I'd be giving up more pay." It became clear to both of us at this point that I didn't know what I wanted for next year, and our conversation ended with my promising to tell him what I wanted within the next two weeks.

I guess what I want, must have, is a quarter off, and it sounds like I can get it. Fall quarter. September, October, November. Finish *Jemmy*. Finish *Callahan*. Start another.

March 19, 1978

The previous night I dreamed that I was to model a suit in a fashion show. I went to the show thinking I was to talk about my book, but when I got there I was told to go backstage and put on the suit the emcee was wearing. I went backstage and waited for the arrival of the suit, a heavy gray suit which the emcee was taking off onstage. It took me a long time to put it on, and everyone was very impatient with me, even disgusted. The emcee's legs were a lot longer than mine, and I had to pull them up to my armpits and fasten the belt over my chest. How much I resemble Anthony Perkins, I said to myself, as I stepped out on the stage [American film and stage actor, 1932-1992].

I guess Anthony Perkins was in my dream because on a recent evening I was standing in the air terminal outside Watertown, South Dakota, and a TV with faulty color (everyone's face was the color of V-8 Juice) was showing some sort of tribute to Henry Fonda, and the man I was with said that he had enjoyed *Murder on the Orient Express*. (I don't remember what the connection was between the movie and Henry Fonda), and I said I liked it too. I liked seeing Anthony Perkins after not having seen him for many years.

The last time I had seen Anthony Perkins was the night my elder son was born, May 26, 1957. I went to the hospital to see my wife and son; then I went to Bagley, seventeen miles away, to see *Fear Strikes Out*, the life story of Jimmy Piersall, the crazy man in the Red Sox outfield. Perkins was Piersall.

I never saw the Red Sox play baseball, but I saw the Boston Braves. This was at the Polo Grounds in New York in 1948. I was spending the month of August with Uncle Neil and Aunt Ruth and my cousins O'Neil and Peter in the luxurious fastness of Westchester County, and I was being driven places and shown things that I daresay no one of my age (fifteen) and place (Plainview) had ever

seen before. Also in that house that summer was Great-aunt Eliza-
beth, a peerless great-aunt if there ever was one. She took me to
Radio City Music Hall and by ferry to Staten Island. She took me
to the top of the Empire State Building where I put my Brownie
Kodak up to my eye and snapped what I thought was going to be
the picture of my life, and when I got it back from the drug store,
the prints were disappointingly small; all of New York City was
crushed into a rectangle not much larger than a postage stamp.

March 27, 1978

Rest. I must have been given, in my upbringing, a hell of a large
dose of the work ethic, the manual-labor ethic. How else do I explain the guilt I feel when people around me are working—digging
in the garden, running the vacuum cleaner, painting the neighbor's
house—and I am sitting here writing? When the sun is shining and
world outside my window is busy—the neighbors raking, birds
nesting—I feel like a shirker. I don't want to rake or paint a house,
or dig in the garden, or build a nest, yet the sight of such industry
makes me feel as if I should want to rake, paint, dig, and build.
Maybe that's why nasty days please me so when I'm writing. I can't
be expected to be out there raking when it's raining, can I? I can't
be expected to build myself a nest in a tree in the middle of winter,
can I? What I'm getting at, Dick, is the fact that in order for me to
write, leisure is necessary not only for me but for the world at large.
If, when I sat down to write, the whole world lay down for a nap,
I'd feel a hell of a lot better about writing. I would be getting ahead
of the world.

Flaws. The foregoing partly explains why I can better endure
long stretches of cloudy weather than I can long stretches of sun. The
world is so intimidatingly up and doing on sunny days. But that's
only part of the explanation. The other part is something I've felt
for a year or so and haven't been able to put into words. It has to
do with my feeling inferior to good weather. This goes beyond feeling inferior to the people who are industrious in good weather. This
is feeling inferior to the weather itself. I remember trying to explain

this to a neighbor last fall. He's a photographer, and he stood at my back door asking if he could use my red maple as a background for a portrait he was to do. It was a dark and misty day. He said, "What a nasty day," and I said, "Yes, I love it." You realize, Dick, there aren't many neighbors you could say this to, but this neighbor is patient with my unorthodox ways. He said, "You do? What do you love about it?" I said I loved not having to be my best for a change. We had been having a lot of crisp, golden days—autumn days so still and bright and lovely that I was beginning to feel tarnished and unworthy, and I was greatly relieved when the sky darkened and the mist came brushing against my window. The pressure was lifted from me. I no longer had to shine. What strange spell or occurrence in my childhood or wombhood accounts for my feeling challenged by the sun? Anyhow, I have been trying to put this in words for some time (I think my neighbor the photographer only partially understood), and now I find that the poet Philip Larkin has already said it. He's got a line in his latest collection of poems in which he says that the trouble "with perfect weather is our falling short." That's exactly what I've been meaning to say. I was glad to find it said in so few words, and I was glad to learn that I wasn't one of a kind.

March 29, 1978

The last word in this version of *Jemmy* is "family." I just now wrote it. The first word is "Out." Between "Out" and "family" are 55,250 other words too numerous to mention. Suffice it to say they include a lot of *the's* and *and's*.

April 1, 1978

My tolerance for administrative duties is nil. To have to handle file folders or make a business call on the telephone goes against something very fundamental in my nature. Put me on a committee and circuits go awry in my head. As little as writing is allied to classroom duties, I believe it is much less allied to administrative duties.

Let me go back to the original subject, administration. There I was at twenty-two entering graduate school at the University of

North Dakota, scarcely aware of what graduate school was all about, entering perhaps more out of parental pressure than ambition, my University-trained mother and my sixth-grade educated father urging me onward and upward. The campus was hot and the lines were long and the English faculty was spooky. That is, they scared me. I have never since run into a group of people who looked so much like the cast of a third-rate, black-and-white horror film. There was the anemic doctor with his bullet-shaped head and his terrible teeth. From Harvard he was, and head of the department, and determined to make this campus in the beet fields, "the Harvard of the West." There was the sadistic doctor with his cankerous cheeks and his sniffling nose and his every utterance laced with poisonous sarcasm. There was the huge and lopsided Dr. Margaret Somebody, who spoke with a lisp and whose eyes were crossed. Honest to God, Dick, as I write about it now, my heart begins to beat faster, kicking with excitement against my ribs: the excitement of fear. Nobody I knew was working for a Master of Arts in the discipline of their undergraduate major. Everybody I knew was working for a master's in school administration. I mean, dozens of my teaching colleagues in those years were aiming to be principals and superintendents, and I was thought to be odd because I was in English. And I can see why they thought of me as odd—stuck over there in Merrifield Hall where those spooks were, sent on stupid errands to the stacks (when was *Comus* first performed [*Comus*, a masque (dramatic entertainment involving dances and disguises) written by English poet John Milton, performed in 1634]? where was Adelaide Crapsey [American poet, 1878-1914] born?), reading books by the dozen, writing papers by the score. When I showed up for my third summer of punishment, the head of the Department was amazed and disappointed. "The way our program works," he told me, "is that we try to discourage you from coming back. We work you until we don't think you can stand it any more. You must be a very persevering young man, Mr. Hassler, to have come back for the third time." Persevering, hell. Stupid was the word for me. One by one the five candidates I started with dropped out, either finding more humane treatment at another university (the English Department at the U. of South Dakota was said to be actually friendly) or shifting their major to school administration. I stupidly hung in there till they gave in and awarded me my degree six years later. I hated every class, every paper, every day I spent on that campus. I came out scarred. My friends in school administration came out about as jolly as they were when they went in.

April 2, 1978

But if I had forsaken the spooks in the English Department and gone the way of my friends, the administrators, I believe I would have been scarred just as deeply, for they were studying nonsense of another kind. Occasionally I enrolled in an education class and accompanied my friends to the education building and was appalled at the subject matter. In one class that met in an auditorium at 7:30 in the morning, they were memorizing the thirty-six purposes of education. The thirty-six purposes of education, Dick, can you imagine? There they were, committing to memory these long infinitive phrases beginning, "To provide. . .," "To facilitate . . .," "To encourage . . .,"—three dozen groups of words so abstract.

April 17, 1978

You are indeed a monumental jogger, as your postcard from D.C. makes clear, jogger for all seasons, a seasoned jogger, a jogger in the eyes of God and your fellow man, a first-class jogger as opposed to the second-class jogger who only jogs at home and does not run a step when he is away on business. I'm not sure I have my terms right here. I'm sure about your being first-class, but I'm not sure if I should be calling you a jogger or a runner. I understand this is an important distinction, and the men and women who at this very moment are running twenty-six miles in Boston (are you among them, Dick?) are definitely runners and not joggers. Me, I'm a walker. For a year or so recently I was a cycler, and before that I was nothing, but now it's clear beyond a doubt that I am a walker. About a month ago I tried running and didn't like it. Running did something disturbing to my brain and gut. It bounced them around, was what it did. It jarred my brain and jiggled my gut, and what I disliked most was that it made me breathe fast. It seemed like I was doing nothing but breathing. If I wasn't breathing out, I was breathing in. So I'm going to stick to walking for the foreseeable future, and as soon as I get someplace where there are a lot of monuments, I'll be a monumental walker.

Last week one night I dreamed that it was my day of execution, that at the stroke of 6:00 p.m. I would be shot through the head at close range by the chairman of our English department. He would use a revolver. It was my worst nightmare in recent years. My emotion was not resentment (I seemed to understand the justice of my punishment) nor was it regret (whatever my crime, it was what I had to do); my emotion was sadness at having to leave life at 6:00 p.m.—a sadness so strong that I was brought almost to tears and began to thrash around in bed and woke myself up. I awoke to the light of dawn and couldn't believe my good fortune, my reprieve, the joyous prospect of living through middle age to old age and dying in my sleep when I'm eighty-eight. [Jon died on March 20, 2008, ten days before his seventy-fifth birthday.]

April 20, 1978
Back to my office then, to read student papers, to try to catch up, to get ahead, to put my schoolwork behind me. Here's a paper by Priscilla—telling of the time in high school when she witnessed her physical education teacher beat up one of his students, a shy boy who was afraid to ask a girl to dance (on rainy days they danced in the gym); Priscilla's determination to squeal on the teacher; she circulated a petition to expose him; she got leaned on, hard, by the principal and his henchmen; she had been taught our institutions operate democratically—thus, the petition; she learned they operated according to who leans hardest on whom. She gave up. Here's a twelve-page paper by Jane about the night her lover died; he was walking along the left side of a highway south of Brainerd when a pickup traveling the same direction crossed over to his side of the

road, struck him, dragged him two hundred feet, then backed up over his head; her search for him through the night—it was twenty below zero—and her learning of it from a deputy sheriff. Here's a paper by Margaret Ray concerning her sister's seventeenth birthday party, which was held in her hospital room five days before her death. (Had enough, Dick?) Here is Betty's account of the time she was five and her parents left her with a mean aunt when they went on vacation. Here is Marie's account of a hitchhiking trip from Los Angeles to Bismarck in the late '30s. Here are seven or eight more papers which I skim through quickly, trailing my red pen over the pages, making them look read and "Corrected"—papers about fish-netting, camping out, paying a fine for speeding, staying at the Radis-son Hotel, going into therapy after surgery on the leg muscles, and trying to drive an old Chevy with a cracked distributor cap. I can't recall a freshman composition class that was as candid as this class, so ready to tell me about their sorrows and sins—page upon page of death and loneliness, disillusionment and longing—and most of it delivered in a steady, unemotional, clear-eyed prose. Paragraphs breaking exactly where they should. Hearts where they shouldn't.

Then out to my blue car and home, where I eat four cookies and a bologna sandwich and open my mail: a bill from J. C. Pen-ney. Then out and away with my dog on a leash, down to the river along a muddy trail and past a young man with a bb gun shooting beer cans and uphill to the cemetery [Evergreen Cemetery in Brain-erd], where I read the short names as I pass, needing as I do a name for Callahan; I'm looking for something Irish and of one syllable. Quinn? Lynch? Dunn? Shea? [Jon finally chose Shea.]

To bed now. An article by D. Keith Mano [American writer, 1942-] in *Esquire* on "Being Short." It's written in the old (but not too old) *Esquire* style cultivated by Gordon Lish [*Esquire* fiction editor, 1969-1977] and Nora Ephron, a breathless, staccato, tape-recorder style which I find refreshing on page one and tiresome on page two, suffering from the one great fault of the *Esquire* style: exhibitionism; the writer seems to be saying, see how clever I am. [Please refer to September 29, 1977, entry.]

Jemmy is finished. What version is this? The fourth? The eighth? I have no idea. I'm sure that certain pages of it have been written sixteen times. I am typing up my clean copy now at the rate of twenty pages a day. I'm on page eighty. In seven days I'll get to page 220, where it ends. It's now called *The Maiden of Eagle Rock*. A young adult book. Fifty-five thousand words. A better book than it was when I was describing it to you last August. But good enough for public consumption, public display? There's an editor at Atheneum who will answer that question. I do hope the answer is yes.

April 23, 1978

Me, I'm still doing the same old things, locked in the classroom just long enough each day to take the edge off my desire to write, scheming how I might buy a quarter off next year, looking forward to the expanse of free time between early June and Labor Day, considering how I might go about repairing my bathroom before the walls cave in, waiting for my kids to grow up, answering letters from readers who tell me Miles Pruitt should not be dead, painting an occasional picture of a farm in winter, reading my students' halting compositions, avoiding faculty meetings, going for long walks with an old dog I inherited, taking out the garbage, and struggling in my journal to keep pace with my life.

Now it's back to the larger novel, which began in August and stopped in November. I'm on page two hundred and it's full of interesting characters, but I don't understand it. Thus far, I don't see the core, the main thread, the climax. It's about an old retired teacher—sort of an updated *Goodbye, Mr. Chips* [a 1934 novel by English author James Hilton, 1900-1954]. I may call it *Hello, Doctor Shea*. If I do, it will be the fourth title it's had thus far. Though I don't understand it, I like it a lot. It's do or die this summer.

May 10, 1978

Peter [Simon in final version] Shea, Jean Kirk, Douglas?, Hattie Norman, Mrs. Valentine Biggs, Jacob Nelson, Linda?, Barbara Shea, Jay Johnson, The Odmers, Donald Stearns, Doodle Novotny, Mrs. Kibbikoski, T. S. Testor. I am at school but my mind is at home, turning over the names of some of the characters in my novel. These mentioned above are alive and kicking; a dozen others are just as healthy and hopeful, but I have forgotten their names because they're on pages I wrote last October and November and only glanced at since.

But it's hard to concentrate on your novel when across from your office someone is teaching a girl how to sit on a chair, as Virginia Major [?] is doing at the present time. "Don't plunk yourself down like that, Jenny. Get up and do it over again. Sit down lightly on the front edge of the chair and then push your seat back. If you're going to cross your legs, now is the time to cross them. Cross them quickly as soon as you sit down." Well, I ask you, how do you write fiction with this going on eight feet away? Your mind is suddenly full of the girl's legs, the girl's seat. Are they good legs? Is the seat trim? Or has the girl grown up on potato chips and hot chocolate, and is her seat broad as a buggy seat? Is she dark or blond? I think she's blond. I hear her voice and I think it's the voice of a blond, not a straw-haired blond but more of a caramel-haired blond. Her voice tells me that her hair is rather long and her complexion is clear. I like her looks a lot. I think I'll get up from my typewriter and go across the hall and ask her if she'd like to step into my office, sit on my chair, push her seat back, and cross her legs.

May 19, 1978

I would be cutting my lawn and writing to New Hampshire more regularly but my novel is getting in my way. Not that I'm adding much to the word count—I haven't time for more than a paragraph a day—but it does occupy my mind. I do believe that one whole compartment of my brain (the writing compartment) has come through these six months of teaching unimpaired. I am so happy.

May 23, 1978

Between my leave and sabbatical I have earned slightly over two years' salary during the last three years, and I have spent my writing money to make up the difference. Which is as it should be, I guess. I mean, after all, isn't that what writing money is for. To buy time for writing.

June 3, 1978

My destiny is to sit at my typewriter with my curtains open when it's rainy and shut when it's sunny. This is where I belong. How old was Proust when he retired to his cork-lined room? I understand Proust better than most people I read about. I know the pull of the enclosed room, the hermitage, the cell. It is where I want to spend my life. I exaggerate, of course. I am still, to some degree, social, and I realize that without intercourse with the rest of humanity I would eventually run out of things to write about (my writing being almost totally concrete and dependent upon my sensory perceptions), yet in the life I am expected to lead the proportions seem wrong. The proportions between social intercourse and solitude. Between my duty to the outside world and duty to my inner self. What portion of my life am I allowed to spend at my typewriter? I would guess ten percent at most. Ten percent is not enough. I am working to increase that proportion. Someday I want it up to fifty percent. So far I have wiped out my social life. I mean social life in its narrow sense: parties and fishing trips. I have dropped out of the Knights of Columbus and the Brainerd Art Club and the Minnesota Rural Artists and the North Country Arts Council and all else that smacks of gathering in rooms with a lot of other people. But that, after all, does not wipe out very much in terms of time. Perhaps ten percent of my life was spent in that sort of thing; no, not ten; more like five. In the next few days teaching will drop away. That's a big chunk of about thirty percent. My family obligations amount to twenty-five percent, and there's no way of reducing that. So here we have the proportions of my life:

$$\begin{array}{ll} \text{Sleep} & 30\% \\ \text{Teaching} & 30\% \\ \text{Family} & 25\% \\ \text{Writing} & 10\% \\ \text{Leisure} & 5\% \\ \hline & 100\% \end{array}$$

Now with teaching out of the way for twelve weeks, I will double my writing time. I know from past experience that only ten of that thirty percent can be used for writing. Family demands will overlap it by ten percent, and painting will come back and take five percent, and rest will require the remaining five. Thus, when teaching stops, the thirty percent it required is parceled out in this manner:

Writing 10%
Family 10%
Painting 5%
Recovery from having taught 5%
_____
30%

Which means that my summer proportions look like this:

Sleep 30%
Family 35%
Writing 20%
Rest/Leisure 10%
Painting 5%
_____
100%

Yesterday I went to the Holiday Inn [Brainerd], where a fly-by-night business-machine company from St. Cloud was displaying typewriters, and I gave a fat man in a red tie $140 for a reconditioned Smith Corona portable electric. It is a sister to this machine, but elite rather than pica because elite was all they had. Then this machine it may be older or it may be newer, but it could not have possibly had more use. So now I have two machines, one for Brainerd and one for the cabin, and I will no longer have to lug this typewriter back and forth. This fine old overworked green machine stays home, and its new sister goes north to stay. Arriving at either place, I can sit down to write without so much as plugging in a cord. I will have to adjust to the difference in type size, for as I mentioned before elite has a somewhat different effect on what I say. It seems to make me more voluble, more copious in my descriptions of things, and that is probably good for early drafts of things. I must remember to compose on the new sister, and prepare my finished manuscripts on this old brother.

June 9, 1978

Two days, thus far, of uninterrupted writing, which is to say uninterrupted writing from 8:30 when I finish breakfast till 2:30 when
I quit my typewriter whether I want to or not. The first day I began
Novel Four all over again. Page one. The first day I sailed through
the first twenty pages, and today I sailed through the second twenty
pages, which takes me almost to the end of Chapter One. Which
means that Chapter One after these many rewrites is pretty smooth.
I expect to finish this work this summer, Dick: typed in its final
draft by Labor Day. I will have no excuse not to if I can maintain
this kind of solitude.

June 15, 1978 – Nevis

I am back at the lake, writing. I'm on page 80 of Novel Four. So
far it's good. It's on my mind as I go to sleep at night, and it's on
my mind when I awake in the morning. Which means, I hope, that
I'm writing in my sleep. Sinking into Novel Four has made me a
dull person to be around. I seem to be spreading the several sides
of my personality among the several characters in the novel, and it
hasn't left me much of a personality in real life. I bore people I chat
with, and I bore myself. And if I don't pick up the pace of this letter,
you're going to be bored to read on.

June 24, 1978

This summer my family seems to be doing well in my absence. All
they require, at this stage of my fatherhood, is that I leave them
with both cars and a certain sum of money each week.

July 31, 1978

Novel Four, entitled *Simon's Night*, stands five-sixths finished.
Which is to say that I have written the last word of Chapter Five,
the word being "death," and I have yet to write the first word of
Chapter Six, which will probably be "Valentine," which is the first
name of Mrs. Bigg's dead husband. Will I have the final draft typed
and ready by the time I fly to New York on September 5? If I don't,

will there be any reason for me to fly to New York on September 5? I think I can do it, but only by not wasting a single minute between now and that day—by composing, revising, and typing through August at the rate of ten or twelve hours a day. But not today, I guess. I got up at 7:30 intending to get right to work on Chapter Six, but my urge to write to Portugal [?] was stronger than my urge to write fiction. In some ways it's nice to be on the last chapter, but in other ways it's nerve-wracking. The end is in sight, which is nice, but endings have never been my strong suit, and after all this investment of time and energy, I could blow it as easily as save it. This morning I felt I had to take a breather and step off into the free and wide-open spaces of letter-writing. Once I'm into a novel over 200 pages I feel as though I were bound from head to toe with black electrician's tape.

I see a statement on page four [of this particular letter—I don't know what this refers to] that may need explaining. When my parents are at the cabin I don't stop my manual labor after an hour and a half because despite their eighty-one and seventy-seven years they are two of the hardest working people I know. When they're at the cabin they're seldom sitting still; they're watering, hoeing, painting, trenching, cooking, cleaning, and all that. I'm ashamed to sit down with all that going on around me.

As edgy as I feel now at the tail end of my novel, I don't envy you at the front end of yours. I wrote the first two pages of *Simon's Night* twenty-eight times before I was able to go on to page three.

August 13, 1978

It's a day a lot like yesterday, except it isn't Saturday. It's Sunday. It's ninety degrees. I'm in my den, working on *Simon's Night*. Yesterday and today I revised part three and saved it from being the weakest part of the novel. Now I'm afraid part one is the weakest. Part one is a hell of a place to be weak. My last part, part six, isn't so hot either. Hell of a place to be weak, part six. But two through five are strong. I really believe that. Sometimes, as I'm working on part two or three or four or five, skipping around, revising here, deleting there, adding over there, I feel very confident. I think it's publishable with a doubt [*sic*]. But then I work on part one or part six, and I say, what a shame, to have written such a poor novel. Then I weigh one and six against two through five, and I conclude that it's a success. One of these days when I type the final word on twenty-pound rag (the final word is "love"), I will be satisfied. I will be proud of the work as a whole and only uneasy about small parts. I'm guessing that day will be August 28th. I finished the first draft about a week ago, almost exactly a year after I began, and as first drafts go it's quite complete and clean. I mean I'm not doing a whole hell of a lot of changing in the second draft. Only about fifteen to twenty revisions per page, only about 6,000 scribbled changes in all.

Writing has come to be such a large part of my day, of my thinking, that my friend Jim has seen fit to warn me about the dangers of withdrawal, from real life, that is. I seem to have a hell of a capacity for being single-minded when the writing is going well and I don't try to keep in touch with people. A week ago two friends came up to the cabin to see me. My first visitors of the summer. They are not friends of the first magnitude, but I was happy enough to see them and catch up on whatever gossip I had been missing in Brainerd. Yet along about ten p.m., though I had noticed their overnight bags in the car, I said, "Would you guys like a cup of coffee before you start back?" Mean, Dick? Ruthless? Yes, I believe so. But though it was mean of me, I don't regret it. We were sitting there at the cabin, having taken care of all the gossip I wanted, and I was thinking of the next morning's segment of writing (I had it all mapped out in my mind exactly what I wanted to write), and I knew if these two fellows stayed the night, the morning would be lost. They would want to sleep later than I, and then there would be the matter of breakfast, either at the cabin or in town, and then we would linger over our farewells, and I would finally get to my typewriter about four hours late, and some day when I came to die my life's work would be four hours short of being complete. Compulsiveness, meanness, ruthlessness. Novel Four is changing me, Dick; it has taken its pound of flesh, or rather (I suspect) its pound of geniality. But watch me spring back. Once I lay this work on Harriet's [Jon's agent] desk, I'll embrace the world once more. Watch out, Dick, I'll hug you.

August 16, 1978
In bed last night I read Philip Roth till eleven, then awoke this morning at six and was out here at my typewriter by seven. I spent five hours typing my final draft of *Simon's Night*, and turned out about thirty-five pages. That isn't spectacular typing by anybody's standards, especially considering that the copy I'm typing from required relatively little revision as I go along. Seven pages an hour. That's been my best rate for a long time now. Seven pages an hour of final draft quality, which is to say only one or two or three inked-in corrections per page when I proofread. My opinion of a piece changes drastically as I type a final draft. I think it's great. I think it's mediocre. I think it's worth so much pigeon shit. Right now the typing stands arrested on page 126, and at this moment I think the novel is slightly better than mediocre.

What will take this novel's place in my life? Why, another novel. And how soon? By early December, I hope. That's when my quarter's leave begins. All arrangements made before the year begins.

August 17, 1978
Behold, it's two days later. The top half of this page was interrupted by the neighbor [I believe that his name was Roy] who bicycles past my cabin every evening and stops, if he sees me, to talk. And I mean talk. This man talks at length on any subject you want to bring up. The poor guy is newly retired from his job and newly transplanted from the city and he's starved for talk and diversion. Taxes, elections, plumbing—any subject will do; he'll give you his views and point out how they differ from the majority view and how his views have shifted over the past ten years. He has very little education and an open mind, and he should have been a lawyer instead of a janitor. He never grows tired of pleading his case. Anyhow, by

the time he left, I had more energy for letter-writing, so I went to bed with Graham Greene, having finished Philip Roth, and drifted off at about eleven. Then up yesterday morning, breakfast, typed till noon, cheese and crackers, typed till two-thirty, painted a few square feet of the cabin wall, went back to typing, drank a can of diet cola a cheap and tasteless brand that gives cancer to rats—then painted two pictures, two twelve by sixteen inch oils, a lake and a farm, both of them keepers. Then supper: two potatoes, one pork chop, one link of Polish sausage, one orange. Then Graham Greene till the lights went out and a colossal thunderstorm came up over the lake, several different strata of clouds, each strata a different shade of blue or rose and each moving swiftly in its own direction. A roll of thunder that lasted thirty minutes non stop. Then five minutes of hard rain. Then the storm passed into the next county and all was still in the gloaming—the leaves hanging heavy and still—and the lights came on again. I proofread the day's typing up to page 162, then went to bed.

August 21, 1978
And now it's some days later again. Damnedest thing the way the days go by, the relentless passage of mornings and afternoons and nights, and August is damn near over and I have two weeks to finish my novel and press my shirt and get my ticket to New York. I'm flying on the day after Labor Day which is the 5th of September. On the 6th I'm seeing my agent, beloved Harriet, in the flesh. Hi, Harriet. Hi, Jon. I wonder if we'll think of more to say than that. On the 7th I'm seeing, indeed, lunching with my editor at Atheneum. Judith Kern is her name. Hi, Judy. Hi, Jon. I wonder if we'll think of more than that to say. On the 8th I'm flying home, touching down in Brainerd in the evening and stepping off the plane and looking around and saying, in the dark, where did the summer go. Here it's the 8th of September and school starts in three days, and I have just finished a great big novel and delivered it to the judgment of Harriet and Judith, and now I'm ready to live a little and here the summer is all gone. I'm ready to rip off my shirt and beat the sparse

hair on my pale chest and kick up my heels and by God school starts in three days. Well, what the hell, if I hadn't wanted to spend the summer writing, I wouldn't have spent the summer writing. It's my heart's desire, writing, and I figured that's what summer was for and I wrote with a passion. I daresay not a single day since June 1 has passed without this novel on the front burner of my cooking little brain. Understand the brain in that metaphor is doing the cooking, not being cooked. Which reminds me, Dick. My writing gets less figurative by the day, by the season. You never saw such unadorned writing as the stuff I'm turning out these days. *Staggerford* looks positively baroque by comparison. Or rather, yes, you have seen such unadorned writing. I sent you a few pages of it last week. Simon and Barbara. Simon and Linda. Literal. Too literal to my taste. I'd like to be a little more playful, a little more figurative, a little more crazy. I can be that way sometimes in letters and short stories and parts of novels before I know they're going to be parts of novels, but when I'm writing full tilt across vast swatches of fiction, I seem to write as though I had no imagination except for the things people do and the things people say. I don't seem to compare anything to anything. I write, "This is something so-and-so did, and this is something so-and-so said." Next page. "And then so-and-so went and did this, and so-and-so's friend said this, and so-and-so replied by saying this." Next chapter. What I'm getting at, Dick, is that some chapters aren't so hot. I wrote you about that last time. I said my opinion of my stuff goes from hot to cold. No, it wasn't last time. I said it in this very letter. Page 2. Well, it was days ago I wrote it, so it seems like last time. And after I wrote it I got your letter about how your opinion of your stuff goes from hot to cold—your cursing weeping account of how gremlins got into your stuff. What can one do? The only sensible way of handling that gremlin problem is to do just what you claim to be doing at the end of your letter: to put onto your novel "as much weight as it can carry." That's exactly what I try to do in the first stage of writing a novel: simply pack plow stack add pile stuff as much as I can possibly think of onto the story line until the line sags and threatens to break from the weight. That's about all I did last fall. I had the fall off, as you may recall, and I spent three months right here piling, packing, stuffing scenes into the entity I imagined as a novel about an old man. I didn't even know what the old man's name was at the time, or what would become of him, but by December I had 50,000 words and I put them in a box and went back to school. Instead of opening the box and peeking inside once in a while through the winter and spring, my attention was unexpectedly turned back on *Jemmy* by an interested editor. So it wasn't until June that I opened the box. I took it to the cabin and I tipped it over on my writing table and out came the most various lot of scenes and dialog, more than I could control. Fiction all over the tabletop, some of it dropping off onto the floor and crawling away. Some of it got away but I saved what I could and said, "This summer I am going to impose some sort of order on you, you myriad pieces of fiction, you," and that's what I did. I'm on page 270 of the final draft.

Oh, there is so much about *Simon's Night* I didn't know when I was at the twenty-thousand-word point. And at the fifty-thousand-word point. Now I'm on page 170 of the third draft and I know a lot. For one thing I know it really ought to be written once more before I let anyone see it, but I am resisting that urge. This draft goes to New York, with all its frailties intact.

August 27, 1978, "A" [Jon had dated this entry and the two following with the same date. I kept the dates as Jon had typed them, adding "A," "B," and "C."]
Then the morning after Labor Day I'm getting on a plane and flying to New York for three days—an impulsive act by which I mean to mark the division between summer and fall, between writing and teaching, between freedom and regimentation. I poured the entire summer into Novel Four, which goes by the name of *Simon's Night*, and day before yesterday I typed the last word of the last draft. I'll deliver it to my beloved agent Harriet Wasserman on the 6th, and the next day I will lunch with my editor at Atheneum, Judith Kern. After all this time, how illuminating it will be to meet these women.

I've been dreaming about them lately. Harriet the other night was old and red-haired and she sat on my lap. Judith was young and good-looking, and after lunching with me her colleagues wouldn't let her back in her office—something about the company she was keeping. Most of my time in New York I spent remodeling my hotel room—plastering, painting, etc. What does it all mean?

Having so recently finished *Simon's Night*, and having been so intensely involved with it, I find it hard to say anything very general about it, hard to say what it's worth. Between its first word (It) and its last word (love), there are 96,000 other words. Simon enters and escapes from the Norman Home (that's where Smalleye lives) in the course of the six days of the novel (Monday through Saturday—on the order of *Staggerford* in this regard). Thus it's about a man who discovers it's not time for him to crawl under a rock and die after all. I saw this theme from the beginning and built the novel around it. What I didn't see at the beginning, and what grew to be a second major theme, is the business of Simon's marriage vow and his life-long effort not to break it even though his wife seems to give him good cause to do so. In my nightmares I fear that this novel doesn't have one iota of contemporary appeal. The fashion now is youth and broken vows. This is a book about an old man and an old vow. Well, whatever it's worth, it's done and I'm breathing easier.

August 27, 1978, "B"

This trip to New York is strictly an impulsive act, a fling. And an investment, too, for I suspect if I show myself to be of flesh and blood, rather than only a voice on the other end of a long-distance call, Harriet and Judith may subconsciously wish to do a bit more for me when it comes to promoting my fiction.

Unlike *Staggerford* this is an upbeat ending, a happy ending that depends somewhat on coincidence, and I'm not sure it's believable. If I had written the novel another time (a fourth time) it would no doubt be better, but I imposed this Labor Day deadline on myself (probably an unwise thing to do) and so it must stand as it is. What I'm hoping is that it has enough merit to tempt a publisher into giving me a contract—then there is always time for a rewrite before publication.

August 27, 1978, Sunday, "C"

You never read anything so scathing in your life as the review devoted to *Staggerford* in the *Times Literary Supplement* of London. The reviewer dismembered the book, character by character, and when he was done he pissed all over them. Even in *The New York Times* review last summer (which was by far the most negative until now) the reviewer, Joyce Carol Oates, found a few good things to say, but this guy Bailey of London has delivered himself of a savage piece. Well, it's balanced by six favorable reviews that came out earlier, including reviews in the *Sunday Observer* and the *New Statesman*.

Hey, Dick, I'm done with *Simon's Night*. I think it's pretty good, at least until the end, where the plot gets resolved in a manner that leaves me vaguely dissatisfied. I have never been good at endings. The ending of *Pinecone* had to be written seven times before the editor at Frederick Warne was satisfied. The ending of *Staggerford* had to be revised for Atheneum. *The Maiden's Tale* was completely revamped before she sold herself to a publisher. *McCall's* is currently hanging fire on a new short story because they don't like the ending. They haven't liked the ending since mid-July and I haven't done a thing about revising it because I was submerged in *Simon*. I think my inability to handle endings carries over to real life too. I remember saying goodbye to a pretty girl in Albuquerque last year. She accompanied me to my car, and as I turned, saying goodbye, in something of a pirouette I tripped on the sidewalk and damn near fell on my ass. Ending my summer at the cabin yesterday and hauling to Brainerd everything I thought necessary to a writer. I left behind my writing table and my writing chair. I brought my typewriter and paper and a pile of various notes and mss. But I am writing this on the ironing board. Leaving you at your parents' house in Minnieska, I found it difficult to time my waving and final words so that they worked out perfectly with my backing up and then going forward with my car. Endings throw me. I want to be graceful.

I don't want to fall on my ass at the end. I daresay it's more nearly acceptable to fall on your ass in the beginning or in the middle than it is at the end. In the beginning or the middle there's still time to prove you're not a dolt. At the end you have no choice but to exit a klutz. I guess that's one of the things that seems wrong about death.

I took up and rejected lots of titles before I hit on *Simon's Night*. I hit on *Simon's Night* while driving in my car. I put on a hell of a lot of miles in a year's time and I try to think about my writing as I drive but I seldom succeed; I'm lucky if I have one profitable thought about my writing in 10,000 miles. But coming home from the cabin about three weeks ago (as I made the turn from hiway 33 to hiway 64, as I looked across the hayfield of the farmer who cuts his hay with a team of horses), I thought of *Simon's Night*. If the book is publishable, and I have no assurance that it is, I'd be surprised if the editor requested a different title. Like you, I like it.

August 30, 1978
It's three days later now, Dick, and I have a sad story to relate about my writing. Thus far, two Agatha McGee stories authored by me have appeared in *McCall's*, and early this summer *McCall's* suggested to Harriet that it would be nice to have an Agatha McGee Christmas story, and around the 4th of July I wrote such a story and sent it off to Harriet. On July 24 she wrote back to say *McCall's* would take the story if I improved the ending. There seemed to be two things wrong with the ending: 1) Miss McGee's triumph was too easy and 2) the other major character, an unwed mother named Janet Raft, is sort of shouldered off stage in the last six pages. Would I revise the ending, they wanted to know. Yes, I said, I would revise it, but not immediately. I was into the home stretch with my novel and I couldn't divert my attention from it right now. Perhaps I would have a revision ready by late August. Well, yesterday *McCall's* called me up to remind me that this was late August and where the hell was the revision? I'm about to write it, I said. I just finished my novel last Friday. But this was the week we were

supposed to see it, they said. (Actually these words were not said by they: they were said by Helen Del Monte, Fiction Editor.) What kind of a deadline are we looking at, I said. That's just it, she said; in order to insure getting an illustration done for the story and getting it into the Christmas issue, we should have had it this week. I'm flying to New York on Tuesday, I said. I'll have it then (cocky of me, what?). Well, she said, of course we'll be happy to look at it next week, but we may have to use something else instead. I'm sorry, I said, I understand, I said, it was simply impossible for me to mumble mumble, you know, too bad, mumble, mumble mumble. I'm sorry, she said, you understand how we here at *McCall's* mumble mumble mumble, deadlines and so forth. Yes, well, good-bye. Goodbye. I hung up thinking I had done my best and failed and there's no shame in that. But now the next morning I feel sort of bad about it all. What she was telling me was that I had just let $1500 slip out of my hands, and as much as I need money, that isn't what really bothers me. What really bothers me is that I am no longer the dependable writer *McCall's* thought I was. I don't know how many times you can risk being undependable—maybe only once—before a big operation like *McCall's* throws you overboard. Am I paranoid, or was there actually something in Helen Del Monte's tone that said, "Vengeance is *McCall's*!" Now, in conclusion, let me add this. When I hung up the phone I wasn't sure if I had been executed or if I had only been threatened with execution. She didn't come right out and *say* that next Tuesday was too late. She said it *might* be too late. So what I'm going to do now, it being 8:30 a.m. and my mind beginning to respond to the caffeine I'm feeding it, I'm going to go to work on the revised ending right now.

Looking back over that story, I see that I have made too light of the lost $1500. I need that $1500, damn it.

September 2, 1978

So it's lunch next Wednesday with Harriet and it's lunch the next day with Judith Kern of Atheneum. There are a number of things I would like them to tell me:

If I keep producing a book a year (short books alternating with long books), how long will it be before I can buy my way out of the classroom?

How did *Staggerford* sales compare with other first-novel sales?

Why did *Staggerford* not arouse the interest of any paperback houses? [A very good question--finally, in August 1986 Ballantine did print a paperback edition of *Staggerford*, currently in its 28th printing.]

Who are Harriet's more prominent clients?

How many copies must be sold before a book is considered to break even? To be a modest success? To be a best seller?

Is it typical writers' paranoia, or am I correct in thinking that both Atheneum and Warner leave something to be desired in matters of promotion?

Does anybody care if I type my final drafts in elite rather than pica?

If *Simon's Night* is bought by Atheneum, will they bring it out simultaneously with *Jemmy*?

How can I convince Atheneum's promotion director that if their salesman is on his toes he could sell a hell of a lot of books around Minnesota?—my books.

Is this the time to send a copy of *Simon's Night* to my editor in London?

I have a very strong desire to write a short story, but not the strength. I am going through my post-partum lassitude. I am also short of sleep. This weekend two of my kids will disappear to campuses at a distance and I hope to resume regular hours in bed. I believe "need my sleep" is the phrase that applies here, the phrase a favorite of those who, like me, operate at half speed if last night's sleep fell short of eight hours. "My" sleep, they say, that sleep being something they owned and was stolen, or something owed to them by a debtor who wouldn't pay up. Well, I do, Dick, I need my sleep. I'm going to get some right now.

September 3, 1978

Now by order in my fiction I do not mean that I work all my fictional events into contrived or happy endings. I mean that every time I complete a sentence (and how many sentences are there in *Simon's Night*? 3,200?), I have achieved command of a thought, I have ordered another small segment of my thinking. I don't ask much more of life than the ability to do that. Some dark bread and jam and a decent typewriter and a priest once a week and a friend to write to and the ability to put my thoughts down in sentences that make sense—that's enough. That's life to my liking.

September 9, 1978

"Who are some of the other writers you represent?" I asked Harriet. We were lunching in the Rose Room of the Algonquin, not at *the* round table, but at a round table nevertheless, and Harriet had just pointed out Mario Puzo's editor [Puzo, American writer, author of *The Godfather*, 1920-1999], who was seated in the corner with his blue shirt open at the collar. "Well, there's Saul Bellow," said Harriet, "I represent Saul." Holy mackerel, I thought. Wait till she sees Dick Brook's stuff; she'll like it. Brook and Bellow are alike in the way they intellectualize experience (though not so much alike that Brook should be worrying about it in his letters to Brainerd). Bellow was put on earth to introduce Harriet to Brook's style of narrative. And that wasn't all I thought when she mentioned Bellow. I thought about the passage in *Simon's Night* where Simon makes a disparaging remark about Bellow's writing.

"And Eudora Welty," said Harriet. "I represent Eudora. And Jean Stafford and Anne Tyler and Reynolds Price. Reynolds Price thought *Staggerford* was a very great work until the end. He thought the ending was a terrible mistake from a literary point of view. And I represent Bernard Malamud. I had dinner here last night with Bernard. He brought me his new work, which will be published in February." Harriet said a lot of other things, such as how disappointed she was that *Staggerford* failed to find a paperback publisher and how she had gotten her degree from Hunter

College in political science and intended to be a lawyer but was sidetracked into agenting and now she's forty-one. She must be rich. Imagine her income from guys like Bellow and Malamud at ten percent. She said that although the firms share the same address on Park Avenue, no one from *McCall's* will speak to anyone from *Redbook* and vice versa. She says she came to Minnesota once when she was in charge of a touring baroque trio. She went to Duluth and (of all places) Grand Rapids.

Harriet read *Simon's Night* overnight and called me at the hotel the next morning to say she thought it was good overall, but there were two rather important characters (Jean and Douglas: young lovers) who failed to be convincing. She also had a little trouble believing Simon's rejection of Linda in Ireland—turning away from his adulterous affair with the lovely Linda. "But you will try to sell it for me?" I asked, feeling low, being somehow more deeply affected by her criticisms than her praise. "Oh, yes," she said, "overall it's very good. Simon himself is wonderful. And so is the Indian, and you have some very funny scenes indeed, and I will represent it with enthusiasm."

"Do you believe the ending?" I asked. "Simon's going back to live in his own house? His wife's return to that house? Were you bothered by those two events happening simultaneously, bothered by the coincidence?"

"No...NO." She said in her slow manner of speaking. I was pleased to hear that because I have come to distrust the endings I write and I was worrying about this one. (In fact, to be frank, I have been worrying about this quite a bit the last few days. Here I was going to New York with this novel I felt incapable of judging. What if it didn't come anywhere close to *Staggerford* in the estimation of Harriet and of Judy Kern at Atheneum? What if I was a one-novel novelist? What if I was told I had written my best two years ago and that I should go home and forget about trying to make my way in the Big Apple? And besides all that, there was the matter of Miss McGee. I was carrying, along with the novel, a revision of "The Holiday Vigil of Agatha McGee," which I had been led to believe might be too late for the Christmas issue of *McCall's* even if it was good enough, which I had begun to doubt. Sitting there on my bed high over Seventh Avenue, with the phone to my ear, I came to realize—and be frightened by—what a climactic point I had come to. I had come to New York with these two manuscripts, one little, one large, and I had no idea what they were worth. My worth and my worthlessness were of equal balance. A no from *McCall's* would tip the balance and make me sad. A no from either Harriet or from Judy Kern would tip over the scale itself and I would plunge into despair.)

So at least I had this word from Harriet: that she thought it was a worthy work, though her praise was definitely reserved and qualified by her misgivings. And then after hanging up on Harriet I betook myself to the offices of Atheneum and met my editor, who turns out to be a slinky young blond with crimson fingernails that extended an inch and a quarter beyond the tips of her fingers. Her skin is a darker brown than the walnut stock of my old shotgun; not that Judy Kern is black—she's white (I think) but she has lain on beaches all summer, and her hair is kinky from having bathed in the ocean all summer. On her walnut left wrist were four golden bracelets. On her fingers were several rings of gold, silver, and jade. Her eyes were blue. She was short. She may have been twenty-six. She may have been thirty. She said one of her main interests in life was shopping. She said certain friends had tried to interest her in religion but the Jewish prayers were so interrupted by commas that she much preferred shopping to religion. I am trying to think of words besides slinky to describe Judith Kern. Ironic. Cynical. Tough. Flippant. Talk about the odd couple. You can't imagine an odder couple than Kern and Hassler. We went to lunch. It was 86 degrees, and over her gypsylike skirt and blouse she wore a street-length shawl and led me out into traffic where I thought I would be killed, and I stepped back to the curb as she went forward. "What's the matter?" she called. "You chicken?" I mumbled and waited for the light to change to green, which struck her as cowardly despite the taxis and busses bearing down. "They never run over you," she said; "it requires too much paperwork." We went to a restaurant called The Scoop and sat shoulder to shoulder at a table, and I ate chicken salad and she ate something slippery and aquatic dipped in something spicy. I drank Coke and she drank something with seven or nine words in its name, and when it arrived it looked like a glass of water. We talked for three hours, but it was a different sort of conversation than the three-hour talk I had with Harriet—harder, mostly. I mean it was not a natural sort of ramble. I seemed to be trying very hard to think of the correct or amusing thing to say next. Not that I didn't enjoy it—who doesn't enjoy a challenge now and then?—but we are two people on entirely different wavelengths, and I'm afraid if I ate many lunches with Judith Kern my digestion would go to hell. ["Also, one time she (Judy) called me at home to ask me a question. We'd discussed this before. She said, 'I forgot the answer. I had a stroke.' It was only a figure of speech, I learned after I had sent her a get-well card. So you see, we weren't on the same wavelength," *Conversations*, p. 58.] After lunch we went back to the office and I met the assistant to the editor who is going to bring out *Jemmy*. This assistant is a down-home type girl from Indiana and we had a comfortable chat. Then it was back to Judy's office to say goodbye. Leaving her, I had the definite impression that *Simon's Night* would have to be pretty rotten for her to turn it down. I have an editor there who, though our backgrounds and attitudes are far apart, is predisposed to my writing. So predisposed is she to like *Simon's Night* that she told me she planned to publish it in late spring or early fall. So what does that mean? What if she finds Jean and Douglas unbelievable? What if she doesn't like the way Simon denounces Linda in Ireland? Will she turn it down? Will she ask for a revision (which I would be glad to do)? Will she buy it? And if she turns it down, having been so predisposed to like it, will that not mean it is a great failure of a book? As you can see, dear friend Dick, I am not yet over my fretting ... but my New York visit ended with the scale tipping in my favor. Before checking out of my room yesterday, Harriet called to say she had a Christmas present for me. "What?" I said.

"Don't you know?" she said.

I had no idea. On the phone I'm the next thing to an imbecile.

"*McCall's* is buying 'The Holiday Vigil of Agatha McGee.'"

Imagine my delight. I ran down the street to St. Pat's [Cathedral on Fifth Avenue] and stood for a moment before an image of Sweet Jesus, who has had to listen to a million prayers of supplication from me, and I said a word of thanksgiving. So buoyant was my heart that on the way home the pilot had trouble keeping the plane down to the 35,000-foot level at which he had intended to fly.

Another thing Harriet told me in that last phone call was that Judy Kern was going to read *Simon's Night* over the weekend.

September 16, 1978

School years were more interesting a quarter century ago when I began to teach, because when I was a brand new teacher I wasn't teaching by conditioned reflex, which I seem to be doing now, nor was I preoccupied by my fiction. In those days I had no fiction. In those days I lived one life, not two.

What do you want to hear about first? Do I start with a twenty-five-year history of myself as a teacher, or do I move right into the news about *Simon's Night*? Yes, that's what I thought you'd say: get my bragging over with first. So, all right, Atheneum will publish *Simon's Night* in '79. That's two in '79. That's four novels in three years: *Four Miles to Pinecone* and *Staggerford* in '77; *Jemmy* and *Simon's Night* in '79. Now what I want to know, Dick, is why do I feel something less than ecstatic? Why, when I got the phone call about *Simon's Night*, did I continue doing what I was doing (defrosting the refrigerator at the cabin) instead of celebrating? You know what I think, Dick? I think that I have become so damn stoical that I am incapable of experiencing joy. I'm not saying that I'm incapable of experiencing happiness, for this news about *Simon's Night* makes me very happy, but my happiness resembles peace rather than joy. What I mean is that I feel a very satisfying peace at the core of me, and that is a highly desirable feeling, but for a moment or two it would be fun if I could get my spirits to soar. Well, I'll settle for peace. It's a peace damn near passeth understanding.

Anyhow, Thursday morning I found myself with no classes, and I got into my car and drove to the cabin. I stopped in Pine River and ate two pancakes and three links of sausage; then I got back in the car, and as I was driving between Pine River and Backus, I had an intuition about *Simon's Night*. I felt confident about it. It was a strong confidence, the likes of which I seldom feel. A voice at the back of my brain spoke to me, saying, "Listen, Hassler, there is a hell of a lot of good writing in *Simon's Night*, and whether or not it's your masterpiece it's got more going for it than a lot of the stuff you've been reading lately, and since Atheneum is certain to recoup their investment (given the number of readers who liked *Staggerford*), they aren't likely to reject it." This, as I say, was between Pine River and Backus. An hour later, arriving at the cabin, I called home to ask David if I had left the fire on under the teakettle (I had the nagging feeling that I had started to make a cup of coffee before I left—a cup of coffee I didn't remember drinking), and David said no, no fire on the stove, and then he said Atheneum was going to publish *Simon's Night*. He said Harriet had called to say that. He said I should call Harriet. David, too, is a stoic. David, though interested (mildly) in my literary ventures, would never have gone to the extreme length of calling me on the phone to tell me this news (and even if he had, he wouldn't have found me, for he thought I was at the college), but as long as I had him on the phone, he decided it was worth mentioning. "Did she say anything else?" I asked. "No, that's it," said Dave. "Did she know who you were?" I asked. "Yeah, she said I must be your son." And what did you say to Harriet: "I said I was." I mean what did you say when she told you about the book? "I said I'd tell you."

So I called Harriet from the cabin. She was on another line, but she interrupted the other party to tell me, briefly, the facts. Judy Kern at Atheneum was taking *Simon's Night*. Judy Kern didn't think this would be my "breakthrough" novel (this remark doubtless tempered my joy), but she wanted to publish it anyway because she was so fond of Simon. She was offering a $4500 advance, was that all right? "Yes," I said. "That's great." (As you know, I am tongue-tied on the telephone and my remarks are limited to three or four phrases, "That's great" foremost among them.) Harriet said there would be some revising to do, and I said I expected that. She said I would be hearing from Judy. "Well, once again, Harriet, thank you so much," I said. "It's my pleasure," said Harriet, in her normal impassive tone, as though her happiness (like mine) took the form not of ecstasy but of peace. I believe we are kindred spirits, Harriet and I, and up there on the fifteenth floor overlooking Fifth Avenue, she has cultivated her own field of alfalfa.

Now let us consider this remark of Judy Kern's about this not being my "breakthrough" novel. If we assume that all editors are looking for a breakthrough novel, then we can conclude that *Simon's Night* is not what Judy had been hoping for. Somehow it does not fulfill her expectations. I do not resent that, nor am I sure I believe that she is correct. All along I have felt that this work was one draft short of being what I wanted it to be, and given the chance (which I now will get) to rewrite it once more, I can add the touches that might lift it to a higher level, I can say the things that might give it power. In my mind I have a checklist of about twenty details I mean to investigate and perhaps change, and I intend to do something a little more intense with the ending—this last because there are three or four points in the novel where the reader is moved more strongly than he is at the end. I would like the end to cause the strongest movement in the reader's heart. As it is, I think it's an adequate ending, but with a little work I would like to make it more than adequate. I would like to make it powerful.

September 23, 1978

We're two weeks into fall term, and I'm feeling overworked. I'm teaching five classes. Shit, I might as well have stayed in high school. No, I don't mean that. Only here at Brainerd Community College can I buy my way out for a three-month period when my writing income allows. That's a nice feature of BCC. Saving money is the highest good. My replacement—some housewife with an old B.A.

in English—will teach for half my salary, and the other half can go to the man who blacktops the parking lot. But when I'm teaching, I'm teaching hard. At Bemidji the teaching load was twelve hours a week, here it's fifteen and this quarter it consists of these:

4 credits – freshman English (literature)
4 credits – freshman English (composition)
3 credits – American literature survey
3 credits – poetry
1 credit – novels of Graham Greene

Comparing notes with a high school teacher the other night, I was reminded of the killing workload I left behind when I moved from Park Rapids High School [1959-1965] to Bemidji State College [1965-1968]. She's teaching two classes of remedial English to sophomores and a novel class to seniors and a speech class to juniors and a writing class to a mix of ages, and after school she rules over the detention room. With no hope for a quarter off. That's a tough way to make a living.

The *Simon's Night* contract arrived today from Atheneum. It requires me to write the novel over and send them two copies by October 30. Holy balls, and me with my fifteen hours of classes.

October 2, 1978, "A"

But getting back to Harriet and Judy. Harriet turns out to be forty-one years old, and judging by the number of prominent writers she represents (Welty, Bellow, Malamud, for three) she must be wealthy. I mean ten percent of Bellow's work alone would give you quite a bank account. She's short and sort of dumpy and altogether human. Then there's Judy. She's short and shrill and slinky. Her fingernails are 2 ¼ inches long and covered with glistening red enamel, and they curl at the ends. So arrested was my eye by those remarkable fingernails that I can tell you nothing else about her appearance except that in spite of the heat (86 degrees) she wore a shawl that hung from her neck to the sidewalk. "Have you ever been to Minnesota?" I asked her. She said, "The closest I've been to Minnesota is Pittsburgh or Chicago, whichever's closer."

October 2, 1978, "B"

Now, Gail [former student—refer to previous journal—December 27, 1977], we take up your case. Comparing your letter of last May and your letter of last week (mailed in another stolen envelope), I see that you did not fulfill your wish to be flying to France but you did accomplish the more important goal: writing a story. Now being published in *The New Yorker* is a very worthy aspiration, and I think you should take that story out of the bureau drawer and address it to the fiction department at *The New Yorker* and see what happens. I know of no shortcuts to being published in *The New Yorker*. It's one of my ambitions, too, but I never got any more response than the innocuous printed rejection slip. I know a man whose submissions elicited personal responses from the editors, which proves that there are readers employed by *The New Yorker* who will respond to stories of a certain quality. I gave up and turned to book-length works. But by all means mail your story out. It's hard for editors to read a story that's sitting in your bureau. To read it, they first have to find you and then they have to find your bureau . . . but I don't mean to joke. I understand why it's in the bureau. In the bureau it's safe. In the bureau it can't be rejected. But you have to learn to think of your art as separate from the artist. A rejection of that story is not a rejection of you. When I was first mailing out stories, I found it helpful to have three or four out at one time; that way one single rejection didn't seem all that traumatic; I could still be hopeful about the others. And by the time the next one was rejected, I had the first one back in the mail again and I could be hopeful about that—which is only one reason for a writer to have a backlog of his writing behind him, a bunch of writing, a lot of writing. That way no single work is dangerously precious.

October 3, 1978

My hotel was near the theatres. I saw *The Gin Game* [1978 Pulitzer Prize-winning play by D. L. Coburn, American playwright, 1938-] with E. G. Marshall and Maureen Stapleton. It's the play about old folks that opened a year ago with [Jessica] Tandy and [Hume]

Cronyn, who are now on tour with it. The curtain went up and there was the front porch of the Norman Home. In Act One Marshall buffs his shoes with a Kleenex, just as Simon does in the first chapter of my novel. Indoors the old folks are watching a kids' program on TV—another scene stolen from my novel. It was a superb performance of a better-than-average play. Another night I went to *Deathtrap* [by Ira Levin, playwright and novelist, *Rosemary's Baby*, 1929-2007] with John Wood and Marion Seldes, which I didn't like as well. A murder mystery, sort of contrived. Broadway is the sleaziest street this side of Juarez.

If and when you go to New York, don't try to get into the Museum of Modern Art on Wednesday or the Public Library on Thursday or the Metropolitan Museum on Friday morning. Those are the days I tried and those are the days they're closed. I did get back to the Museum of Modern Art another day, where I decided my favorite pieces are Rodin's *Balzac* and Monet's room-wide spread of water lilies.

October 27, 1978

I haven't been very faithful about writing lately, have I, Dick? The reason is that I'm into education up to my bellybutton. Remember when you were in education. Try hard, and you will recall how you used to leave the house in the morning and go to work at a college where you had an office to yourself and a secretary to yourself and a faculty of your own and you were deeply into education—perhaps up to your belt; certainly not up to your bellybutton. Nosiree, I'm the one who is up to his bellybutton. I may have complained about this before, but I'll say it again: I have five preparations this quarter. I have been grousing and murmuring and straining at the harness, and now I discover that I have been assigned (as though in retribution of complaining) six preparations for spring quarter. Six! For God's sake, I haven't had six preparations since I was in Fosston [high school in MN where Jon taught from 1956-1959], and even there I might not have had six. No, as a matter of fact, I didn't have six. I had six classes each day and, among them, three preparations. I can't keep up this pace in Brainerd. I'll retire during winter quarter to my den, to my typewriter, to my walks in the woods, to my coffeepot, and along about March I'll get comfortable with writing, I'll get to feeling strong and clever in my handling of the language and indifferent toward my handling of real life—and I'll get up from my typewriter and go back to the college for spring quarter and pow! Six preparations. How can I face it? How can I keep this up for two and a half more years, until I bail out in '81. I may not be able to keep it up for two and a half more years. I may not bear up under another year of five and six preparations. Well, Hassler, how about one more year then? How about quitting in the spring of '80, instead of '81: Could you hold out until the spring of '80? Yes, I believe I could. [Jon received a Guggenheim Fellowship in spring 1980 which allowed him to resign from Brainerd Community College. Bob Spaeth, the dean at Saint John's University in Collegeville, MN, invited him to teach two classes per semester, Minnesota Authors and Creative Writing, which he did from 1980 until his retirement in 1997. Jon dedicated his 1997 novel, *The Dean's List*, to Bob, "In memory of my dean / Robert L. Spaeth / 1935-1994."] I'd have to, in fact, considering what St. Ben's [College of Saint Benedict in St. Joseph, MN] is charging for Liz's tuition. Don't talk to me about tuition, says Brook. Brook is busting into this conversation at this point and saying, Don't talk to me about tuition; I wrote the book on tuition; I pay out millions in tuition; my four children are all scholarly and all need tuition at one time and will continue to need it for years to come. I concede that, Dick. I realize that you know all about tuition, that your income is mostly sniffed up the noses of bursars; I grant you that. But at least let me say that St. Ben's is raising their tuition $500 next year, and that increase is such a small portion of the total that it's hardly worth mentioning. So one more year. Yes, I'll continue in the classroom one more year. I suspect, Dick, that since you are a more reflective person than I, idea is the controlling element in your letters—more so than in mine. In mine, form plays a large part. Shapes are important to my thinking as I write, never mind if there isn't an arresting thought in twenty pages. You can be sure that I will say scarcely anything interesting about the motives and consequences of hunting, but I will strain to give my reminiscences some shape.

And that reminds me of a third extraneous matter, and don't ask me what the connection is between the previous assertions in this letter and what follows. When I went to New York, I had three people in mind whom I thought I should call. I went to the trouble, before I left home, to find out the telephone numbers of these people. [Jon's original included this: "???? A page about calling old friends include or not? October 30, 1978, page 3."]

November 22, 1978

Two weeks from Friday my duties at the college end. December 8, Feast of the Immaculate Conception. Then, as you did six months ago, I will put the college out of my mind and devote my thoughts to myself: my past, my future, and how they relate to my fiction. My past. I must continue to mine my past. Daily I must dredge up memories. I think this is the year for dredging up Plainview and making something of it. My boyhood, grades five through twelve, as seen from a distance of twenty-seven years. I had thought that this would be the year for a shorter, less demanding novel, and maybe it will prove to be just that, but at the present time my instincts tell me to go to work on something deep inside me, something at the core, something ambitious, something emotional, something bordering on the sentimental, something that goes back to a time before my life was flawed, something pre-1956 [*Grand Opening*]. And my future. I must think about my future. I must work out a timetable of sacrifice. How much, and when, shall I sacrifice for my fiction? By making June of 1981 my target date, am I waiting too long to quit? Is there any possible way for me to squeeze more than one free quarter out of the 1979-80 school year? That sort of thing is what I've got to think about.

This quarter I have had an occasional thought. Every two weeks I have been permitted thirty seconds of free time for thinking, and

I have devoted that time to imagining potential pieces of fiction.

I imagined these:

A Miss McGee novel [*A Green Journey*].

A novel based on my visits to the friend who sickened and took seventeen years to die of sclerosis; my progress through life as measured by his decline [*The Love Hunter*].

A novel about the relationships among a few selected college instructors, played against a background of declining enrollment [*Rookery Blues*].

A novel using as its scheme, or shape, the procedures of a search committee, hiring a dean, a president, or a superintendent. Perhaps the search committee in *Staggerford* looking for a successor to Superintendent Stevenson [eventually *The Dean's List?*].

Men of the Morgan, the Morgan being a run-down hotel and the men being three or four permanent, run-down tenants including a retired turkey grower and a guy named French, both from early short stories ["The Staggerford Murders" and another novella, "The Life and Death of Nancy Clancy's Nephew," published as *The Staggerford Murders* by Plume/Penquin in 2004].

The Plainview experience, whatever the scheme [*Grand Opening*].

A young-adult novel.

So there are seven ideas exerting, on me, seven different degrees of appeal. Today "Visits to a Friend" ranks right up there with "Plainview." The more thought I give it, the more possibilities of plot I see. These could be the two duck-hunting friends of my last letter. The three-in-a-blind idea could be the beginning of the novel: two young teachers starting out their careers, their marriages; the one arrested at a certain point by his illness and the other going on, going through changes, changing jobs, changing wives. Perhaps what I should do one of these days is embark on another of my life-story letters and take up, instead of hunting, my relationship with Bob Nielson, from the time we met in Fosston in 1956 until the day we buried him in 1977. Yes, that's what I'll do, and if it runs to twenty or thirty pages like the last one did, I have the skeleton of a book. I would call the book *Visting Bob* [eventually *The Love Hunter*], except of course his name in the book would not be Bob, and except of course the first titles that occur to me are never keepers. At the present time *Venables the King* sounds absolutely stupid. [Jon's next novel turned out to be *The Love Hunter*, published in 1981.]

Jon vacationing at Dick Brook's home in New Hampshire

J ON HASSLER, author, educator, playwright, and painter, began his
  writing career at the age of thirty-seven, completing fifteen works
of fiction and two works of nonfiction. His novels include *Staggerford, A Green Journey, Dear James,* and *North of Hope.* Jon
taught English in high school and college for forty-one years, ending
his academic career as Regents Professor Emeritus at Saint John's
University of Minnesota. He died in 2008 after a long illness, though
he continued to write novels until the end.

JOSEPH PLUT RECEIVED his bachelor of arts degree in English from
Saint John's University, Collegeville, Minnesota, and his master of
arts degree in English and Comparative Literature from Columbia
University, New York. Plut met Jon Hassler in 1968 when both were
in the English Department at Brainerd Community College (now
Central Lakes College) in Minnesota. Plut taught English and hu-
manities for thirty-six years at Brainerd. His previous book was a
collaboration, *Conversations with Jon Hassler.*